All Our Love

A Collection of Stories that Speak to the Heart

Coordinated by Novel Grounds

Marcia
all my love
Robin Green

All Our Love

Juli Valenti

Rene Folsom

Brooke Cumberland

Vicki Green

Melissa Collins

Felicia Tatum

Jettie Woodruff

Marie Wathen

Brandy L. Rivers

Sarah M. Cradit

S.L. Dearing

ISBN-13: 978-1496178039 | ISBN-10: 1496178033
First Edition Paperback

Compiled by Megan Gallt Novel Grounds
www.novelgrounds.com

Juli's Elite Editing

Edited by Juli Valenti with Juli's Elite Editing
https://www.facebook.com/JulisEliteEditing

Phycel Designs
Graphic Arts & Web Development

Cover Created by Rene Folsom with Phycel Designs
www.phycel.com

License Notes

This book is licensed for your personal enjoyment only. This book may not be resold or given away to other people. If you would like to share this book with another person, please purchase an additional copy for each person you share it with. If you're reading this book and did not purchase it, or it was not purchased for your use only, then please purchase your own copy. Thank you for respecting the hard work of these authors.

This book is a work of fiction. Names, characters, places and incidents are products of the author's imagination or are used fictitiously. Any resemblance to actual events, locales, or persons living or dead, is entirely coincidental.

A Thank You from Novel Grounds

To all those who find solace in that coveted moment in a novel—I hope you enjoyed this. I hope you reveled in each of the eleven stories contained in these pages. Thank you for reading. For those of you searching for the type of love you find in books, don't lose hope. It's out there.

Thank you, Rene. This would never have happened without your help. I am lucky to have gotten the chance to work with you. I learned more and more each step of the way, and I look forward to even more in the future. You are invaluable in the literary world, invaluable to all the readers out there, and, most of all, invaluable to me. This anthology is the product of a small idea I had that you took and blossomed into a real work. I can't thank you enough.

Thank you, Juli. You were a huge part of this anthology and bringing it to life. I am SO thankful that you agreed to be a part of it and that I got to have the pleasure of working with you. You are so talented and you don't even see it. I can't wait to watch your writing career blossom with more novels. It will be our pleasure at Novel Grounds to aid you how we can. *Hint Hint*

My dearest Amy—thanks for being my cheerleader and for always asking what book is up next every time you got the chance. Novel Grounds wouldn't be what it is without you. I can't believe this Anthology is complete!

To all the authors that took part in this… Thank you. I will never forget how much fun we had putting this together, including the fifty comment posts where we went back and forth about book things. It was an adventure and I am so glad you all were on the ride with me. It would never have become what it is without you. Keep writing—your stories change lives. I know they have changed mine.

Last, but not least, thank you to my husband for listening to me gush over each of these stories day after day. I'm sure you enjoyed every second of me talking about how great these women are, and how desperately I need to go to a book signing to meet them. I love you and I swear they really are just THAT good.

Table of Contents

All Roads Lead to Jackson
Juli Valenti

"Oh, you've *got* to be kidding me!" Raven exclaimed, hitting the steering wheel as her car sputtered to a stop on the ruddy dirt road. "Reliable, the guy said. Gas efficient, he said. Bullocks."

Not knowing what else to do, she shut off the engine on the now-worthless rental vehicle. Go figure, Murphy's Law—if something bad could happen, it would, and did, to her.

"Well… wasn't this a wonderful idea, Rave? You're now stuck in the middle of backwards nowhere, alone. Oh, and look at that, you have no signal either, so you can't call Triple A," she argued to herself, holding her cell phone toward the roof and ignoring the fact that she probably looked insane from the outside. Not like anyone would see her anyway. She'd been driving for hours on that stupid road and she hadn't seen a single car or truck. Come to think of it, she hadn't seen *any* sign of human life… she did see a cow, though, so that had to amount for something.

Folding her arms over the top of the steering wheel, she put her head down, debating what few options she had left. She could call her mom—no, wait, she couldn't. Raven refused to listen to her mom and her '*I told you so's* about traveling alone, and to places she'd never been. Anything would be better than that. She could always take a nap in the car… but then again, it was nine o'clock in the morning. She'd gotten up at six after spending the night in a tiny motel, so she wasn't tired. Unfortunately, that motel, and town, was more than three hours away in the opposite direction; heading back was definitely not a good choice. Sighing, she knew she only had one other option open to her; she was going to have to walk.

"Joy," she muttered as she snatched the keys from the dash and climbed out. Frustrated, she slammed the car door much harder than was necessary. It felt good for a moment, until she realized she'd left her purse in the passenger seat. Ruining the gumption she'd felt a moment before, she sheepishly opened the door, leaned over, and grabbed her purse. For the first time today, she was grateful no one had been around to witness her little show.

"These boots are made for walkin'," she told herself wryly, glancing down at the high-heeled, dove gray boots she wore. They'd always made her feel pretty, though, today, she just felt silly. Shrugging and deciding to make the most of it, she took off down the dirt road, absently pressing the lock button on the key fob. No use in someone getting in and stealing what few possessions she had left. Nope.

Keeping her eyes down, she put one foot in front of the other, ignoring the endless expanse of red dirt in front of her. Raven had never seen a red dirt road before; she'd heard of them, of course, but always thought they were an urban legend. *What made the dirt so red?* Shaking her head, she decided it didn't matter. It was what it was. A bird screamed loudly overhead, pulling her gaze up to follow the sound.

"A Raven," she said aloud. "How appropriate."

She watched, in awe of her namesake. Its wings were fully extended, its beautiful jet-black feathers fully exposed. It was lovely to her, even if her mother had a hilarious sense of humor when she'd named her after such a regal creature.

Raven, despite sharing the same name, was nothing like the bird flying overhead. Actually, she was the exact opposite. She had long blonde hair and pale, un-tannable skin. The bird was graceful and she was awkward, uncomfortable in her own skin most times, as well as clumsy. The only part her mom seemed to get right was the sometimes-bad omen part. If something bad was going to happen, it was more than likely going to happen when she was around. No, she wasn't bitter... huh uh, no way. Okay, maybe she was, but she couldn't help it. Her mother was graceful and she'd always felt like she'd been adopted.

"Things are going to change," she declared, doing her best to keep her steps steady, moving quickly to avoid a pot hole the size of Nevada. Of course, when she'd dressed that morning, she hadn't known she would be hiking in the countryside, but there was nothing she could do about it now. She smoothed her blue and cream accordion peasant skirt, pleased that it was lighter-weight than jeans. Paired with a sky blue spaghetti strap tank top, she looked nice, even if she was starting to sweat. The morning was cool, but the sun was soon going to be high in the sky, and, she knew, it was just going to get hotter. She needed to find a town and fast. Raven wasn't naïve enough to believe that she wouldn't need water, or that she could hike for miles without getting tired. Her goal was to just keep moving, just keep going. She'd stumble across something, she had to.

* * * * *

"GOD BLESS AMERICA!" Raven yelled after she tripped over another rock and landed face first in the dirt. Oh, she'd stumbled across something alright... but her own feet wasn't exactly what'd she meant. Now, her hands were scratched and bleeding, her ankle throbbed where she'd twisted it, and her boots were killing her feet. To top off the disaster, she'd been walking for miles and come across nothing. Zilch. Not a single person, cow, nothing.

Down, depressed, and beaten by the country landscape, she collapsed into a heap on the grassy side of the road. Pulling her boots off, she massaged her sore and blistered feet, being careful not to touch the huge lump that was forming on her ankle. She moved quickly, pulling her right boot back on before it swelled to where she couldn't put it on at all. Better to have it on than be stuck barefoot. There was no way she could walk barefoot on the gravel... she could barely walk now.

Checking to see if her luck had changed, she pulled her cell phone out of her purse, examining the screen. Still no service. Sighing, she tossed it back into her bag and dug around, hoping she'd find something to snack on, but no dice.

Raven decided she may as well get comfortable for a while, give her poor feet a rest. Of course, as soon as she'd gotten comfortable, she heard a familiar roar. Feeling like a dog, her ears went on high alert as she listened harder, hoping she wasn't imagining things. She heard a loud crunching, followed by the same roar, and she could've jumped for joy if she wasn't prone and hurting on the ground. The sound of an engine got louder, and panicking, she jumped to her feet, wincing at the pain in her ankle. Moving forward, she waved her hands, probably looking absurd, but not caring. This hillbilly's truck was going to stop for her, it just *was*.

Luckily the driver saw her and slammed on the brakes, sending gravel and debris up in a huge cloud of dust. Sure, it went all over her, but she was beyond being worried about it. She was so relieved to see another human being, she could've cried.

"Are you freaking crazy, lady?" a male voice shouted from the truck before he opened the door and stepped out. His voice was deep, a southern accent clear as he moved in a rage toward her.

The dust cleared and she got a good look at him. Wow. He was tall, really tall, and tan. Dressed in a red flannel shirt with the sleeves cut off, ripped blue jeans, and a pair of cowboy boots, he was the epitome of country boy. His shirt was left unbuttoned and Raven found it hard to pull her eyes from the muscles of his stomach.

Gathering herself, she tore her gaze away and upward. From what she could see of his face, the part that wasn't covered by a large straw hat, he was handsome. She could see his piercing gray eyes, even from the distance they stood apart, his full lips, and his strong jaw. *I'm in trouble,* she thought. Her mouth went dry and all logic left her.

"Are you okay?" the man asked, his words more gentle this time, almost melodic.

Yep, big big big trouble.

"Actually," she started, swallowing hard before taking a deep breath. "I'm sort of... stuck."

"Stuck?"

"My rental car decided to die on me. I didn't know what else to do so I decided to walk... but that was *really* a bad idea. Have you seen these boots? They're seriously not meant for hiking; I keep tripping over rocks and potholes and my own feet. I hurt my ankle really bad when I stumbled, my hands are bleeding, I'm hot, and I'm starving," she told him, fully aware that she was rambling but unable to stop herself. She was worn out and desperate.

The stranger stared at her for a long moment before removing his hat, exposing dark-as-night cleanly cut hair, and scratching his head. He seemed to be debating something internally and Raven kept quiet. She held her breath as he nodded, his decision made.

"Would ya like a ride?" he asked her, the words sounding weird in his thick accent.

"Yes!" she exclaimed immediately.

"Ya don't know where I'm going to," he answered her, rubbing his chin with his hand while cocking his head to the side, looking at her oddly.

Raven didn't care where he was going. Anywhere had to be better than the never ending hell she was walking now, and she told him so. At her words, he smiled and her breath caught.

"Gorgeous," she whispered, flushing when his eyebrows rose and she realized she'd spoken aloud. "Um..." she tried to come up with something clever or witty to distract him from her foot-in-mouth slip, but failed. Instead, her mouth opened, closed, and then repeated the gesture.

Shrugging, she pasted the best smile she could conjure on her face and extended her hand.

"I'm Raven," she introduced herself.

Country boy continued to stare at her for a long moment before he blinked and took her offered hand.

"I wouldn't have expected your name to be Raven," he responded and she rolled her eyes. She heard it all the time, it was nothing new to her. Hell, she'd heard it her entire life.

"I know. My mom has a great sense of humor, wouldn't you say? I seriously doubt she thought I would look the exact opposite of her."

Not waiting for him to say anything else, she did her best impression of a runway walk to his truck. Sure, the whole swagger was probably completely ruined by the fact that she was limping and swaying to one side from pain, but a girl had to try. She thought she was doing well, too, until she stumbled.

Before she could hit the ground, strong hands grasped her by the waist, keeping her from getting more dirt road rash. Faster than she could have thought, he scooped her into his arms, cradling her as if she weighed nothing. Breaths coming fast she peered up at his face, finding concern and a hint of amusement in his eyes.

"I'm Jackson," he said, carrying her toward the truck.

"Jackson..." she mumbled, pressing her face into his chest, breathing in his scent. *Man, he smells good.*

"My momma, too, had a sense of humor," he said wryly.

Confused, Raven brought her eyes back to his. Correctly reading her expression, Jackson's smile grew as he placed her on the passenger seat.

"Darlin', don't you know where you are? You're in Bolton, Mississippi, right outside Jackson." He handed her the seat belt and she quickly buckled herself when he shut the door. Raven watched as he crossed the front of the truck, moved back to her previous spot in the grass, and scooped her purse up from the ground.

Once back at the truck, he climbed in, flashing her a mega-watt smile and handing her the designer bag. Barely glancing at it, she dropped it to her feet, wincing as it hit her injured ankle. The roar of the engine was loud as he turned the key and it startled her.

"Ya sure you're alright?" Jackson asked her as he shut his door and put the large vehicle into gear.

"You know... now that you ask? I'm pretty crappy right now," she complained, leaning down to remove her boot. It was funny: she'd loved the boots before... but now she was almost sure she hated them.

Sighing at the relief of pressure, she dropped the boot and examined her ankle. It was even more swollen than the last time she'd looked at it, and it was turning a technicolor purple. It hurt to even look at it, let alone touch it.

"You broke it good," the man beside her said, startling her. He was peering over at her in between glances at the road, his forehead scrunched in concentration. "I know somebody; we'll head there first."

"First?"

"Well, I'm sure not gonna just drop ya off and abandon ya there."

Raven smiled at his southern charm, the way his lips screwed up at the thought of leaving her somewhere alone. *Country hospitality at it's very finest*, she thought, content for the first time all day.

* * * * *

"Well, good news, little lady. It's not broken; you have a pretty nasty sprain though. I'll give you a brace to wear and I suggest staying off your feet for a week or so. Use ice for the swelling and try to keep it elevated for a bit, hm?"

Raven was pleasantly surprised that Jackson had gotten her right in to see a doctor, especially when she found out that Dr. Moore was the only one in town. Her surprise in learning that he was Jackson's cousin was even more so.

She smiled at the doctor and nodded, telling him that of course she would stay off it for a week. No way was she really; she was just placating him until she could get her rental fixed and be out of backwardsville USA. Apparently Bolton Mississippi was an 'it' town, with a grand population of 568—they even had a twenty-four hour 7-Eleven now, or so she'd been told. Hooray.

Dr. Moore narrowed his eyes at her before speaking again. "Do you have a place to stay in town? I'd like you to come back next week to check on it, make sure the muscles have healed correctly."

She opened her mouth but Jackson beat her to the punch.

"She's gonna stay with me, Cousin. I'll make sure she comes back. We got ourselves a runner here; luckily she ain't able to run very fast... or far... or at all, really," he said, smirking at his family member before turning an eagle eye on her.

Something fluttered in Raven's stomach at his words; what, she wasn't quite sure. Anger that he'd assumed she'd agree to stay with him? Excitement that she was going to stay with him?

Crap, you just acknowledged you were going to stay with him, she scolded herself. *Only mentally,* she argued back, despite knowing it was the truth.

"Good deal, Jack. Make sure she does as little walking as possible, especially today and tomorrow. Oh, and Raven? Don't wear those boots," Dr. Moore said, pointing to the offending footwear on the floor, "until the day you can walk with no limp, understand?"

"Yes, Sir," she answered, her voice small. She felt like she was being scolded by her mother. He probably didn't know that she wasn't planning to wear them *ever* again.

Thanking his cousin, Jackson helped her stand without putting pressure on her wounded ankle and walked her slowly back outside. Raven protested, needing to pay the doctor, but he waved her off.

"Houston won't accept your money—ain't his style," he said, ushering her into her seat.

"Houston?" she asked, feeling woozy from the pain.

"The doctor, my cousin?" he said, peering at her closely. "You're turning green… it hurting that bad?"

The way he said it made her pause. She felt like such a wimp, but it did hurt; especially since she'd thrown her purse to the floor, right on it… again. *Wimp, wimp, wimp.*

"No, it doesn't hurt," Raven lied, trying to plaster a smile on her face. She knew she wasn't very convincing, but she hated being weak. You'd think by now she'd be used to stupid injuries like this, but noooo, they still hurt like the bloody dickens!

Jackson merely chuckled and shut her door, moving to clamber in beside her. Without speaking another word, he started the truck and drove them to a tiny building that announced "Perscriptions" in big blue lettering. The building was obviously old, age turning the color from white to a dingy brown, but the sign was definitely new.

"Your sign is spelled wrong," she noticed, laughing.

When he didn't join in, she turned to face him, seeing that he was turned toward her, a wry look on his face.

"What?" she asked, feeling self-conscious. She knew she was a hot mess from the road to Hell, but she hadn't cared before. Now she wished she'd taken a few moments at the doctor's office to make friendly with some water. *Damn, you've got it bad, girlfriend.*

"First time I heard ya laugh," he stated, his mouth turning up. "Awfully cute."

16

Raven blushed, praying that the dirt on her face would cover the scarlet her cheeks were turning. Pale skin had its advantages, but blushing wasn't one of them—she always looked like a cherry tomato. Miraculously though, the pain she'd been nauseous with just a few moments before, vanished at his words, being replaced with butterflies in her stomach. *You're acting like a schoolgirl, Rave, get a hold of yourself!*

"You stay here, I'll get your meds," Jackson said, clearly taking pity on her and not mentioning her embarrassment. Not having the strength to argue about it, she merely nodded.

Closing her eyes, Raven leaned her head back on the seat. The warmth from the sun felt divine, warming her from her middle outward. The doctor's office had been freezing, especially after she'd been sweating, and she welcomed the heat. She would've done a lot right about then for a shower and a nap, not necessarily in that order. It was creeping on three in the afternoon and apparently pain made her sleepy.

With the sun soothing her, she allowed her mind to wander, mentally replaying the past few weeks' events. When she'd come home to her apartment and found that her ex-boyfriend had stolen most of her things, she'd freaked out. Raven hadn't dated Todd long, maybe two weeks, and she'd made the decision for them to part ways rather than continue the nightmare they'd been in. It had become glaringly obvious after three dates that he wasn't for her; he was a jerk, controlling in all the wrong ways, and gave her a creepy vibe in the pit of her stomach. He'd demanded that he order for her when they went out to eat, regardless of whether she liked what he chose or not, as well as trying to get her to change how she dressed. He'd told her if she was going to be with him, she had to be pristine, which had puzzled her. That particular meeting she'd worn a black Versace dress paired with Jimmy Choos—definitely not slumming clothes.

Todd hadn't been happy that she'd dumped him and, somehow, he'd gotten into her apartment. He stole most of the items that were of worth there, including her clothes and her jewelry. As far as brains for a thief goes, he was slightly lacking... he left a note. Hell, he'd even *signed* the note. She shook her head at the thought of what it had read:

Rave, as much fun as your name sounded, you weren't. I figured you owed me, so I took what I deserved. I'll be seeing you. –Todd

When she'd called the police, angrier over the theft than the threat, and they'd discovered who the perpetrator was, the officers' faces had turned white. Apparently, *Todd* was more than the investment banker he claimed to be. He was part of the mob, and a dirty part, at that. The detective who contacted her afterward informed her that Todd was the one who was called in to clean messes, oh, and that he was good at his job. He'd kindly suggested she get out of New York for a while. When she'd asked how long "a while" was, he'd simply shrugged at her and smiled apologetically.

Taking their advice, Raven packed some of her remaining possessions, luckily Todd hadn't taken *all* of her clothes, and rented a car. Not having a single clue of where to go—she couldn't take her problems to her mother, despite her demands that she come there—she'd gotten into the car and started driving. Streets passed in a blur, whole towns flying by her before she'd even been aware of them. There was something freeing about aimless driving, going wherever the world took her. She'd lived in the city for as long as she could remember—her only sights being skyscrapers and bright lights. Now, she was learning to enjoy more than that: the lush colors of the world around her, even the beauty of the stars framed in a night sky, uninhibited by the lights of the city below.

Of course, she was also realizing the ugly parts too—like the parts of the country that went on forever, with no one in sight, nowhere to stop and use the bathroom, or buy a latte.

"And stupid dirt roads that jump up and hurt people," she said aloud, grumpy.

Reminded of the dirt road that had caused this whole mess, Raven's thoughts drifted to Jackson. Who was this gorgeous, kind, *hot*, stranger that had taken her in like she was part of his family? He didn't ask questions, well, he did, but not about her family or her past, or where she was even from. He was obviously well liked by the small town, everyone who saw him waved as he drove past them. *Does it surprise you? Hell, you just met him and you like him.*

She sighed. There was something about this man, more than just how he looked, that drew her to him. The *something* that had been missing from nearly all the men she'd met and dated in the past, he had. Raven enjoyed his company, even when nothing was said between them. It was rare, for her, to instantly like anyone too. Most of the time she preferred the company of a good book, especially since she was awkward and had a tendency to not shut up. Like she had today.

Oh God, that poor man. Reliving the conversations they'd shared, she realized that she hadn't even given the guy a chance to decline her. She'd been so set on being rescued that she'd taken the knight by the sword and demanded to be saved. *Well... I've never been the damsel in distress type, I guess.*

* * * * *

"Who the hell is *that!?*"

A shrieking voice jolted Raven awake. She hadn't realized she'd fallen asleep and it took her a moment to recognize her surroundings.

Oh yeah, Jackson's truck, she observed, shaking the fog from her head.

About three feet from the front of the truck, she spied a woman animatedly speaking to Jackson while he stood with his hands in his pockets, his demeanor screaming nonchalance. Raven could tell that this girl was *not* happy that she'd been sleeping in his truck, if her pointing and motioning toward her was any indication. Raven closed her eyes again, faking sleep and trying to catch their loud, and very public, argument.

"Who she is, isn't your business, Jenny," Jackson replied coolly.

"The hell you say, Jackson! You're my –"

"Not your anything, anymore. We haven't been together in over two years," he cut her off, his voice hard. Raven's eyes opened, unable to help herself as she stared at him, enthralled.

The woman named Jenny opened her mouth, as she remained frozen in place, dumbstruck. Shaking her head, she propped her hands on her hips before regaining her bearings.

"You'll come back to me, you always do. Doesn't matter how many women you take to your bed—I'm the one for you."

"You were never *the one*," he answered her, his voice so soft that Raven had to strain to hear him at all. She was seeing another side to the country gentleman who'd rescued her, and damned if she didn't find it attractive. "You were a *distraction*."

"That woman –" Jenny started again, pointing toward Raven, but Jackson held up a hand to stop her words.

"Enough!" his voice was loud, shocking the crowd who'd stopped to watch the drama unfold between the two. "*She* is none of your fucking business, Jennifer Mae, so drop it. *We* are done—we've been done for a long time. If you so much as come near Raven, or me, I will call Sheriff Tate and have ya arrested for harassment. I've been nice to ya, ignored your crazy, but I can't anymore. Enough, Jenny."

"But, Jackson," she said, clearly upset by his words.

"No buts, Jenny." Without saying anything further, Jackson turned on his booted heel and strolled toward the truck and Raven. He'd buttoned his shirt at some point, his skin no longer on display, and for that, Raven was grateful. Not because he was less distracting, but because she didn't want *Jenny* ogling him. *Quite the green-eyed monster, eh Rave?* She wasn't quite sure where the jealousy came from—it didn't make sense, not even to herself—but it was there nonetheless.

Catching herself staring, she quickly squeezed her eyes shut, feigning sleep and praying he hadn't seen her watching the explosive interaction between the two. She heard his sigh as he climbed into the truck then there was nothing but silence. Raven waited but when there was no movement, she opened her eye to look at him. Jackson sat, his arm rested on the wheel, his hand massaging his forehead.

"I know you're awake, Raven," he said quietly, not lifting his head. "How much did ya hear?"

"Pretty much everything, I think... but it's not my business," she answered him, yawning.

"Jenny and I," he started to explain, but she shook her head.

"You don't owe me anything. We just met five hours ago—it's not like I'm your girlfriend or something. You're just being nice and helping the gracefully challenged city girl."

Jackson chuckled before meeting her eyes. "I still want you to know. She and I dated; it went well for a while but she turned into a stalker. She followed me everywhere I went and would ask me a thousand questions every time I talked to anyone that wasn't her. It got old really quick."

"Jackson, really, you don't have to tell me about her. I get it, you dumped her and now she's psycho crazy nuts."

This time, he burst into full-blown laughter, the sound bringing a smile to her face. By the time he'd finished, his face was red and his eyes leaked.

"In only one sentence ya got it pretty good," Jackson said between gasping breaths. "Psycho crazy nuts, yep, fits."

Still smiling he started the engine, handing her the white paper bag with her pain medication and a bottle of water. Grateful, she palmed one of the pills, swallowing it down with a large drink. The water wasn't cold, but she couldn't complain.

They drove in silence and Raven relaxed once more into her seat, idly watching as they passed through the small town. There was very little traffic, people preferring to walk together with their children instead. She saw a mother with a baby on her hip inspecting a barrel of tomatoes, the local grower selling his wares. It was peaceful, she decided, the slow pace of this tiny nowhere place. *I could get used to this,* she thought, surprised at herself. She'd always loved the fast paced life she'd led… but maybe this could work too.

"Home sweet home." Jackson's voice interrupted her musings and she was surprised to find them parked in a driveway. Flicking her eyes up and out the windshield, she took in his home.

A sprawling wooden cabin was tucked among massive weeping willows, the branches lovingly brushing the building's outer walls and roof. Flowers lined the driveway and front walk, colors brightly welcoming any guests or passerby. It wasn't a large house, but it wasn't small either; it blended in perfectly with the surroundings and looked like it'd been built just for this area, this place, and it was magical to her. She'd never seen anything so perfect, so out of a storybook before, and for a moment she couldn't come up with any words.

"Wow," she said dumbly, her eyes taking in every detail; forest green wooden shudders open to show flowy cotton curtains blowing in the country breeze, the wrap around deck, complete with a porch swing, matching the walls to perfection. It was obvious within moments that he took great pride in his home.

Jackson flashed her a face-splitting grin before he hopped out and moved to help her out. Once he'd opened her door, he scooped her back into his arms and carried her to the front door.

"Can you reach the handle?" he asked her, zero strain in his voice at holding her weight. She moved carefully, not wanting to unbalance him, and turned the knob.

"You leave your house unlocked?" she inquired incredulously as the door opened to a neatly kept entry.

"No one is going to steal from me here, from anyone. Bolton is better than that," he remarked, propping her purse on one of the pegs sticking out of the wall. Raven shook her head, irrationally wanting to scold him for his naivety, but she refrained. It wouldn't do any good, she could tell by the hardness in which he'd spoken. He hadn't chastised her, more like he tried to reassure her that the problems she'd had in New York City wouldn't happen in the small world they were in.

Closing her mouth, Raven allowed Jackson to carry her like a child through his home. She marveled at the completeness of it; his place was homey and comfortable. She took a deep breath as he placed her on a plush suede couch, the smell of pine and cinnamon filling her, soothing her.

"This okay?" he asked, untangling himself carefully so no to jar her.

She nodded, watching him fuss around, straightening things that didn't need to be adjusted. Absurdly, her eyes watered and a tear fell. Raven wiped it away quickly, hoping he hadn't seen. She wasn't sure why her eyes were leaking, why her heart ached. Sure, she was in a strange place, completely out of her element, but she was used to being independent—she shouldn't be such a mess. *Get your stuff together, Rave, seriously. What the hell is wrong with you?*

Jackson turned at the sniffle she tried to hide, his face concerned. He was at her side immediately, peering down at her.

"Raven?" Just one word, one name, her name, and she was lost.

"Gah! I'm fine—my eyes are just leaking, it happens from time to time. I suffer from Leaky Eye Syndrome, you know... nothing to worry about. It's not contagious," she quipped, drawing on every ounce of self-preservation she could muster.

Though his lips quirked, he didn't smile. He simply gazed at her, the crease in his forehead deepening. Bending, he pulled the coffee table close and perched on it, his concentration never leaving her.

"Talk to me," he commanded, his voice soft but firm.

"Did you know that okapis live in Africa... and that they're part of the Giraffe family, NOT the Zebra family?" she asked, deflecting his command and remembering the tidbit from past games of Trivial Pursuit.

"No, didn't know that... not that I know, or care, what an okapi is. That's not what I mean and ya know it. Talk to me, Rave." His tone had changed this time, turning hard, unyielding, as he used her nickname. Hearing it from him caught her attention like nothing else could have. When she still didn't speak, he made a motion with one hand, waiting. One look at his handsome face and she knew that he wasn't going to let her keep quiet.

"Okay... but you really may need to know about okapis some day," she answered, changing the subject quickly at the stern frown he gave her. "I lived in Manhattan my whole life, until recently, when a dirty cleaner man decided to half threaten me after jacking my stuff. I left, and, voila, here I am. I can't feel my foot because I'm pretty high on the pain medication your cousin doctor gave me and I can't stop staring at you. Did I forget anything? Oh yeah, and I don't really have Leaky Eye Syndrome, I made that up—it probably doesn't really exist. I'm not sure what's wrong with my eyes, they're just stupid."

Raven knew she was rambling, completely embarrassing herself, but she couldn't help it. There was something about this man, this ridiculously beautiful man, that put her at ease. She'd known him all of ten hours and felt like she could trust him.

"You can't keep your eyes off me?"

Go figure that *would be what he latched on to out of all that,* she scolded herself. She really needed to work on her brain to mouth filter. Jackson chuckled at her, the sound warming her from inside out. Dropping her head back onto the arm of the couch, she kept her lips firmly pressed together. She knew anything else that may possibly slip out would only be worse. Raven had always said what she meant, as she thought it. Of course, it had gotten her in trouble in the past but she never really cared... until now, with Jackson. She didn't want him thinking she was a nutcase, even though he probably already did.

"Okay, so ya got in with some bad people, it happens. I meant it when I said that you're staying with me, at least until your ankle heals and Houston gives the all clear. You're safe here. Go on and sleep, I can tell you're tired."

Her eyes had grown heavy and it seemed like a lot of work to open them, but she did, allowing herself to fall into his sparkling eyes. Raven didn't want to sleep just yet; she liked hearing him talk, lulled by the sound of his 'you're's sounding like 'yers'. It was quaint and foreign... and completely freaking sexy.

"Nope, not sleepy," she yawned, her words sounding weird and the side of his mouth quirked up.

"Hmmm," he mused, standing and meticulously moving the table back to its proper place. Jackson walked to the corner of the room, gathered an acoustic guitar, and slipped the strap over his head. "How about I sing to ya until your medicine takes over?"

"You any good?" she asked him, raising her eyebrow with effort before closing her eyes completely. *Please, please, let him be awful,* she begged.

"Nope, I sound like a dyin' dog," he retorted, strumming a chord. Raven smiled at his adopted sarcasm. *He's learning fast.*

Before she could say anything more, he started to sing; his voice was haunting, almost painful to hear, as he serenaded her with the familiar melody. Music had always been a lodestone to her, and hearing Taylor Swift and The Civil War's 'Safe and Sound' done acoustically, with him singing, was hypnotic. It was like he had a direct line to something inside of her and was pulling it, soothing it, caressing her from within. A lone tear trickled out of her closed eye, trailing down her cheek, the warm wetness altering her somehow.

"Come mornin' light, you and I'll be safe and sound."

She drifted off to sleep, warm, content, and completely captured by his voice. Raven didn't know why, or how, even, but she *knew* she was safe with Jackson. That knowledge allowed her the most peaceful sleep she'd ever experienced.

* * * * *

It had been three days. Three stinking days of lying around, gimping around, and looking around. Raven was bored, frustrated, and really tired of doing all three. Never one for idle lazing, this forced injured vacation was a rough pill to swallow.

The only thing that kept her from going completely crazy was Jackson. Gahd, that man... he was sweet and kind, attentive, and *so* not real. No man could possess the traits he had, along with his looks, and not be a pleasant daydream. At least, that's what she kept telling herself.

"Did my blanket offend you somehow? I'm sure you don't have to strangle it to get your point across," came his musical voice from the doorway.

Raven looked down at her hands, finding them balled up and knotted in the woven blanket draped across her. Sighing she let it go, smoothing the wrinkles in the fabric.

"I'm really, *really*, bored," she told him, frowning. "Why don't you at least have a TV? Aren't boys in the south football fans?"

Sure, the gorgeous man can smile at her grumpiness all he liked, his eyes glinting, but he hadn't been the one stuck on a couch for days. He got to go out to his barn and work, building furniture, or so he told her. She'd learned a lot about him since she'd met him: he was an only child, his parents had passed away a few years ago and left him everything, he'd started his own furniture company because he hated 'going to work,' and he'd gone to college at NYU. The latter had surprised her—she just couldn't see the gorgeous country man in the big city.

"Let me see your ankle," Jackson instructed, not commenting further on her bad attitude. Sitting on the opposite end of the couch, he lifted her leg and inspected the annoying injury. Raven's breath caught as his fingers gently touched her skin.

"Hurt?" he asked, as he gingerly prodded the swollen and bruised skin. She shook her head, distracted by the warmth radiating up her leg and settling in her belly. His gaze met hers before he began massaging her ankle. Raven stopped breathing, all tension flowing out of her body. *Oh hell,* she silently cursed, simultaneously praying he'd keep touching her, and stop.

"It's, um, it's fine today," she stuttered as his hand moved, covering more of her bare leg. She flushed, grateful that he'd lent her a razor when she'd bathed, but embarrassed that she was still wearing his boxers and white tee-shirt.

"Hmmm." The sound was a husky murmur as Jackson's hand caressed its way up her leg, meeting the hem of her borrowed shorts. *Oh Jesus.* Raven's heart pounded loudly in her chest and she clamped her lips together, afraid the sound of it would escape. Her eyes closed and she relished in his touch. No man had made her feel like this—like there wasn't enough air to breathe, no thoughts, only sensation. It was almost too much.

"Jackson," she started, the words dying when his hand grasped her face and drew it to him. She had just enough time to suck in a breath before his lips were on hers.

His lips were soft but demanding, giving her no choice but to return it. *Yeah, right, woman... you keep telling yourself you have no choice,* she chastised herself even as she opened her mouth to give his tongue access. Jackson explored her, tasting her, taking her over. He tasted so good, felt so good, and she wanted more.

"I'm hungry," she blurted loudly when he broke the kiss for a moment. Her chest heaved and she felt lightheaded. Raven was also very aware that his hand still lingered on her inner thigh, goose bumps forming on her skin from the intimate touch.

"You're hungry?" he asked, gray eyes lustful as they traced her face.

Warmth flooded her, filling her cheeks, and she broke eye contact, her gaze falling to her hands still clutching his biceps. *Wow, he's muscular,* she thought idly before snatching her hands back and clasping them tightly in her lap.

"Raven?"

"Errr..." she said unintelligibly, not having a single clue what to say to the gorgeous man in front of her. She'd never tell him she was afraid, because she wasn't... that's just silly. Okay, maybe she was a little. Hell, she hadn't even known this man a week, and she wasn't Cinder-freaking-ella. She DID NOT meet 'Prince Charming' and fall in love over a shoe, or a sprained ankle, in one night and live happily ever after. Fairy tales didn't exist. Right?

"Rave," Jackson's voice was close, so close; his words brushed her face, drawing her gaze back up. He looked confused now, his forehead pinched and his eyes no longer clouded.

"Yeah, I'm hungry... for food... yeah," she rambled, blushing even more. "I want to eat. Is that okay? Jeez, you're holding me captive on your couch—you could at least feed me."

He stared at her for a long moment before slowly withdrawing his hand, his fingers tracing her skin as he pulled away. The absence of his warmth hit her immediately and she shivered, despite the temperature of the room being normal.

"Okay, darlin', you win... for now. Come," he instructed, cocking his head toward the door. Raven hesitated, staring up at him, desperate to ignore the not-so-clean thoughts now running through her head. Such an innocent word yet she was thinking like a randy teenager.

"We're going to get food," Jackson elaborated, a huge grin flashing across his face as he read her expression.

"Oh." Did she sound disappointed? Maybe. "Sorry, but I can't go dressed like this—I mean, your underclothes are lovely, and quite comfortable, but not really five-star appropriate."

"Dunno if ya noticed... but we don't really *do* five-star 'round here. Jackie's down the road sure has some mighty fine pancakes, though."

"Pancakes? For dinner?"

"That a problem?" Arching an eyebrow at her, he moved across the room, gathering a large brown paper bag and bringing it to her. "Here, though, this should fix your black-tie requirements."

Raven glanced from the package in her lap, *man it's kind of heavy*, then to the man in front of her. A mixture of excitement and trepidation filled her, and, feeling like a small child, she tore it open to peer inside. Soft burnt orange fabric lay folded neatly, the color vibrant against black cloth and an underlying bulge beneath it. Her fingers caressed the material, almost reverently, before her gaze met Jackson's again, confused.

"I thought you'd need something to wear until we can get the things from your car," he said, shrugging.

"You bought this?" she knew her voice sounded skeptical, she just couldn't help it. Men where she was from didn't do anything nice, let alone go *shopping* for someone... unless it was their wife and they feared for their lives. Well, except if they wanted to get a little somethin' somethin'...

"It's no big deal," he said. "That there's a dress—the girl at the store said with the length you'd probably want those tight pant things, so I got those, and a pair of strappy shoe-things that girls like since you can't wear your boots. Get dressed so we can go, 'kay?"

The look on his face was clear: don't make a big deal out of this. Not understanding him, or his intentions, she decided to go with it. Besides, she was dying to see what he actually chose. After a long moment she nodded and his sigh of relief was clear.

"I'll wait for ya on the porch," he said and turned away.

"Jackson," Raven called out, before he took two steps toward the door. He turned, eyebrows raised. "In case I'm a jerk and forget... thank you."

The smile he rewarded her with made her flush, and she turned back to the contents of the bag to hide it. *You've got it bad when you're stuck in the house,* her brain sang and she mentally snapped at it to shut up. She heard the screen door shut and hobble-stood, careful to keep her weight off her tender wound. *Tis only a flesh wound!* she quipped mentally, trying to keep herself from thinking too hard. Raven didn't want to think. She wanted to go out with the man of her dreams, in the clothes that he actually chose for her, and not worry about whether he had dirty secrets or if he wanted into her panties, erm, his boxers.

Moving as quickly as she was able, she slipped into the gifted outfit, sighing at the delicate caress against her skin as she swayed in the dress before struggling into the black capri-length leggings. It was quite short and she was pleased the store-girl had instructed him to get the pants. The last item in the bag was a pair of bejeweled sandals, strappy shoe-things as Jackson had called them, only they were more. They were gold, with topaz gems that matched almost perfectly with the orange color of the dress.

"I've gotta thank that girl," she thought aloud, before strapping them on. The highest strap fell well below the ugly bruising and swelling of her ankle, making her smile as she peered at them on her feet. He really did think of everything. Random thoughts of her very manly Jackson in a country women's boutique had her giggling, until unwelcome flashes of jealousy coursed through her at the idea of the girls flirting with him. Plus, it was a small town—she could only imagine what people were saying by now. What his ex-girlfriend might have heard. This could be a problem.

"Well, piss," she swore as she pulled a mirror out of her purse and ran a tiny travel brush through her hair. "She's just gonna have to get over it. Over him." Giving up on styling, she pulled it up, creating a loose chignon at the top of her head and allowing some strands to fall and frame her face.

As she limped to the door with her purse tightly in her hands, she mentally prepared herself for war with Jenny. Raven reached for the handle, only then realizing she'd called Jackson *hers*.

"Ha. Raven, you may just be Cinder-freaking-Ella after all, eh?" she chastised herself aloud, before walking out and grasping Jackson's outstretched hand.

* * * * *

"Ya look really pretty," Jackson whispered in her ear as he guided her into the small mom and pop restaurant. One arm wrapped around her waist, Raven was very aware of how they looked together: a couple. Secretly she was pleased and his compliment, in a public place, even, made her grin from ear to ear.

"Jackson!" a woman's voice carried across the dining area, and Raven looked up to find an elderly looking, apron-wearing woman excitedly making her way toward them.

"I'm sorry about this," he muttered quietly to her before smiling up at the oncoming lady. "Hi, Mrs. Wallace."

"Dear boy, how many times I gotta tell ya to call me, Momma Walla—everyone else does," she scolded him lightly as she reached to hug him. The gesture was returned, albeit awkwardly, as Jackson refused to release Raven.

"Sorry, Mrs. Wallace."

"Hmph," she retorted, slapping his free arm lightly. "Anyways, I'm glad to see ya here and with such a lovely girl, too! Always said Jenny was bad for you."

"Jenny and I haven't been together in forever," he answered the older woman, his tone hard.

"You know that, and I know that, but that girl just can't get it through her skull that you don't want her," Mrs. Wallace wiped her hands on the little white apron before turning to Raven. "Oh my, how careless of me! I'm Dolly Wallace, though most everyone calls me Momma Walla in these parts—except for Jackson here. Manners so deep in him, no one could ever break them from him."

"I'm—" Raven started to introduce herself, holding her hand out, only to be cut off again.

"Raven, right? I know. You're the talk of the town; a pretty young stranger coming along and stealing this good 'ole boy? Talk of the town, indeed," the woman said, ignoring Raven's outstretched hand and pulling her into a tight hug. Raven didn't like that people were talking about her, but just ten minutes ago, she knew they would be.

"Can we get some pancakes, Mrs. Wallace?" Jackson asked, carefully extracting Raven from the elderly woman. "Raven here is under the impression you can only have them for breakfast," he added, winking at her and lightening her mood.

"Pish-posh," Mrs. Wallace huffed, ushering them to a small booth along the wall. "Momma Walla's hotcakes and grits are good all the time—day and night. You two just sit tight, I'll be right back."

Just like that the woman was hurrying off, to the kitchen, or so Raven assumed. After a moment she realized that she hadn't gotten to order something to drink and asked Jackson about it.

"She'll be bringing coffee, OJ, and water. If ya want something else, just ask when she comes back."

"Oh, okay," she said, looking around and taking in the dark room. The tables were covered in red gingham tablecloths, all the chairs mismatched wood with custom homemade looking cushions on them. With the dim lighting in the place, Raven almost felt like she was at her grandmother's house or something, waiting on dinner to be ready.

"I'm sorry."

Jackson's truly apologetic tone brought her eyes up. He was always so cool, well, hot—*that's beside the point, Raven!*—that the sound of his voice sounded so wrong. She quickly suppressed the urge to offer him anything to be happy again. *Focus!*

"For what?" she asked, allowing her confusion to be heard. He hadn't done anything wrong and she couldn't understand what he was sorry for.

"That the town is talking about ya. I hate when they talk about me, can't imagine how it feels for someone not from here."

"Oh, that. Well, there's not much to say anyway. I'm not all that interesting, and if the worst they have to say is that I've stolen you? Well, put me in handcuffs now," she said jokingly, trying to lighten the mood.

"You can't steal what is freely offered."

His voice was so soft this time she barely caught what he said. *Crap, what do I say to that?!* Raven was used to, well to put it bluntly, assholes. Men didn't want to be stolen... they wanted free reign, like horses, didn't they? Choosing to not embarrass herself by telling him that she wanted to steal him, among other things, she kept quiet, instead listening to the country music playing. She vaguely recognized the song, but she couldn't place it—she just wasn't well versed in the genre.

"Dance with me?" Jackson asked, standing and moving to help her up from the bench seat before waiting for her acceptance.

"Jack, how am I supposed to dance when I can barely stand? You're just waiting for me to face-plant into the wooden floor, aren't ya? Here I thought you were a southern gentleman, not funny, mister," she rambled, nervous. She was *not* a dancer... she was barely a walker. This would only end badly—she'd horrify him and he'd go running for the hills. *Well, miss wishy-washy, what do you want? Do you want him to want you to steal him? Or do you want him to leave you be to grow old with forty-four cats and alone somewhere?*

Taking her into his arms, he placed one of her hands behind his neck before pulling her tightly against his body. He held the other hand gently and swayed them, taking most of her weight onto himself, instead of letting her put it on her injured ankle.

"Raven, I'd never take joy in you falling. Hell, I'd never let it happen. To be honest, I'm happy that the cleaner guy failed so badly with you."

She harrumphed at his words. Todd had been the world's largest mistake, one she wanted to forget. Surprisingly, in the past few days, she had, completely. She'd forgotten that he was mafia, that he'd threatened her, and that she'd been forced to leave the only home she'd ever made for herself. She didn't even mind being all gimpy around Jackson—he seemed to accept her. All of her: her sarcasm, her complete inability to open up, and her lack of coordination.

"I like ya, Raven, I do. It's as if 'suddenly there came a tapping, as if someone gently rapping, rapping at my chamber door,'" he quoted and Raven stood still, no longer dancing.

"Edgar Allen Poe? Are you going to continuously recite 'Nevermore' to every question I ask you?"

"No, because I could see a 'Forevermore' one day, with you. Not today, 'course, we just met. But I could see it. I've never met a girl like you—one who spoke her mind. A girl who knows who she is, accepts it, and just is. I admire you."

Raven was unsure how to handle the fact that he'd basically just told her that he could see a real future between the two of them, effectively cancelling out the just wanting a little somethin' somethin' she'd thought earlier, and focused on his latter words. *He* admired *her*? What was this, the twilight zone?

"Why, on God's green Earth, would you ever admire me? I'm a complete contradiction. My name doesn't match how I look, I'm completely ungraceful, putting it nicely, and you only even met me because I'm so poorly coordinated that I apparently don't know how to walk on a dirt road. Why are dirt roads so dirty, anyway?!"

"Raven?"

"Yes?"

"Shut up," Jackson said as he lowered his mouth to meet hers. For a moment, she forgot that they were in the middle of the restaurant, that Mrs. Wallace was going to be bringing them food, she forgot everything. She let the man that was quickly stealing *her*, kiss her.

"Ahem," the elderly woman's voice came from beside them, and Raven jumped like she'd been hit. Jackson, though, just kissed her forehead before turning his gaze to Mrs. Wallace and her hands full of plates. His southern manners kicked in quickly and he moved to take them, placing them on the table and thanking her for the food.

Raven, on the other hand, was more confused than ever. *You're not confused, you're cynical,* her inner voice scolded. She sat, staring at her food, regardless if it meant her manners were bad. She wasn't sure she could look at the small woman, or Jackson, for that matter. Her thoughts drifted to his words. He could one day see a forevermore with her, and damn her if that didn't sound just ducky.

* * * * *

How do six days feel like six years? It had been two days since the breakfast-for-dinner event, and everything had changed since then. After they'd finished their meal, Jackson had taken her home, put on a movie, and they'd innocently snuggled on the couch. It was one of the most amazing moments of Raven's life.

The day after he'd taken her 'out on the town' which took all of about an hour to see the 'sights,' and, if she was being honest, she'd barely been paying attention to her surroundings. She'd been paying attention to her man. Yes, she could say it now… she wasn't sure how it was possible, but she had it bad for him.

Now, here she was, dreading tomorrow and her doctor appointment. It was likely that she'd be given the all clear—she could walk now and the swelling and bruising was slowly, but surely, going down. That concept should've made her happy, but now, it was making her nervous. Raven didn't want to get the rental fixed, get back in, and start her aimless driving now. She'd been going, without knowing where she was heading, but now she knew where she wanted to be. When she thought of a new home, a place to make her happy, she thought of this quaint little town, with this southern man, this simple, slower-paced life.

That was even taking in the scuffle she'd had with Jenny a few hours ago. The god-awful crazy woman had come over right after Jackson left to go into town for more work supplies. She tried to give Raven the whole "me cavewoman, my man, you go" lecture; it hadn't worked, obviously, and she'd given her a piece of her mind, even advising her to see someone to cure the 'issues' she had. Raven hadn't mentioned that there's no cure for bat-shit-crazy, but hey, Jenny didn't know that. She'd even gotten her to give Jackson's spare house key back—score one for the New York Bitch!

The sound of tires on gravel caught her attention and Raven stood, adjusting the orange dress he'd purchased for her. This time, she'd decided against the leggings, allowing the soft fabric to brush her bare thighs. For a moment she despaired that she was so pale, slightly jealous of Jackson's gorgeous tan, but she brushed it off. *Never concern yourself with things you can't change*, she chastised herself. She knew that Jackson liked her as she was and that was enough for her. Besides, she had *plans* for today. She wasn't balking away today; she'd never been meek or shy, and yes she'd made some tainted decisions in the past, but Jackson wasn't a mistake, or a bad decision. *Mom always says to make up your mind and stick to it.*

Raven's head shot up as the screen door opened, the setting sun spilling onto the floor, framing his masculine shape. From where she stood, he was shadowed, silhouetted, only his outline clear. Despite having been out, his shirt was off, held loosely in his hand—she'd learned that unless being dragged to church or to dinner, the man never covered his chest if he didn't have to—it was one of the many things she liked about him. She smiled at the thought and did her best sexy saunter up toward him, the whole time praying that she wouldn't fall or trip and look like a fool. Luck was on her side, though, and she made it to him unscathed, her hands immediately drawn to his bare stomach, her fingers tracing the outline of his muscles there.

"Raven?" he asked, the question sounding strained as his skin twitched at her touch.

"Hmmm," she hummed, moving her hands around to his back where she drew circles on him. He was slightly sweaty from the humid heat and she liked the way her fingers glided over the contours she found. Still not answering him, she pressed her lips together and kissed his chest, delighting in the way his breath sucked in and caught. *Damn he's fine.*

"Raven," he said again, this time the word was a statement and not a question; he was obviously trying to get her attention, but she didn't want to talk. She could have laughed at herself—isn't that what most men thought when women wanted, to talk? Shrugging inwardly she turned her face up to his, the tables turning as she lost her own breath at the fire she saw in his eyes.

"I missed you," she answered honestly, her hands stilling.

It was his turn to murmur in, what? Agreement? Approval? Raven wasn't sure, but he could think whatever the hell he wanted as long as he made that noise again. Jackson stared down at her for what felt like an hour, though was only a few seconds, before he dropped his shirt and kissed her. His hands held her face in place as if she'd pull away, *fat chance, that.* When she responded, an encouraging sound coming from her, he released her face, only to wrap his arms around her, crushing her body to his.

Jackson's hands were hungry as they grasped her, his hands traveling up and down her body like he wasn't sure what he wanted to do first. Raven's hands clasped around his neck, holding on for dear life, her fingers playing in his hair. He broke the kiss long enough to all but throw her against the wall, and Raven couldn't help the moan that escaped her before his lips took hers and he stole all breath from her lungs. His body was hard against her, strong, all male muscle and she relished in it. Funny thing was that she hated losing control, had always rebelled in it, but with Jackson, it was right and she was damn near in heaven. She wanted him, it was that simple. Hell, she had since day one; it was like each day that had passed only made her want him more. Initially it was his body that attracted her, then his mind, his voice, now, it was all of him.

"Jesus, Raven," his words came muffled, his lips leaving hers and traveling down her neck, kissing and nipping. Jackson's large hands pinned her at the waist, his fingers digging into her hips, both of them breathing hard.

"I want you, Jackson," she whispered, afraid to speak any louder. The things the man could do to her just by kissing her. He was driving her freaking insane and if he didn't do more soon she was going to scream, or cry, she wasn't sure which.

"I'm not a sleep 'em and leave 'em type, Rave."

"I know," she gasped, his kisses never ceasing as he spoke, making it hard for her to think clearly. "I'm going to stay in Bolton for a while, I think I could really like it here... but we're going to need to have a long talk about Jenny."

"Jenny?" he stopped for a moment, his eyes meeting hers. She could see the desire in them, now mixed with confusion regarding his ex.

"Later. Now," she demanded, more than likely not making any sense. She knew what she meant though, and apparently so did Jackson, because he bent, lifted her legs around him, and started walking them through the house toward his bedroom.

Once through the doorway, he tossed her onto the bed, forcing a startled squeal from her. His lips quirked at the sound as he toed off his boots and moved to her, his gait sure and really, *really*, sexy. He stopped at her feet, slowly unbuckling the strap to her sandal and letting it fall to the floor. Jackson repeated the gesture with the other and ran his hands up her ankles, his touch soft on her injury. Raven squirmed, unable to help herself, as his hands trailed up her legs and played with the hem of the dress he'd purchased for her.

He said nothing, merely locked eyes with her, and at her nod, he gripped the delicate fabric and pulled it up over her head. Throwing it haphazardly onto the hardwood floor, she watched as Jackson's hungry eyes trailed her now bare skin. She felt a twinge of guilt for not warning him that she'd forgotten under things, well, hard to forget things she didn't have at the moment, but still. Then again, the carnal appreciation on his face was well worth the surprise.

"You're seriously overdressed. While I appreciate the removal of your shirt before coming home, you could have done me the same courtesy of your pants. I mean, it's a matter of public service… except, only for me, so I guess private service," she quipped after he continued to blatantly stare at her body.

His hands moved quickly to his belt, fingers fumbling for a moment on the large silver buckle before he pulled hard and unbuttoned his pants. Raven had never seen a man scramble so fast to undress and she had to smile—his gaze never left her body. Frantically kicking to free his foot from his jeans, he lunged for her, allowing his weight to rest on his elbows while he towered over her. He was hard against her and she squirmed, not wanting to wait longer for him. There would always be more time later.

"Rave," he groaned, resting his forehead on hers. "Foreplay, darlin', give a man a chance."

She shook her head, mentally begging him. "Don't need it. Please, Jackson," she pleaded after a second, wanting him, needing him.

He peered down at her for a moment, concern plain on his face, but nodded, reaching between them to roll on a condom and positioned himself. When she arched to meet him, he took pity on her and entered her, pure bliss filling her as he did. *Holy fuck, I've died and gone to heaven,* she all but sang in her head. He was perfect for her, his body filling her completely, and she stilled to let her body adjust. Todd had been, well, tiny. Jackson? Not so much, and damn if she wasn't pleased as punch. He lowered his head and kissed her, his mouth owning her as his body moved and did the same.

His motions were rhythmic, knowing, and completely confident. It wasn't long before she felt her body quicken and she was begging him for wholly different reasons. When she let herself go, he followed shortly after, shouting her name in his deeply southern accent. While she was floating down she thought how sexy it would be to record that sound, the absolute awe in his voice. Jackson rolled off her and pulled her to him, settling her in the crook of his arm and Raven closed her eyes, fully happy here in the backwoods of nowhere.

* * * * *

The bedroom was dark when Raven awoke and the other side of the bed, empty, cold. It was clear that Jackson hadn't been there for a while and for a moment she questioned her decision to sleep with him. *No. No second-guessing... you both wanted it, and you want him, for more than just today.*

A soft melody drifted to her ears and she got up, wrapping the sheet around her and tiptoeing into the living room. Jackson sat in a wooden chair, clad only in a pair of boxers, strumming his guitar and humming quietly to himself. The light in the corner of the room was clicked on the lowest setting, bathing the room in an almost unreal glow. Raven couldn't help but stare, watching the man she'd allowed to steal her, in awe of him. He was amazing, talented, handsome as hell, and with a mind to match. He was truly the whole package... who would've guessed he'd be in the middle of nowhere, just waiting for her.

"Jackson?" she asked as he finished the tune he was playing before he could start another.

"Mmm, hey darlin'," he smiled at her, propping his guitar against the couch and opening his arms to her.

She couldn't help how pleased she felt; she'd been irrationally worried that he'd change his mind. Moving carefully, she slipped into his opened arms and positioned herself in his lap, resting her head on his shoulder. Jackson slipped his arms around her, holding her tightly, and kissed her hair.

"What're you doing out here? I expected you to be in bed when I woke up... bad form leaving a girl to wake up alone. Just saying," she teased.

"Sorry if I worried ya. I slept for a while, but it was early when we... er... fell asleep. I don't need much to get by."

She murmured a sound of agreement against him, relaxing as she listened to the sound of his voice. Raven loved his voice—when he sang, she couldn't focus on anything but him. She knew she'd have to be careful about that in the future though. If he were playing, talking, making any sound at all, she'd have to make sure she wasn't trying to do something—chop vegetables, cook, walk, you know, anything that could hurt if she got distracted.

"Did ya mean it when ya said ya were gonna stay in Bolton?"

Jackson's words were light, but the tone wasn't. *He's afraid you lied to him to get him to make love to you.* She nodded, deciding that every woman he'd ever dated sucked if that's the first thing he'd think.

"Of course. I'm not sure what will happen to me here, but I've decided to take a real chance. I was planning to get somewhere that Todd and his mafia friends couldn't find me, and I got there. Really, who would look here in this tiny town no one knows exists for me? Plus, you're here and I'd like to explore a possible forevermore too."

The beautiful man holding her let out a relieved sigh and Raven realized she didn't even know he'd been holding it. How could he think that she would just love him and leave him? That's not how she rolled. Well, she didn't really *roll*, rolling was dangerous for someone as accident-prone as she was. She walked, really, really slowly.

"I really like you, Rave. I'm glad you'll stay. Don't make plans for day after tomorrow," he said, his fingers moving to play with a loose lock of her hair.

"Why?"

"I'm gonna take ya to Jackson tomorrow. We're goin' shopping. You definitely need some underwear if I'm supposed to mind my manners."

Raven laughed as awesomely bad mental images swarmed her of Jackson taking advantage of her on the small streets of Bolton. She was as happy as she had ever been and couldn't think of anywhere she'd rather be right now. Raven had made a lot of mistakes in the past, bad decisions, but they'd all brought her to where she was now. Sure, they may not know where they would be, or where they would go, but that was okay, she was content being here. Besides, here in Bolton, all roads lead to Jackson anyway.

Juli Valenti

Author Dedication

For my husband, Marc—Thank you for teaching me that all my roads lead to you. You're always going to be my Prince and I love you more than the best fairy tales.

About Juli

Juli Valenti grew up in Arkansas and currently resides in Florida with her husband and two boys. Working a full time job, as well as owning her own editing company (Juli's Elite Editing), along with a full time family, her life is crazy but she wouldn't have it any other way.

Juli is currently working on several true-life inspired novels, a couple short stories for anthologies, and collaborative build works. Keep your eyes peeled!

Follow Juli

Website: http://www.authorjulivalenti.com/

Facebook: http://www.facebook.com/authorjulivalenti

Read More from Juli

A Little Broken: http://amzn.to/1gBvaWb

Bad Girlfriend

Brooke Cumberland

Chapter One

Sunday

There's nothing like a big slap of reality to get your life in check. The whole *"you only live once"* and *"live like there's no tomorrow"* couldn't be more true for me. At least now, I knew.

I broke up with my boyfriend recently. He didn't deserve it, but it was inevitable. It had to happen. There was no point leading him on. I just saved him years of grief.

"Kate, don't do this. I love you," he pleaded kneeling in front of me. I knew he did… and that's why this was hard, but it was like ripping a band aid off. I just had to do it.

"Sorry, Kyle. I don't love you anymore," I lied. If I told him the truth I knew he'd promise to stay with me, but in the end, he'd only resent his decision.

"I can't believe this." He brushed both hands through his hair as he stood up. He paced back and forth in front of me. I tried to remain calm, not affected. I turned off any emotions—like an empty shell.

"You're a bad girlfriend, Kate. I can't believe you'd do this." He walked toward me, his face directly in mine. *"You're a bad girlfriend… I'm lucky to be rid of you!"* I knew his words were spit from anger. I understood. He gave me everything—and in return—I couldn't give him anything.

I thought about the words he said to me only a few months ago as I drove up north for the week. Bags packed in the trunk with a week's worth of clothes and necessities. I still missed him, but I knew in the end it was what he deserved—better than what I could ever give him.

Kyle was supposed to come up with me on this trip, but now it was welcomed silence.

The silence made me feel numb. Numb to the facts. Numb to reality. It's what was best and gave in to what my destiny held.

The truth was that I didn't want Kyle changing his life plans for me. He graduated at the top of his class in law school and had just been hired as a law clerk, working under a judge. It wasn't exactly something you took a year off from. I could never let him jeopardize his career after all his hard work.

* * * * *

Going to my cousin, Natalee's wedding for the week was finally my chance. My chance to be spontaneous, wild, and carefree. It was possibly my last chance. *And I would enjoy every moment of it.*

I cranked the radio as I allowed the wind to blow my long, just dyed blonde hair—one of the numbers on my list—everywhere. My shades helped the sun stay out of my eyes as I drove with the top down, and with 90-degree heat, it felt amazing.

Fast Cars and Freedom started to play on the radio. I cranked it as loud as it'd go as I sang along with the lyrics. *Perfect song...*

I finally arrived to my cousin's house—no make that *mansion.* Natalee's father was a wealthy businessman and after he passed away, Natalee inherited all of it. Her mother passed away when we were both little, so she was used to getting everything she wanted. But for being a little princess, she was definitely the sweetest girl I knew.

"Kate! Katie, is that you?" she screamed from the door as I pulled up to the house. She was wearing a baby blue sundress, looking beautiful as always.

"It's me," I called back as I got out and slammed the door behind me.

She flailed her arms as she ran toward me, pushing me back against the car.

"A bit much?" I laughed, wrapping my arms around her.

"Sorry! I'm just so excited you are here, Kate! Oh my god! Your hair! I love it! Oh my god, there's so much to do!" I could tell she was a bundle of nerves by the way she was rambling.

She grabbed my hand and helped me back up. I walked to my trunk and grabbed my two suitcases before slamming it down.

"Well, I'll help anyway I can." I smiled back sincerely.

"Thanks for being here, Kate," she said genuinely. "You're all I have."

Oh god.

To hear her say those words made this whole situation a living hell. I wished I could tell her, prepare her for what was to come, but I couldn't do that to her. Not when this was suppose to be the happiest time of her life.

"I'll always be here for you, Nat." I let her wrap her arms around me again as she squeezed me once more.

"Okay, enough of this girly crap. Let's get you inside and settled in."

I smiled back and followed her in, inhaling slowly as I braced myself for this week.

She showed me to one of the guest rooms I would be staying in. Apparently, her fiancé, Trace, would also have a guest staying in the house.

"So, this is your bathroom. It's stocked with everything you need—shampoo, soap, shaving gel, *condoms*." She winked.

"Condoms? Really?"

"Hey, I'm just trying to be a good host. I won't judge." She laughed.

"Good to know." I laughed with her.

After the tour, I told her I needed to shower and nap for a while after my long drive. She told me dinner would be ready at six—and by dinner she meant the caterer would have it ready by then—and to make myself at home. I thanked her and tossed my luggage out on my bed, digging around for a razor and toothbrush. I walked out into the hallway to the linen closet and grabbed a couple towels. She had the absolute softest, fluffiest towels I'd ever felt.

Yes... yes this will be nice. I grinned at myself for how cheesy I was being, but I couldn't help it. Staying with Natalee was like staying in a five-star hotel.

I walked back to my room and locked the door. Stripping down, I tied my hair up in a knot, and wrapped a towel around myself. I turned the shower on as hot as possible, allowing the steam to take over before I dropped my towel and stepped in.

After a few minutes, I heard banging and immediately jerked around. I opened the curtain just enough so I could peek out.

A man—*a very sexy man*—was standing at the sink, brushing his teeth. *With my toothbrush!*

"Um, hello?"

He looked up vaguely, with no concern at all. "Hello," he managed as he continued to brush.

My eyes widened as I looked from left to right, wondering if he was being an ass or was just seriously clueless.

"Can I help you?" I snapped, holding the curtain tighter to my chest.

"Not unless you have aftershave? Forgot it." I saw a smirk form on his face. *He was messing with me.*

"Get out!" I snapped again. "Didn't you hear the shower running? That means someone is in here."

"Sorry Doll Face. Door wasn't locked."

"Yes it was," I argued.

"Not mine." He shrugged and pointed to the door on the other side of the bathroom. "Joint bathrooms," he confirmed.

Son-of-a-bitch. Natalee managed to tell me every detail about the house *except* this apparently.

"Fine, I'll be out in a minute," I huffed, closing the curtain. This was awkward. I couldn't shower knowing there was a stranger in here.

"Take your time, Doll Face." I could hear the amusement in his voice.

"It's Kate," I announced. I didn't hear anything after, so I assumed he left.

I turned around to wash my face under the steam of water. "I'm Gabe." I heard him announce. Spinning around I saw his head peeked in through the curtain.

"Oh my god!" I screamed, grabbing the curtain from the other end to cover up my body. "What the hell are you doing?"

"Well, how can we have introductions if I don't see your face?"

"Seriously, get out!" I pushed a hand against his hard chest, hearing him chuckle as he finally backed up.

I placed my hands on the curtain and stretched it out as far as it'd go, shaking with nerves.

What the fuck was that…

"You have nothing to be embarrassed about." I heard him say after a while.

What was he still doing in here?

"Are you some kind of weird freak who gets off on perverting women? Because if you are, I'm going to kick your ass." I shut the water off and reached slowly for my towel that was on the hook.

Oh, come on… what the hell?

"Where's my towel?" I barked. "Give it back."

I heard him laugh again. *Ugh, seriously?*

"Fine." I rolled my eyes at this little game he was playing.

I grabbed the curtain and whipped it open. After hearing a loud clank from the rods, I stepped out. He was holding the towel securely in his hands, with a big grin of victory.

"You play dirty," I said, walking toward him. I grabbed the towel from his hand as he stayed frozen in place. "Two can play that game," I announced before reaching the door and exiting.

What an ass.

After getting dressed and mentally preparing myself, I met Natalee down in the kitchen at five-thirty. I forwent taking my nap, unable to turn my mind off after my meeting with Gabe.

She was with Trace and Gabe already... *great.* I walked in unannounced, hearing their conversation. Natalee was joking around with them as I heard laughter.

"Oh my god, Katie!" Her eyes widened as she tried to hide her laughter.

"He told you."

"I'm so sorry! I forgot that teeny tiny detail."

"Apparently," I snorted, annoyed.

"Don't be mad, Kate. Gabe was being a perfect gentleman about it. He's real sorry." Silence filled the room. "He's *real* sorry, aren't you Gabe?" She spun around to stare him down.

"Of course," he said genuinely, but I saw right through him.

"Good to know." I walked closer. "Oh, Nat. Gabe was looking for something—" I turned and smirked at Gabe before I continued. "Yeah, something like hemorrhoid cream? And since you practically have a pharmacy, I figure who better to ask." I smiled back at Gabe. I could tell he was ready to die.

He stayed nervously silent as Natalee assured him it was completely normal and that he shouldn't be embarrassed. Gabe and I kept eye contact as she ran to the linen closet and returned with a brand new tube.

"Here, honey. This'll make you feel better." She handed him the hemorrhoid cream as she patted his hand sincerely.

"Thanks," he responded through clenched teeth. Natalee and Trace excused themselves, leaving Gabe and I alone in the kitchen.

"Is this you getting even with me?" He pointed to the tube, eyebrows raised.

I nodded and grinned. "But don't think you're off the hook," I retorted. "You saw me naked."

"And wet," he added.

Fabulous.

"It's embedded into your brain, isn't it?" I crossed my arms.

"Like my favorite food." He smiled wide.

Ass.

"Perfect." I rolled my eyes before turning on my heel and walking out.

Who the hell does this guy think he is? Just met and already he was under my skin. And the fact that he was hot as sin didn't help either.

The four of us gathered around the dining room table. Apparently, more guests weren't supposed to arrive for a few days... *just great.*

I ended up sitting across from Gabe. His continuous stares were starting to creep me out. I tried to figure him out, but with his cocky smile and attitude, all I could conclude was that he was probably a man whore.

However, he was exactly what I needed right now. Someone to have fun with without letting him get attached... or myself attached for that matter.

I couldn't do attachments right now... or *ever*. It just wasn't in the cards for me anymore. My life's destiny had been chosen and now it was up to me to live like there's no tomorrow... *because there might not be.*

Chapter Two

I watched Gabe intently as we ate, twirling my fork around in the pasta that lay on my plate. I tried to seduce him with my eyes. I watched as he reciprocated the act, hardly taking his eyes off me.

I pulled my lower lip in between my teeth as I watched him. It was so sensual— watching him enjoy eating—such a pleasurable act. And then I began to think of giving him pleasure and what it would be like to watch him during it.

I realized by now I was practically drooling all over him right in front of everyone. I cleared my throat, needing to erase the thoughts out of my head.

"So Kate, why don't you tell Trace and Gabe about your *new hobby*?" Her voice was filled with amusement.

"It's not a *hobby*," I corrected her.

"Um… you're naked on a pole. I don't know what else to call it." I heard Gabe choke on his food as soon as Natalee finished speaking. I grinned at the thought of him getting choked up over the word *naked*.

"Okay, now I've got to hear this," Trace interrupted.

"It's an exercise *class*." I shot my face toward Natalee. "And I'm not naked. I'm in my workout clothes. It's pole dancing."

I saw Gabe's shocked face in the corner of my eye. His mouth dropped open a little as I mentioned the words *pole dancing*.

"It's healthy and gets you in shape," I clarified.

"Yeah…" Natalee's voice lingered. "That's a stripper." She laughed.

"I don't get paid!" I laughed. "And call it whatever you want. It helped get me this," I bragged as I shimmied my hand up and down my body. Natalee snorted and laughed again. I looked over and saw Gabe's flushed face, his eyes mesmerized.

After dinner, Natalee attacked me for wedding preparations as the boys did their own thing. She had everything displayed in a thick binder with pictures and diagrams.

"So what do you think?" she asked as I flipped through the pages.

I nodded my head and smiled at her. "It's beautiful, Nat. I'm really happy for you." My eyes welled up with tears as I began to think how I'd never have this. I quickly dismissed them before Natalee started to question my sudden emotional breakdown.

"You alright, Kate?"

"Yeah, of course." I waved a hand in her direction. "I'm just so happy and excited for you!" I wrapped my arms around her, embracing her in a tight hug. "You are very lucky," I whispered.

She pulled back, looking directly into my eyes. She stared at me for a moment before she said, "Don't worry, Katie. You'll get this too someday." She sounded sincere and it nearly broke my heart.

"I know," I lied. I swallowed and pushed the rest of my tears away.

Once we finished looking through her binder, we got right to work. She had table favors to make yet and after a half hour of working, she left to recruit the boys.

"So Gabe, how do you know Nat and Trace," I asked across from him as we all sat on the floor wrapping little bows around the favor bags.

"Gabe and I were frat brothers," Trace explained, grinning.

"Ahh… fraternity, huh?" I smirked. "That explains a lot."

"What does that mean?" Gabe asked offended.

"Just explains it." I shrugged. I loved that I was getting under his skin.

"You should've met Gabe back in our college days. Man he was a riot!" Trace laughed, shaking his head at the memories. Gabe's face immediately turned red as he looked down.

"Really? Well, now I'm intrigued." I continued what I was doing, making sure I kept my eyes on Gabe.

He was a character that was for sure. He seemed part good-guy, part bad-boy. And I could definitely work with that.

"Gabe was like a God. Senior year he jumped from the roof to the pool—biggest stunt ever done!" Trace cracked up as he told the story. Apparently, it was some kind of dare, alcohol was involved, and he was trying to impress a girl.

"Gee, thanks man." Gabe chuckled as he patted him on the shoulder.

He stood up and said goodnight to us before heading upstairs. I needed some alone time after our busy day, so I told Natalee I was heading to bed as well. I said goodnight to them both before heading up to my room.

I looked out my window and got a brilliant idea. Putting on my flip-flops I tiptoed downstairs without being caught.

I walked down to the pond that sat behind the house. The moon was bright and shining right over the water. It looked beautiful and on hot day like today was, I couldn't resist going in.

I threw my shoes off and stripped off my clothes. *Skinny-dipping.* Bucket list number three. I walked to the edge and dipped my toes in, giving my body a few moments to get use to the temperature. As I removed my hair tie, I allowed my curls to fall loosely down my back.

I smiled as I looked up at the moon, memorizing it so I wouldn't ever forget. It was big, bright, and for some reason, gave me hope.

I walked further into the water, submerging my entire body. I swam out further, getting my face and hair wet. I floated on my back as the calm water lay under me.

Skinny-dipping a success.

I'm not sure how long I floated, but suddenly the water was wavy and distracted me from my peaceful moment.

I sunk low in the water and saw someone swimming toward me. He stood up, the moonlight shining over him. *Gabe.* He looked breathtaking. His biceps were filled with tattoos that bled into his hard chest. He was built for sure. Looking lower, his abs confirmed it. *He's ripped.*

"Didn't anyone ever tell you not to skinny dip alone?" he said as he swam closer.

"Who says I'm skinny dipping?" I perked an eyebrow up at him.

He bit his lip before responding, "Well, the fact that all your clothes are laying in the grass is a pretty safe bet that you are."

I raised a brow at him, suspiciously. "Or you saw me."

He chuckled lightly before responding, "Or I saw you. Yes. I did."

I shrugged casually. "You're just seeing all kinds of me naked today, aren't you?"

He swam closer, within inches. "What can I say? I'm good at being in the right place at the right time."

"Apparently," I said, my words just above a whisper. My mind was too busy taking him in. His scent, his body, his mouth—*oh his mouth.* I had the sudden urge to kiss him, but I didn't. "Is this you getting even with me?" I took a step back, needing the distance.

He thought for a moment, a sly grin appeared on his face. "More of an opportunity."

I laughed at his honesty. "It's my first time," I said, breaking the tension. His eyes widened. "Skinny-dipping," I clarified. "I wanted to try something new."

"And?" he persisted.

"It's exhilarating," I said honestly.

"It is."

We swam around each other in circles, each of us unsure of what to say or do. I wasn't usually the type to pounce on a guy I just met, but at this point, what did I have to lose?

Finally, I couldn't take it anymore and wrapped my arms around him. Our bodies came in contact and his arms automatically wrapped around my waist. I pressed my head against his forehead, just brushing our lips, but not quite touching.

I inhaled slowly, closing my eyes. *Take a risk*, I reminded myself. *Live like there's no tomorrow.* I fought with the facts that I didn't know him but that I was so fucking attracted to him. *Be spontaneous,* I reminded myself again. But in the end, the latter won.

On a whim, I crashed my lips to his. It didn't take long before we synced our mouths, massaging our tongues together.

Oh hell, he had an amazing mouth. One hand gripped my neck, forcing us closer. Our kiss was hungry, *desperate.* He tasted incredible—a mix of sweet and musky. He was all male—*demanding and eager.* His kiss was aggressive, and I took it willingly. It felt like forbidden fruit. *Kiss a guy without knowing his last name*—bucket list number eight—but in the end, it felt right.

His other hand grasped my hip, clutching me tighter as if I might run out of his grip. I tightened my hold around his neck, letting him know I wanted this, too.

Eventually, the only sound in the air was our panting as we broke from the kiss. It was heated, and for a moment, I contemplated letting him take all of me.

"Wow..." he breathed out finally. His hold was still firm on me, but as I loosened my arms, he eventually let go.

"Yeah." I swallowed.

"Sorry, I shouldn't have—"

"It's fine," I interrupted. "I liked it," I admitted, embarrassed. "A lot."

He exhaled slowly, looking torn before responding, "So did I."

I chewed my lip nervously, not exactly sure what to say next.

"I don't normally kiss girls I've just met, just so you know," he spat out quickly.

"I find that hard to believe," I teased.

"No, really. I was a dumbass in college, that's for sure, but I didn't just make out with girls I hardly knew," he responded sincerely.

"Oh, so like the second date?" I quipped.

His head fell back as he laughed. "Is that you getting even with *me*?" And just like that we fell into an easy banter, splashing and testing each other.

"You need to walk out first," I informed him.

"Why me?"

"You've seen me naked *twice* now. It's my turn."

"Ohh... is that how we're playing this?" He cocked an eyebrow. "How about we go out at the same time?" he counter-offered.

"You think I'm falling for that? No way."

"What? You don't trust me?"

"In general? No. In getting another chance to see me naked? Yes. So out you go."

He shrugged playfully. "You drive a hard bargain, Kate." He winked and swam back to shore. I slowly followed behind, getting the perfect view of his ass.

Yes... that man definitely works out.

Chapter Three

Monday

I woke up in a much better mood than yesterday, especially after getting a full night's rest, and probably due to the fact that Gabe-*Something* kissed me last night. It felt good to laugh again—it felt like it'd been months since I had. It was one of the reasons I made my bucket list. After accepting my diagnosis, I decided I needed to make the most out of what I was given.

"Kate, I'm sorry, but without treatment you have six months to a year, maybe a little more. I'd say once you start getting severe symptoms, it'll be very close after that."

I remembered the day like it was yesterday, my doctor was on the verge of tears. She constantly said how I was too young and how it was a shame my diagnosis wasn't caught earlier.

Well... that's what happens when you can't afford health insurance. It was the ugly reality—*survival of the fittest*—or in my case, survival of the richest.

I hadn't been feeling right and because Kyle made me, I decided to make an appointment with a doctor. Once he couldn't figure it out, he sent me to a specialist.

A half a dozen tests and thousands of dollars later, I was finally diagnosed.

Stage three bone cancer.

Treatable yes, but it had already spread too far. I didn't want to be connected to a machine, and I wasn't going to put my father through that again. I'd already watched my grandmother suffer before watching my own mother suffer. I wasn't going to let that be me.

There were things I could do to help with the pain. It wasn't horrible yet, but some nights became unbearable.

However, I wanted to live. Yes, I was dying, but for the rest of my time here, I was going to live *free*. I had my bucket list and, as soon as I completed it, I'd know that I had lived. And that, I could be content with.

* * * * *

"Morning, sunshine!" Natalee flashed a bright smile as I walked into the kitchen.

"Morning," I mumbled back, my eyes still adjusting to the light.

"You look good bedhead style," Gabe teased. "Suits you."

I flashed him a look. "Thanks."

"Hey, you be nice to my cousin! She's been through a lot—"

"Nat, it's fine," I interrupted. I knew she was talking about Kyle and my mom, but I didn't want Gabe knowing anything about me. That wasn't what this was about.

"We have a lot to do, so eat up."

The table was spread with French toast, scrambled eggs, ham, toast, and a variety of fruit. It was like a freaking buffet.

"If you keep feeding me like this, I may never leave," I joked, grabbing a plateful of food.

Natalee smiled as Trace flashed a concerned look.

"Don't worry, I'll be quiet as a mouse." I smirked, giving him a hard time.

The four of us ate together, laughing and talking about the day's plans. Apparently, I had to get fitted for my bridesmaid's dress. Natalee hired a tailor to come right to the house since I didn't make it to any of my appointments.

"You can't get away from me, missy! You are wearing a *dress*." She pointed a finger at me in a warning tone.

"It's not *a* dress I'm worried about, it's *the* dress."

"It's a themed wedding, Kate."

"I know." I laughed. Natalee had a thing for themes. I remembered each year she sent a Christmas card with a themed picture. Even for Halloween her and Trace dressed up as some kind of theme—famous couple, popular singers, cartoon characters—so it wasn't a surprise when she told me she was doing a roaring twenties theme for her wedding.

"The flapper dresses are totally cute, Kate. You have lean legs and a big chest. You'll be smokin' hot!" she declared with amusement.

"Is the hairpiece really necessary?" She turned and stared me down. "And the purse? All really necessary?"

"Yes," she replied sternly.

"Fine," I sighed. "Know I'm doing this because I love you."

She wrapped her arms around me. "I know. I love you, too."

* * * * *

"So how brutal was it?" Gabe asked. I looked up from the book I was reading and saw him leaning against the doorframe with his arms crossed. He was staring intently at me, and I couldn't help wondering if he was thinking about our kiss still.

"Torturous, thank you. I look ridiculous."

He grinned as he pushed himself off the doorway and started walking toward me. "Somehow I doubt that." He sat down on the bed next to me, making me suddenly aware of the pulsing that was occurring in between my thighs.

"Make yourself at home."

He smiled, but didn't move. Damn he had a gorgeous smile. It was easy to get loss in it if I didn't remind myself to look away.

"So, what's your story?" he asked.

I dropped the book in my hands and gave him a suggestive look. "What's my story? I don't have a story," I lied. "What's yours?"

"Oh no, you go first." He adjusted himself on the bed as he inched closer.

"You saw me naked—*twice*. You owe me this." I folded my arms in protest.

"Alright, fine." He cleared his throat. "What do you want to know?"

I thought for a moment before responding. "Okay. If you were told you only had a week to live, what would you do?"

"Oh, we're getting deep here." I raised my brows at him. He laughed. "Deep in conversation," he clarified.

"Sure." I laughed with him. "It's just a question."

"Okay, well, I'd probably do some fucked up shit. Ride an elephant, sky dive, bungee jump, fly around the world just to say I did it, eat like shit."

"And on the last day?" I asked weakly.

He looked at me first before answering, "I'd tell everyone who was important to me how much I loved them. I'd make sure they knew before I left," he responded quietly. My heart sunk. I wished it were that easy. I wished I could say goodbye, but if I told anyone now, I know they'd all look at me differently. I'd be the sick girl, the one who needed taking care of. They'd treat me like I was breakable, and I didn't want to be *that* person. I wanted to live my life, however long I had left.

"What about you?" he asked interrupting my thoughts. "What would you do?"

I swallowed and carefully answered, "I'd make a list. I'd make sure to check them all off."

"Yeah? What's on the list?" he asked as if we were really playing this game of only having one week left. *How ironic it wasn't a game for me...*

"Well... just thinking off the top of my head..." I lied. "I'd want to learn how to climb a tree."

"Climb a tree?" he asked surprised. "That's pathetic." He chuckled.

"Shut up!" I laughed with him and pushed him. "I never learned."

"Really?" I shrugged and looked down. "Okay... get up. That's absurd."

I couldn't tell whether he was joking or not, so I didn't move. He jumped off the bed and grabbed my hand quickly. He rushed me down the stairs and out the door.

"What are you doing?" I squealed.

"Everyone needs to know how to climb a tree," he informed. "C'mon, I'm going to teach you."

I felt the sexual chemistry between us as soon as he grabbed my hand again, like it was fragile and could break if he let go.

He released my hand and spun me around, facing the tree. "Grab that branch." He pointed to the one on my right. "And that one." He pointed to the one on my left. "Then prop your right leg up as you push up."

I tried to do as he said, but I had little strength in my knee to pull myself up. Suddenly, I felt his hands on my ass, pushing me up just enough to reach the branches and lift myself up.

"I bet you're enjoying this."

I heard him laugh, but he didn't respond.

"Is this you getting even with me?"

"Keep reaching for the branches and use your legs to lift yourself up," he said, avoiding my question, no longer able to reach me.

"Okay…" I breathed out. Once I got started, it was pretty easy to keep going, even through the mild pain. "Hey, I'm doing it!" I squealed, proud.

I heard ruffling behind me and felt him approach me. "What are you doing?"

"Just making sure you don't fall. I can't be liable for any broken limbs." He grinned. *God, that smile.* I took an extra second to admire his mouth, his very *perfect* mouth.

I reached a thick branch and wrapped my legs around it, securing myself against it before releasing my hands.

"Wow…" I looked out and above at how high we were.

"Are you okay? You aren't going to pass out on me are you? I mean, I'll carry your ass down if I have to, but it won't be easy," he asked amused.

"Are you always a cocky ass?" I tilted my head to the side. He sat on the branch across from me, giving me a perfect view of his body.

"Nah, not always."

"Just to random girls you make out with?"

"Yeah, I guess so. It's easier than pouncing on you," he said playfully with a serious look. *God, what was this guy doing to me?*

I shook my head and laughed. I reminded myself I couldn't get emotional with him. This *could not* go anywhere, but I could have fun. Yes. *Be Spontaneous.* Bucket list number four.

"I don't mind," I whispered. Carefully, I shimmied myself closer to him on his branch and brought my hand to his cheek. It was flushed and it was easy to see he had the same desires as me. As I leaned in for a kiss he cupped my face with both hands, kneading his fingers into my hair and bringing my mouth closer to his.

He controlled the kiss, first soft and slow, then fast and aggressive as if he couldn't get enough. I reciprocated, needing his kiss just as much. I allowed his tongue to explore my mouth, kissing and sucking as desperation and need grew in between my legs. I ached for him so fucking bad. This wasn't normal for me—I didn't throw myself at guys. I made Kyle wait two months before I gave in to him. We were only together ten months, but back then I wanted a future—to make plans. But now—now there were no plans. *And no future.*

One of my hands explored his body. I gripped the ends of his t-shirt, slowly roaming over his chest. His body was warm against my cold hands. It felt amazing—all muscle.

He freed one hand and cupped my neck, urging me in closer. He deepened the kiss, sending shivers down my entire body. It was nothing like I'd ever felt before—*a mix of lust and desire.* I wanted to give him everything right now—*all of me.*

"Kate..." he breathed out, panting. He rested our foreheads together, closing his eyes. I breathed with him, syncing our rhythms. "We should get down before we fall." He was right. The way we were clawing at each other on top of a tree was probably not the best idea. But fuck, it was hot.

"Right," I panted out, already missing his lips.

He climbed down first, jumping off the lowest branch. He told me to jump and that he'd catch me. I was nervous as hell, but I went with it anyway—*take a risk.* Bucket list number two.

"So how was your first time?" he asked as we walked back to the house hand in hand.

I snorted as his innuendo. "It was great. Everything I imagined," I played along.

"Glad to be of service." He smiled wide as he led me back up to my room. "Goodnight, Kate." He kissed me gently before reluctantly releasing me. My body felt empty without his touch and suddenly I realized... I liked him. *A lot.*

Chapter Four

Tuesday

Natalee dragged me into town after our breakfast. She was on a mission to find something *blue.*

"It's tradition," she informed me for the second time. I huffed and teased her for following all those corny rules. "You'll understand that someday, Kate. You'll want all the traditions and ridiculous flowers and be picky about colors and venues." She smiled sweetly at me. "Someday you'll be dragging me around looking for stupid wedding things too."

This was harder than I thought—it kept getting harder the longer I kept it a secret.

"I'm sure I will." I faked a smile. The day consisted of rummaging through flea markets, looking for something she could pin in her hair, wear on her ankle, and old, large picture frames. When I gave her an odd look about the frames, she informed me it was for pictures— snapping a picture of the two of them *in* the frame.

It was kind of unique once I understood the purpose. After a while, I loosened up and enjoyed my time with her. It was fun picking out pieces and looking through old stuff.

"So... what's the deal with Gabe? I mean, have you known him long?" I asked casually as we drove back on the highway.

She turned her head slowly at me and grinned. "You like him." It wasn't a question.

I shrugged casually, not giving anything away. "I think he's nice."

"Kate Wesley! You can't lie to save your ass!" She chuckled. "You think he's hot, don't you?"

"I... think... he's fine looking."

She slammed on the breaks at the next stoplight and stared me down. "Spill."

For the next half hour until we arrived back to her house, I told her everything about what happened with Gabe and after the shower scene. I didn't tell her how I felt exactly, but I told her I definitely enjoyed kissing him. I didn't want to give too much away, because there really wasn't anything to give away. This wasn't for real. It was just a fling. Nothing more could happen.

Damn... that really did make me sound like a bad girlfriend.

Kyle's words echoed in my head as I helped Natalee bring in all her bags. I wasn't Gabe's girlfriend, obviously, but I was probably leading him on to think there was the possibility of more.

We entered the house to find Gabe and Trace wrestling on the floor.

What the hell?

Gabe was shirtless and only wearing a pair of sport shorts. He easily pinned Trace to the ground, shouting in victory.

"Do I even dare ask?"

"Just a little initiation." He grinned. It warmed my heart immediately, making me forget my mini meltdown just moments earlier.

"Initiation into what?" Natalee interrupted.

"Into manhood! Getting married! Ya know... I need to make sure he's up to the challenge."

I laughed as I see Natalee's face heat with anger. "Oh god... you walked yourself right into that one," I told Gabe.

"What?" he asked as he helped Trace up.

"Marriage is a challenge, huh?" Natalee eyed Gabe curiously.

I laughed as I left the conversation. "I'm going to put your bags upstairs."

Once I was done unloading, I walked to my room and took a shower. It had been a long day of walking around in the heat.

The hot water felt amazing. It released all the tension in my shoulders and back. I closed my eyes as I imagined my life only six months ago.

Happy. Free. Young.

The sound of the curtain opening made me spin around quickly. Gabe walked in uninvited with a cocky smirk on his too-adorable face.

"Can I help you?"

"Well... if you're offering."

I got so lost in his smile that I couldn't even react when he leaned in and kissed me. He pressed me back against the wall, one hand cupping my face, and the other leaning on the wall behind me. The water sprinkled over us as we explored each other's mouths. It didn't even creep me out that he just walked in uninvited, rather, it was welcomed... *very welcomed.*

His hands roamed up and down my sides, cupping my breasts and rubbing over my nipples until they were hard. I hadn't felt like that in so long, *if ever.*

The sensation grew, making it impossible to stop the moans that escaped my mouth. I felt him hard against me, pressing right into my stomach as if to ask for permission.

"Gabe..." I breathed out, panting with desire and need. My body quivered as his lips move down my jaw and to my ear, where he teasingly pulled the lobe into his mouth.

"Oh god... yes." I allowed my head to fall back as his lips trailed down my neck and to my breast. He sucked the nipple hard, making the sensation teeter on the verge of pleasure and pain, pleasure taking over any and all pain.

"What do you want, Kate?" he growled as he tongued my breast. I couldn't respond. I could hardly fucking breathe. His mouth moved back up, landing on my neck before he spoke again, "Tell me, Kate. What do you want me to do to you?"

I wanted him—*all of him.* I didn't care that I just met him two days ago. I didn't care that I didn't know his last name or any personal information. I only knew that I wanted this. I wanted him.

"I want you," I managed to say as his kisses and touches became more aggressive and needy. "I want you to fuck me," I finally said.

"Are you sure?" he whispered in my ear, licking the lobe and sending shivers down my core. "Are you sure that's what you want?"

"Yes. So fucking sure."

His mouth landed on mine in an instant. I gave into the desire, the need my body wanted. His touches were so sensual and masculine as he reached under my ass and lifted me up. My legs immediately wrapped around his waist as he lined us up perfectly, entering me as he leaned us against the wall once more.

I gasped as he thrust in hard. "Oh my god... yes..."

"Say it, sweetheart. I wanna hear you scream," he demanded in a raspy voice. God, just the way he talked turned me on.

"Gabe... harder..."

"God, that's so fucking sexy, Kate." He went in deeper. "You're so fucking sexy." He crashed his mouth to mine again, kissing me as he went in deeper and harder.

I arched my hips to greet his, begging and desperately needing more. No matter how hard or deep he went, I needed more.

"Jesus... shit, Kate," he growled loudly as he came inside me. I came with him, clawing my nails into his biceps as I waited out the storm.

"Wow..." I breathed out. I wasn't expecting that. *At all.*

Chapter Five

Wednesday

I woke up with Gabe's legs intertwined with mine. The sun shined in and I couldn't help the stupid, giddy smile that flashed across my face. Waking up with Gabe—*naked Gabe*—was exhilarating.

"Morning, beautiful." I looked over and saw Gabe's bright, smiling face.

"Morning."

"So what's on the agenda today? Being held captive by Natalee all day?" He stretched his arms over his head, flexing every muscle in his upper body.

Nice... very nice.

I stared a moment too long as I enjoyed watching him.

"Knowing Nat, probably." I laughed. "What about you and Trace? Big wedding plans?" I teased.

"God, I hope not. I was kinda hoping to sneak a day with you."

"Really?" I asked. "Hmm... that could be arranged."

He leaned in and kissed me until I practically forced him out of my bed. "We need to get dressed. Natalee will send a search team for me soon if I don't at least show my face."

I put on sweats and a baggy sweatshirt before going down to the kitchen. If I was going to play 'I have cramps and can't leave the house' routine, I needed to be dressed for the occasion.

"Aw, that's too bad, Katie. Are you sure you don't want me to stay home with you?" she asked after I told her.

"No, don't you dare. I'll be fine by tomorrow. The first day is always the worst." She eyed me suspiciously. I was worried she saw right through me, but eventually she told me to go back upstairs and rest.

Whew… crisis averted.

I snuck into Gabe's room quietly and told him it was all set.

"So what's your plan for me today?" I asked as I crawled onto his bed, corning him against the bedrail.

"Oh well… I could think of *a lot* of plans for us today." He grinned, grabbing my hips and pulling me against him. "However… I want to get out of this house for now."

"Alright." I smiled sweetly at him. He was truly a unique kind of guy.

"You need to tell me more about yourself first." I froze, worried he knew something. "From the other night…" he clarified. "What are some more things you'd do if you only had a week to live?"

I sat back and thought of the rest of my actual list. Surprisingly this week alone, I'd done almost half of them—*be spontaneous, take a risk, go skinny-dipping, kiss a guy without knowing his last name (and more, apparently), and climb a tree.*

"Um, well I have two," I admitted.

"Spill it."

"First, I'd eat sushi and then I'd sing karaoke. I haven't done either."

"Have you been living in a hole? I mean, seriously? Every college aged girl needs to have sung karaoke at least once."

"I didn't do the college thing," I admitted. I didn't want to give him details, so I continued, "Plus, who wants to go eat sushi alone? I mean, who's going to hold my hair when I throw up?"

He laughed and said, "Okay, then it's settled. Let's go."

We talked and laughed the entire drive to the city. He was so down to earth and easy to talk to, I almost forgot my entire situation. I almost forgot that this wasn't real—that this was just for the week and that by Saturday I'd be driving back home to my reality. But for now, I would enjoy every moment I had with him.

We arrived at a little Hibachi grill that was right downtown. "I've heard this place is great." He grabbed my hands and ushered me inside.

We were seated and handed two menus. I read over everything and was completely confused on what to order.

"I give up," I said, surrendering my menu.

"Let me order for you," he offered genuinely. "I'll hook you up." He winked.

I listened as he told the waiter our order. He spoke with extreme intelligence, like he had a background in literature, maybe? He was very thorough on our order and a part of me was intrigued to know more.

"So what did you major in?" I asked.

He leaned over the table and crossed his arms. "Guess," he said with amusement.

"English?"

"Nope."

I bit my lip as I thought some more. "Literature?"

"Colder."

"Sociology?"

"Warmer."

"Hmm…" I thought for a moment and then it hit me. "Psychology."

He smiled. "Yup. What gave it away?"

"Your mannerisms. You're very thorough and give very good… directions on what you want." I tried to say it without sounding perverted, but it was the truth. His instructions on simple things—climbing the tree, swimming, sex—were very detailed.

He shrugged lightly, grinning. "Or I could just be a man who knows what he wants."

Our food arrived and I was immediately intimidated on where to begin. "Here," he said as he handed me some sauce. "Try this."

I did as he said and about died in sushi Heaven when I tasted it. "Holy shit," I mumbled with food still in my mouth. "This is incredible."

As we ate, we laughed and teased each other. We fed each other from our plates, trying different sauces and combinations. It was amazing at how easy it was to just be with him.

"So, it's your turn now," I told him. "We have to do something that's on your list."

"I don't remember that being one of the conditions."

"What? Afraid you'll chicken out in front of me?"

"No, of course not. Afraid *you'll* hold me back is all."

"Oh really!" I threw a piece of food at him. "Try me."

"Okay… but first… we sing karaoke!" he announced.

"Fine." I laughed. "But don't think you're getting out of yours!"

"I won't."

He drove us to a small shack of a bar. It was completely dead with only a couple older men sitting at the bar.

"Hey, can you turn karaoke on for me?" he asked the bartender. I could tell he was batting his eyes in hopes of getting what he wanted.

"It's not nice to use your behavioral modification skills on people to get what you want."

He laughed lightly. "Sorry, sweetheart, but four years of college and living with drunken men, I earned the right."

"Okay, fair enough. But just know it's not going to work on me."

"We'll see."

Once the bartender had everything set up and stopped to drool over Gabe for a second, she informed us how it worked. Since no one was around to work it, we had to do it ourselves.

"Easy enough?" We both nodded.

"Alright, what's it gonna be?" he asked, flipping through songs.

"Hm… Benny and the Jets." I smirked.

"Amazing choice." He smiled back, looking for the song.

"Get ready," I warned, pointing at him with the microphone. "I make no promises to be good."

I closed my eyes as the song started, soaking in the moment. It felt good to let loose.

I began singing, nerves still at bay. I kept my eyes focused on Gabe and soon I was dancing all over the stage. I didn't care that I sounded and looked like a fool, I was having a blast.

I saw him laugh as I got a few of the words wrong and tripped over the damn microphone cord. He surprised me when he grabbed the other microphone and joined me. He held my hand as we bellowed out the words, completely off key.

My heart ached as the song came to an end.

"Holy shit. That was so fucking fun!" I wrapped my arms around his neck, thanking him for making me do this.

It became extremely real and emotional for me knowing this was my actual list. It wasn't just a game for me like it was to him. I cursed my stupid body for getting cancer.

Fuck this sucks.

Sing karaoke and dance like nobody's watching—Bucket list numbers ten and eleven.

Done and done.

Chapter Six

Thursday

Today was dress rehearsal, so between people coming into town and Natalee having me run around all day, I hadn't had a chance to see or speak to Gabe.

Yesterday with him was one of the best days of my life. So carefree. So liberating. Gabe had shown me in so many ways how desperately I wished I didn't have cancer. Before, I accepted it and now—now I hated myself for getting into this situation—*falling for Gabe.* And I was.

How crazy was that? I met him four days ago and I was already falling for him? *Shit.* I can't. I really can't.

Natalee's other bridesmaids showed up, all from her sorority house back in college. As soon as they walked in, screams and *Oh my god's* filled the room.

I stood in a circle with them as they gossiped about their latest news. If only blurting out, *I have cancer* was easy. But I knew that wasn't really what I wanted to do. I wanted Natalee to enjoy her moment, she deserved to be happy.

By the afternoon, we were all dressed and ready to go. The rehearsal was at three and then we had dinner reservations at seven. Natalee gave us instructions once we arrived to the church. We all carried the bags of supplies into the room where we were all going to be getting ready for the ceremony.

My eyes finally met Gabe's and I held his eyes for a moment until Natalee's voice interrupted. I felt so distraught that we hadn't had anytime to talk. It felt as if we never had the past three days together.

"Kate, you're up here with Nathan." She pointed at me to come forward. Nathan was Trace's brother. Since I was the maid of honor and he was the best man, we were last in line of seven couples. Gabe was three couples up, paired up with Yasmine. She had long, luscious black hair and dark-toned skin. I could hear her giggling as her arm was looped through Gabe's. I rolled my eyes at how pathetic she looked hanging all over him. A fury of jealousy overcame me as I watched them walk down the aisle.

As soon as rehearsal was over, we headed over to the restaurant for drinks and dinner. Once again, I couldn't seem to get five seconds with Gabe. Either I was being pulled one way or he was being pulled the other way.

I tried to look like I was having fun, flirting and talking with the other guys around. I tried to stop looking over to see if he was watching me, but he never was.

Well fuck this shit.

I turned my body away from his so I was no longer tempted to watch him. I talked to the other girls surrounding me who were asking me stupid questions like, *do I have a boyfriend, what do I do for a living, what do I think about the wedding so far?* I mean, really? That wasn't the most important thing in this world. At least not to me.

* * * * *

I was relieved to finally be back at Natalee's house after a long, draining day. I slipped into my room without being noticed and sunk to the floor against the door.

I reminded myself, *just two more days.* I could do this. I stood back up and walked to the bed where my luggage was laying. I grabbed a t-shirt and yoga shorts before heading into the bathroom.

Once I was done brushing my teeth and getting ready for bed, I walked back into my room, tossing my clothes on the floor. Before I could get into bed, a hand covered my mouth. I was being pressed against a hard body. I didn't have to look to know it was Gabe. I recognized his scent.

"Shh…" he whispered in my ear. His other hand grazed my sides, pulling me closer against him. His nose nuzzled my neck, barely kissing the soft skin.

"I missed you today," he said. "I haven't stopped thinking about you… and then to see you in that dress. Good God, Kate. I was hard all night," he growled in my ear, sending shivers down my body and in between my thighs.

Sweet Jesus, I missed his mouth all over me. And to finally have him again was fucking phenomenal.

"Did you miss me today?" he asked seductively, taking my earlobe between his teeth. I nodded, his hand still covering my mouth.

He spun me around, pressing us closer into each other. I could feel his arousal against me as his mouth covered mine, kissing me into a blissful oblivion.

"Gabe…" I whimpered out, wanting him desperately. I didn't know if it was the contact I needed most, or just the reassurance that he needed me as much as I needed him.

"Tell me what you need, Kate," he purred against my mouth, backing us onto the bed.

"I need you." I panted. "I want you." I pressed my fingers through his hair, pulling aggressively. We fell on top of the bed as he knocked us over. No longer able to maintain my desire for him, I quickly stripped him down. He reciprocated and soon we were both naked on the bed together.

He lowered his body while his mouth wandered down my chest, stopping at my breasts and sucked the nipple until it was hard. He continued his path down my torso, landing in between my thighs.

He used his knee to spread my legs apart, giving his mouth more access to me. He plunged his tongue inside, shooting sensations up my core. I hadn't expected him to do that, but I definitely didn't complain.

"Oh god... yes," I panted out. He forced two fingers in as his tongue continued to assault me. He sped up the pace, not giving up until he felt my release. "Gabe... god, yes..."

He climbed up my body, kissing me softly before entering inside me. We moaned out in unison, but Gabe pulled out shortly after.

I watched as he leaned over, looking for his wallet. "No... I want to feel you. Just you," I pleaded. At that point, there were no concerns about using protection. I was clean and on birth control and if I contracted anything from him, I wouldn't be alive long enough to care.

"Are you sure?"

"Yes... so fucking sure. I want to feel you."

He complied and entered me again, deeper this time. I wrapped my legs around his waist, pushing him harder against me. No matter how close we were, it didn't feel close enough. I wanted more.

"Is this what you want, Kate?" he growled against my mouth. My eyes shot open to him looking directly at me.

"Yes, more than anything."

He continued thrusting inside me, deeper and harder until we both came in unison, crying out in ecstasy. My entire body quivered as I came down, already needing him again.

Chapter Seven

Friday

It was the morning of the wedding and surprisingly, everything was going smoothly.

Natalee was shockingly calm. The caterer, florists, and band all made it on time. I knew I wouldn't get much time with Gabe today, which was probably for the best. I didn't want to hurt him by having to tell him this couldn't go any further than this week. *Or perhaps it was to protect myself.* However, last night was incredible and the perfect goodbye.

Once the ceremony was over, we all stayed around for pictures. Gabe and I snuck glances at each other anytime we could. The smile on his face was breaking my heart, because I knew this would be our last day together.

And it was breaking my heart.

I tried to push the thought out of my head as I watched Natalee and Trace together. She couldn't stop smiling, and I could tell how happy they were going to be together. She looked perfect in her twenties themed-wedding gown and feather-headband in her hair.

I jumped as I heard Gabe whisper from behind me, "You look gorgeous."

I spun around and saw his perfect smile. His eyes were embedding into mine and for a moment I felt like breaking down and telling him everything. But I didn't. I swallowed the emotion and told him he looked stunning.

"Dance with me later," he demanded. He winked as he was whisked away by Yasmine.

"It's time for our couple pictures," she said in a thick accent. *Ugh, skank.* She had just met him and was already all over him.

But I couldn't really judge... could I?

"Find me later," he called out one last time. He had a look of lust in his eyes and it about broke me.

I turned on my heel and found a private spot behind a tree. I allowed the tears to fall down my face as I realized what I'd done. This was supposed to be simple, fun, and spontaneous. This was never meant to hurt anyone—but now it was too late.

After the dinner, I told Natalee I'd be right back. She barely nodded in response as family and friends consumed her with congrats and well wishes.

I snuck out without being seen and grabbed a taxi back to her house. I couldn't do this and I felt awful about ditching Natalee on her most important day, but if I saw either of them again, I was going to break down and confess everything.

I cried the entire drive back. I so badly wished I could redo this week, but if I was being honest with myself, this was one of the best weeks I'd ever had. Meeting Gabe was special, fate almost—too bad it would never lead to anything. This is why I had to leave. I couldn't do goodbyes. I couldn't see Gabe's face when I told him it was over and couldn't lead to anything more than what we've already had. I just couldn't do this to them, or to myself. This was for the best, just bow out gracefully and peacefully, and avoid anyone getting hurt.

Once I finished changing out of my dress and packing the rest of my belongings, I left Natalee a note on her bed. I apologized for leaving and told her I'd call her after her honeymoon. I made sure to turn my phone off so I didn't have to deal with her calling me constantly.

I thought I could do this. I thought I could do one more day, say my goodbyes tomorrow, and be just fine. The truth was however, that was a bunch of bullshit. I couldn't cross number one off my Bucket List and it was the most important one—*Don't fall in love.*

* * * * *

"What the hell are you doing?" I heard a deep growl from behind me. *Shit.*

"What are you doing here?" I asked as I looked Gabe in the eyes. He wasn't supposed to be here, *dammit.*

"You disappeared. Natalee asked me to come looking for you."

Shit. I didn't think she'd do that.

"It's hard to explain. I have to go." I grabbed my bag that was sitting on the floor and aimed for the door.

He stood in front of me, blocking me in. "So that's just it? You're leaving without as much as a goodbye? Am I not worth at least *that* much?" I saw the pain in his eyes and hurt in his tone. I looked up to the ceiling, keeping the tears in.

"Gabe, listen…"

"Don't you fucking dare. Don't you fucking 'Gabe, listen' me. I want the truth," he demanded. He grabbed my wrist; his voice was filled with anger.

"I don't do goodbyes, Gabe. You and me can't happen, okay? It's just easier this way." I jerked my wrist from him and walked past him.

I heard him behind me as I turned the door handle. "For who, Kate? Who's this easier for?"

"Trust me," I barely managed out. "This is easier for *you*."

I whipped open the door, not bothering to shut it behind me. He followed me out and continued to watch as I threw my bag in the trunk and walked to the driver's side door.

"Kate, please," he pleaded. "Don't do this," he growled. I saw the hurt in his face. It killed me. I hated myself for doing this to him, but it wasn't supposed to end this way. He wasn't supposed to get attached.

And neither was I.

He pinned me against the car door as he pressed his body into me. He cupped my face as he forced me to kiss him. I didn't fight him, rather I allowed him to have this one last kiss.

"You can't tell me you don't feel something, Kate," he whispered. "Please don't leave." He rocked his forehead against mine, squeezing his eyes shut.

I cursed myself for looking up at him. I couldn't fight back the tears. They came in full force, streaming down my flushed cheeks.

"I. Can't." I said firmly against his mouth. "Please, just let me go. Forget you ever met me. It's easier this way."

He pushed himself against the car and released me. I could tell he wasn't going to let me go without a fight.

"Why? Just tell me why? Was I just a fling? Was it just sex? I mean, God, Kate. Just man up and tell me. Don't worry about hurting my feelings, but at least be honest with yourself. You can't deny the fact that you feel something for me."

Before I could respond, thunder echoed through the sky as rain started to pour over me. *Just great.*

"Answer me!" he demanded.

The tears came stronger, unwilling to let up so I could speak clearly. "Yes! I like you, Gabe! I'm falling for you! This is why this can't work, don't you understand? I'm not good for you!" I screamed out over the rain and thunder that bolted around us. "You deserve better," I said just above a whisper.

He leaned in, putting both hands against the car, trapping me in once again.

"Don't you think I should decide that? If you're good enough for me?" I shook my head, looking down. "I'm a big boy, Kate. I can make my own damn decisions. And right now, I'm not letting you go that easy. You understand? I want you!"

I closed my eyes, completely sobbing in his arms now. "Why won't you let me in, Kate?" he whispered against my ear. "Please."

"Trust me Gabe when I tell you this." I looked up into his eyes, which were filled with tears of his own. "I want you. I want this more than anything. But I-I can't give you that. I won't be *around* for that."

He pushed away from me again, pacing in front of me as he brushed his hands through his hair, slicking his hair out of his eyes.

"I'd be a bad girlfriend," I began to explain, but I couldn't seem to get the rest out.

"Are you sick?" he asked, interrupting my thoughts, and for the first time ever, I admitted it.

"Yes…" I whispered.

"Please tell me this isn't you getting even with me or some bull shit, because that'd—"

"It's not."

He stayed silent a moment before speaking again. "What's wrong with you?"

"I have cancer."

I looked up, just brave enough to look at his face, but not his eyes. I could tell his face was flushed and swollen. I swallowed as I anticipated his next move.

"You're not getting treatment." It was more a statement than a question.

"No. It's spread too far." I lowered my head again, shame filling me for putting Gabe through this.

"Jesus Christ, Kate! How could you? How could you *not* tell me?"

"I haven't told anyone," I responded quickly. "Not even Natalee."

"You're joking."

I shook my head no, my voice lost. I half expected him to kiss me and tell me it was okay, but I knew better. I didn't deserve that.

He cursed before turning on his heel and walking back into the house, the slam of the door being my cue to get the hell out of there.

I cried on and off as I drove myself home. That wasn't the goodbye I wanted, *needed* from him. But then again, I didn't deserve one either.

Chapter Eight

Gabe

I couldn't comprehend the words that Kate confessed to me. They didn't make any sense to me. She couldn't be sick. *She was so beautiful, so full of life.*

I called Natalee moments after I left Kate in the rain. I couldn't think straight. But now I was and I never should've run off like that. I didn't want to be without her, sick or not.

I gave Natalee the safe version of what happened with Kate, not wanting to tell her horrible news on her wedding day. Rather, I put the blame on myself, telling her I fucked up and that I needed to get to her immediately.

As soon as I had her address, I jumped in my car and started driving. I could hardly think of what she just told me, but I had to find her again. I couldn't let that be our goodbye.

I pulled into her driveway, my hands sweaty from gripping the steering wheel so hard. I brushed a hand through my hair, fixing it the best I can. *Oh fuck it.*

I raced to her door and pounded on it, begging and pleading for her to open. I had hope when I thought I heard her, but it was her locking the door.

"Kate!" I pounded again. "Please, just let me in!"

I heard her sink to the floor against the door. I knew she was being stubborn, thinking that this was best for me.

"Dammit, Kate! Let me in! I need to see you. Please!" I stopped pounding and rested my hand flat against the door. "Please, Kate. I can't *not* be with you." I was crying like a fucking fool, but I didn't care at that point. Kate made me feel more in the last week than I'd ever felt in my entire life. She hadn't a clue what she did to me. No girl had ever made me feel that way before. *Not ever.*

And it wasn't because I was a heartless dick—it was because those other girls weren't *the* girl for me. But Kate was. She was *my* girl.

I sunk to the ground, keeping one hand on the door. Minutes passed, hell maybe even hours, but I didn't move. I wasn't leaving until I saw her. I was fighting for her no matter what.

She finally opened the door. I could tell she was overwhelmed with me being there, but I couldn't even think about that as I slammed her against the door and took her mouth. I kissed her deeply, passionately, gripping her hard so she wouldn't get away.

She panted as she released the kiss. I didn't budge, not willing to let her go without speaking to me first.

"I'm not running away, Gabe. You can let me go. I promise."

I released her wrists and sensually grabbed her hands. I brought them to my chest and looked into her eyes. "Please, Kate. Let me be here for you. Let me make this decision. Let me be strong for *you.*"

The tears in my eyes didn't rest as they came back for another round. I could tell Kate was doing the same, obviously crying since she left Natalee's house.

She nodded slightly and looked up at me. "Okay..." she said quietly. "But Gabe... please don't be here just out of pity. If you're here, it's because—"

"I'm all in, Kate. God, don't you see that? I fucking promise you—I'm. Not. Leaving. I want you. I want you no matter how I get you, but I know one thing's for sure, *I'm falling for you.* I don't know how that's possible—" I laughed lightly at the irony. "But I have. This last week has forever changed me, and I'm not willing to let you go without a fight."

She shook her head in disbelief. "I'm falling for you, too, Gabe." My heart clenched as I heard the words roll off her tongue. "I'm falling so hard for you in such a short amount of time, and it's so damn scary and hard for me to let you in," she breathed out. "You deserve better—you don't deserve this—" She continued before I could interrupt. "But I don't think I have a say anymore. No matter how much I told myself not to get attached, I did—I did so fucking much." I watched as she fought with herself. "But I'm willing to try—if you want me..."

"Yes..." I quickly responded. "I want as much time with you as you've got. Whether it's a week or a year, I want it. *I want you.*"

I didn't let her respond because I couldn't take it anymore. I scooped her up in my arms and carried her into the house, kicking the door shut behind us. If this was my last time making love to her, I was going to do it right,—slow and sensual—exactly what she deserved.

* * * * *

Kate and I married six months later. It was the first day she started showing more intense symptoms—extreme fatigue, chronic pain, weight lost—a year on the dot since she was fully diagnosed. I knew then I couldn't let her go without her being my wife. We spent those six months doing crazy activities—bungee jumping, skydiving, trying different foods, traveling—exploring as much as we could when we weren't locking ourselves in our hotel room—*together*. Kate wrote a new bucket list, and I made sure she crossed every damn one of them off, including *walking down the aisle.*

God, she was beautiful that day. She began losing weight rapidly and couldn't stand up as long anymore. She was weak and couldn't always tell me what she needed. But no matter what, I made sure she finished her list.

Bucket List number thirty-three—*Live with no regrets.*

Chapter Nine

Kate

Spending those last days with Gabe was everything I could've ever imagined. I always thought I'd be alone, not wanting to be a bother to anyone.

Natalee and my dad never treated me like a sick cancer patient, which I was grateful for. They were upset at first that I had kept it a secret, but they understood my reasoning. Knowing that we watched my grandmother and then my mom battle cancer, they knew I'd never want that for them. And I never wanted that for me, either.

Gabe never left my side. His mood and voice was always cheerful, making sure I was always comfortable and even when I couldn't tell him what I needed, he always *knew*. He never resented meeting me, in fact, he thanked me everyday for allowing him in my life, for allowing him to love me. And every moment we had together was worth everything I ever fought for.

Bucket List number twenty-four—*Fall hopelessly in love.*

And I did.

I wasn't exactly sure why I had let Gabe in after I swore I wouldn't, but it was the best thing I ever did. Because being alone wouldn't have been worth it. Letting him in had been.

Bucket List number twenty-five—*Give every reason as to why being a bad girlfriend paid off...*

Meeting Gabe.

My only reason.

Dear Gabe,

By now, I'm long gone. And I wish I could console you on how you must be feeling right now, but if anything, I hope this letter gives you closure.

I can't tell you how happy you've made me. Meeting you was never supposed to happen, but fate had different plans for us. I want you to know you made my life worth living so much more than I ever thought possible. You never let me feel sorry for myself and for that, I thank you. You always encouraged me to do everything I set my mind to. You never forgot to tell me how much you loved me. But when you said you loved me, know that I loved you more.

Since meeting you, I wanted nothing more than to be able to make a difference before leaving this Earth and because of you, I had. Meeting those sick children reminded me how grateful I was to have the time I had. I had 24 years. 24 amazing years. It wasn't the quantity of life, it was the quality. You gave that to me. In the last months of my life, I had never been happier. When I first found out my diagnosis was terminal, I imagined my life filled with dull, unimportant moments. But you made my life worth living. You made me want to fight for as long as I could. So thank you. Thank you for loving me. Thank you for loving me despite what I had to offer you. Thank you for loving me so I knew what true love felt like. And most of all… thank you for letting me love you back.

And please don't forget to live. Don't be sad for too long. I want nothing more than for you to be happy again.

I'll always be by your side…

Yours always,

Kate

* * * * *

There will be an extended full-length version coming soon. Stay tuned.

* * * * *

Brooke Cumberland

Author Dedication

To anyone who gave love a chance… no matter the outcome.

About Brooke

Brooke Cumberland is a stay-at-home mom who writes full-time. She lives with her husband and wild toddler in the frozen tundra of Packer Nation. She's the author of *The Riverside Trilogy* and *The Spark Series*. When she isn't writing, she's playing with her daughter and chasing after her crazy black lab. You can find Brooke on Facebook, Twitter, and on her website.

Follow Brooke

Website: http://www.brookecumberland.com/

Facebook: http://www.facebook.com/brookecumberlandauthor

Read More from Brooke

Flame: http://amzn.to/1jcsH8k

Coming Home

Melissa Collins

Chapter 1
2014
Sophie

"Okay, Annie. I promise. I'll get you the princess fruit snacks you like." I can't help but roll my eyes at my three-year-old daughter's insistence on buying the pink kind and not the blue ones—saying that the 'blue ones are for boys and boys are icky.' "Can you put Grandma on the phone, sweetie?"

A cacophony of noises stream together in the background—the television playing too loudly, toys crashing all over, but the noise doesn't bother me; it's par for the course in my house. Besides, I know that the girls are well taken care of when they're with their Grandma. "Hey, Mom."

"Hey, Sophie. How's work going?" Hearing the exhaustion in my mom's voice presses down on the weight of guilt I feel from needing her to watch the girls while I work. More than anything, I wish I didn't have to rely on my mom to babysit. But since I'm on my own, I have no other choice. Mom doesn't seem to mind, always saying that spending time with her twin granddaughters keeps her young.

"It's good. Been kind of a quiet night so I should get off early. If I do, I might stop at Target on the way home; the girls need a few things and it's just easier to stop there without them. Do you mind?" I always feel bad asking for more of her time, never wanting her to feel like I'm taking advantage. Being a single mother means you have to rely on other people. I just wish I didn't have to rely on her so much.

But she's all I've got.

"Of course, sweetie. They'll probably be in bed by then, anyway. Take your time." Annie and Alex's cries wail out loudly in the background. They're probably fighting over the Cinderella Barbie doll, as usual. Maybe she'll splurge and pick up another one tonight while she's shopping. "Gotta run, Soph. See you later." Her mother ends the call abruptly, her words of discipline cut short as the line goes dead.

Knowing better than to worry since the girls are always getting into some kind of trouble, I hang up with Mom, and make my way back to the main room of the diner. I only have five tables left and most of them are just about done. I drop them the checks and clear their plates, but when the last table straggles, my shift runs a bit later than I expect.

"So much for that leisurely stroll through Target," I mumble to myself. It's a rare event that I can go shopping without the girls hanging all over me, but at least I can still go. After my last table leaves, I grab my things, punch out, and race over to the store so I can maybe make it home before Mom is fast asleep on my couch, yet again.

I mentally flip through the list of everything I need as I scan my cart. Counting items off on my fingers, I'm pretty sure I've remembered everything, but I'd put twenty bucks on me having to come back tomorrow—with the girls. Sometimes, I feel like I practically live here.

Just as I'm about to walk toward the checkout, I remember that I wanted to get Annie that new Barbie. "Lucky," I whisper to the doll through the thin sheet of plastic separating us. "You found your Prince Charming." Finishing my thought, I toss the doll into the cart.

"Hey, Soph," a warm voice melts over me from the other end of my cart. Only one voice has ever had that effect on me. Only one voice has ever made my body tremble and my heart race. Only one voice has ever broken my heart.

Slowly, as if I'm afraid to face the inevitable, I lift my head and see Rhys Baker, my first love, gripping onto the end of my wagon. A similar look of shock is also plastered to his face. As the scent of his familiar cologne wafts over to me, I'm immediately taken back to ten years earlier when Rhys stole my heart.

Chapter 2
2006
Sophie

"Sophie, your date is here," my mom calls up to me as I put on the final touches to perfect my prom look. My light blonde hair falls in loose curls past my shoulders. The rhinestone-tipped bobby pins add little glints of light that sparkle like the stars. Taking one last look in the mirror, I swipe on some light pink lip gloss before dropping it in my silver clutch.

As I walk down the stairs, I hold the front of my long, Greek goddess inspired silver-grey gown up, careful not to trip over it. When my mom catches sight of me, she clasps a hand over her mouth, trying to contain her gasp of happiness. "Oh, sweetie," she runs her hands up and down my arms before tucking a strand of hair behind my ear. "You look stunning."

"Where is he?" I can hardly contain my excitement.

"He's in the study with your father. You know how he can be." Mom's look of sympathy does little to abate my anger. My father, the high-level investment banker, has always treated me like one of his investments. Sheltered and untouched is how he wants me to remain. Needless to say, our conflicts have escalated a lot this past year. I want to believe it's because he loves me so much that he just wants to keep me safe—so much so that he doesn't know how to let me be my own person. He doesn't know how to deal with me becoming a young woman who needs room to grow. But I'm not so sure that's the real issue. Watching his little girl grow up and talk about leaving home has rankled his ultra-conservative side—a side which I'm certain is coming out full force in a lecture to my date, Carter Anderson.

Dad walks Carter out of the study, clapping a strong hand on his shoulder. Carter mouths "wow" to me and I stifle a giggle. Knowing my father would have more than a few select words for Carter is what made me suggest we just meet at Lila's house. She's been my best friend for as long as I can remember and she's hosting a huge prom send-off party—you know the kind where half of the school is invited and you take half a million pictures in front of a gigantic limo.

My father would have none of that.

"I brought you this." Carter looks at the red rose corsage in his hands and then up to the thin straps of my dress. Fumbling with the pin, he looks back and forth between the flowers and my dress, catching my father's angry glower from the corner of his eye.

Way to be subtle, Dad.

I roll my eyes just as Mom swoops in to save the day. "It can go on her wrist too." She smiles, pointing at the elastic band hidden beneath the petals. As she leans in to kiss my cheek, I whisper, "Thank you."

Looking like he's just survived the Spanish inquisition—which probably isn't far from the truth—Carter stands awkwardly next to me as Mom snaps a few pictures. Fifteen minutes later, Carter and I step out into the humid summer air, under the persistent stare of my father paired with the loving gaze of my mom, and walk toward his car.

He opens the door for me and I slide into my seat. Leaning into me before closing the door, he presses his lips softly up against my ear. "You look beautiful," his warm breath gives me chills even in the warm summer night. When he steps away and walks around the front of the car to his side, I see my father glaring from the front porch. Carter sees him too as he gets into his seat.

"He's intense," he says as he buckles his seat belt.

"Intense?" I scoff. "An over-bearing, over-protective, stick-up-the-ass is more like it." We both laugh at my description as we pull away from the house.

While we all make a super-huge deal out of prom, the reality of it is that it's nothing more than a dance in the high school gym. No big, fancy ball at a hotel or anything like that. 'Simple' pretty much describes everything here in the middle of nowhere. That's the only way I can sum up our small town of Westfield, Maine; unexciting, tiny, and absolutely lifeless.

As we pull into the parking lot, excitement bubbles in my chest. I rush us through the requisite things—getting our table number, posed pictures with the photographer, rushed hellos to a few of our teachers who are here as chaperones. Really, all I want to do is get into the gym and find him.

Rhys Baker—my boyfriend.

Carter is just the front for tonight, a beard, if you will. Carter is actually my boyfriend's best friend posing as my date for the night. If Rhys would've shown up at my house, my father would have chained me in the basement. He finds me the second I enter the streamer-covered gym, his mocha eyes roving over my body from head to toe as a lopsided smile pulls at his lips.

"Hey, beautiful," he coos in my ear, pulling me into a tight embrace.

"Hey, yourself. You clean up real nice." I press my hands against his traditional black tux.

"Thanks for helping us out, man." Rhys bumps fists with Carter.

"No problem, you know I don't mind. But, you might want to think about breaking it to your old man, Soph. Six months posing as your boyfriend is getting old."

Rhys bellows a loud laugh. "Yeah, well, it's only another two months before college and then it won't matter, right babe?" He coils his arm around my waist and pulls me to his side.

"Yep, only fifty-eight days until we're on our own." I smile up at him, getting lost in the twinkle of his eyes. As the only son of the town drunk, Rhys would never be good enough for me, according to my father that is. Rhys has dealt with a crap-load of pain and anger in his life and he's got the temper to prove it. He keeps it in check most of the time and being captain of the wrestling team helps where that's concerned. It gives him an outlet and a place to belong, but my father wouldn't understand any of that.

All my father would see is a tall, dark, bad-boy from the proverbial wrong side of the tracks, with tattooed muscles and searing eyes who could only possibly want his daughter for all the wrong reasons.

I see a lot more than that, of course. Yeah, the tattooed muscles and the easy-on-the-eyes stellar good looks are fantastic, but they're really just a bonus to the funny, kind, and genuinely good person I know he is.

"It's about time! We were staring to think you weren't going to make it." Lila barrels into me, distracting me from my dreamy staring. We jump up and down and squeal with the girlish delight of two best friends who have known each other a lifetime.

"So daddy dearest let you out of his sight for a few hours, huh?" She quips playfully, but in reality, he was pretty close to not letting me go.

"Can we just not talk about him tonight?" I sigh, more than frustrated at his sheltered mentality. "I'd like to enjoy the night."

Without warning, Rhys pulls me out onto the dance floor. Swaying in his arms, moving my body against his all night is the perfect way to enjoy myself.

"I don't want tonight to end." My words get lost against the lapels of his jacket.

"I know." Rhys sweeps my hair over to one shoulder and leans down to press a soft kiss to the crook of my neck. "But just think," I look up at him when his words take on an excited rather than regretful tone. "Next weekend is all ours."

Lila's parents have a lake house and, if you ask my parents, that's where I'll be next weekend. It's not entirely a lie. I will be there, but so will Rhys. Since my parents know nothing about him, they never asked if he would be there.

Is it sneaky? Sure, but I'm tired of being stuck under my father's thumb.

Getting agitated just thinking about him, I puff out a frustrated breath and lean back into Rhys. "It'll be okay, Soph. We'll figure it all out, but, for now, let's just dance and forget about it all."

So that's what we do—hold onto each other until the clock strikes midnight when the twilight dreams of princesses turn back into reality.

Chapter 3
2014
Sophie

Turning toward him, I'm not surprised at all to see a gorgeously muscled man standing before me.

"Hi," I croak—two simple words stick in my throat as my first love walks the remaining two steps toward my cart.

"I thought that was you. You look," he scans me head to toe and nervousness like a million butterflies settles in my stomach. He settles on my face, which I'm sure is tinted a nice shade of pink under his heated inspection, before finishing his sentence. "Absolutely stunning."

A loud chuckle passes my lips as I look down at my grease spattered waitress uniform of hideous black pants and a too-big white button down shirt—oh, and the no-slip, thickly soled black shoes are hot, too. "And you're a liar."

He laughs and nods, but then that damned sexy smile spreads slowly across his face as he stares into my eyes. "Yeah, the clothes look like shit, but you," he takes a step closer, "you look as beautiful as ever."

Not quite knowing how to deal with that compliment in light of our past, I tuck a few loose strands of hair behind my ear and stare at the ground. "Anything good down there?" He jokes.

"Nope, not really. It's just been so long, I don't know what to say." I fidget with a few things in the top seat of the wagon, nervously trying to calm my suddenly jittery hands.

"A little over eight years," he admits, a touch of sadness coloring his words. "How have you been?"

"Good, I guess." I lamely shrug my shoulder. "When did you move back?"

He shifts his weight from one leg to the other before answering. "Last week, maybe two." There's no need to ask when I moved back.

I never really left.

"I was going to look you up, see if you were still here..." there's guilt in his words, like he's done something wrong by bumping into me at the store rather than try to find me. His voice wavers and he crosses one arm under the other. I watch the movement, captivated by the bulge of his bicep as it pulls the fabric of his black t-shirt. Why stop there? My eyes travel down the rest of his arms, along the cords of muscle that move under his inked forearms, down to his hands—just thinking about his hands makes my face turn read all over again.

Then I catch sight of the hand-basket dangling from the end of his fingers. "Never pegged you for much of a Barbie man?"

Sheepishly, he looks down at the basket. "Oh, that's for my niece." A knot of confusion twists at my brow—he doesn't have siblings.

"Carter's daughter." He clarifies and my confusion washes away.

"Oh my God, Carter is a dad? I bet that's a sight to see."

"Yeah, it is. You have kids?" The last part is more of a statement than a question as he scans my cart.

"Twins, actually, three year old girls." As the last word comes out of my mouth, I see him sneak a peek at my left hand as it grips the shopping cart. "Single mom," I mutter, answering his unasked question. Not wanting to open that particular can of worms, I glance down at my watch.

"I should get going. My mom has the girls and I hate to keep her later than I really need to." As I move my cart to go around him, he shuffles in front of it.

"Wait." He stands next to me and his familiarly strange scent invades my senses as he towers over me. "It's been close to a decade. There's no way we can catch up in ten minutes." He pulls out his cell phone. "Can I have your number? Maybe we can get together?"

Despite all the reasons I shouldn't give him my number, I debate the idea of just walking away for all of two seconds before giving him my digits. My phone rings in my pocket a second later. He quirks an eyebrow at me, a dimple forming in his cheek as he smiles. "Now you have my number too. No excuses."

He steps closer still, not that there's much space between us anyway. When he's less than a centimeter away from my ear, I feel his breath, hot and steamy on my neck. His full lips press a sweet kiss to my cheek, lingering there for a second more than they should. "I'll call you soon. Goodnight, Soph."

Chapter 4
2006
Rhys

"You sure you have everything covered?" Carter asks for the millionth time as he's lying on my bed, tossing a baseball in the air over his head.

I shove a t-shirt and pair of jeans into my bag, unfolded and scan the messy surface of my dresser. "Yeah, we're good. Sophie went through everything with her parents, and Lila's parents will technically be there."

Carter sits up and shoots me a shit-eating grin. "I'm just looking out for you, man. Mr. DeMarco is some serious shit. I'd hate to see you guys get caught."

"We're not going to get caught. We've been keeping everything hidden for six months now and we're almost in the clear, so would you just keep your hole fucking shut and let me finish packing." I rake a nervous hand through my hair because as much as I'd like to avoid the topic of Sophie's dad finding out about us, it's pretty much the only thought racing around my brain.

"Seriously, though. How are you guys getting away with this? Lila's parents don't know about you two and aren't they tight with Sophie's parents, too?" Carter leans against my desk, placing the baseball back in the plastic ball holder where it usually sits.

"You know, if I wanted someone to point out how fucked up this whole situation is, I would have invited Sophie's dad. I thought you were on our side?" I'm trying my best to keep my temper in check, but honestly, being reminded of all the reasons we can't be together is not helping.

"I am, dude. Sorry. Just worried for you two I guess." He flops down into the chair as we hear my drunk-ass father stumble through the front door.

"Rhys!" My father bellows from the bottom of the stairs, the thud-thud-thud of his heavy boots ringing loudly through the empty hallway. When we hear the bathroom door slam into the wall behind it, rattling my bedroom wall on the other side, we wait to hear dear old dad stumble to catch his balance before the door slams shut, shaking the nearly destroyed frame. The sounds of his retching fill the hall.

I used to be ashamed of him. I used to hate having him as my father. That was before I stopped caring. Carter has been here often enough to know the drill. Dad stumbles through the door, looks for me, pukes his brains out before finding me, and then passes out in the bed, forgetting about me completely.

"Let's get out of here." I toss my duffle bag over my shoulder and drop it into the backseat of my Jeep Wrangler when we get out to my driveway. A few minutes later, I pull up to Carter's house and head off to the lake.

* * * * *

The lake house is huge, so huge in fact that Lila's parents occupy an entirely different wing than the girls. The plan is simple. I'll text Sophie when I get there and she'll let me in through the sliding glass door off her and Lila's room. Lila said she'd sleep out in the family room that connects the two sides of the house. This way she'll be able to intercept her parents when they come home or if they go to check on her and Sophie.

Even though we seem to have all of the bases covered, my eighteen-year-old brain is riddled with worry. It's all a pretty big risk.

As quietly as possible, I climb up the back deck stairs connecting to Lila's room and Sophie opens the door for me.

"Hey, Romeo," she reaches up on her toes and kisses me, pressing her body against mine as she does. I quirk an eyebrow, not getting her new nickname for me.

"Seriously? Romeo. You know as in *Romeo and Juliet*—the balcony scene. Did you pay attention at all in Fredrickson's English class last semester?" She pokes me in the arm, mocking my lack of interest in most things related to school.

"Nope, that's why I've got you," I band my arm around her waist and lift her up to my lips. She squeals as her toes come off the ground and I use my mouth to silence her.

"Shhh, you have to be quiet." Her eyes widen into saucers, remembering just how careful we need to be.

"Is Lila downstairs already?" I toss my bag into the corner and lock the door behind me.

"Yep, we're all covered. It's just you and me." Her last words are seductive as fuck.

"Are you sure about this, Soph?" I run my hands down her bare arms. She's wearing a tank top and shorts that are so short they look more like underwear than shorts—I love them. Lacing our fingers together between us, I lean my forehead against hers.

"Yeah, I'm sure. We've waited long enough and," she pauses for a moment, looking up at me through her thick, long lashes. "I love you," her voice is barely above a whisper, but the sincerity of those three little words can be felt down to my toes.

"Babe, you know I love you, too." I cup her face in my hands, tenderly, pressing my lips to hers. "But that doesn't mean we have to... I don't want you to feel pressured."

"No, I don't feel like that at all. I just... I want to be with you and I'm ready." Her mouth silences any protest I was about to speak. She rests her hands at my waist, toying with the hem of my t-shirt. As she arches up to mold her mouth to mine, her top slides up the soft curve of her waist, exposing the sexy expanse of skin on her lower back. She's got those two little dimples right above her ass—damn, those are fucking hot.

Walking with her still in my arms, I bring us over to the bed, stopping before we fall down onto it completely—and noisily. Her fingers tremble as they reach for the waistband of my cargo shorts. Not so deftly, she unclasps the button and unzips the fly. Her hands slide under the thin grey fabric of my shirt, roaming over my chest and abs.

I mirror her movements, running my palm across her flat stomach, inching up her small ribcage, tracing dangerously close to the underside of her breasts. Her abs tighten and her breath hisses through her teeth as my thumbs stroke her nipples over the lace of her bra.

"Ah, Rhys," she sighs into my ear, forcing my groin to twitch to life. Since it's no longer restrained by my shorts, my rock-hard erection presses in between us, only the thin cotton of my boxer briefs separating us.

Her tongue plunges into my mouth as I toy with her breasts. No longer able to go without touching her actual skin, I pull her tank top over her head and unsnap her bra in one swift move. My large palms cup her soft curves and she melts into me. "God, I love your hands." She moans as I tease her pebbled nipples. Her back arches and instinctually, I lower my mouth to taste her.

The coarse rasp of my tongue across her heated skin causes her to grind against me as she threads her fingers into my hair. As I move to the other breast, she releases my hair and moves her hands lower— down my neck, over my shoulders, across my back and around my stomach before tentatively grabbing my cock.

I push up into her small hand. "Fuck, Soph." My sounds of pleasure spur her on and she slides a hand under the waistband, lowering my boxers over my hips. Her skin against mine, it's like silk on silk. She works me into a frenzy—long, hard strokes that have me about to lose all pretenses of control. "Soph... Oh God... your hands..." She feels me tense, knows I'm close—we've been here before. She stops, looking up into my eyes, searching for something— a reason to stop or maybe permission to go on. But I see it in her eyes, she wants this. Fucking hell, I want this.

We silently nod our agreement before I lower her to the bed. I slide off her shorts and stare, slack-jawed at the sight before me. We have *not* gone this far before—this is the first time I've seen her in the dim glow of a bedside light, completely naked—and simply breathtaking.

"Fuck, Soph... you're... I don't even know... Beautiful doesn't seem like it's a big enough word." I scrub my hand over my face, still in disbelief at how perfect she looks sprawled out on the bed.

"There you go with that Romeo stuff, again," she grins at me, making no attempt to try and cover herself. While most girls I know would absolutely loathe the idea of being naked, Sophie's never been self-conscious; she's always embraced who she is and what she looks like.

Now, I can tell why.

"I'll show you Romeo," I arch an eyebrow and kick my shorts and boxers to the floor. My erection springs free and I feel a huge bubble of pride when her eyes widen.

"Beautiful isn't enough of a word for you either, Rhys." Her words pummel my chest. I feel them somewhere deep down—this thing we're about to do, it's so much more than two kids "doing it;" it's more than just rebelling against the parents who think we shouldn't be together.

It's about being with someone because they love you for who you are, not for who they think you should be.

I cover her body with mine and revel in the feel of her skin sliding against mine. "You're so soft everywhere," I mumble against her lips, my hands skimming across inch after inch of creamy skin.

"And you're not," she arches her hips up into mine as she pulls my lower lip between her teeth.

Unable to hold back any longer, I reach down to the floor and pull a condom out of my pocket. After sliding it on, I let my fingers do some exploring, reaching in between her thighs.

Teasing, stroking, massaging, I bring her to the edge of her control within minutes. Watching her writhe in pleasure by my side is something I'll always love doing, but honestly, right now, the idea of being inside her, has my brain going all sorts of crazy.

I roll on top of her. She opens her thighs to me, wrapping her legs around my waist. I search her face for any sign of a last minute hesitation and thank God when I can't find an ounce of it.

My tip nudges her open and her nails dig into my back. "Shh, relax, babe." I press hot, wet kisses to her neck and collarbone, sending goose bumps racing across her skin. I rest my elbows on either side of her head and rain kisses across her breasts before pulling her hardened tip deep into my mouth, forcing her to push up into me.

"Holy fuck," my words are muffled against her breast. Her body stiffens as we both feel a tight pinch. "You okay?" Concern colors my words as her wince of pain tugs at my heart. She nods and searches my face for something—that she hasn't let me down, that this is the right thing to do. I'm not one hundred percent sure.

"I'll do everything in my power to make sure that's the last time I ever hurt you, Soph. I promise." Her throat works to swallow her tears as she pulls my face down to hers.

Our body moves together—not-so-perfectly in-sync, but beautifully nonetheless. When we collapse together, a mass of tangled limbs, the only sound that fills the room is that of our collective and erratic breaths.

Falling asleep with her spooned in my arms makes my world feel complete. It makes anything seem possible—even us. Despite all of the running around and hiding we've had to do, in this moment of sated contentment, it feels like our time has finally come.

Now, all we have to do is survive the rest of the summer.

Chapter 5
2014
Rhys

"You didn't tell me Sophie still lived here, dick." I shove a six-pack and a poorly wrapped Barbie doll into Carter's hands as he opens the door to let me in.

"Nice to see you, too, asshole." He claps a hand to my shoulder, closing the door behind me. "And for the record, I didn't tell you because you didn't ask. And, just in case you forgot," he pauses, sweeping his hand to the side where the boxes are stacked at least five high, "we only just moved back."

"Fine, you win." I hold up my hands, mock-surrender style.

We walk into the kitchen and he hands me a beer. Twisting the cap off, he eyes me suspiciously. "How'd you find out?"

"Fucking ran into her at Target of all places. It was…" I take a deep pull from my Bud, unable to find the right word to finish that thought. "Awkward at first, but," I take another pull from my beer, "it was really good to see her. I don't think I ever really stopped loving her." I admit quietly as Carter's wife steps into the kitchen.

"Hey, Emily." She smiles brightly at me as Maya, their two-year old daughter, bounces excitedly in her arms. "Hey, birthday girl."

"Unka Ree," Maya squeals, nearly falling out of Emily's arms.

I pop a kiss to her head before handing her the present I brought. "Here you go, sweetie." I put her down so she can open it.

"Oh *another* Barbie, just what she needs," Emily jokes as Maya sprints into her playroom to add it to her collection of dolls.

Carter hands me a tray of meat and a few more beers and we head out to the grill. "So you *think* you still love her?" Carter hedges around our earlier conversation, obviously digging for more information.

I shrug my shoulders, not really wanting to get into it. "I don't know. So much came back when I saw her." I pause for a moment, "but then again, I don't think any of it left me."

"Of course it didn't, man. She left without a trace. One day she was in your life and the next she was gone. That's not easy to get over." He casually flips a few burgers as my head spins back to ten years ago when my world was flipped upside down.

"Yeah, no shit. That's what fucked me up for so long." I won't get into all that here with him. He already knows my demons. He already knows how after she vanished, I spiraled out of control, drank my way through college, slept with pretty much anyone who would spread their legs, barely graduated by the skin of my teeth.

Life gets fucked up pretty bad when the one girl you've ever loved, the one girl who's always seen you as you—not the troubled son of the town drunk—the only girl you've ever trusted with your heart just leaves in the middle of the night without ever saying goodbye.

"So when are you going to see her again?" Carter asks, shaking me out of my silent anger. When I don't answer right away, trying to avoid the topic all together, he laughs. "Oh, cut it, asshole. You know you're going to call her. You know you're going to finally get to the bottom of what happened. That's why you moved home."

A humorless laugh fills the space between us. He's right. She might not be the only reason I came home, but I won't lie. Seeing her again definitely isn't a bad thing. There are only so many failed relationships you can handle without healing the scar that just keeps bleeding.

* * * * *

After Maya's party, I head home. Alone with my thoughts, I have to admit that I feel like a shit. Wallowing in my own self-pity isn't a pretty sight. But so much went unsaid when I ran into Sophie.

Eight years.

Carter is right. Eight fucking years is way too long to leave something like this unresolved.

Spurred on either by my anger over what happened, or by my anxiety to see what she has to say, I dial Sophie's number.

"Hello?" She sounds harried, rushed.

"Hi, Soph." When she realizes it's me, I hear her muffled gasp.

"Hi," she says with a bit more warmth in her voice. "Hold on one sec." I hear the ruffle of sheets and blankets through the line as she kisses her girls goodnight. Shit, I didn't even think about what time it was. I just dialed, the need to talk to her overwhelming me.

"Sorry, had to tuck them in," her words are still hushed. "I... I didn't expect to hear from you," she adds as the click of a door sounds out behind her.

"I said I'd call. I'd never go back on my word." Those words come out harsher than I'd intended, her betrayal fresh in my mind. She stutters over a few attempts of how to respond, and I realize I'm being an ass. No amount of anger is going to change what happened.

"I'm sorry. That was low."

"No, you're right." Frustration and sorrow are clear even in the simple sound of her sigh. "I'm the one who's in the wrong here." Her admission catches me off-guard. "There's so much that I need to say to you, that I need to explain about that night, but I can't do it over the phone."

Part of me wants to volunteer to go over there now—to hash this out tonight, but I know I can't just invite myself into her home after eight years. Plus, I'm not the one who has to apologize. This is in her hands.

"I'll make arrangements for the girls to spend the day with my mom. Can we get together for lunch?" Her offer sounds plagued with guilt and my earlier frustrations soften quite a bit.

"Lunch sounds good." She lists off the directions to her place—not the same home she grew up in, not the same home where our relationship burned and crashed to the ground.

Chapter 6
2006
Sophie

"Oh my God! What happened?" Rhys stumbles to my front porch, his eye swelling shut, shades of purple and blue shading his skin.

He eyes the hallway from the opened front door. "Are you sure they're not home? This is safe?"

Grabbing him by the arm, which I now realize is shaking, I pull him into my house. "Yes, I'm sure. I wouldn't have told you to come over if they were here. They just left for dinner and a movie. They won't be back for a few hours. We're good." I tilt my head to the side, offering him a sympathetic look as I direct him back to the kitchen. After situating him on a barstool, I hand him a bag of frozen peas wrapped in a dishtowel and slide him over a bottle of water.

I slide into the seat next to him and place my small hand on top of his still shaking one. "Your dad?" I ask the unnecessary question. He nods, his neck tense, his body vibrating in anger.

"He was so fucking drunk. I tried to help him, tried to get him inside without too much commotion. Then he caught sight of my new tattoo," his fists ball up with tension under my hand. Rhys is one of the oldest in our grade, turning eighteen months before most of us. But even if he wasn't, he looked like more of a man than a teenager and he would have easily passed for legal tattoo age anywhere. In our small, quaint, conservative town, Rhys' tattoos just fortified his pre-established bad-boy image. It's difficult not to be labeled a bad-boy when your father is constantly drunk, starting fights at the local bars—some nights, even managing to start the fights in his own home. I guess tonight is one of those nights.

"I don't know how he made out her name, but he did, and in an instant he became enraged. His arms were flailing all over the place and he took me by surprise. Got in a few good punches before I could calm him down enough to pass out on his bed." He flips over the bag of peas, searching for a colder spot to place on his now deep-purple bruise.

"Oh, honey. I'm so sorry. I don't know why he treats you the way he does." His slammed fist against the cool granite countertop makes me jump in my seat.

"He treats me like this because I remind him of my mom." His voice booms through the kitchen, bouncing off the walls around us. "He does it because I'm a worthless piece of shit!"

As he stands from the stool, the legs screech angrily across the tiled floor. "I can't wait to get the fuck out of here." He runs a more-than-frustrated hand through his medium length inky, black hair, pulling hard on the ends.

"You'll go bald by the time you're twenty, if you keep that up, honey." I step to his side and loop my arms around his waist. He smells like beer, from his father I'm sure. Draping his arms around my shoulders, he tucks me under his chin and presses his lips to the top of my head.

"Maybe, but at least I'll have you, right?" He means for the question to come out light-heartedly, but I can hear the seriousness of his undertone. From the moment we became friends and then more, he was always afraid of losing me, always afraid that we'd be found out by my too-concerned-with-appearances-to-actually-care-about-who-a-person-really-is family that we'd be ripped apart before we had a chance to really be together.

"Without a doubt, Rhys. You will always have me," I stretch up onto my toes and softly press my lips against his.

We both freeze, paralyzed by the sound of the front door clicking shut. We scramble for a moment, but it's no use. The front entry way opens up right into the joined family room and kitchen.

"What on Earth?" My father's loud voice, shrill with anger, stops us dead in our tracks. My mother stands at his side, hand covering her still-gasping mouth. "Sophie Grace DeMarco, explain what is going on right this second."

I open my mouth a few times, like a guppy gasping for precious oxygen, but my brain just won't work. In my infinite wisdom, I go with, "You're not supposed to be home yet."

"Well, we're here now," my father glowers at me, stepping toward Rhys. "And who the hell do you think you are? You're that no-good son of what's his name, Andrew Baker, right?" My father steps in between Rhys and me and even though he's a solid six feet tall, my father, at six-three, towers over him intimidatingly. It must be because of the encounter he's just had with his own dad, but Rhys, who would normally stand his ground and find some semblance of level-headedness, actually cowers under my father's cold, hard, malice.

"You smell like alcohol. You've been drinking." It's not a question but an accusation that falls from my father's lips. "What are you doing with this derelict, Sophie? Didn't your mother and I raise you better than this?" He waggles a finger in my face, his air of superiority suffocating me in the process.

I look to my mother for some kind of support, some warmth and protection—that's what mothers are for, right?

But when I get nothing from her, I straighten my spine and stare up into my father's cold, hard eyes. "I love him, Dad. We've been together..."

His flippant huff of dismissal cuts me off mid-sentence. "You're a fool. You don't know love."

"We do..." Rhys stands up for us, moving toward the heated exchange going on between my father and me.

My father turns on his heel and stares aggressively into Rhys' bruised face. "You're not good enough for her, and you never will be."

From behind my father, I'm silently begging for Rhys not to get involved, not to spur him on, not to say something he'll regret, but it's all in vain.

"We're leaving this shit hole of a town for college in just a few days and there's nothing you can do to stop it." My world crashes all around me as Rhys says the one thing he never should have said.

"No," I gasp audibly as my father chuckles maniacally at Rhys' admission.

Grabbing Rhys by the collar of his thin t-shirt, he drags him to the front door. "Like hell you are. Now get out of my house and leave Sophie alone." He pokes Rhys hard on the chest on the last word, emphasizing his point.

If I would have known that when my father shut the door on Rhys' pained face, that it would be the last time I would see him, I would have sprinted after him and run away right then and there.

Chapter 7
2014
Sophie

I shouldn't be this nervous, yet I am. No matter how much time passes, no matter how many times I remind myself that I was just a kid, it still kills me that I gave up on us without a fight.

Or maybe I did fight, but it just wasn't hard enough. I mean at eighteen, when you're still under your parents' roof, what control do you really have? I always knew my parents cared about appearances and impressions more than anything, but I never understood how shallow they were until they kicked Rhys out of their house and out of my life.

My pointless mental ramblings and non-stop pacing are abruptly interrupted by the soft tapping on my door. Taking a deep breath, I straighten my spine and hope for the best.

"Hi." My heart pounds in my chest and my mouth goes dry just at the sight of him. Tight, dark jeans paired with a cotton t-shirt that molds to the planes of muscle across his chest always was my favorite look on him. He smirks as he catches me staring, a heated blush creeping up my neck and face. "Come in."

"It's a nice place," he adds as he steps past me and into the living room.

I stifle a chuckle. "Sure if you don't mind stepping over the mound of toys."

We make our way into the kitchen and sit at the table, staring awkwardly at each other for a few quiet moments. When neither one of us seems all too ready to start the "what the hell happened to Sophie eight years ago" story, I ask the lame-ass, "What brings you back to Westfield?"

He leans his long body back in the chair, crossing his arms over his broad chest. "I wanted to start my own business, a gym, actually." I smile brightly at him.

"That's fantastic. Had you always planned to do it here?" I fold my arms on the table in front of me.

"Nah, actually I had planned to do it down in North Carolina," just the mention of where we were supposed to end up together feels like a punch to the gut.

"You went there, I'm assuming." My words are quiet as shame washes over me. That was our plan—our young, naïve, filled-with-hope plan.

"I did but I didn't make it through my first semester at UNC. They frown on drunks who rarely go to class. I lost my scholarship and ended up going to a community college by Wake Forrest where Carter went. We got an off campus apartment in his junior year. If it wasn't for him, I doubt I would have finished at all." He scrubs a hand over his face, reliving a past he seems to want to forget.

"So why didn't you start your gym there?"

"My dad died." He adds a lamely shrugged shoulder to his words.

"I'm so sorry, Rhys."

"Don't be. He drank himself into an early grave. He's got no one to blame but himself, but since I was all he had, I needed to come back up here and take care of everything. Carter just moved back so I figured I'll sell the old house and use the money for the gym."

He absentmindedly stares out the window, gazing at the birds flying in and out of the bird feeder in the back yard. "That was the girls' idea. They love animals."

"What happened?" He whispers softly. His eyes still glued to the hot pink bird feeder staked into the soft lawn.

"We were so young," I sigh, a lump of emotion quickly forming in my throat. His eyes fall to me and there's so much emotion there, so much that I need to fix and now's as good a time as any.

"Please know that I tried to get to you." He shoots me a look of disbelief across the table. "Rhys, believe me, please. I did. I fought and cried and actually tried to leave the house, but he wouldn't let me. I mean, I can't say I blame him—I was raving mad. And really what choice did I have?"

"I loved you, you know that?" He asks, pointlessly. Our love for each other, even at our young age was never the question. "You were the only good thing in my life for a long time back then and you were just gone one day."

It's after that last sentence that the full weight of the last eight years hits me in the chest. I've had time to figure it all out, time to understand why finding him never happened.

I take a deep breath and let go of everything. "After my father kicked you out, they searched my room. I felt like I was a prisoner going through room inspection or something like that. They found my phone." I see the look of recognition flicker across his beautiful face.

"You mean?"

"Yep," we share a knowing glance. "All of those pictures and texts, the emails back and forth. They found it all." My face heats just thinking about the things we would send back and forth to each other—we spent more time away from each other than with each other some days and a dirty text or a sexy picture was sometimes the only bright spot in our days.

Besides, we were horny teenagers who thought we would never be caught.

"But, I thought…"

"Oh I did. I kept it as well-hidden as I could, but when they ransacked my room, there wasn't much I could do."

He reaches his hand across the table to cover mine softly. "I don't understand why they treated you like that."

Here comes the big revelation and it's something I've never told anyone—something with which I've only recently come to terms.

"I wasn't his daughter." I let that hang out there between us. Rhys opens and closes his mouth a few times, his brow knotted in confusion trying desperately to comprehend what I've just told him. "He didn't know until I was three and I didn't find out until that night."

"What the hell?" His voice is a growl of pained confusion.

"Mom had an affair—actually a one night stand is more like it. My father was the only man she had ever been with and when things turned bad, she couldn't suppress the need to… I don't know… rebel, I guess. Mom and Dad spent some time apart and that's when she got pregnant with me. When my father begged my mother to come back to him, she went willingly because she loved him, but also because she was afraid that she wouldn't be able to provide for me as a single parent. So, she told him I was his and they patched things up as best as they could. Then when I was three, my father was up for partner at his law firm. I guess things were stressful with him working all the time and my mom being on her own after all. They fought and fought and fought and one night it came out that I wasn't his. He hasn't treated me the same since. My mom had nothing so she had to stay and since my father was so concerned with looking the part, with playing the perfect family, he let us stay." I huff out a flippant laugh at my use of the word "let." He forced my mom to stay, really—froze all of her accounts, and threatened to publicly shame her by telling all of her high profile friends that she was a slut. I guess my mom always had to know, at least a little, he would never reveal her truth—that would make him look bad, but she stayed nonetheless.

"You said high profile? There isn't much that's high profile about Westfield." He says dully.

"Yeah, that was all before we moved. After the initial blow out, I guess they patched things up enough to move on. They moved out here after my father relocated with a smaller firm. It was less stress on him in a small town and he was getting older. I think my mom enjoyed knowing that her secret was safe, no one here would really know. But it didn't stop my father from being way too over the top with keeping me… I don't know, isolated, I guess. He was always afraid I would turn into my mother and that's why he wanted to keep me away from guys like you." I huff loudly, recalling that night from eight years ago with such vividness it may as well have happened yesterday. "That's why he flipped his shit when he saw you here that night."

I feel like a weight has been lifted off my chest, but I can't imagine the weight that's still sitting on Rhys'.

Chapter 8
2014
Rhys

"A boy like me," I chuckle sarcastically. God, what a fucked up case I was back then. But, it's not exactly like my life was handed to me on a silver platter.

"So what happened after they found your phone?" I know it should be the least of my concerns after everything she's just dropped on me, but I need to know.

"All hell broke loose," she answers swiftly.

"I waited for you at the dorms, you know. When you didn't get in touch with me after your dad caught us, I waited for you and I tried to call—probably thousands of times a day."

She reaches for my hand—a gesture of sympathy, I'm sure, but I can't deny the tingles that travel up my arm, little sparks of electricity. Throwing caution, and perhaps all of my good sense, to the wind, I lace my fingers through hers and give them a gentle squeeze. She smiles at me, the kind of smile that reaches her hazel eyes, making them crinkle in the corners.

"We moved away from here right after that blow out, me and my mom, I mean. My world came crashing down around me that night. We left the next day so please understand that I didn't look for you right away not because I didn't love you, but it was because I just couldn't. I was running." She admits quickly. "That's why I never got in touch with you. She'd had enough of my father by that point. When she saw you here, she'd nearly had a panic attack thinking about what he was going to do. I had no clue about him not being my biological father until that night. She also told me that she'd been saving her own money for years on the off chance that she ever left him. Seeing him seethe at the two of us, and then dealing with the nearly volcanic eruption after you left must have been enough for her. We moved down to Miami for a few years. I went to a community college; mom got a job with her old college roommate as a receptionist in some office."

This time she's the one who squeezes my hand, searching my face to make sure I'm still with her, because, yeah, it's a fucking lot to take in. "I never got your calls because my father smashed my phone and then by the time all the dust settled in my life and I tried to get in touch with you, you must have already flunked out. I was only a kid; I had no clue where to start." A stray tear slowly streaked down her cheek.

"When I saw you the other night, I thought I was losing my mind. The only way I could know for sure it was you was by touching you, like you were just a ghost or something like that," I admit sheepishly.

She huffs a laugh. "Believe me, I didn't think you were real either." Her eyes soften and she offers up a sad smile. "I can't tell you how long it's weighed on me that all this time went by without being able to tell you how sorry I was for letting this all happen. It's all my..."

"Don't you dare finish that sentence. It wasn't *all* your fault," I slide my chair over, shimmying up beside her. "I could have looked harder, could have done more to find you, but it was easier to be drunk—guess that's just part of my DNA." I let that sit there, pregnant in the air between us. "Like you said before, we were a couple of kids who thought they could rule the world. The world just had other plans."

"That brings me to the other part of my story," she mutters, tucking a few strands of long chocolate-colored hair behind her ear.

"Your girls, you mean." I clarify and a huge, warm smile graces her face.

"I was young and stupid—par for the course, I guess. Anyway, Eddie was a nice enough guy, a decent boyfriend. We got together right at the end of college. A few months after we started dating, I got pregnant and before long there was an Eddie shaped hole in the wall. He couldn't get away quick enough."

What a dick! "He left you with twins," I grit out angrily. What kind of man does that? I bite my tongue, swallowing the rest of the insults I want to say.

Sophie rolls her eyes and laughs at my little outburst. "Eddie is far from a man. He was really just a boy—only twenty-one at the time. I wasn't going to make him stay. I saw how well that worked out with my own parents. I told Mom about it right away and we decided to move back to Westfield. Our money went further up here anyway, and, despite the memories this place has," she shoots me a knowing look, "it's a great place to raise a family."

With everything laid out and bared before us, we both take a deep breath, leaning back in our chairs, gazing out at the beautiful spring day before us.

"That's a lot of shit to deal with," I mutter.

"Yeah, tell me about it—a lot of baggage to deal with. But, please believe me, Rhys, I never meant to hurt you the way I did… it was just how things worked out." I nod at her. The sadness for how our past has been written must be evident on my face.

She stands and walks over to the sliding glass doors, wrapping her arms around her waist. She must get lost in her own emotions for a moment. Her shoulders start shaking and I hear quiet sobs filter over to me in my chair.

I step behind her, draping my arms over her delicate shoulders. She stiffens at first, not sure how to react to my touch. But, when I feel her back melt into my front, I press a sweet kiss to the top of her head. "Your hair smells the same," I whisper into her mocha and caramel-colored locks, a small smile curling at my lips.

"Is it okay to tell you that I've missed you?" She asks tentatively as she turns in my arms to face me.

Looking down at her eyes, I see a sparkle there—the light and livelihood that I've missed for so long. "I've missed you too," I admit and a spark of something hugely significant passes between us.

I bring my hand to the side of her neck, cupping it gently as I stroke her jaw line with the pad of my thumb. She leans into my touch and my chest thuds like crazy. When her lips press into the calloused skin of my palm, it's as if all time and distance has evaporated. No longer two young kids, we stand before each other two grown adults, absolved of our pasts, in search of a future.

"Soph," I nearly growl her name, feeling the soft, tender kiss she places on my hand. "What are you doin?" Her eyes close slowly as she nuzzles into my hand.

They flicker open, staring up at me, filled with so much emotion I don't even know where to begin. "I don't know," she says with more sincerity than I had expected. "I just know it feels right. Being here, with you—even if all we do is talk some more, it's just *right*." The warmth of her contented sigh washes over my skin. I angle her face up to mine and search her eyes for any hesitation. When I can't find an ounce of it, I lower my lips to hers.

The slow, erotic pulse that passes between us is almost unbearable. Her lips press against mine as I mold mine to hers—it's hot and heavenly, a perfect combination of sweet and spicy. When I trace my tongue along the seam of her lips, she whimpers and nearly goes limp in my arms. Opening to me, I slide my tongue in her mouth, reveling in the hot, velvety feel of her soft and willing mouth.

Her taste.

Her feel.

God, I devour her mouth like a starving man at his last meal. The honest truth is that this kiss is a meal I've been waiting on for far too long.

Cupping the back of her head, I pull her closer to me, coiling my other arm around her waist. When she nips on my lower lip, a rumbled growl of pleasure erupts from my mouth. Glancing over her shoulder, I see the playroom off to the side of the kitchen.

Too many small plastic pieces will get stuck in places if we go in there, so I loop my arm under her knees, lifting her in one fell swoop. She squeals and laughs a little before nuzzling into the crook of my shoulder.

"Upstairs," she whispers into my ear.

With more speed than I think I've ever moved with, I'm standing in her room, holding her in my arms at the foot of her bed.

I want to ask if she's sure about this, if she has enough time before her girls come home, if she thinks this is a good idea, but my mouth is only functioning for one thing right now—kissing her sweet lips.

With careful precision, I lower her to the bed and with a harried rush, she sits up and pulls me down with her. "I don't need slow, Rhys. I need you."

She pulls at my shirt, tugging it over my head roughly. Deft fingers quickly unsnap my jeans and a small hand dips into my boxers, stroking my erection slowly.

"Fuck," I call out, shoving up into her hand. She pushes my jeans down over my hips and when I lean back on my calves to shimmy them down the rest of the way, she moves quickly, kneeling before me on the mattress. Using just the tip of her tongue she licks me from root to tip, back and forth again and again.

I lace my fingers into her hair, pulling it out of her face. "Damn, Soph." Her lips wrap around my dick, taking it as far into her throat as she can. Catching the fiery look in her eyes, I can't help but wonder if I'm not the only one who's been starving all these years.

"Too close... I'm too close..." I pull away from her and drag her legs out from under her body.

She's naked in about two seconds flat—our clothes a rumpled pile on the floor.

I press my body against hers, resting my elbows on either side of her head. I dot her ear, neck, collarbone, and shoulders with heated kisses, loving the sight of her skin raising in goose bumps with every touch of my lips. After nuzzling my nose against the hardened tip of her breast, I lick and nip at it. Drawing it deep into my mouth, I feel her push her hips up into mine. I stop at the other nipple, paying it the same attention as the first, before capturing her mouth in a searing kiss.

"After all these years, you're still the most beautiful woman I've ever seen." A blush creeps across her chest and neck at my words.

"Still a Romeo even after all this time," she jokes, grazing her fingers through my day-old stubble.

"Oh, I'll show you Romeo." I waggle an eyebrow before descending down her body—neck, breasts, stomach, hipbone.

She spreads her legs willingly. "I've wanted to do this for so long," I mumble against the soft flesh of her inner thigh, inhaling her sweet scent. "God, if you taste half as good as you smell..." I can't think of anything to complete that thought, because when the tip of my tongue licks through her hot flesh, I lose all sense of rational thought.

Feeling Sophie writhe beneath me with each rapid flick and smooth stroke of my tongue is like finding heaven. Two fingers easily glide into her tight pussy. Massaging and stretching her, I find her g-spot and work my fingers back and forth across in perfect sync with my tongue.

Her nails dig into my back before scratching at my scalp. She grinds into my face shamelessly, calling out my name. I feel the tiny flutters build into rolling squeezes as her orgasm builds, gathering strength like an impending storm.

"Rhys... Rhys... oh God... I'm..." Before she can get the last word out, she comes with spectacular beauty, barely able to contain her ecstasy.

I crawl on top of her, a wicked smirk pulling at my lips. "Please tell me you have a condom."

She fumbles in the bedside table and just when I think she's going to come up empty, she finds one buried behind a few magazines. She tears it with her teeth and reaches between us to roll it down over me, causing me to grind against her hand once more.

I slide into her inch by fucking agonizing inch, stretching her with every movement. "Fuck, Soph... you're so tight."

She looks up at me shyly, admitting, "It's been a while."

I lean back down on my elbows, molding my lips to hers as I glide in and out of her, never all the way in and never all the way out—short, hot strokes, preparing her.

"Now, Rhys... God, I want all of you now," her nails dig into my ass on the last word, pulling me into her.

"Ahhhh, so fucking tight," I growl in her ear before sinking my teeth into the soft flesh where her neck meets her shoulder.

We set a grueling pace—driving, pounding, really. She thrusts up into me and I drill into her as if we're both trying to bury ourselves deep inside the other person.

My pleasure builds, a slow tingle gathering at the base of my spine, pulling my balls tight against my body. "Sophie... Sophie..." Her name falls from my lips in time to my final thrusts.

"Oh God... Rhys..." she calls out as she falls over the edge with me.

Sated and calm, we lie in each other's arms, reveling in the feel of just being close to one another again. She presses a soft kiss to my chest as she curls into my side. I wrap my arm around her, pulling even closer still, as I press a kiss to the top of her head.

"So what do we do now?" She asks cautiously.

Running my fingers through her hair, I stare up at the ceiling. I can't say I wasn't thinking the same thing, but honestly, I don't know what comes now. "What do you want to happen?"

I feel her chuckle softly. "You know, answering a question with a question is, like, breaking the first rule of conversation."

I laugh with her before finally conceding. "Truthfully, I'd like to see you again."

"I'd like that too," she looks up at me with doe eyes and a fully bared soul.

We both stiffen as we here keys jingle in the door downstairs. Four feet quickly and loudly race through the door, followed by who I'm assuming is Sophie's mom.

"Caught again," she laughs, softly tracing her fingertips through the light dusting of hair on my chest.

"Looks that way."

As we get dressed, a touch of tense silence descends upon us. "Are you sure Soph? I could sneak out..."

She cuts me off, silencing me with her lips. "Stop," she says, pressing a finger to my lips. "Mom is different, I promise, and so am I." She wraps her arms around my waist, pressing her cheek to my chest. "Maybe we can be too?"

"Different?" I clarify.

"Yeah, different, but the same. Maybe."

Lacing our fingers together, I pop a kiss to her forehead. "Different but the same sounds like the perfect combo for me."

As we reach the bottom of the stairs, Sophie calls out, "There's someone I want you to meet, Mom."

At this point, all I can hope for is a better reception than last time.

Melissa Collins

Author Dedication

Thank you so much to Novel Grounds for giving me the chance to write this story. It was so challenging and fun to write. And a huge thank you to my family for giving me the time to discover and explore my passion.

About Melissa

Melissa Collins has always been a bookworm. Studying Literature in college ensured that her nose was always stuck in a book. She followed her passion for reading to the most logical career choice: English teacher. Her passion for writing didn't start until more recently. When she was home on maternity leave in early 2012, she read her first romance novel and her head filled with the passion, angst, and laughter of the characters who she read about it. It wasn't long before characters of her own took shape in her mind. Their lives took over Melissa's brain and The Love Series was born.

Follow Melissa

Website: http://www.melissacollinsauthor.com/

Facebook: http://www.facebook.com/melissacollins.author

Read More from Melissa

Let Love In: http://amzn.to/1e0Then

Cora's Plantation

Jettie Woodruff

Chapter 1

"Hello," Kadyn answered her ringing phone.

"Kadyn Wellington! What is going on there? I just got an email, informing me that you were under academic probation. What's this all about?"

"It's nothing, Mom. I copied and pasted a little, that's it. It's not a big deal."

"It *is* a big deal. Isn't that the same as cheating? How do you expect to have a career in politics with a record like that?"

I never wanted a career in politics. "Mom, its fine. It's not going to be on my record; I've already talked to my professor about it. Don't make it out to be some big thing. I've got to go, I'm walking into class," Kadyn lied, tossing her phone to the bed with a deep sigh. She was never going to make it through her senior year—she didn't even want to. For once in her life she just wanted to do what she wanted to do, not what the political Wellington's wanted her to do. She wasn't like her sister; she wasn't into public speaking, campaigning, and she sure as hell wasn't trying for an intern position at the white house.

She glanced at the time, noting that she hadn't actually lied to her mom—she really did have to get to class. She hated this class, not that she didn't hate all of them. Mr. Rodrigues was so boring—she never knew what he was talking about. She groaned thinking about the controversial subject that she was going to have to debate against Candace Long. They were in Chicago, why did they need to debate about the racing industry being forced to use biofuels. Kadyn didn't care. She'd never even watched a race.

"It's not about the race, Kadyn. It's about the argument," her dad had tried to explain when she complained about it. She knew that but

still didn't care. She wanted to go to nursing school and take care of little babies. She didn't want to follow the line of her political parents, or her sister who was obsessed with all the political bullshit too. Her sister Janelle was three years older, just got her masters in political science, and would be interning at the White house. Her parents were so proud and often talked about how Kadyn, too, would get an internship there as soon as they witnessed how dedicated Janelle was. She would never be that dedicated. She just wanted it to be December already so she could take a break from school.

This was college, she was supposed to be partying and living it up. Unfortunately, it wasn't that kind of school—students even dressed in business attire to attend class. She'd been looking forward to getting away from her parents so she could wear cool jeans and hoodies. That didn't happen; instead, her school was full of nerdy, dedicated, wannabe politicians. It sucked, and her roommate didn't help matters any. She always had her nose in a book with the television on the campus's political station. Needless to say, Kadyn had ear buds permanently placed in her ears.

* * * * *

"Are you sure I'm in the right place?" Anderson asked, gazing out the windshield to the old stone archway leading to some sort of plantation.

"Does it say Wellington in gold letters?"

"There's not really gold anymore; this place is rough, Charles."

"That's why we're going to get it at a steal. Some old bat inherited it back in 1955. Offer one million. From what I have researched, she's alone. I guess she has some high class, political son in Detroit, he doesn't even visit her. I'm sure we'll be signing papers in no time."

"How much land did you say was here?" Anderson asked, looking around as he drove up the dirt road.

"Over 700 acres—more than enough for a luxurious golf resort that will make us both very rich. You just secure the deal and let me take care of the rest."

Anderson started down the long lane of weeping willows, wondering if the old house was even still standing. All he saw was dried up cotton fields that hadn't been used in quite some time, probably years. The manor was at least three miles in, sitting alone, nestled in overgrown trees and some sort of ivy that had taken over the right side of the house.

This was his chance, the big opportunity that he had been waiting for. He could see the potential in the mansion. The architecture was brilliant, nothing like you would see in a modern house. The house was charged with emotional symbolism. Anderson opened the door of his expensive BMW, straightening his tie as he visualized the entrance. Lori would love it there, well, maybe not yet, but eventually. It wasn't like they would be living there anytime soon. The old hag was still breathing.

"You got business here?" The old lady asked, looking down the barrel of a shotgun.

Anderson held up his hands. Jesus, the old woman was crazy. "Sorry ma'am, I didn't mean to frighten you. My name is Anderson Paine. I'm doing some research on Alabama plantations. I was hoping to talk to you about your home," he lied.

"Watcha wanta know?" she asked sternly, not dropping the gun.

"Well, I'm absolutely amazed by the architecture," he replied, sliding his hands into his dress slacks, trying to ease her trepidation. That part wasn't a lie; he was in awe of the rundown mansion, maybe for other reasons, but he was no doubt intrigued by what this place could be.

The old lady lowered the gun and opened the wooden screen door, causing a creek and a thump from the walker that she pushed in front of her.

"Could I come in? It's a little chilly out here," Anderson offered.

"I suppose you look like a nice young man. I'll make some coffee," she offered. It was a frigid day for that part of Alabama. The earlier rain left a lingering damp chill. Cora probably shouldn't have let the stranger come in. Truth was, she got lonely out there all by herself. She hardly ever saw people anymore, hadn't in years. She saw Tommy

Price once a week and that was it. He never stayed to visit though; he'd drop off the one bag of customary groceries, gallon of milk, and occasional household necessities. He was just a young boy with no need to associate with Cora Wellington.

Anderson walked behind Cora, noticing her feet dragging and scuffing across the floor. He wondered what was wrong with her, other than her eighty-something year old age. His eyebrows rose when he caught sight of the interior of the home. It wasn't near as rundown as it looked on the outside. Granted the whole place was covered in dust and cobwebs, but it was obvious that she couldn't do any of the cleaning. He observed the double staircase also covered in dust. He was sure it had been a while since anyone had ventured up the steps.

"Do you have something to write with?" Cora asked, heating a kettle of water.

"Something to write with?" Anderson asked.

She turned and glanced over the brim of her glasses. "You wanted to know about the plantation. You gonna remember it all?"

"Oh, I have something in my car. I wanted to make sure this was okay before I got it out."

Cora walked over to a beautiful cabinet, housing an elegant set of china. She opened a drawer with arthritic hands and took out a yellow legal pad.

Anderson took a pen from a cup in the center of the table and accepted the pad of paper.

"Have you always lived here?" he asked, not writing.

"I moved here with my in-laws when my husband was drafted. I had become with child and my husband didn't want me to be alone."

Anderson smiled at her description of her being pregnant. "This was your husband's childhood home?"

"It was. I married Ross Wellington in 1947. He was killed when our son was just over a year old."

"And you stayed with your in-laws?"

Cora looked down to her worn out slippers and smiled. "I married Randal Wellington when Arden was not quite a year old. Randal was Ross's younger brother."

Hmmm, Cora Wellington had a past. She married her husband's brother? "You only had one child?"

"We tried, it just never happened."

Anderson asked a lot of questions, mostly about the house, the land, the taxes, and the deed. He listened intently as the old lady rattled on and on about her home, the grounds, the cotton crops, and her only son, whom she hadn't seen in over a year now. He was busy, she understood that. He had a political career, and was too busy to be bothered with her. He didn't think the lady was ever going to shut up, still he listened. He had to; but what he really wanted to do was explore the place, see what he was up against.

"Do you think I could take a look around?" He finally asked after two and a half hours. That should've been enough time to win her trust.

"I suppose it would be okay, only the downstairs though," she countered. "It's a big house. You might be here a while. Maybe if you come back, you can explore the upstairs."

Anderson had a feeling she was fishing for him to come back. She seemed to like his company, or any company, really.

"I have nowhere else to be. I don't mind having my presence graced by a beautiful woman like yourself at all," he flattered.

"Oh, you go on now," she rosily gestured with her hand, dismissing him to snoop around her house. "You can go down to the cellar if you want," she nodded to the wood door in the corner of the kitchen,

"Is it haunted?" he teased.

"More than likely, I haven't been down there in 40 years."

* * * * *

Three more days of finals. Kadyn couldn't wait to get out of Chicago. She was looking forward to the warmer weather and would be content if she never saw another snowflake in her life. Plus she hadn't seen her Grandma Cora since June.

"Hey dad, did you get my plane ticket?" she asked, tightening her winter coat around her, trying to shield from the brisk wind whipping through her skin.

"Plane ticket?" he asked.

"Yes, to Grandma's remember? You said it would be okay to go there during Christmas break."

"Oh, didn't you talk to your mother? We're spending Christmas in Washington this year."

"No way. You guys are just going to go there and attend a bunch of charity and Christmas parties. I am not spending my two weeks off in Washington with a bunch of politicians."

"You are one of those politicians, my dear child," Arden reminded her.

Not by choice. "Dad, I've already told her I was coming."

"How? She doesn't even own a phone. You haven't talked to her in six months."

"I told her when I was there in the summer I'd be there for Christmas."

"You're going to have to take that up with your mother. I've got to go Kadyn, I have a board meeting. Call your mom."

Kadyn was going to Alabama if she had to buy a bus ticket herself. There was no way she was spending Christmas with a bunch of social climbing politicians. She stomped down the sidewalk of the campus, furious at her family. Why couldn't she have been born into a circus family, had a waitress and a banker for a mother and father, anything but this. She'd been to more campaigns, charities, social events, and election parties than any twenty-three year old girl should have been to in a lifetime.

"Why don't you watch where you're going?" one of her classmates yelled as Kadyn plowed into her, sending her bag and books to the sidewalk.

"Sorry," Kadyn replied. She didn't know the girls name, just the face. She didn't know anyone's name except for her roommate, Kathrine. Their parties consisted of library meetings and debates they did on their own in circles because they wanted to. Kadyn attended one of those debates. She didn't care about that subject either. It didn't matter to her one way or another whether or not same sex marriage should be legal. To each his own.

The girl gathered her things and stormed away. Kadyn only snorted and shook her head. She spent her ten-minute walk back to her dorm, freezing and arguing with her mother. She got about as far as she had with her dad. Her mother had it all planned out: they were going to spend a week in a house with Marla and Thomas Black, their political friends. She wasn't even sure of their titles, but knew they were both high up there on the list of representatives. She didn't care, she wasn't going. Their son was always trying to get her to go out with him, and, of course, her parents loved the nerd to death. She wasn't about to spend a week listening to Garett Black talk about Obama Care.

* * * * *

"I've been there three times in the last month. She's not going to crack. She won't sell, Charles," Anderson implored, trying to get his stepfather to understand that this lady wouldn't budge.

"Bullshit," Charles yelled, his fist coming down hard on his desk. "I have investors waiting to hand over their money. It's almost Christmas—get your ass back there and get me a deal. That's an order."

"I'm not going back to Alabama right now. It's Christmas. I promised Lori I'd spend a few days with her in New York."

"You're going to Alabama. Have you ever come out and bluntly asked the old bat, you pussy? You also need to put that girl of yours in her place. You let her control you too much."

"I don't need to just come out and ask her, she's told me a hundred times it's staying in the hands of a Wellington. We already know she has no family. We'll get it from the son; he doesn't want the place. And I do not let Lori control me."

"You do, Anderson. You're a Paine. If I would have known you weren't going to be able to control your women, I'd sure as hell thought twice before giving you my name."

"You adopted me when I was *five*."

"And you've seen me with enough women to know what the hell you're supposed to do with them. You're twenty-five—you shouldn't even be tied to one girl. We got her daddy's hotel, you're done with her. Get the fuck out of here. I've got work to do," Charles demanded.

Anderson stood to leave, shaking his head as he closed the door. Charles was already on the phone, setting up arrangements for Anderson to be in White Forks, Alabama in three days. *Great.* He was going to spend three days pretending to listen and give a shit about this lady's history. Lori was going to be pissed.

Anderson decided to try his upper hand that very evening. He's watched his step dad control four different wives, maybe that was why he had four different wives, including his own mother, but nonetheless. They did as he said, when he said it.

"I can't believe you, Anderson," Lori yelled, really yelled. Yep, she was pissed. "You do this every time. I don't even know why we make plans—you're just going to cancel them, anyway."

Anderson stood from his seated position at the head of his table. His fist came down hard, just like Charles would do.

"That will be the last time you raise your voice to me," he angrily spoke through gritted teeth. "Do you understand me?" he asked, grabbing her up from her chair.

He guessed there was an act to this controlling thing, or maybe a certain kind of girl. Lori wasn't that girl. She slapped him across the face and stormed out of his high-rise apartment. Anderson stared after her with his hand covering the stinging sensation on his cheek.

"Well, that went well," he said as the door slammed loudly.

* * * * *

"What do you mean you're in White Forks," Elaina yelled through the phone. They were scheduled to board a plane in three hours; Kadyn was supposed to be on the plane that had just hit the ground.

"I took the bus. I'm spending Christmas with Grandma," Kadyn said for the second time.

"I can't believe you right now, Kadyn. What were you thinking? Garett is expecting you to be there."

"Garett? Really mom. You'd rather I spend Christmas with some geek than my own grandmother?"

"That *geek* is your future. Your grandmother isn't even going to know you're there."

"Yes she will. She is as smart as you are, if not smarter, and I assure you, Garret Blake is not my future."

"Get a cab to the airport, I'll order the ticket," Elaina ordered.

"No. I'm not spending Christmas in Washington. I'm going to Grandma Cora's," Kadyn argued and hung up just as the bus pulled into the small town. *Aha, White Forks*, she smiled, breathing in the country air where the weather wasn't what you would call warm, but she'd take the fifty-eight over the twenty-one she left in Chicago any day. She looked up to the sun, letting it relax and warm her face while she waited for the attendant to retrieve her bag.

She thanked the lady and threw her backpack over her shoulder, walking toward the road to her grandma's. She stopped off at Thompson's diner and got a cup of his delicious hot chocolate with melted marshmallows for her walk. She could have gotten a ride; she knew several people around there. She didn't want to, though, enjoying the peaceful walk in the superb weather. It was a beautiful sunny day, and it felt good to be there and away from the rat race of Chicago. It wasn't that far, maybe four or five miles, which would take her an hour or so if she strolled and took her time. That was her plan. She was going to enjoy the fresh air and the scenery.

"Hey, little girl. I didn't know you were coming. How are you?" A man asked, rolling down his truck window.

"Hi, Buck. I'm well. How are you?"

"Never better, get in, I'll give you a lift."

"Nah, I kinda want to walk. I'm used to that Chicago weather; I'm enjoying this too much to ride. You think maybe you could stop by later and give me a jump? I'm sure that thing hasn't been started since I was here in the summer."

"Sure thing, kiddo. Might not be until tomorrow, is that okay? Going to watch my granddaughter in her school Christmas play."

"Yes, that's fine. I'm sure I won't be going out today."

"How's your dad?"

"Same ole dad," she smiled.

"Still trying to be the president, eh?"

"Yeah, something like that," she agreed.

"See ya later," he called when she fished her ringing cell phone from her pocket.

"Hey, they sick you on me now too?" Kadyn asked, waving to the older gentleman.

"Why do you have to be so difficult? It's Christmas, Kadyn."

"Exactly, Janelle, its Christmas. Grandma shouldn't spend it alone."

"Mom wants you here, Kadyn."

"I refuse to spend my break around all those people. I'm staying here with Grandma Cora."

"Why would you want to stay in that haunted house with that old kook?"

"That's so wrong, she's is your grandmother too. You'd rather hangout with a bunch of people who are only in this world for themselves than to be with your family?"

"Kadyn, your family is going to be there, remember? I'm your sister. I haven't seen you since Thanksgiving. Why do you have to be so weird?"

Me, weird? "That was only three weeks ago. I'm not coming, Janelle."

"Fine, whatever. I told mom I was wasting my time."

"I'll call you in a day or two."

"Mom and Dad are not happy about this."

"Yeah, they'll get over it. I'll talk to you later," Kadyn said, not giving her sister time to respond before hanging up.

She did enjoy her quiet walk along Steiner road, all the way to the lane leading to her grandmother's house. She enjoyed *that* walk even more. The weeping willows down the long lane were so dramatic, the atmosphere felt almost theatrical with a personality. Kadyn thought about being a little girl and skipping down that road with her grandmother when she was a small child. Of course, it wasn't often. They rarely visited, even growing up, and, when they did, her mother was ready to leave in a day or two.

Once Kadyn got a little older, her dad did let her and her sister visit alone more. They would stay a couple weeks in the summer, but that too changed once Janelle got older. She didn't want to stay in the boring mansion with no internet, or cable television. She wanted to stay in Detroit with her friends. Kadyn still came though. Her grandmother was probably the closest person she had in her life. She never fit in with her family's high-class snobs; she never fit in at her private, all-girls school. She was always backward and stuck to herself.

Kadyn blamed her backwardness on her upbringing. She'd never been normal, not the kind of normal she envisioned anyway. Her family activities included inaugurations, debates, public addresses, political speeches, and more social events than she cared to remember. Her parents were always on to her to pay attention. When she was twelve she asked for the hot new *Harry Potter* book for her birthday. She got *The Politics of Direct Democracy: Referendums in Global Perspective*. It was exactly what all pre-teen girls wanted.

Coming to Grandma Cora's was the only time she ever got away from the craziness of her family, their friends, and colleagues. She loved it; her mother hated it. She thought she needed to be in the limelight, exposing herself to important people. She needed to know the right people to insure she had a head start on her career... the career she never wanted.

Her reminiscing was interrupted by the black BMW coming up the lane. She stopped and looked back, wondering what a fancy car like that would be doing coming to her grandmas.

"You lost?" she asked, as Anderson rolled down his window.

"I was about to ask you the same question," he smiled.

Wow, what a powerful smile. "I'm not lost, my grandmother lives here. What's your story?"

"Your grandmother?" *Shit!* She never once mentioned a granddaughter, only a son. This could be bad.

"Yes, you know her?"

"Sort of. I was just going to visit her. You want a ride?"

"No. I can see the house. I'm fine. How do you know my grandmother?"

"I was doing a story on plantations around here a month or so back. She filled me in on a lot of information and we just kind of became friends. She doesn't get many visitors."

"Who do you write for?" Kadyn asked suspiciously. She didn't believe him. Writers were starvers; he did *not* make enough money writing to buy that car.

"I write for a lot of people."

"So you freelance?" Freelancers didn't make that kind of money, either. This guy was up to something, Kadyn decided as she continued to walk while Anderson crept, following.

"Yeah, you could say that."

Kadyn continued with the probing questions and rudely kept walking once they were at the house, not waiting for him to exit is car. He was beside her before she had her key out of her bag.

"Grandma!" Kadyn called. They both ran to the kitchen when they heard a moan.

Cora was spread eagle on the hardwood floor.

"Grandma, are you okay? Did you fall?" Kadyn asked, kneeling beside her.

"No, I'm dying."

"Why? Do you have chest pains or something?"

"No, I'm just dying."

"Did you purposely lay down here?"

"Yes, I told you, I'm dying."

"But why are you on the floor?"

"I didn't want to die standing up."

Kadyn smiled and shook her head, happy that she was okay and just being a little senile. "Can you wait till I go back to school to die? I came to spend Christmas with you."

"Oh, I guess so."

"Help me get her up," Kadyn requested, looking up to Anderson. Not hesitating, he helped her pull the frail lady to her feet and into a chair.

"Don't do that again, Grandma. You're going to get down there and not be able to get up one day."

"Where's Arden?" Cora asked.

"Dad didn't come, Grandma. He's working."

"I told that boy to go to school. He wouldn't be working in that field, had he listened to me."

Kadyn smiled up at the stranger. "I don't think she's much for company today. Maybe you could stop by in a day or so."

Anderson didn't want to come back the next day. He had just driven all the way from Atlanta. He wasn't going back yet. He had to find out what was going on. Charles would be wanting an update. This girl could mean trouble. Nah, surely not. She was from the big city. She wouldn't want this place. He just needed to stay focused and not fret over issues that weren't there.

"I was planning on going back into town and cooking for her tonight. You eat, right?"

"You don't have to do that. I'll take care of it," Kadyn assured him.

"I wasn't going to do it because I had to. I was going to do it for Ms. Cora here. I promised her my famous lasagna," shit... what the hell was he saying? He didn't cook. He had no idea how to make lasagna. It was fine. She wasn't going to let him stay anyway. He could tell.

"Kadyn, you're not being very hospitable. Where are your manners? The boy wants to make us dinner. We should let him... besides, he's cute. Don't you think he's handsome, Kadyn?"

"Grandma!" Kadyn scolded, feeling the blush burn her cheeks.

Anderson laughed. "Okay, it's settled. I'll be back in a little bit. Is there anything else I can pick up while I'm out?" *Besides a cookbook?* He thought.

"I'm sure there is. Can you wait a few minutes while I check for things she needs?"

"Sure, I'm in no hurry."

Kadyn walked around the kitchen, writing a grocery list as she looked through the cupboards. Anderson raised his eyebrows. He didn't know he was grocery shopping, he was just picking up a few things.

"Grandma, where is your checkbook? I need to give--" she stopped, looking up, forgetting his name.

"Anderson," he helped.

"There is cash in the nightstand by my bed," Cora explained.

Kadyn walked into the room that used to be the den. *Ugh*, she smelled, taking in the scent of her grandmother's room. It needed a good cleaning and probably clean sheets.

"Oh, my God, Grandma," she said out loud, scooping up handfuls of twenty dollar bills. There had to be a couple thousand dollars there. She took three of them and headed out.

Waiting until Anderson left, she turned to her Grandmother. "Grandma, where did you get all that money? You can't keep that kind of money lying around."

"Tommy cashes my estate checks for me every month. I have to get them cashed. Someone took my car keys."

"Give him a deposit slip and let him deposit them. I'm going to talk to him before I leave. You can't keep that money in your nightstand like that."

"What if I need some cash?"

"We'll keep some out for you," she promised, knowing she should never need it.

* * * * *

"Please tell me you have good news. I'd like to get this thing going by February," Charles answered his phone.

"Not really. I sort of have bad news," Anderson replied, holding his breath and knowing what was coming.

"What do you mean? Don't fuck with me, boy. What the hell is it?"

"Her granddaughter showed up here."

"Granddaughter? I thought she just had a son."

"You did that research, not me. She has a granddaughter. I'm sure of it."

"Is that the only grandchild?"

"I don't know yet. I haven't really had the time to talk to her yet."

"How old is the girl?"

"I don't know. I'd say twenty, maybe."

"Perfect. Take her to bed."

"What?"

"You heard me. Sleep with the girl. Get her on your side, take control, and wait for my instructions. Find out about the will."

"I'm having sex with her granddaughter? She doesn't even know me... she's not going to let me touch her. You're crazy."

"You have three days there. Get in her pants and start the process. You want me to give you control of the whole resort project, but you can't control some twenty year old puss?"

"Charles, I am not going to try to get in the girl's pants. That's absurd."

"You will, I'm sure of it. I'll call you tomorrow. Find out about the will."

"CHARLES!!!!"

"Goddamnit," Anderson yelled, tossing his phone to the passenger seat.

Chapter 2

Cora was napping in her recliner when Anderson returned with the groceries. He carried in the bags, wondering where Kadyn had gone.

He had them almost put away when she emerged carrying a laundry basket of sheets.

"You better not let my grandma see that," Kadyn nodded toward the bottle of wine while snapping a pillowcase and folding it.

"She doesn't drink wine?"

"I've never known her to drink any kind of alcohol. She says it's the devils blood."

"I guess I better make sure she doesn't see it then," he smiled with a wink.

What the hell? Was he flirting with her? Hmm he was kind of cute. Okay, he was hot as hell, but she wasn't looking.

"Your famous lasagna, huh?" Kadyn said, spying the cookbook on the counter.

"I forgot my recipe back home," he lied.

"Sure you did," she accused, walking out to put the clean sheets on Cora's bed.

Anderson procrastinated, taking as long as he could in the kitchen. He listened to Kadyn interacting with her grandmother in the next room, sounding more like the adult than Cora did. She was determined to turn the heat over to air because it was the 4th of July; Kadyn argued with her and told her it was almost Christmas and she couldn't turn the air on.

"Then we need a fire. We have to have a fire for Christmas."

"We will, we need to get someone out to check the chimneys before we build a fire."

"Charlie was just here. He ran that brush thingy down all of them. We can build a fire."

"I'll talk to Charlie tomorrow, just to be sure, okay?"

"No, we need to build a fire. Go look out back. He brought all that wood for me."

It was a little chilly in the house, and a warm fire and book on her iPad sounded pretty good. Kadyn went to the kitchen to get her phone. She wasn't building a fire until she talked to Charlie himself.

"Hmm, it smells delicious," she said coming into the kitchen.

"I'm actually kind of proud of myself," he smiled, looking at his loaf of bread, ready to bake.

"Why? Because you really don't have a famous lasagna recipe?" she asked.

"I do not," he smiled, trying to flirt. She turned and walked out. Damn she was tough. Maybe she wasn't into guys.

After talking to Charlie and being assured that he indeed came out and took care of the chimneys. Kadyn started a fire in the living room. She cleaned off the dining room table, moving stones and pebbles, shaking her head. Why was her grandma bringing them in the house? She wiped it clean of dust, and set it for their supper. She was hoping it was almost done. She was starving.

"Need some help?" she asked, more for the benefit of her hungry stomach than his.

"Nope, I think it's ready. Do you want a glass of wine in a coffee cup or something?"

"Sure," she smiled, thinking about it. A full belly, wine, a cozy fire, Grandma sleeping in her chair, and a good book—that's the kind of Christmas she was hoping for. Anderson would leave right after supper, she would shower, and curl up under one of her grandma's handmade quilts. She couldn't wait.

Anderson's lasagna was actually pretty good. Kadyn listened to her grandmother talking about the county fair that she raced horses in last week and won. She was starting to worry about her. She'd really gone downhill since the summer. She was pretty forgetful even then, but this was different. She was talking like it was 1965, believing everything she was telling them. Anderson even asked questions as if he believed everything she was saying.

"Grandma, you haven't barrel raced in many years," Kadyn tried, giving Anderson a look to stop encouraging her. Cora stood and walked to the other room with her cane. Anderson glanced at Kadyn, wondering what she was doing.

She returned carrying a medium sized trophy.

"There. Don't you tell me, young lady," she ordered, handing the trophy over to Kadyn.

Kadyn looked at the first place gold plate and then the date, 1961, White Forks County Fair. She didn't argue. She only smiled and set it aside.

"Thanks for the visit, and stopping by," she said, getting up and cleaning dishes, dismissing Anderson to be on his way.

"I can help clean up," he offered.

"No, I've got it. It's dark out. You can go. Thanks again," she said, walking away with dishes in hand. He followed carrying in the pan of lasagna.

"I'm not leaving you with the mess," he assured her.

"Do you live close?" she asked, wondering where he came from.

"Not too far from here," he lied, trying to think of his next lie before she asked.

"Where do you live?" she asked, pulling the foil off to cover the leftovers.

"Carroldon," he replied, remembering the town right before White Forks. Kadyn gave him a look; only outsiders called it that, the locals called it Carol Dawn. That was what it was originally. The town was named after a woman from the early twenties who had fought to get the railway through the town. She didn't say anything, deciding to let it go, but knew this guy was up to something. He didn't live in Carol Dawn, and she didn't believe he was a freelance writer either.

"You can go," she practically ordered.

Shit. He didn't want to go. He didn't want her to be there. He was hoping to find a will, find out exactly what this old woman had. He could have done it, had this mysterious granddaughter not showed up. Now what? Charles was going to explode.

Anderson said goodnight to Cora and saw himself out.

"You have good news?" Charles answered on the first ring.

"Not exactly. I need more than one night. The girl is suspicious," he replied.

"Did you do what I ordered?'

"No. I just met the girl."

"Yeah, and your point? Where are you?"

"Heading back."

"Like hell you are? You get your ass back there and take care of that girl."

"I can't just go back to the house. She'll call the cops."

"You're such an idiot. Do I have to do all of your thinking? Pull the car over, walk back to the house, and tell her your car broke down."

"I can't do that, Charles. She knows people around here. She's just going to call someone to come and bail me out, besides, it just started raining. I'm not walking back there."

"Perfect."

"What?"

"It's raining, she'll feel sorry for you. Is she cute?"

"What?"

"Never mind. It doesn't matter. Get your ass back there and take care of business. I want that property."

"CHARLES!!!!" Anderson yelled to the dead phone again. Stupid bastard.

He pulled over about half way down the lane and looked at the outside temperature, reading forty-five. Forty-five and rain. *Great.* He shut his car off and did a quick search on what to do to make the car not run without damage. Hmm, that's an easy fix, he thought before popping the hood, and removing the fuel pump relay. Sliding back in, he cranked the key. Nothing. Now all he had to do was hike back to the house.

Kadyn took a quick shower in the downstairs bathroom, the water barely warm. She needed to get someone out there to check it. She dried off, quickly, freezing from the cool air hitting her already cold skin. She thought about her father and how he seemed to be neglecting his own mother. She shouldn't be left alone anymore and he acted as though he had only one thing on his mind, getting votes. She wasn't sure what to do. How did she go about getting someone in there to stay with her grandmother? She was only twenty-three; she didn't know what needed to be done.

Kadyn pulled on dark blue, worn sweatpants, her favorite pair, a plain white tee, and an ugly grandma-looking purple sweater. It was her grandma's, but she was freezing. She went out to the empty living room where she had left her grandmother, working a word search puzzle. She wasn't there. Walking to her room, she quietly opened the door, finding her snuggled in bed. Smiling, she closed the door behind her. Powering on her tablet while she threw a couple pieces of wood on the fire, she groaned. Crap. The battery was dead. She dug through her bag, groaning again, realizing she didn't have the charger. So much for her relaxing night with a book and Anderson's wine.

She froze when she heard the knock at the door. It was nine o'clock, who in the world could that be? Walking over to the door she peeked through the side window, seeing Anderson, soaked to the bone.

"What are you doing?" she asked, opening the door.

"Burr, my car broke down. I figured it would be closer to walk back here than it would be into town."

Kadyn didn't believe him. He had a brand new BMW. How could it just break down?

"Can I come in?" he asked, obviously freezing to his core.

Kadyn stepped aside with a peculiar look. He walked past her and straight to the fire. He'd worry about everything else when he was dying from hypothermia.

"Hope you don't mind," he said, removing his wet shirt. Whoa… she did mind. She was still a female after all.

She tossed him the afghan from her grandma's chair. "I was just going to have a glass of your wine, want one?" she offered.

"Yes, that would be great," he replied with chattering teeth, wrapping himself in the blanket.

Kadyn poured them both a glass of wine and joined him in front of the fire.

"Thank you," he said.

"Aren't you going to call someone to come and get you?" she asked, not-so-subtly letting him know that he wasn't staying.

"No, I'm staying the night. I'm sure Grandma Cora would insist."

"You can't stay here. What are you up to? What are you doing here? And don't give me some line about being a writer, either. I don't believe that story for a second; a good-looking guy like you doesn't just go around visiting lonely old women. You have a motive."

"Good looking guy, eh?" he smiled a sexy smile.

"What's your last name?" she asked for whatever reason. At least if he turned out to be some sort of murderer she would have a name. Oh, wait... she'd be dead.

"Paine. Anderson Paine."

"My dad says you should never trust a guy with two last names."

Anderson laughed. "Actually, that's never trust a guy with two first names."

"Oh, answer my question. And you're still not staying here."

"I have to, unless you're going to make me walk to town in the rain."

"You're not serious. You are a stranger; I'm not letting you stay here. I'll call someone."

"Who are you going to call? It's late."

Anderson was right. She wouldn't call someone to come out on a cold rainy night like tonight. That still didn't change the fact that she didn't want him there.

"Okay, you can stay in the cellar," she teased, sort of.

"No way in hell. I went down there a couple weeks ago. Something transparent lives down there."

Kadyn couldn't help but laugh. She'd never heard a ghost described as transparent before, although she guessed that it fit. She hated that cold dark basement too, always had.

Kadyn and Anderson drank the entire bottle of wine. Anderson didn't feel it all. He always had an alcohol tolerance. Kadyn did not. She was a little intoxicated and told him more than she meant to about her life.

"So why are you letting your parents dictate what you do with your life?" he asked. "I mean, what would you do if you didn't follow the political footsteps of your parents?"

"Nothing. I'd move here with my grandma, and take care of her and this place."

"Why would you do that? You're so young and pretty. There's a whole world out there."

"Yeah, well I'm not like most girls," Kadyn admitted, looking down at the last drink of wine hidden in a coffee cup. She was a little uncomfortable after the pretty comment. She didn't really do guys, not like most girls did.

"Do you have a boyfriend?"

"Now, you're getting personal. Do you have a girlfriend?" she countered.

He snickered. "I don't think I do. Well, I did. She sort of slapped me across the face a few days ago, and I haven't heard from her since. So I would say no."

"Why did she slap you?" Kadyn boldly asked. It was the alcohol, no doubt.

Anderson didn't want to answer her questions. He was the one that was supposed to be asking the questions. Charles was going to be on his ass first thing in the morning, and he didn't know any more now than he did before he met Cora Wellington, other than the fact that she had this granddaughter he never knew existed.

"I guess I can be somewhat of an ass," he smiled a flirty smile.

"Nah... Really?" she responded, her words dripping with sarcasm. He laughed, deciding to try his luck and moved closer to her lips with his own. Of course she stopped him by placing her hand on his chest.

"Whoa," she quietly protested. "We should probably get some sleep," she suggested, coming to a standing position from the warm floor. "I'll get you another blanket for the couch," she offered.

Anderson smiled and nodded. He wasn't supposed to like her, not really, anyway. He did like her, though, and the moving in to kiss her wasn't all an act.

It was nothing, he decided, as he lay on the sofa, staring at the burning flames. He'd done the same thing with Lori when he swooped in to take over her father's hotel. She'd been around for nine months now.

Kadyn slept in the room across from the den where her grandmother slept, staring out the window to the windy downpour of rain, contemplating what had just happened. Anderson was up to something. She could tell. She knew it. He wasn't there to befriend her elderly grandmother. Nonetheless, she couldn't help but notice how handsome he was. He wasn't like the guys from her private high school or the political college she attended. He had a dark edge to him, something she couldn't quite put her finger on.

* * * * *

Kadyn knew she had to do something about her grandmother the following morning when she woke. She was no longer safe to stay alone at the plantation.

"Grandma! What are you doing?" Kadyn shouted, pulling her from the front lawn. The rain hadn't let up at all, coming down in buckets the entire night. Flat drops splattered on the saturated ground, leaving puddles with nowhere else to go.

"We have to get the cotton picked. It will rot in the ground," Cora protested and then stopped dead in her tracks, seeing her granddaughter. "What on earth are you doing out here in the rain, Kadyn? Come on, get inside before you catch your death," Cora coaxed, turning the tables.

* * * * *

"Is she okay?" Anderson asked concerned. He really was concerned. He liked Cora and couldn't believe her family would just leave her alone in her state of mind.

"Yes, she's okay. I've got her in dry clothes covered up in front of the fire."

"I made her some hot coffee," Anderson nodded toward the brewing pot.

"Thank you. Do you want to take it out to her? I'll start some breakfast."

Cora was confused the entire day. Kadyn even called her dad, concerned with leaving her grandmother alone. He, of course, wasn't alarmed, and was too busy to talk at the time. He was in the middle of debating a very important issue.

Once Kadyn fed her grandmother scrambled eggs, she was out like a light, nestled in front of the fire under her handmade quilt.

"She's out," Kadyn announced, walking to the table to join Anderson. "Wow, is this rain ever going to stop?" she asked, watching the rain pour down the eve of the house and onto the drenched front yard as she washed the few dishes in the sink.

"Not according to the weather. Aren't we supposed to have snow? It *is* Christmas," Anderson teased, taking the dish from Kadyn to dry. Kadyn looked up and locked eyes with him as the dish traded hands. Abruptly, her cell phone rang, breaking the unwanted trance.

"Hello," she answered the familiar number.

"Hey Kadyn, this is Buck. I was heading back to jump your car, but it doesn't seem to look like anyone is coming in or out of there with a vehicle anytime soon. Do you know there is a BMW over the bank out here?" Buck asked. "Yes. It's a friend of mine. What do you mean?"

"The road is washed out pretty good on this end. I can bring you groceries on my four wheeler if you need them, if this rain ever lets up, but you're not getting out of there in a vehicle for a couple days."

"No, that's okay. We have enough food to last a few days. Thanks, Buck. I'll talk to you in a day or two."

"You're welcome. If you need anything, you just give me a ring."

"Where is your car?" Kadyn asked Anderson, hanging up.

"I told you. It's broke down at the end of the lane."

"I don't believe that, but I do believe that it is washed over the bank."

"Why?"

"One of the locals was coming back to jump my grandmother's car for me. The whole road is washed out. Did you leave it over the gully?"

"I don't know. It was dark and raining. What do you mean it's washed over the bank?" he asked in a panic. That was a sixty thousand dollar car.

"We'll get one of the locals to pull it out, but not until this rain stops. We can walk out if you need to meet someone to pick you up. I'm sure you need to be home for Christmas."

"What are you doing for Christmas?"

"Um, staying here with my grandmother."

"I'm staying too."

"Don't you have family to get home to? I'm sure you have something better to do than to stay in this old plantation full of transparent people," Kadyn nervously smiled, trying to hide the fear of being alone with this guy for who knew how many days.

"Not really. My mother is spending Christmas on a yacht with her new boyfriend, and my stepfather is, well, who knows what he is doing, but I'm sure his plans don't include me. What about you? Shouldn't you be with your parents? Do you have siblings?"

"I have a sister, and my parents are spending Christmas in Washington with some stuck up political family. I'm not about to do that."

"Then it's settled. We'll spend our pathetic, lonely lives here together with Grandma Cora. I can't think of a better place I'd rather be," he smiled a sparkling white teeth smile. "Are there any Christmas decoration around here? We should put up a tree," he giddily offered.

"There are decorations, but no tree. We always cut real trees… we could do that," she smiled, getting the idea.

"Do what?"

"Go cut a tree. Do you have other clothes with you?"

"Yeah, in my stuck-in-the-mud car."

Kadyn found raincoats and umbrellas for them and led Anderson to the barn to find a saw.

"We're really going to cut a Christmas tree?" Anderson asked, unbelieving.

"Yup, that one right there," she pointed to the edge of the woods. It was the closest one to the house and not overly big. They should be able to manage it. "Let's walk out and get your bag first."

Buck wasn't exaggerating a bit. The expensive BMW was definitely stuck in the mud and not going anywhere. Kadyn slipped walking down the small slope, sliding on her butt, now wearing a new layer of mud. Anderson laughed at her.

"Okay, come on, city boy. Let's see you maneuver your way down here," she teased, looking up to him. He failed miserably, knocking her feet from under her as he, too, slid down the slant, landing her body on top of his. The umbrellas tangled, and their bulky raincoats slid together.

"This sucks," Anderson alleged, moving a loose strand of wet hair from Kadyn's face. She stared down at him briefly before swiftly jumping up. Her eyes moving to his lips didn't go unnoticed, and Anderson knew for sure he could take her if he wanted to. Why didn't he want to? He should have been jumping on the chance. He liked her, that's why. She wasn't some stuffy bitch like Lori was, or the girls he was used to being around and dating. Kadyn was down to earth, plain and simple. She cared about someone other than herself. Anderson wasn't used to that.

Anderson laughed with Kadyn like he'd never laughed before. Neither of them could get enough traction to make it up the bank and slid back to their starting position numerous times before making it to Anderson's bag, tossed to the gravel road.

"Well, that was fun. We're a mess," Anderson stated, looking down at his wet, muddy clothes and then to Kadyn's.

"It's all your fault. If you wouldn't have feigned a broken car, we wouldn't be out here in this mess," she accused.

"I'm glad I faked it, Kadyn. I'm very excited to spend Christmas with you and Cora. There is nowhere else I'd rather be," he assured her, looking from her eyes down to her muddy boots.

"Why, Anderson?" she asked, still not looking at him.

"Why what?"

She did look at him that time, with a look that told him to stop playing her as stupid. He took a deep breath and told the truth for whatever reason. This was so not what he was supposed to be doing. He didn't even know this girl, she was ruining everything. Cora was getting worse by the day. He was sure he could get her to sign her name and be done with it. He didn't want to.

"I'm supposed to come here and get your grandmother to sign over the house and land for a new golf resort," he explained, stopping her response by turning her to look at him once he saw the fury on her face. "Let me finish before you go kicking me in the groin or something," he begged. "Don't worry. I'm not interested in taking anything from you or your grandmother. Maybe a couple weeks ago, when I didn't think of her as a human being or know that you existed, I was, but not anymore. I'm probably going to be homeless when I tell my stepfather I'm out of this, that I refuse to help him take the plantation from your family, but I'll live with that."

Anderson had no idea what he was saying. For just an instant, he imagined him and Kadyn living there and taking care of the plantation together. It was stupid, he knew it was, but he still felt something around her he'd never felt before which was stupid too. For Pete's sake he didn't even know the girl.

"I should knee you in the nuts," Kadyn threatened. "You've been coming here for weeks lying to convince my grandmother into signing over her house?"

"Yes, and I'm sorry. You have another issue that you need to worry about," Anderson stated, wanting the heat off him.

"What?"

"Your grandmother. I don't think you should leave her alone anymore. I'm afraid something bad is going to happen."

Kadyn sighed audibly. "I don't know what to do. Who do I even call for something like that? It's obvious my family doesn't care enough to help," she whined, taking a step back from Anderson. She had to, she felt a very strong urge to lean into him, kiss him in the rain like some Hallmark commercial or something, and wrap her arms around him.

"Let's get out of the rain. I'll help you."

"Why?" Kadyn wanted to know. Why would this stranger want to help her with her grandmother? If he was being honest, than there was really no need for him to stick around and help her do anything. There was no way she would let him or anyone else ever touch that plantation.

"Because I like you, and I like your grandmother. You can't go back to school and leave her here alone. Something's going to happen to her."

"Let's go cut a tree," Kadyn suggested, changing the subject. She was freezing and wanted out of her wet clothes.

* * * * *

Cora was having a better evening and once the tree was dried out enough to set up, and both the youngsters were dry and warm, Cora insisted on making supper for them. They both tried to protest with no avail.

"No, now you two love birds take care of decorating the house. I'm looking forward to having some yuletide spirit around here. There hasn't been any in years," she smiled, and lifted the needle to the record, beaming from ear to ear as the Christmas music echoed throughout the room.

Anderson smiled at Kadyn, liking Cora thinking they were lovebirds. He could easily be in love with her. Kadyn smiled back at him. She could see that too, but it was crazy. Wasn't it?

"We have to go to the basement," Kadyn announced, breaking the news to him.

"Uh-uh. No way. I'm not going down there."

Kadyn laughed and shoved him in front of her toward the kitchen.

"Hmm, grandma, it smells delicious in here. What are you making?" Kadyn asked, shoving Anderson through the door to go first.

"You'll see," Cora boasted.

"I'm scared," Anderson teased. Well, maybe he wasn't really teasing, but it did make Kadyn laugh and he was quickly finding that he liked to make her laugh.

"We'll just get the tree decorations and lights. There's nothing down here but... What's that?" she whispered.

Anderson turned, heading back up the stairs. He didn't want to know what it was. His sudden spin on his heels landed him at the same height as Kadyn. She laughed at his cowardness and then got quiet, realizing how close their lips were. She was the one to lean in, probably just to see if he would move in too. Of course he did.

"You should probably leave," Kadyn whispered to his lips, right after a mind blowing kiss that left her weak in the knees.

"I can't. My car's stuck in the mud," he quipped softly, causing her to snicker. "And we have a Christmas tree to decorate."

"Then turn around and get the box before you kiss me again," Kadyn tormented, still leaning into his strong chest.

"Is it me, or are you more afraid of *you* kissing me?"

Kadyn didn't answer. She wanted to kiss him again and did just that. He watched her moisten her lips with her tongue and part her lips as she kissed him, moaning in his mouth this time. He moaned too, sure he'd never been kissed like that before, not with the emotions that followed anyway. Jesus. What was going on with him? What was going on with her?

They both had a wonderful time decorating the tree, listening to Grandma Cora explain each and every one of the ornaments and where they had come from. She knew where, or who bought every last one of them. For supper they had breakfast because Cora had gotten a little confused on the time, but it was delicious, and nobody made homemade biscuits as well as Grandma Cora. Their happy time was interrupted by a phone call that Anderson didn't want to take.

"Hello," he answered, leaving the two ladies alone, walking into the kitchen.

"You got us a deal?" Charles practically yelled in the phone.

"No, there's no deal here. You're going to have to find someplace else."

"Like hell I am. Did you do what I said? Did you get in the girls pants?"

"No, Charles, and I am not going to. She's got a meeting with an attorney tomorrow morning to take over the estate. She's not going to sell you this property, and I'm not going to trick her into it either."

"What the hell is wrong with you? Of course you are. You're going to get me that property or you're going to be living on the streets. Ever work at McDonalds before? I will ruin you. You will never spend another penny of my money. You got that, Anderson? You get that deed, and that's an order."

"I'm pretty sure I can survive without your money. Goodbye, Charles."

Anderson hung up. He knew he could come crawling back and Charles would pick up, controlling his life like he always had. For the first time in his life, though, he didn't want that. He didn't want Charles' money dangling over his head. He wanted Kadyn, as crazy as that sounded. He wanted a girl he'd just met.

"You okay?" Kadyn asked, pushing open the swinging door to the kitchen and seeing Anderson's expression full of sadness.

"Yes, I'm fine. Let's go put the star on top of the tree."

Kadyn smiled when she felt his hand on the small of her back, not understanding the feelings transpiring between them, or were they only coming from her and not him at all. She still had to be cautious. She knew what he was doing and she wasn't about to let her guard down long enough to let him swarm in like a bee family and take over the plantation.

Kadyn's guard was let down, crashing to the floor as soon as Grandma Cora turned in for the night. Both Kadyn and Anderson snuggled in front of the sofa, enjoying the crackling fire.

"The rain stopped," Anderson pointed out, looking toward the window.

"Good, maybe we can get your car out of the mud, so you can be on your way."

"Do you want me to be on my way?"

"I need you to be on your way," she admitted.

"What if I didn't?"

"Didn't what?"

"What if I didn't 'be on my way?' What if you didn't 'be on *your* way?' You hate school. You hate what you're going for and you don't want to follow in your parent's footsteps. Let's move here, take care of your grandma, and do something with this place. I'll just work for you."

"You're crazy," Kadyn laughed, but couldn't help feeling a little excited about the notion of what he was saying.

"I'm not crazy. Let's do it. We've both been doing what makes other people happy our entire lives. Let's make *us* happy. Let's do it, Kadyn."

"Do what?"

"I don't know. What can we do here? I'm not sure about cultivating cotton."

Anderson watched Kadyn get up and walk to the kitchen. She came back with a notebook and pen.

"Not that I am agreeing to anything, but say we did do *something* here, give me an idea," she coaxed with pen to paper.

"Bed and breakfast?" he offered as she wrote.

"Horseback ranch," she added to the list.

"Four-wheeler trails."

"Camp ground," she went next.

"We could turn the barn into an animal shelter, go around the United States and rescue animals."

Kadyn's pen stopped as she looked over to him bewildered. "Anderson, I actually *love* that idea. Do you like animals?"

"I love them, but was never allowed to have any. I have a cat, now, Romeo, that I picked up when he was just a kitten," Anderson snickered. "I still hide him when I know my stepfather is coming around."

"Want to hear something funny?"

"Of course."

"I rescued a cat too. Her name is Juliet, and I, too, hide her when my parents come around."

"That is funny. Romeo and Juliet. That's not coincidence, Kadyn. I think it's fate trying to tell us something."

"We don't even know each other. This is so crazy," Kadyn assured him, dropping the notepad to the floor and moving to his lap, one leg on each side of his legs.

"I don't care if it's crazy. Let's see where it goes," Anderson offered, running his hands up her shirt and to her back. Anderson parted her lips with his tongue, exploring her mouth, and gaining an erotic moan from her. He moved his weight, shifting her from him and moving her to the floor.

"Anderson, we can't do this. I don't *do* this until after at least three official dates," Kadyn protested. She didn't really do this at all. She'd only been with three guys since she lost her virginity at seventeen. Only one of them had gotten lucky the first night, and that was because she'd let alcohol get the better of her. She was sober this time, and wanted Anderson more than she'd ever wanted anyone in her life. It really was crazy.

"How long's it been since you've had an orgasm?" Anderson asked.

"What time is it?" Kadyn smiled.

Anderson pulled back and looked at her, shocked.

"What? You're the one that had to go and take your shirt off last night," she blamed.

"You?"

"Yes, I did."

"Thinking about me?"

"Don't flatter yourself," she teased, but, if she was being honest, that was exactly what she'd been thinking about while she pleased herself.

"Let me, Kadyn," he begged with some sort of low raspy voice that just happened to send chills to her groin area.

"Do what?" she feigned ignorance.

Anderson didn't reply. He slid his hand between the elastic of her sweats and right to her slippery wet folds, sending her eyes to the back of her head. Anderson was good, Anderson was damn good. He knew exactly what he was doing and where to do it. He had to move his mouth to hers in order to muffle the noise of her intense audible orgasm.

As soon as Kadyn was coherent enough to look at him she flipped him over, towering over him now. She released his already erect shaft and stroked him, knowing full well what to do. She wanted to take care of him too. And she did, wishing she could break her rule and let him release his pleasure somewhere besides the palm of her hand. She didn't though, and he respected her and didn't try.

* * * * *

They spent the next four days together with Grandma Cora, laughing, and discussing the animal shelter they were planning on manifesting from the plantation. Cora even got excited about it. She loved the idea of animal life on the farm once again. She hadn't had so much as a dog in over fourteen years, and missed having all the stray kittens around hoping to get a free pan of milk from one of the cows. She liked the idea of having Kadyn around more, and even Anderson. She liked him.

Charles was *furious*. He wanted the plantation; he had plans for it. Anderson was letting some stupid girl get in the way of everything, or so his stepfather thought. Charles had his brand new BMW towed away, changed the locks on his apartment, and froze his credit cards. A week ago, Anderson would have cared. He didn't care about money for the first time in his life. He cared about Kadyn… and Grandma Cora.

"Hey, Mom," Kadyn answered the dreaded call.

"Hi, you all set? Your dad is making arrangements for you to fly back to school tomorrow."

And here it comes. "I'm not going back to school."

"What do you mean, you're not going back to school?"

"I'm staying here with Grandma Cora."

"Kadyn, you are going back to school and you will be on that plane tomorrow. I will make your dad sell that place and stick her in a nursing home before I let you do this."

"You can't. Dad is no longer the executive of the estate; I am. We took care of it a few days ago. There's nothing you can do about it, Mom. I'm staying here with Grandma Cora."

"Kadyn! Listen to how ridiculous you sound right now. You are going back to school and getting your degree in political science, just like your sister and your father and I. I've had your life planned for you before you were ever born. You're *not* doing this."

"You can't plan my life. I am staying right here. I'm never leaving the plantation and there's nothing you can do about it. I have to go," Kadyn said, hanging up, not because she was tired of arguing with her mother, well, that too. Kadyn noticed the pink fuzzy slippers, toes up, lying in front of the sofa.

"Grandma! What are you doing? Stop doing that," she ordered as Anderson came into help, *shirtless and wet.*

"I'm dead," Cora assured with closed eyes.

Kadyn couldn't take her eyes from Anderson. She had the strongest urge to touch his damp chest, and was having an extremely hard time controlling her emotions when he was around.

"You're not dead. Come on. Get off the floor."

"I want to die right here."

Kadyn and Anderson pulled Cora to her feet and sat her in her chair. She instantly closed her eyes.

"Fine. I will just die right here."

"I'm making lunch. Can you wait until after you eat?" Kadyn asked.

"Okay," she agreed with closed eyes.

Anderson smiled at Kadyn, locking eyes in an emotional stare.

"Look, Kay," Anderson beckoned, taking Kadyn's wrist while she set the table.

She smiled at him calling her 'Kay.' Her grandpa used to call her that when she was a little girl. Her smile grew when she saw that he was searching Craigslist and a whole litter of abandoned kittens needed a home.

"Let's go get them after lunch."

"We can't both go, Anderson. One of us has to stay here with Grandma."

"Okay, I'll go. Do you think we can get your grandma's car started?"

"I'll call Buck and see if he can come over and get it started."

Christmas Eve was the beginning. Christmas Eve started the arrival of many neglected animals. Kadyn, Cora, and Anderson made the kittens a bed in the corner of the barn, served them warm milk, and Anderson even tied a yarn ball for them to play with.

By spring the barn had been transformed into an elaborate animal shelter, housing seven different species, including two lamas. Kadyn couldn't have been happier. She was not only in love with her sophisticated animal shelter, but with Anderson as well. They spent hours in the barn with Cora, who, with proper medication, was doing much better. She still had her confusing moments, but loved to spend time in the barn being with her animals.

Kadyn sipped her coffee, letting the spring air and bright sun warm her face. She never dreamed she'd ever be where she was at that moment. It cost her though. Her family didn't call, come around, or even call to check on Cora, but she was okay with it. She was happy and couldn't see herself anywhere but right there with Anderson and the animals.

"You okay?" Anderson asked, wrapping his arms around her.

"I am more than okay. I love you," she smiled, leaning into his chest.

"I love you, too. How about you come back to bed with me for a little bit?"

"Hmmm, sounds great, but we have a barn of animals to feed."

"How about you come back to bed with me and then we'll feed the animals."

"Didn't I just take care of you sometime during the night?"

"You did, but that was just an appetizer."

"Where's Grandma?"

"Asleep in her chair with both Romeo *and* Juliet."

Anderson led Kadyn back to bed and made slow passionate love to her, staring deep into her soul as he moved himself in and out of her, becoming one. Neither of them could be happier than they were.

* * * * *

Kadyn woke Cora from her sleeping slouch in her favorite chair for breakfast. Cora sat up and placed her hand flat on Kadyn's stomach.

"You know this is a little girl, don't you?" she proclaimed and stood.

Kadyn's eyes went right to Anderson's wide stare. Cora left them alone, both with agape mouths.

"Kay?" Anderson questioned, but she didn't speak. Her hand had replaced her grandmother's, covering her stomach as she let her mind wonder. Was she late?

"Kadyn?" Anderson questioned again, placing his hand over hers.

"I don't know. I am a couple days late, but that doesn't necessarily mean…"

"It does! It does, Kadyn! We're going to have a baby; I know we are. Grandma Cora said so."

"Anderson, we can't have a baby. We've only been together for five months. This can't be."

It could be, and it was. Cora Dawn Paine and Lucas Wade Paine were both welcomed nine months later. Now the couple was absolutely sure they couldn't be happier. They were married that summer with a small group of people from town and a lot of animals, right there on the plantation. Cora brought them together. Had it not been for Cora, Anderson would have never known true happiness. He would still be scamming people with his manipulative stepfather, whom he never spoke to anymore. Kadyn would be working for some politician and would have never felt the love and attraction she did with Anderson and her new little family.

All because of Cora.

Jettie Woodruff

Author Dedication

This short story was the hardest thing I have ever had to write. I tend to get very wordy when it comes to my writing. This was a challenge for me to stay under twelve thousand words. I want to dedicate this short story to my two girls, Megan and Amy. Both Megan and Amy have been amazing supporters for me throughout my journey. Thanks guys. You're my rock.

About Jettie

Jettie Woodruff is a practicing physician and has been a Civil War buff for decades. No. Not really, she is not a doctor nor is she a Civil War buff. She is however a goof-off and has a hard time being serious for too long.

Jettie enjoys a challenge when it comes to her writing, concentrating on trying to pull every emotion possible from her readers. She wants you to be pissed off, questioning your sanity, depressed, happy, and hopefully turn your mind from wanting to cut the villain into tiny little pieces to loving him by the end of the book.

Underestimated was her first dark endeavor. It went to number 24 on Amazon's bestsellers list. After many requests, *Underestimated Too* is in the making and expected to release in March 2014.

Follow Jettie

https://www.facebook.com/JettieWoodruff

Read More from Jettie

Underestimated: http://amzn.to/1lAUhbQ

Fated Love
(Others of Edenton: Book 2.5)

Brandy L. Rivers

Chapter 1

Christian sat up straight. He was drenched in a cold sweat, his breath coming in great gulps. He kept seeing the pool of blood, torn flesh, and Delilah's scarlet hair lying around her pale face as her amber eyes stared up at him. She kept telling him to go, but he couldn't.

The alarm kept blaring at him, and he blindly shut it off before trudging to the bathroom for a shower.

He much preferred the dreams where he woke up in her warm embrace, looking through a haze of red because her hair was still draped over his face, bathing him in her vanilla and jasmine scent.

One of these days I'll grow a set and ask her out.

He knew they were meant to be, but he was still waiting for the right time to tell her.

Delilah wasn't like any other woman. She didn't look through him, only seeing his strange behavior. No, she saw him for who he was, and seemed to genuinely like him.

His hold up was that he'd seen the guys she went for: big, bold, and confident. All the things he wasn't.

* * * * *

There was a knock on Delilah's door, pulling her from sleep. She was still wrapped in a blanket on the couch, her Kindle lying beside her. There was a massive kink in her neck.

Delilah was tempted to scoot down, get comfortable, and go back to sleep to dream about Christian and all the things she wanted to do to him.

This time the doorbell rang. Yawning, she stood and moved to the door to look through the peephole. Rebecca shifted from side to side while wearing a nervous smile. She did have two coffees in hand.

Is she friend or foe today? Rebecca generally looked out for herself, and Delilah had been burned a few times because of it. They had been friends once but she no longer trusted Rebecca after catching her with a boyfriend more than a year ago.

They both claimed being too drunk to think straight. She let it be and walked away, done with both of them. Delilah hadn't been invested in Todd, but Rebecca's betrayal hurt.

Now they were neighbors and Rebecca claimed she was trying to mend their friendship. Delilah didn't know what to think.

Rebecca knocked again.

Sighing, she opened the door. "Morning."

"Good morning," Rebecca said, much too chipper. "Can I come in?"

"Uh, yeah. Sure."

She stepped back, and Rebecca came in, taking a seat on the couch.

Delilah pulled the blanket tighter before closing the door. She sat down on the chair and accepted the offered cup of coffee.

"So, how was it?" Rebecca asked in her bubbliest tone, sitting on the edge of the couch, watching Delilah intently.

"How was what?"

"Your date. I know it was a couple days ago, but you never drop by anymore." There seemed to be real regret in Rebecca's expression.

Unsure what to think of her intentions, Delilah went ahead and answered. "With Lance? Disastrous. It lasted all of about fifteen minutes."

Rebecca's mouth fell open. "Why? What happened? I thought you liked him."

Delilah snorted. "I thought I did, until I realized he was only after one thing. We went to the movies, and before the lights even went out, he was trying to grope me."

"So? He got a little fresh. Nothing wrong with that." Rebecca giggled.

"No," Delilah insisted. "He got downright grabby, reaching under my shirt and wasn't listening to the word *no*. It ended with me punching him when he wouldn't stop. That's when I walked out."

Rebecca's expression fell. "No wonder he was complaining."

"I don't even want to know." Delilah fell back in her seat and took a slow sip of her coffee.

Shaking her head, Rebecca told her, "He called you a tease, and he was saying even worse. I thought maybe he was just disappointed because you didn't just roll over for him, but now I'm worried."

Delilah's blood ran cold. He'd also been following her for the last few days, but she hadn't led him on. A date didn't give him the right to have his way with her. "I already told him not to bother trying for round two. I'm not interested, regardless of what he thinks."

Sweeping her hair behind her ear, Rebecca sighed. "I told him that he should leave you alone. Your Dad wouldn't hesitate to put him in his place. He just laughed at me."

Staring out the window, Delilah wondered what the hell was going on with her frenemy. One minute she seemed excited about Delilah's possible relationship with Lance, and next, she's concerned.

What the hell? What am I supposed to do with that?

Delilah was almost tempted to tell her Dad about Lance. Sure, he would make Lance leave her alone, but she hoped just ignoring him would work. She didn't want to have to rely on her dad's position in his pack, or his job, to protect her from a sleazeball.

Rebecca changed the subject, back to being bubbly. "Are you still going to your interview today?"

"Yup. I should probably get ready." If she had time, she'd go visit Christian. He always managed to brighten her mood and leave her smiling, even if he never came on to her. She was starting to think she needed to stop waiting on him to ask her out, and just ask him herself.

Chapter 2

The warm breeze brushed past Delilah, shifting her silk dress across her legs. It was silly, but she hoped Christian liked her outfit. She decided that if he didn't make a move, she'd ask him.

Footsteps sounded behind her and she glanced over her shoulder. Her stomach bottomed out when she saw Lance a block away with his eyes trained on her.

Why the hell did I ever date him?

Ever since that night, he was always showing up, following her with a dark scowl on his face. Delilah couldn't believe she was the first to turn down his advances. Who the hell wants to deal with an overbearing asswipe?

Lance was the typical, cocky, high school jock who was too hot for his own good. He was twenty-three now, going nowhere in Edenton, and he still thought he was God's gift to women.

Now that she saw how he really was, she was disgusted by him and herself. Him for being a pig. Her for not seeing it sooner.

She turned the corner and caught a glimpse of him closer than before. Her skin crawled, and she started to regret not telling Dad.

Her father was a giant burly officer who would likely make Lance shit bricks. Maybe it was stupid, but she wanted to prove that she could fight her own battles.

Lance needed to get over himself. She wasn't interested in a quick fuck, as she had told him at the end of their pathetic attempt at a date.

He was closer, and she could hear his heavy footfalls closing the distance. She held her breath as she slipped into A Good Book.

Lance wasn't fond of books, so she doubted he would bother coming in. And she was right. Delilah shut the door and Lance kept walking, his eyes sliding over her greedily.

"Fucker," she muttered as she flipped him off. She sighed in relief as she crossed the room, and slid into the seat at the counter.

Christian's velvet smooth voice pulled her from her thoughts. "Good morning, Delilah. Are you okay?"

Too bad he wore a frown, and his golden brown eyes narrowed on her in concern. She had been looking forward to his sweet, shy smile that brought out his dimple as he ducked his head, causing his dark blond hair to fall into his eyes. One day she would give in to temptation and push his hair off his face to stare deep into his eyes.

Man, I have it bad.

She couldn't help smiling at him. "Hey, Christian. I'm fine, but I can't figure out why the Captain of the Asshole Squad keeps following me around."

He shrugged, one side of his mouth lifting as humor flashed across his expression. "Would you like your normal drink?"

The tension slid from her shoulders. He had a way of wiping out the worry, the stress, even the anger. It felt good to be around him.

"Mmm, you know I do," she murmured.

These were her favorite moments of her day, getting to watch him while he made her coffee. He was long, lean, but in great shape. He practiced yoga, of all things, but man, did it leave him looking good.

He bent to grab the carton, and looked up at her with that shy smile if his. Her insides turned to jelly. She couldn't stop her own grin and he ducked his head as he straightened to steam the milk.

He didn't look up when he asked, "Are you sticking around to look at books?"

"No." She sighed, regretting that she really didn't have time. "I have an interview in just a bit. I might come back later though."

"Good, I like your daily visits," he admitted as he glanced away.

"Think you might..." Lance walked back by the shop and she trailed off.

Christian frowned at the door. "Would you like me to walk you to your car?"

She did, but not for that reason and she had walked anyway. "No. I'll be fine. I might just duck out the back."

"Oh, okay." His expression dropped clean off his face as he handed her the drink. "Be safe. He's giving me a bad vibe."

That gave her pause. Christian had a knack for sensing things. He never claimed being psychic, but he always knew just what to say or ask, as long as it didn't have to do with asking her out.

She slid her money across the counter. "Are you busy tonight?"

He shrugged. "I thought I might lose myself in a book."

What she wouldn't give to be able to read him better. She couldn't tell if he was interested but shy, or if he only liked what he saw but didn't want a girlfriend.

"Well, enjoy your book." She stood and gave a little wave before slipping down the hall and into the alley. She hoped Lance wouldn't notice her disappearing act.

* * * * *

Christian wanted to smack himself as he watched Delilah walk out of the shop. The question had been on the tip of his tongue, and then he chickened out. Again.

I'm such a pussy.

"Hey, kid," Tremaine called as he came from the back. "You need to just spit it out. She wants you, but she's not convinced you really want her."

"I know," Christian muttered. "I just don't know what to say."

"So, Del, want to go out with me... would work." Tremaine winked as he started toward an aisle.

Christian narrowed his eyes. "That why you haven't asked Liz out, in what... 20 years? Probably more?"

"Look, we're not going there," Tremaine warned.

"Yeah, yeah, 'cuz that shit's complicated." That was the same excuse Tremaine had used for years.

"That doesn't even scratch the surface."

Christian slumped against the counter. He didn't understand why the two of them didn't *un*complicate their situation.

Years of being in love, and neither Tremaine nor Liz would venture there. Christian didn't understand why they both tried to push him into action with Delilah when neither of them could see what was right in front of them.

As for Delilah, it wasn't time, or maybe it wasn't right yet. He had a feeling that things would work out soon. Maybe that's why his tongue was always tied.

Chapter 3

Delilah knew that Christian's shift was nearly over. After thinking about him all day long, she was out of patience. She was going to ask him out. Worst he could say was no, but she had to know what he really wanted.

She hurried down the sidewalk and peered into the window. Rebecca was there, leaning in close to Christian, whispering in his ear.

Her heart sank as she watched the exchange. Christian's eyes closed and he nodded. Maybe he wasn't all that interested in her.

The urge to strangle Rebecca flittered through her head. It wasn't the first time and probably wouldn't be the last that she backstabbed her. The part that stung was that Rebecca told Delilah to go for it before the whole Lance incident.

Why the hell don't I ever learn?

Her heart was being crushed as she turned on her heel, and headed back the way she came. She walked right past her building and kept going to the park, then back to the woods. The further she went, the faster she walked, until she was practically running.

* * * * *

"I need to lock up," Christian insisted for the third time.

His teeth ground together as Rebecca leaned in, tiptoed up and whispered in his ear, "You really do want Delilah, don't you?"

His eyes closed and he nodded. He sucked at lying and it was pretty obvious to begin with.

Rebecca leaned back, her eyes wide. "Not me?"

"I've told you I wasn't interested in you every single time you asked. I'm sorry, Rebecca, but that's not changing."

Her arms crossed over her chest and she pouted. "Fine, point made."

A chill traveled up his spine, and he knew that he needed to be in the woods, and he needed to be there now.

"I'm locking up now. Please, leave," Christian nearly growled.

"All right, all right. No need to get pissy." She slunk out the front door.

Christian gritted his teeth in annoyance as he shoved it shut and locked it.

Rebecca glared back at him before stomping away. The prissy little blonde reminded him of a whiny toddler.

He didn't have time to concern himself with Rebecca or her bruised ego. Something far more urgent was waiting in the woods. The details were fuzzy, just beyond memory, but the same nightmare had woken him up in a cold sweat every night for weeks.

* * * * *

One clear detail clicked in Delilah's head. Christian's fists had been bunched at his sides as if he were ticked. Maybe she read the whole scene wrong.

She slowed, and then stopped as she tried to catch her breath. Maybe Rebecca was only trying to seduce Christian. Or maybe that wasn't even what was going on at all.

Letting out a heavy sigh, Delilah started back toward the park when she heard the growl.

"Shit," she whispered, then shook her head.

Stupid, stupid, stupid. Werewolves can hear everything.

Trying to be smart, she ducked into a cluster of trees to avoid being seen, but she knew he would smell her. There was a reason she ended her date with Lance at the first sign he'd be a pushy bastard. She didn't stand a chance against a werewolf.

Her father had insisted his girls carry a gun. Her mother helped her find a nice custom Sig Sauer p239 that fit her hand and packed a punch. Delilah wasn't afraid to use it.

Hell, Dad taught her to shoot the damned thing. Granted, she had only ever shot at the range, but she was prepared to defend herself.

Ever since that dreaded date, she'd been carrying it concealed. *Daddy would be proud.* Or not, seeing how he would bitch that she should have told him. Apparently, he would've had a point.

Taking a deep breath, she pulled the weapon from its holster and took aim in the direction of the snapping branches. The snarling growls were closing in. She saw the heap of fur barreling at her and fired, once, twice, thrice, and once again for good measure.

The beast took a silver bullet to the face, the shoulder, and two in the chest, but his momentum drove her to the ground. His massive jaws clamped around her wrist and his claws drove deep into her gut.

Her wrist was broken, and her abdomen was torn open where his claws had plunged into her. That all hurt but it was nothing compared to the virus burning its way through her veins like a wildfire. The liquid flame was agonizing. She screamed out, her vision flickering to black even as the full moon called to her.

* * * * *

Christian heard the rapid gunfire. He pushed himself faster, trying to get to Delilah. The dream came back to him in vivid detail, but it didn't prepare him to see Delilah bleeding underneath the giant werewolf.

He collapsed to his knees beside her, heaving the wolf to the side as Lance's corpse started to shift back to his human form. His face and most of his chest were blown away. There was no coming back from that.

She cried out as the claws were torn free of her body.

"Christ, I'm sorry, Delilah," Christian whispered. He pulled his shirt over his head and tried to pack her gaping stomach. Everything inside was still in place, nothing but shredded skin by some miracle. Still, he could *see* her insides and there was so much blood.

"Del, I'm sorry," he murmured, holding the cloth tight to her stomach.

She nodded, her brown eyes fluttering open. "Hurts like a bitch, but you got to go, Christian. I feel the shift coming." Gasping for air, her eyes went wide as she stared up at him. Then she screamed, "Go! I don't want to hurt you."

Determined, he cupped her cheek with one hand, and stared into her eyes. He knew how this played out, and he wasn't leaving her side. "Listen to me. I'm not going anywhere. I'm staying right here with you. I'll be fine. You won't hurt me." He knew it. He'd seen this entire scene too many times to count.

Her groan was ragged. "I will. No one shifts the first time without tearing apart the first living thing that's weaker than them."

Christian shook his head. "You won't. I promise, Del. Just relax as best you can, and let the shift come. I'm not afraid. I know you won't hurt me."

"How? How can you be so sure?" she whimpered, still trying to fight the change, but the moon wasn't going to let her win that battle.

"I dreamt this. I'm sorry I didn't say anything. I was hoping I was wrong, or that I could prevent it." He looked up at the sky and closed his eyes. "Should have known better." Sighing, he looked back into her brown eyes. "You'll be okay though. Hell, you'll be healed just as soon as you let the change come."

"I won't hurt you?" she whispered. "Do you promise?"

He nodded. "I promise."

"Then, if you're right, when I get through this, I'm taking you out to dinner."

"I have one better for you. When you pull through this, I'll make you breakfast. I'm not letting you out of my sight, and I know you're going to need to hunt soon. Don't worry about me." He knew without a doubt that she would be fine, and that she wouldn't harm him.

* * * * *

The big dummy was calming her, his presence easing her tense muscles. The shift was coming, but she was terrified she'd mangle him when her beast took over.

Delilah whispered, "You should go. I'll be all right."

"You won't hurt me. I promise. You'll shift, you'll hunt down a rabbit or something, and then I'll take you home. You can sleep on the bed. I'll take the couch."

The rejection, even while in agony, was like being stabbed in the heart. She stammered, "You don't want to be next to me?"

One corner of his mouth tipped up. "Oh, I'd love to be, Del. I just didn't know if you wanted me in there when you'll wake up naked."

Naked and wrapped around him. That thought did funny things to her in this state. "Not gonna mind. You're the only thing keeping me calm."

He smiled then. "Then let the change come. Go hunt. Later, when I get you home, I'll curl up on the bed with you."

She trusted him more than anything, but Delilah had heard so many horror stories of new wolves ripping apart their loved ones the first time they shifted.

When he looked at her with his big warm brown eyes, his gaze full of love... *Love...*? She knew he spoke the truth.

Closing her eyes, she stopped fighting. She rolled to her side, curling into him as her body started to shift. Her bones stretched and contracted, fur flowing down her skin as her clothes shredded. Her stomach mended, her wrist snapping into place as it was replaced with a massive paw.

Then it was over, the pain gone. Instead of running off into the night, or even turning to tear him apart, she nuzzled into him. Christian stroked her fur as he softly hummed one of her favorite songs. He let her cuddle up to him like a puppy. A big, monstrous puppy.

"You were always beautiful, Delilah, but you are one gorgeous wolf," he murmured.

She tipped her head up to look him in the eyes. Truth was the only thing she sensed from him. It was more than sight that convinced her.

Probably smell. Oh Lord, that's going to take some getting used to.

"Go on," he told her. "Sooner you eat, the sooner I can make sure you're comfortable with your new self. Don't worry about me."

She nudged his chin with her snout before tromping off in the direction of something that smelled so good her stomach rumbled. Delilah didn't allow herself think as she let her beast take charge.

* * * * *

Christian could have smacked himself. Remembering the dream this afternoon would have helped him plan this out better, but they always faded away in moments, leaving him with blurry images that made little sense.

Too late now.

He needed to make a call while Delilah did her wolf thing.

He cautiously picked up her gun and put it in his waistband. Then he dialed the Police station.

"Edenton Police," Erik answered after the second ring.

"Good, I was hoping it would be you," Christian said. "Look, Simons is going to freak, but Delilah's a wolf now. She killed her attacker, and trust me, he attacked her, but she's still a wolf."

"What? Are you serious? How do you know?" Erik demanded.

"Look, I'm in the woods. I have Lance Range dead beside me. She shot him, but he still hurt her. She's fine though. She just shifted for the first time, and I'm going to take care of her."

"The hell you are. We'll lock her up in one of the silver cells and Simons and Slater can deal with her in the morning. It's too dangerous."

"Maybe I shouldn't have called you," Christian muttered.

"You were right to call me. You're out of your league here. She could really hurt you and never mean to. It's her first shift. She can't be stable."

"Erik, really, trust me here. I'm fine. She's fine. I'm taking her home. I've seen this night a hundred times or more."

"Don't leave this to chance."

Christian sighed. "I promised her breakfast in the morning. In fact, I'm going to walk her home now, and make sure she doesn't freak out when she realizes she just shot a man to death, turned furry, and then ate a raw rabbit."

"Shit. You really are serious, aren't you? You watched a new wolf shift, and she didn't touch you?"

His face scrunched up while he tried to think of how to answer that question. "Well, she didn't hurt me. I helped her through it. Just trust that she's fine, and she's coming home with me."

"Fine, fine. What do you want me to tell her dad?"

"Honestly? I think it's probably best if she tells Simons herself. It's not like you all are going to arrest her for defending herself from a pissed off wolf."

"I can't believe you're sitting there with a brand new wolf pup running around. You're crazy. You know that, right? Liz is likely to chew my ass when she finds out I didn't talk you out of this."

Christian chuckled. "Then don't tell her. It's not like she has to know. Not until it's all said and done. By then, she'll know I did the right thing. She won't freak out about this. She would do the same thing in my shoes."

"Fine. Fine, but if she does go off the deep end, it's your ass I'm going after. Just fair warning, kid," Erik grumbled before hanging up.

Christian shoved his phone into his pocket and stood up. There was a good chance that Erik would be coming after taking care of Lance.

Chapter 4

Delilah trotted back to Christian. The second he was in sight, she slowed down to a walk, dropping her head, attempting to look less threatening.

She was amazed that she was perfectly conscious and seeing through her wolf's eyes. Every wolf who ever mentioned their first shift said that they couldn't remember shit. Most of them took months before they had any control in their furry form.

"Oh, don't do that, Delilah. You can't scare me." Christian walked toward her, wearing a small smile. "If you want to keep Erik from trying to talk me out of taking you home, we better get there now."

She whined, not wanting to deal with anyone knowing what happened just yet. Though calling someone to deal with Lance was probably wise.

Her eyes grazed over Lance's nude and bloody corpse and her wolf snarled. Not even her beast had any desire to be near the asshole.

Christian looked down at Lance and shook his head. "Tomorrow, if you're up for it, I'll listen if you want to talk about it."

She barked once and nodded toward the direction of the park.

* * * * *

Christian couldn't help running his fingers through Delilah's silky coat before he started down another trail that would take him to his apartment a few blocks from A Good Book. He didn't want to chance running into Erik if he could help it. He still needed to formulate a good enough excuse to keep Erik from taking Delilah out of his sight.

Hopefully, Erik would keep his mouth shut until Delilah could talk to her dad herself.

After hearing about the way Simons recently flew off the handle at a very sweet and innocent nymph, he wasn't sure what to expect from the officer. Of course, a Shadow Fae had been messing with a lot of people and their emotions, causing them to do things they wouldn't normally do, but Christian wasn't sure if there were any lingering affects.

He took another look at the gorgeous wolf beside him. Her eyes were a slate gray in this form. Her fur was reddish brown. He'd dreamt of her wolf so many times that she was already familiar to him.

With a sigh, he hurried up his stairs and opened the door. She slipped inside before anyone noticed her.

"Still hungry?" Christian asked. "I have steak in the fridge." He half laughed. "It's funny, you know. I don't eat much red meat. I got it on a whim this morning."

Her eyes moved through the apartment, and settled on the fridge before walking to it.

He took that as an affirmative and pulled the package out. He opened it and set it on a plate on the floor. "Go ahead. I'm just going to grab a snack. I have a feeling we'll have company before too long."

She ate her raw meat while he had a tuna wrap.

There was a knock on the door as he slid the dishes into the dishwasher. "That would be Erik."

He braced himself for an argument as he walked to do the door, and then opened it without looking through the peephole. Erik stood on the other side with a dark look.

Christian leaned against the wall to block the door, and crossed his arms over his chest. "I told you, she was fine here. Let her be."

"You have a brand new wolf in your apartment, Christian. Should I call Liz to straighten your ass out on this subject?"

Delilah sidled up next to Christian and sat her butt down, leaning her head against his hip. He automatically reached down to scratch between her ears.

Christian sighed. "You can call Liz, but she's going to take my side on this. Does Delilah look like she's going to attack me?"

Erik's eyes rounded as he looked at Delilah. "How the hell are you perfectly calm, Delilah? You killed a man, and now you're a werewolf."

Christian cleared his throat. "Lance attacked her. Look, she's a strong woman who protected herself. She couldn't dodge a 300-pound wolf, and he infected her after she shot him. He was already dead by the time I threw him off her. I watched her shift. She's fine to be here tonight."

Erik scrubbed a hand over his face. "Fine. It's your ass if she loses herself." He started down the stairs, but paused halfway, turning to look back at Christian. "Oh, and good luck with Simons. He's going to shit bricks over this, Christian."

Rolling his eyes, he shut the door and locked it. He crouched down to look into Delilah's eyes. "I trust you, Delilah. I know you won't lose yourself."

She stared back at him, her head tipping to the side.

"You tired?"

Her head dipped and she started for his bedroom, which had been left open.

"Sorry for the mess." He stood and walked into the room. When he looked over his shoulder, he found her climbing onto his bed. Trying to lighten the mood, he teased, "I'm going to change. I don't mind if you watch, but I know I'm not built like the guys you tend to go for. So it's probably a good thing that you can't laugh at me." Although, that *was* a fear of his.

He pulled his shirt over his head and turned to dig a pair of sweats out of his drawer. Once he was ready for bed, he turned to find her big slate eyes watching him.

"I'll leave a shirt and sweatpants for you, in case you wake before me and want to get dressed." He tossed the clothes on the dresser and lay back on the bed. She laid her head on his chest and closed her eyes.

Smiling to himself, he rubbed behind her ears before drifting off to sleep.

Chapter 5

Warm.

Safe.

Home.

Delilah nuzzled her face against his smooth chest. The scent of clean male and musk welcomed her. Desire hummed through her veins as her hand tightened around his hip.

Peeling one eye open, she looked up to find Christian sleeping peacefully. The night came back to her, and strangely enough, it only amped her up more.

Fearless, kind, and sweet. He stood up for her when Erik showed up. He came to find her, as if he'd known what was coming.

Her heart swelled, and a new wave of need washed through her. She trailed her nose down his chest and abs as she shifted her body between his legs, pulling his sweats down as she went.

He smelled so good that she licked his already hard shaft and groaned. He tasted better than his scent. Her mouth closed over him and he moaned, his hips shifting.

"Del, come here." His voice was sleepy and rough.

Her eyes flashed up to his. He caught his lip in his teeth and made a sound that brought her closer to the edge.

She released him and pulled his pants the rest of the way off before climbing back up his body. Trailing kisses along his torso as she moved.

Caressing her face, he stared into her eyes. "You sure, Del?" he murmured. "We can't go back if we do this."

She didn't grasp his meaning, but she belonged here, with him, in his arms, in his bed. This was where she wanted to be.

She took his mouth in a kiss, his lips soft, but firm. He matched her passion, his hands tangling in her hair as she straddled his hips and reached between them to position his length at her opening.

There was an ache inside her that only he could soothe. She slowly lowered over him and his head fell back. Wrapping his hand around the back of her neck, he drew her close, his hand sliding up her side as he kissed her slow and deep.

His touch lit her on fire as she started to glide up and down, relishing in the feel of skin on skin, mouth on mouth.

He moved with her until pleasure spilled over, rushing through her. She climaxed with him, and his arms wound around her to pull her flush against him.

She *felt* loved, deep down she felt his emotion. The bond was formed and she knew they were mated. Breaking the kiss, she peered into his eyes and fell into him, letting his love roll into her until her own blossomed.

The realization was so unexpected she bolted off the bed and into the bathroom.

* * * * *

Christian let his head fall back as he closed his eyes. He knew he was in love, he had been all along. The mating only sealed a fate he couldn't regret.

Delilah though, well he needed to talk to her. He probably should have stopped her, but she was the first woman who didn't treat him like a freak.

He rolled from the bed and pulled his sweats back on before grabbing the clothes he left on the dresser for her.

Closing his eyes, he knocked on the bathroom door. The shower was going.

He felt like an ass. He knew what would happen. She wasn't thinking. Now they were bonded and it was permanent.

"Delilah, we should talk."

"You knew," she accused. "You knew what would happen."

"I told you we couldn't go back. I tried to warn you, but that was my first time. You are the first woman who hasn't treated me like some weirdo. And the way you touch me, I was lost to it, but I tried, damn it."

"Shit. Your first?" she muttered. He barely heard it over the water. "Fuck," she said louder. "You're right... you tried. I couldn't think, I needed you so bad I couldn't have stopped if I wanted to." Her voice broke and something slammed into the wall. "Do you hate me?"

"Hate you? No, Delilah. I've been falling for you since that first day you walked into the shop and I banged my head into the counter trying to get a better look at you."

The door opened a second later. She was dripping wet, standing there with red-rimmed eyes. "You what?"

He couldn't help smiling as he cupped her face. "I love you, Delilah. I know that probably seems fast, but you walked into my life two years ago."

She leaned into his palm as she closed her eyes. "Why didn't you say anything?"

His smile fell. "You were with Matt for a long time. You thought you were in love. Then there was Todd..."

Covering his mouth with her hand, she muttered. "Okay, so I have a habit of picking jock assholes. I thought you *knew* what I was feeling about you though. You always seem to know."

He pulled her hand away. "Unfortunately, you weren't always so sure, so I wasn't sure how to tell you. Remember, most girls think I'm a freak, and not the kind they want to get down and dirty with."

"I'm really your first? Aren't you going to regret never having another woman?"

He chuckled low and deep as he backed her into the counter. *Silly woman.* There was no regret. He brought his lips to hers in a slow kiss.

Christian murmured, "I figure it can only get better and that was pretty damned spectacular. I just hope I didn't disappoint you."

Her hands threaded into his hair as she pulled him closer, exploring his mouth with hers.

There was a knock, a firm steady rapping on the door.

She pulled away. "Shit. I hope that's not Dad."

He smiled reassuringly. "No, but it is Slater. I believe Erik called him this morning. Finish your shower. I'll keep him busy until you're ready."

"Right. Okay."

He stepped out of the bathroom and walked to the living room. Taking a bracing breath, he opened the door and boldly met the Alpha's gaze.

Slater's brow arched, his gray eyes piercing his. "You're mated." It wasn't a question. Of course he knew. The Alpha always knew when his wolves mated.

Christian shifted uncomfortably. "Yeah. Look, I know. You would have told me to have someone pick up any new wolf. Well, this was different. She shot that asshole. She shifted for the first time. She needed a friend who would give her comfort. And look, I'm fine, not a scratch on me."

Slater nodded, a smile quirking his lips. "You have some coffee you can make?"

Christian's mouth fell open. "You're not going to jump on my case?"

"What's done is done. You're fine. I'm assuming she's fine. So really, where's the problem?"

That was easier than he expected. Mostly because he half expected Simons to barge up and demand to see his daughter.

"Okay," Christian dragged the word out before turning to make his way to the kitchen. He pulled down the coffee and loaded the grinder before turning back. "So, Erik told you?"

"He did. Said you wouldn't back down. Honestly, considering the circumstances, I would say you were the best choice. Erik means well, but he couldn't soothe her like you did."

A smile lifted his lips as he started the coffee. Slater was watching him when he turned back.

"Don't look so surprised," Slater said. "Mate bonds start forming before sex seals them. Sometimes, even while human, the bond starts to form. You two grew as friends."

Christian nodded as he took three cups down. He just hoped Delilah was okay with everything. Her emotions were too jumbled to get a decent read on them this morning. He knew their future was bright, but the present, well that wasn't so clear.

* * * * *

Delilah stood under the water, trying to sort out what happened. Christian's first time with her and now he was bound to her.

Forever.

Shit. And I took his virginity.

She wasn't sure what to think of that. She wasn't sure about settling down, but she felt the connection, she felt as if she belonged with him.

And what if it's just the mate bond talking, and none of it's real?

She wanted to cry, to scream, to hit something. That wouldn't do a damned bit of good but it was tempting.

Why couldn't I just get my shit together and ask him out ages ago? We could have figured it out without the metaphysical bullshit.

The smell of coffee brewing reached her. She heard the quiet conversation between Slater and Christian.

Sighing, she shut off the water and quickly dried off to get dressed.

She found Slater sitting at the counter while Christian waited on the coffee. Slater's last comment rang true. They were friends, there was love. Even if it was new for her, she couldn't deny it.

"He's right," Delilah said softly.

Christian's gaze snapped to hers, and she saw the hope mingled with the worry. "About?"

"I've felt that connection since I met you. I guess I'm used to a guy chasing me. You waited. You were patient. You made sure we were friends. Then, you did the impossible and came to me when I needed you most. I don't regret this morning, Christian."

He closed the distance and wrapped her in his arms. "Good, because I want to explore *us.* I meant what I said. I do love you. I have since the beginning."

She brushed her lips over his. "I love you too. Sorry I freaked."

"It's okay. We're here now," Christian murmured.

She stepped back from Christian and turned to Slater. "So, I guess you're my alpha now."

Slater chuckled. "Unless you want to move somewhere else. I think your dad would be ticked though. It's going to take him a little time to get used to his little girl being a wolf. Not to mention that you're already mated."

Delilah ducked her head. "Yeah. I should probably talk to him about that. Think you'd come with us? I'd rather not have Dad freak and strangle my mate." Her eyes cut over to Christian. His brow arched, a smirk lifting one delicious corner of his mouth.

"I just got you. I'd rather not die so soon," he teased.

Slater grinned. "Then after some coffee, we should go. Stacey's making us breakfast. They don't know the details, but I did tell them to plan for a couple extra people."

Delilah shook her head and looked up at the ceiling. "This should be interesting."

Chapter 6

After a stop by her apartment, Delilah was dressed and presentable. Christian held her hand as they walked up the front steps to the door.

Slater stood next to her and squeezed her shoulder. "Don't worry. Simons told me once he wished you two were together instead of those assholes you usually date."

Her eyes rounded as she looked back at her Alpha. That was going to take some getting used to. All of it really. She was a werewolf, had to answer to Slater, and all these new senses and strength. She took a deep breath and pressed the doorbell. She figured it was better than barging in with her new mate and Slater.

The sound of feet thundering down the stairs amplified her heart rate. Then her dad opened the door. There was a look of confusion on his face.

She looked up at him with a lame smile. "Hey, Dad."

Simons sniffed the air, and his brow creased as his eyes lasered in on her. "What happened? Was it that piece of shit Lance?"

That wasn't quite the reaction she expected. "Um…" she uttered.

"Come in, come in," he insisted, stepping back and gesturing to the living room. "No need to do this outside."

She crossed her arms over her chest. "First, I'm mated to Christian. Everything sort of happened all at once."

Simons barked a laugh. "Yeah, well, you don't choose who you mate, and Christian is a good kid. Maybe someday I'll tell you about how your mother and I mated."

Delilah shuddered, not really looking forward to that story.

Christian squeezed her hand and nodded inside. She walked in and took a seat on the couch. Christian sat beside her but she snuggled into him, *needing* to be close in a way she hadn't experienced before.

Her father had told her enough for her to know that reaction had to do with being a werewolf. She now had need for physical contact, especially when stressed. And this was stressful, even if it seemed to be going way better than she ever imagined.

"What happened last night, Del?" Her dad asked before taking a seat.

"Well, Lance had been following me because I blew him off. I knew better than to stay on a date with a werewolf when he got too pushy, so I ditched him. He's been following me ever since. Or I guess… he was."

"Wish you had told me. I could have…"

"Don't. I didn't. It's too late now. I avoided him the best I could."

"He still attacked you," Simons pointed out.

She drew in a breath and shrugged. "Yeah. I noticed."

Simons leaned forward, his hands cranked into fists. "What happened, Delilah?"

"Last night was the full moon, and he had followed me again. When I heard him behind me, I shot him. He was too fast though, and drove me to the ground, doing enough damage that he infected me."

Simons' eyes narrowed as he nodded his head. "And Christian? How did you wind up with him and not in a containment cell?"

She grinned then. "Christian showed up before I shifted. He talked me through it. Then he took me home." Delilah looked over at Christian. "You should have seen him. He wasn't going to let Erik take me."

Christian shrugged. "Erik saw that you were fine, so there was no reason to take you."

Delilah blurted out, "The mating was my fault…"

"I think I can fill in the rest." Simons shook his head, his eyes closing. "I really don't want the details."

Delilah blushed, but asked anyway, "So, you're not upset with me? Or Christian?"

Slater cleared his throat. "I'll go check on breakfast. Come on, Christian."

Christian looked deep into her eyes. "Up to you. Want me to stay? Or do you want a few minutes with your father?"

She was torn. She wanted him next to her, but she did need to talk to Dad. "Go with Slater. We'll be right in. I can smell breakfast, and Mom made my favorite."

Christian smiled back at her before standing, and following Slater out of the room.

"Look," Simons started. "You did what I taught you. You protected yourself. You did everything right."

Delilah let out a breath. "You don't think Christian happened too fast?"

Dad chuckled. "Mating happens, and Christian has always treated you well, even before you realized it. I can't imagine a better man for you. So no, I'm not upset."

"Good. I didn't want to disappoint you."

"You haven't. You are doing great for your first day as a wolf, and finding yourself mated. You'll figure out the rest later, but it's pretty rare to mate someone who isn't perfect for them."

"Really?"

"Honestly." He stood up and took her hand, pulling her to her feet for a hug. "It's probably a good thing you killed that loser. I have a feeling Hayden would have had to lock me up if I got my hands on him for any of it."

She laughed then. "That was half the reason I didn't tell you in the first place."

"Well, next time you tell me if someone is hassling you."

"If I don't rip into him first," she answered.

* * * * *

Stacey smiled as Christian stepped into the kitchen. "I heard. Congratulations, young man. You better take good care of my daughter."

Christian swallowed hard as he nodded in agreement.

Stacey's warm brown eyes studied him closely, but she wore a pleased expression. "I know you will. Don't worry."

"I can't imagine treating Delilah anything but well. She has always been everything I want, but was too afraid to ask for." He blushed as he felt Slater's gaze catch on him. Christian knew that sounded cheesy, but it was the truth.

Slater asked, "You knew it was coming though. Right? You're better at seeing than Jess."

"Doesn't mean I believed it. It seems too good to be true. " Christian looked away, a slight smile on his face. "In case you haven't noticed. I don't have any experience with women. I'm not exactly a ladies man."

"You just don't try. I know you've turned Rebecca down several times. I've been there. Other young women have shown interest in you, and you ignore it."

"None of those women were Delilah. She's always been the only one I wanted," Christian replied.

He felt Delilah walk up behind him. Her arms slid around his waist as she whispered in his ear, "Well, you have me. I'm not going anywhere."

He hugged her arms to him and turned his head to brush a gentle but brief kiss over her lips.

Stacey closed the distance and hugged her daughter and Christian both. "Aww. You'll be good together."

Simons cleared his throat. "Yeah, well I don't need to see it," he grumbled as he moved past them to the table.

Slater shook his head. "Now that the air is cleared, I vote we eat."

Chapter 7

Delilah trailed her fingers over Christian's chest and looked into his eyes. "You really have to work?" She asked again. She just wanted to lock Christian in his room and make love to him for the rest of the night. They had spent most of their day in his room since they got home, only venturing out for lunch and snacks.

He caught her hand and brought her fingers to his mouth for a gentle kiss. "I do. You can come if you'd like. That is if you don't have anything else you need to do today."

"You want me there?" she asked softly.

"I do." He chuckled. "You can snarl and snap at Rebecca. Maybe she'll finally take the hint that I'm not interested."

"Is that what she was doing last night?" Delilah knew that sounded catty. She didn't care. She wanted to claw Rebecca's face up for looking at Christian.

Christian's head fell back. "You saw her pathetic attempt to tempt me?"

"Yeah. It's why I went for a walk."

"Shit. I'm sorry. I was trying to get her to leave. I was going to see if I could track you down." He sighed. "I finally got tired of waiting for you to realize I might not be such a bad choice."

She pushed herself up to look down at him. "Aww, you never were, Christian. Why the hell would you think that?"

He rolled her over and pinned her down with a sad smile. "Remember, I know how people feel about me. I see how so many girls would have rejected me if I ever gave it a chance. It sort of kills a guy's hope pretty fast. Besides, I've been a goner since you walked into the shop that first day. I haven't really given any other girl a thought since I saw you."

"But I never would have done that to you."

He dropped a kiss to her lips. "No. Still, you weren't ready. Now, hopefully you are."

"I am." She nipped his bottom lip. "You sure we have to go in?"

Climbing from the bed, he nodded back at her. "Yes. Just wait. Tremaine's going to give me hell. He was telling me yesterday that I needed to tell you how I feel."

She smiled, watching the way his lean muscles moved as he pulled on his clothes. "You know what I always wondered?"

"Probably. Something about Liz and Tremaine? Don't bother asking. All I ever get from either one of them is something along the lines of its complicated."

"What's their story?"

Christian shook his head. "Don't know. I gave up asking long ago. He's always there to pick her up when she's down. She's always watching him like he's her other half. I'm not sure I'll ever figure it out."

"You haven't seen anything for them?"

He snorted. "No. I think there's a missing piece. Something they're both waiting on. Crazy, huh? Except, it's not. I'm not sure we would have worked so well if it hadn't been for me showing up when I did last night. You would probably think I was crazy if I claimed to love you without the mate bond."

She shuddered, thinking back. If she hadn't watched Rebecca throw herself at him, and then storm off, she would be fine, and they might not be together.

Then she remembered Lance, and the realization that she had killed a man settled in. She felt sick to her stomach as she thought about it.

He spun around and knelt at her feet where she was now sitting at the edge of the bed. "Hey, Del, don't do that. It's not your fault. You did what you needed to. He meant to kill you for humiliating him. You're still here, and better yet, you're mine."

Her eyes slid closed as she muttered, "You can read minds too?"

"No, but I can feel what you feel, Del. You just had a wave of guilt so strong it brought me to my knees. I can only imagine what you're thinking about."

A weak smile graced her lips. "You're right, on both counts. It's not my fault, and I shouldn't feel guilty."

"Come on. I promise I'll make up having to work tonight."

"You will?" she whispered.

He nodded but didn't say a word before he stood and turned back to what he was doing. "I will."

Christian came around the corner, Delilah's hand in his, and he froze. Tremaine and Liz stood close, talking quietly. He could feel the love and tension from outside the damned building.

"I really wish they would uncomplicate their shit. They deserve to be happy."

Delilah leaned into him. "They do."

He smiled over at her. "Come on. I better get in there."

They stepped inside, and Christian waved. "Hi, Trem, Liz. Hope you don't mind, but I brought Delilah along for the night." He knew they wouldn't.

Tremaine grinned. "About damned time, kid." He looked to Delilah, and his smile fell. "Wait. What happened?"

Liz looked at him, then her. "Are you okay, Delilah?"

She nodded slightly. "Thanks to Christian, I'm fine."

Tremaine's head cocked to the side. He always had a sense of who was what and what was different. His face cracked into a grin. "You finally got the guts to say something, and now you're mated?"

Liz gave them a sad smile. "I'm happy for you." She sighed as she looked down at the ground, avoiding Tremaine's gaze. "I have plans tonight. Delilah, you're always welcome in the shop. Good night." She slipped out the back.

Closing his eyes, Tremaine leaned against the counter and pushed his fingers through his hair.

"You should say something to her," Christian told him lightly before going to the back room. He figured showing Delilah where her purse could go would give Tremaine a few moments to center himself or whatever he needed to do.

Delilah pulled him close. "You okay?" she whispered.

"Yeah. I just wish Liz didn't push Trem away. I wish Trem would just tell her. I can feel what they feel."

"Is it weird? To feel everyone's turmoil?"

He shrugged. "I'm used to it. It doesn't go away."

"Then you knew I wanted you?"

He half laughed. "You weren't ready. I don't know. Something was holding you back. So I waited. Maybe I shouldn't have."

"Maybe I needed a push."

"I'm sorry…"

She interrupted him with a kiss.

"Stop that. Go, get to work." She gently pushed him toward the door. "Go on."

Christian grinned. "All right then."

She swatted his ass and he looked over his shoulder at her with a raised brow.

"Watch it. I'm at work," he teased.

Shaking her head, she followed him back out.

Tremaine still stood there, but he was staring out the window, a sad look on his face.

Christian moved to stand beside him. "Anything I can do?"

"Nope. I told you. It's not happening."

Christian didn't believe that. Maybe not at that moment, but sooner or later, they'd wind up together. They had to. "Then get out of here. I got this."

Tremaine snorted. He looked at Delilah. "By the way, Rebecca was looking for you earlier. She was worried about you when she didn't see you come home last night. She said something about Lance." Then he paused. "That's what happened? That scumbag attacked you?"

"He did, but my dad taught me how to use a gun. That's why he's not around anymore."

Tremaine nodded, amusement dancing in his eyes. He gave Christian a knowing smile. "I always did like her." He lifted his hand in a wave. "You two have a good night."

He left and Christian took the same spot Tremaine had vacated. "You know, you don't have to stay if you don't want to. It can get pretty boring. It's not like we'll be busy."

"I'm not going anywhere. Besides, I have a *friend* who needs to back off my mate." There was a light growl to her voice that got him hard.

He closed his eyes and took a slow breath. "Trust me. She'll be in tonight."

Her smile was on the wicked side. "Good."

Chapter 8

It was almost closing time, and Rebecca was still a no show. Delilah was disappointed. She felt the strong desire to put her supposed friend in her place.

Christian nodded to the windows as he came around the counter. He kept coming, leaning into her as he pressed his mouth to hers. "We could just show her that I'm taken," he murmured against her lips before taking a slow taste of her mouth.

She spun him around, leaning into him as she deepened the kiss. Only a few hours since the last time they had made love and she needed him desperately.

Delilah had no problem showing Rebecca that Christian was spoken for.

The door opened as she felt Christian's desire, his hands tangling in her hair as he nipped her bottom lip.

"Better stop that. We'll be home soon, and I have a few things I want to do to you before you get back to that." His breath was husky, and she could smell his lust. It was a rich heady scent that made her a little crazed.

Rebecca cleared her throat. "You finally manned up and asked her out?"

Christian sighed as he leaned his head back to glare at Rebecca. "Told you I wasn't interested in you. This shouldn't come as a surprise."

"No." Rebecca sighed and looked out the window. "You two seem happy at least. Hey, do you know where Lance is?"

Delilah looked away, chewing her lip.

Christian pulled Delilah closer. "He attacked Delilah last night. She shot him. He's gone."

"I'm sorry. He left me some creepy message. I didn't know until I got home, after..." She glanced away. "After I had to go push boundaries with Christian. Anyway, he said he was coming after you. When I couldn't get in touch with you, I started getting worried."

"I'm fine, but Christian is officially off limits. He's my mate, and I won't play nice if you try that same bullshit you tried last night."

One pale eyebrow arched as Rebecca smirked. "Don't worry. I was trying to push him into action with you. He made it clear long ago he wanted nothing to do with me. I probably should have tried another route."

She turned and marched out the door as Delilah's mouth fell open. "Is she for real?"

Christian shrugged. "She doesn't seem to know what she wants. I'm going to close up, and then we can go home. One question though." He stole a quick kiss. "My apartment or yours?"

"Yours, if you don't mind. It already feels like home."

* * * * *

Christian cleared the table while Delilah walked back to their room. They had decided his apartment was the best choice. Bigger, and more comfortable.

She pulled her clothes from her body, anticipation making her hot. His shirt landed beside hers as his hands came around her waist. His mouth brushed over her shoulder before nibbling up her neck.

His velvet voice teased her. "Tell me if I do something wrong."

She let out a husky laugh. "Oh, Christian, that you're concerned you'll do it wrong tells me you won't. You aren't out to please yourself, but to please me. I'm confident you'll do just that."

"Oh, Del, just watching you unravel gets me off, and you feel like heaven."

She turned in his arms and opened his jeans, sliding them down his hips with his boxers. "I love you, Christian."

"Love you too," he murmured before backing her to the bed and laying her down.

Brandy L. Rivers

Author Dedication

Sofia, we may not have planned you

And you might be Little Miss Diva

But you're the sweetest little snuggler in the world

And I would never ever trade you

Not for anything

Since Delilah's a spitfire, she might

Be a little like you

Momma loves you

About Brandy

Brandy is a stay at home mom with a wonderful husband and three great kids. They live in the Pacific Northwest. Her obsession with monsters and magic started at a young age, so it only makes sense that she writes about them now. She is the author of the Others of Edenton series.

Follow Brandy

Website: http://www.brandylrivers.com/

Facebook: http://www.facebook.com/brandylrivers

Read More from Brandy

Others of Edenton Box Set: http://amzn.to/1ecpf5Q

Have My Heart

Rene Folsom

June 27th

Dear Diary,

The summer night air is just cool enough to make the grains of sand chilly as they squish between my toes. Sitting on the bank of the lake and looking out onto the water as it shimmers like diamonds in the moonlight, I have just enough luminous glow to help me see the muted black ink of my pen as I scribble on your surface, your pages slightly dampened with dew. As much as I am trying to busy my mind with more inane drivel, I can't help but think of him. The feel of the sand beneath my body reminds me of a more joyous and carefree day not so long ago. The vision of his smile consumes my thoughts and makes me wonder... what is he doing right now? Is he looking up at the same pale moon and thinking of me too? Is he thinking about whether my eyes will shimmer like the undulating surface of the lake? Is he thinking of what it would feel like to hold me just as badly as I want to feel his arms wrapped around my body—protective and strong?

Yes. Just the dream of Blake's thoughts coinciding with mine makes me feel better. In my dreams, no one can take him away from me. His toned body and beautiful mind belong to me... but only here on this tiny piece of paper, hidden in the darkness of night, while the judgmental eyes of this world sleep.

Thankfully, the animals of the night keep me company as I continue to covet my love. The frogs sing songs to their mates, as the crickets join in with a natural harmony only God can create. The constant sounds of a lonely Whip-poor-will cuts through the night air, but doesn't bother the other insects as they continue their serenades.

The singular bird's call reminds me once more that I am alone—through no choice of my own. I am allowing others to dictate my life, and the reality of it saddens me. But, will I gain the strength to stand up to the judgments of others?

The temperature continues to drop as I write the words of my heart on your faithful pages. When a shiver runs through my bones, causing a blanket of goose bumps to spread across my pale skin, I try to think of Blake's warmth enveloping me. His very nature melts the chill from my body, like the sun melts snow during spring.

Feeling the sun's rays on my skin that warm summer day not so long ago is the perfect way to describe how I feel when he looks at me. His honey brown eyes bore into my soul and somehow prove to me just how much he cherishes every moment we have together. The feel of his hand on my cheek as he leans in and places a long kiss on my forehead, the smell of his cologne as he holds me against his broad chest, the sound of his heart beating against my cheek as it thumps in rhythm with my own—are all proof he consumes my every waking moment with power and grace.

The nocturnal sounds of the owl tell me it's time for me to go. No matter where I am, my memories of Blake will continue to warm my soul and strengthen my resolve… One day soon we will be together. Racial judgments be damned.

June 29th

Dear Diary,

The beady condensation sliding along the side of my glass at lunch today brought back some delicious memories of my obsession. Each watery drip cascading down the dark glass of tea had me salivating at the memory of the last time I saw Blake. My stomach flips and flutters with just the thought of him. I know such reactions from a twenty-two-year-old woman are not commonly spoken about. So, as I sat amongst a group of my friends earlier today, I kept my jittery feelings of young love to myself.

Now that I am alone, I feel more confident in scribbling my memories on your ever-forgiving pages. Just the thought of spilling my heart out onto your cream-colored surface gives me new butterflies of anticipation and desire.

Last Saturday began like any other summertime weekend. I bounded down the stairs, wearing a tank and shorts over my bathing suit, eager to enjoy some sun by the lake after getting a few chores done. Considering I slept until ten, I knew I wanted to hurry so I could enjoy some rays before band practice at three.

As I reached the bottom of the steps, I stopped short with the sight of him in the distance beyond my wall of sliding glass doors. There he stood, wearing nothing but his swim trunks, which hung loosely around his hips. Droplets of water beaded on his chocolate-colored skin, dripping each time he took a step toward his friend, while draping a towel around his neck. I knew even if I licked every drop of water from his delicious body, it still wouldn't quench my thirst for him. My life hadn't been the same since he moved in next door a few months back.

I bit my lip and wondered if he knew I was watching his every move. Just as I thought I was getting away with sneaking a peek, he looked directly at me, making my heart momentarily stop with shock. Once our eyes locked, a broad smile crept its way across his face, showing those startling white teeth through his thick, juicy lips.

Like a magnet, I slowly walked to the closed glass door and stared at Blake, watching him converse with his friend as he continued to look in my direction—never removing his eyes from mine. Before I could muster the courage to go see him, my vision refocused on my reflection as the sun shone brightly against the glass surface.

Large, green eyes stared back at me with what looked like fear. I needed to wipe that look of terror from my face before he began to get the wrong idea. My curly, red hair was in complete disarray, and I knew there was nothing I could do about it.

Without warning, a figure approached the other side of the glass and startled me, making me jump like a skittish kitten.

Blake.

As if in slow motion, I watched him reach for the door and gently slide it out of his way so he could reach me. He smelled of fresh spring water and beachy sweat—a heady combination that had me completely speechless as I stared at his soaking-wet form.

"You, my Gwen, have no chance of staying dry," he roared just before bending down and scooping me up over his broad shoulder. To my horror, I squealed like a nitwit teenager. My scream was followed by laughter one would hear from a hyena on steroids.

"Blake, please!" I screamed as I held onto his waist for dear life. My face was startlingly close to his tight rear, and his hands wrapped protectively around my thighs, sending shivers through me at just the thought of him touching me more intimately. I had only known him for a little over a month, but our instant attraction caused our relationship to escalate rather quickly.

"Begging won't help you now, Gwen. I want to see you dripping wet," he joked as he bounded further down the path to the lake. Red strands of curls threatened to choke me as I sputtered them out of my mouth, while laughing and squealing some more.

Feeling his body slow a bit, I knew he was now wading through the cool water. As if the splashing sounds weren't enough of a hint, I could also feel the wetness splatter against my skin each time he lifted his knees and sluggishly ran deeper.

"Blake! My clothes!"

"They're going to get wet too. Plug your nose..."

And with that, he slung me around so I was cradled in his arms and immediately submerged us both under water.

That day was definitely one of the most memorable times of my life—and the most heartbreaking. It was the last day Blake and I got to spend together, blissfully unaware of the evils that lurked behind the scenes of our lives.

July 1st

Dear Diary,

Sticks and stones may break my bones, but words will never hurt me.

All children are taught these infamous words, yet I can't help but ponder their validity. Even a child understands how much name-calling can wound their soul. From an adult perspective, I realize it's not the actual words people spout that can cause pain, but the anger and cruelty behind those words are what I fear. The pain increases when such venomous words are spoken by someone you once considered a friend.

Blake's five-year-old daughter, Maya, is no exception to this hurt. Her eyes show every emotion in clear detail, and the reality of it pains me.

Memories of my time spent with Maya continue to both fill me with joy and sadness. Yes, I have many wonderful recollections of playing with her out by the lake, helping her brush her baby doll's hair, and enjoying a spot of tea over plastic crumpets. But one memory of my time with the little princess continues to plague my thoughts with sorrow, and is ultimately the reason I had to distance myself from the situation.

For her, I'd do anything.

The night of our playful time by the lake, Blake asked me to watch Maya for a couple of hours while he went out with a few buddies. I was always more than happy to spend time with her. Her smile was infectious, and her blue eyes stared back with innocent curiosity.

While I sat comfortably on the couch with a new novel, Maya sprawled her coloring books and crayons across the rug, vigorously decorating each page as if her next breath depended on using every color in the box. Just when I became lost in the fictional plot of lovers reuniting, I noticed a pair of sparkling, blue eyes staring at me— studying me tenderly.

"Hello, beautiful," I said, peeking over my book and meeting her gaze.

"For you," she said excitedly as she shoved a piece of paper in my direction.

"For me? Thank you," I replied, taking the drawing from her hands and examining the figures on the white sheet. Water decorated the background behind a group of three trees, making it obvious it was

a drawing of our lake. Standing on the bank was two dark figures, one significantly shorter than the other, and one yellow figure with fiery red hair. The tall, dark figure, I only assumed to be Blake, was holding a heart and extending it out to the redhead.

"Dats you!" she said excitedly, pointing to the crazy, red hair and beaming from ear to ear.

"It definitely looks like me, Maya. Thank you," I said, pausing and bringing her up on my lap. "And who is this?" I asked, pointing to the small, dark figure beneath the heart.

"Dats me and dats Daddy," she explained as she pointed her stubby little fingers against the page.

"You look so beautiful. And what is Daddy holding?"

"His heart." She put an emphasis on the word his. Her words caught me off guard. She didn't say it was just any old heart. It was his heart.

"And why is he giving his heart to me?" I asked, wondering why she would put it this way.

"'Cause he wuvs you dat much," she said matter-of-factly, adding a little bit of a 'duh' factor to her tone. Her innocent, blue eyes looked up at me with startling clarity, as if I should have known this little fact.

"You think so?" I responded, desperately trying to keep my voice from cracking with emotion.

"I know so," she said with a nod. "I can see it in his eyes," she added, pointing to the face of her daddy in the drawing.

From the mouths of babes comes only truth. Then again, little minds didn't really know the difference between love and lust. Regardless of her understanding, her goodness still tugged at my heart.

Attempting to distract her from the deep topic she considered to be so light, I asked, "And what color are Daddy's eyes?"

"Brown, like his face," she responded. "Why are my eyes not like Daddy's?"

"Because everyone is made differently. You know how you like to color with all the crayons in the box?" I asked her. She nodded with excitement. "Well, God likes to use all the colors in his crayon box too."

The smile covering her face was one of youthful joy—obviously thrilled that God enjoyed coloring just like her.

"C'mon. Let's go hang this beautiful work of art up on my fridge, okay?"

"Yeah!" she yelled, hopping off my lap and sprinting toward the kitchen. "That way you can see me and Daddy every day," I heard her holler over the patter of footsteps against the tile floor.

Following her in, I grabbed a magnet and boosted her up so she could help me hang the picture.

After putting it in place, a quizzical look crossed her face and she asked, "Gwen, what's a nigger?" The 'R' sound at the end rolled off her tongue in an innocent manner, catching me completely off guard in the process.

"Where in the world did you hear that word?" I tried my best not to sound angry with her, but the look of shock that crossed my face could not be avoided.

She flinched before shrugging and saying, "Nowhere."

"Well, Maya, it's not a very nice word and definitely not a word you should repeat. Did you hear it from someone at school?" She shrugged again while walking away, obviously embarrassed she even brought it up. I knelt in front of her to get her attention and tried my best to place a sympathetic expression on my face. "It's okay to talk to me about anything, you know that, right?"

"I don't want to get in trouble," she whined, shying away from my intense stare.

"You don't have to tell me anything if you don't want to. If someone is calling you names, you just ignore them, okay?" I said, trying to make her feel more comfortable, without forcing her to give me details.

"Not me, Daddy," she admitted. "He was mean, and I don't want him to be mad at me."

"He who?" Now I was pressing. The look of terror on her face told me this wasn't just some bully picking on her at school.

"Billy's daddy. He was talking about my daddy and you."

"What did he say?"

"He pointed at me and said he wanted to teach you a lesson and show you why you shouldn't love a nigger and his mutt kid. That's why I asked. I'm sorry." A small tear trickled down her cheek with the apology.

"Don't be sorry," I soothed, picking her up and carrying her back to the couch. *"It's not your fault people are cruel. And thank you for telling me. Best friends tell each other these things."* I tried to keep my voice calm, even though I was anything but. Dread and anger coursed through my entire body. It was all I could do not to lash out with rage at the man.

The man I thought was my friend.

The memory of holding Maya for the last time continues to haunt me. Time spent with her was always so joyous. So the fact our last embrace was brought on by such negativity continues to grate at my resolve to keep my distance.

Her letters and drawings repeatedly plead for me to come over and play. I only hope she isn't blaming herself for my distance.

I have to do everything in my power to keep her safe.

July 3rd

Dear Diary,

Seeing Blake's number glow on my caller ID today is a torturous reminder that I'd ended things with him last week. The turn of events that lead me to this point in our relationship have my cheeks flushing with embarrassment at just the thought. I still can't tell if my actions are justified. My mind is in a constant state of confusion as I continue to absorb the haunting reminders of the past few weeks.

Still, the pain of his absence is like poison. It seeps into my veins until there's nothing left of me.

I am forced to put on a front each and every day—pretend like all is right in the world—a world so full of corruption and hate. This world, and the depravity that gnaws at humanity, has won. I'm no longer with the person I love because so many can't see past our various shades of melanin that make us so unique.

Scribbling on your all-forgiving pages seems to be the only way I can express my love for the man next door. While this may be an outlet that is free of judgment, I still feel empty… lonely. The only reprieve from my solitude is my memories, some of which are not always so kind to my heart. As I sit here now and write about my feelings, I can feel the pitter-patter of my pulse quickening with the recollections. He does this to me.

I remember the evening like it was yesterday—the evening I had to turn him away—an open wound that continues to torture me with every move I make. Pretending he means nothing to me is probably the most agonizing thing I've ever had to do.

It was the day after my talk with Maya. My fingers shook as I fumbled with the screen of my phone. Controlling my breathing became a chore as the ringing sounded through the receiver, and it was all I could do not to break down in a full-on sob. Regardless of my reluctance to let him go, I kept repeating my goal over and over in my mind: I had to protect Maya from my world of corruption.

My insides nearly melted whenever I heard his voice. It was as if he was seductive without even trying. I often wondered if he spoke that way to all women or if I truly was special in some way. I always hoped for the latter.

The dreaded phone call that day was no different. My name dripping from his lips through the phone had my stomach doing summersaults. My eyes fluttered shut, and I sucked in a ragged breath, attempting to reassure myself and willing my voice to work.

My tone betrayed me, and he could tell something was seriously wrong. I could hear his demand ringing through my ears as he said he would be right over. My protests went unheard as he disconnected the line.

At the time, I was stunned. I knew I couldn't resist him when he was near. All it took was the thought of him in my home for my resolve to crumble.

A light rapping on the glass of my back door had my heart pounding.

Stepping through the door, he reached for me. The only possible way I could stay strong was to keep my distance and avoid physical contact. He noticed me dodge his touch, and the look on his face pained me. A mixture of confusion and hurt rippled through his expression, and I would've given anything to make him feel at ease—anything except for his safety.

Suddenly, it was as if he made a split-second decision to disregard my reluctance. Closing the door behind him, he took the few steps toward my near-trembling form. I backed away from him, fearful I wouldn't be able to handle his intense stare at such a close proximity.

"Why are you frightened?" he whispered.

My back hit the wall and I turned my face away from his scrutiny, shaking my head in defiance. The warmth of his strength surrounded me, suffocating me, as he inched closer and braced one of his hands above my head.

I knew I couldn't show him just how much he affected me. Tears would only compound the issue. If he thought I no longer cared for him, then he could go on with his life oblivious—completely unaware of how frayed my heart would be.

A warm finger caressed the side of my face, over my cheek, and down across my jaw until it hooked beneath my chin and forced me to look up into a sea full of molten honey, scorching me with intensity and lust.

"My Gwen, you can't hide from me. Please, tell me what's causing your fear," he pleaded. His mouth was so close to mine, so close. I needed his thick, warm lips upon me more than I needed my next breath. But I knew it wasn't possible. I knew what I had to do, even if it meant I had to suffocate in the process.

With an attempt to seem uncaring, I looked him straight in the eye and said, "We can't—" I faltered. The words became a thick ball of pain in my throat. My eyes stung as I struggled to spit out the vile words.

"We can," he affirmed, still unsure of what I was even attempting to blather about. Obviously, he didn't care. "We can, and we will."

His body pressed hard against mine, pushing my back into the wall with force. I shuddered at the feel of his fingers trailing down my neck, across my collarbone, and to the swell of my breasts, which were rising and falling in response to my rapid breathing.

Flattening his hand out, he held it over my heart and looked me straight in the eyes.

"We will, Gwen," he said, his voice deep with a steady resolve that almost made me wonder if he knew what was tearing me apart. Maya probably had no reason to tell him what she told me. She was so young and confused. Did he even know what his daughter was going through?

I went to open my mouth and argue, but he quickly covered my lips with his long, solid fingers. To soothe the initial blow of shutting me up, he grazed his thumb along my trembling lower lip. I couldn't control myself anymore and opened for him, bringing my tongue out to lick and kiss the pad of his thumb.

Since he stood a good foot taller than my short frame, he dipped his head low and brushed the thickness of his lips against mine. Every time this man kissed me, I lost all control of my senses. I wish I could say I went numb, but the feelings he tore from my soul were quite the opposite. A fire erupted deep inside me, setting off jolts of pleasure through every nerve ending in my body.

And all he had done was kiss me—a simple, sweet kiss that needed no other explanation. My mind immediately began to imagine what it would feel like to make love to the beautiful Blake.

Losing all control and completely forgetting why I had called upon him in the first place, I crept up on my tippy toes and deepened our kiss. It was all the invitation he needed to take control.

Parting my lips, I invited him in and allowed him to consume every fiber of my existence. His intensity increased, our tongues tangling together in a heated mess.

God, he was so wonderful. Words couldn't begin to describe how he made me feel that night. His smooth, yet demanding kiss fogged my mind until I couldn't see straight, think straight—hell, if it weren't for the wall holding me up, I would have surely fallen to the floor in a puddle of desire.

When his fingers traveled down my torso, over my hip, and behind the crook in my knee, coaxing me to wrap my leg around his glorious body, I could feel his excitement pressing against my belly. The sensation sent my mind into overdrive, and I suddenly realized this was a huge mistake.

"No," I blurted out in a near sob. My eyes stung as I forced the tears back and shook my head.

Using his large hands to cup my cheeks, he bent down and gazed into the depths of my soul. "No?" was all he asked. I was sure my single-word refusal took him off guard, because he knew damn well what he did to me.

"We can't—"

"I already told you, Gwennie. We—"

"Don't interrupt me," I hissed, pushing at his chest, desperate for some sort of distance between us. "We can't see each other anymore."

There. I said it. And now I felt like I was going to puke.

"You don't mean that," he whispered, obviously dumbfounded by my sudden outburst.

I felt sick. My mind clouded. My stomach churned. My vision began to close in on itself.

Blake caught me as I started sinking to the floor. So much for making him believe he didn't matter. And so much for making him think I didn't want him around anymore. My body was betraying me as I attempted the impossible.

On the floor, he held me—rocking me as I quietly stained his shirt with salty tears. After a few minutes of attempting to catch my breath, I mumbled into his chest. "We can't see each other. I don't want you to fight me on this. It's final."

"You at least owe me an explanation," he grumbled, clearly not happy with my baffling dismissal.

I shook my head, refusing to speak, worried I wouldn't be able to without the tears spilling out unwelcome once more.

"I'm not leaving until I know what's caused this."

"Blake, please."

"Please, what, Gwen?" he seethed, slightly pushing me away and distancing himself from the quakes that were rattling my body. "You're telling me to get lost and have absolutely no reason?"

I avoided his intense gaze. I knew his eyes were my biggest weakness.

"I thought what we had was special," he said as he attempted to grasp my hand.

I pulled it away like it was fire scorching my skin. Shaking my head, I looked at him with such torturous fear—fear I wouldn't be able to continue with this façade much longer.

"I don't buy it, Gwen. What did I ever do to make you look at me with such contempt?"

Oh, god. He thought I hated him? Good. Maybe that was for the best.

"I need you to leave now," I said, while staring at my fingers knotted in my lap.

I could feel his muscles tense and revolt against the blatant dismissal in my words. Heat radiated from him like an inferno blazing through my very essence.

Before he stood, he reached out and brushed a strand of red out of my face. He then placed a kiss on my forehead—an act that sent all-new thrills through my body with his intimate touch.

The thump of the sliding glass door as he left made my heart stop. With robotic movements, I walked to the liquor cabinet and pulled out a bottle of tequila. My sister rounded the corner at that time and noticed the despair written across my face.

Knowing she'd want to talk, I poured us each a shot, downed mine, and immediately poured another for myself. Dalia threw back her shot and reached for the bottle.

"How are you?" she asked. I had to avoid being snippy with her and just stared at the floor to evade her gaze.

Grabbing my arm, she walked with me into the living room, coaxing me to sit down in the process. After I was four shots in, I finally started succumbing to the numbness created by the alcohol.

Sweet, sweet alcohol.

"You didn't have to do that, you know. You should have told him. He has a right to know." These words were coming from a girl who was hysterical the night before when I told her about my conversation with innocent little Maya.

I just stared into the distance and silently praised the alcohol that was beginning to warm my veins. Dalia sat, patiently waiting for me to finally snap out of my trance.

"I feel nothing. I thought I was supposed to feel something... pain, regret. But instead, I just feel... nothing," I mumbled weakly. Eyeballing the tequila bottle on the coffee table with a sideway glance, I pushed my shot glass toward Dalia and said, "I need more nothing."

I may have felt nothing and even puked up a lot more nothing that night, but I sure as hell feel something now. My bitterness and grief is spilling onto your cream-colored pages like a busted dam. Nearly a week of constant gifts—flowers, notes, and phone calls—his voice begging for some sort of explanation. It's all eating away at me.

Not to mention the beautifully colored pictures from Maya. Each rainbow-filled page rips a new hole through my heart.

Despite my attempts at sacrificing my happiness and diffusing the situation, the hate keeps finding me and is much closer to home than I ever anticipated. How my own friends, people I considered allies, could betray me like this... I have no words.

I'm a shell of a woman, empty on the inside. The man next door is holding my heart captive.

July 4th

Dear Diary,

Holidays are supposed to be so joyous and carefree. Hmph.

My band is scheduled to play at *The Bandshell* today. Yet again, I will be forced to wear a smile in an attempt to fool the inhabitants of this small, hypocritical town. My sister has been avoiding me, most likely because of how difficult I've become. Every word out of my mouth tastes bitter, like my entire life is a lie. I no longer feel the need to look for the beauty in my surroundings. What's the point in doing so if I know it will all be ripped from my life?

The Robert Frost poem, *Nothing Gold Can Stay*, used to be one of my favorites. Now, I despise its words and the reality of its meaning.

The bright sun is causing me to squint as it glares off your pages. Even you want to blind me from the innocence of nature, knowing good and well how vehement it's making me feel. The beautiful nature around me is a stark contrast to the animosity I feel inside. Having a constant reminder of the happiness I'm not able to covet pains me.

In front of me sits a note—a small sliver of paper I found tucked under my windshield wiper yesterday. This note is the exact reason why I cannot risk love. This note is a prime example of why I go through life with a gaping hole in my heart. This note... this note is what makes me punish myself every single day in hopes Maya can lead a normal, safe life.

This note is written in my best friend's hand. Scratch that... my former best friend's hand.

Glad you finally realized that black is not your color.

With a flick of a lighter, I watch as the revolting words go up in flames. The fact he wins kills me inside. I let him beat me down. I let him and his judgmental ways completely shatter my happiness.

I'm doing it all because I will *not* let anyone mar her innocence.

To top it off, I have to play with him at *The Bandshell* tonight.

Adding an additional layer of misery to my existence, I dreamed of Blake last night. Yes, I know it's sad for me to compare a Blake dream to misery and pain, but that's how I feel when I wake up and find out it's just a fantasy. My delusional mind is playing nasty tricks with my happiness, obviously intent on ripping down the walls I have built as a way to cope.

Writing about the dream will only cause my heart to ache even more. So, for now, I will bury myself in my music and attempt to forget about my beautiful Blake.

Still July 4th

Dear Diary,

It's official. I broke up the band. Call me Yoko, but I couldn't continue playing alongside that sad excuse of a man. Not after what he's put everyone through. Not after his cruel words made my little Maya cry.

My Maya—I have to keep reminding myself she's not mine... *he's* not mine.

Blake showed up at The Bandshell *today to hear me sing, which was something he used to do regularly until the most recent events. His face was one of joy, but I could tell it was a mask—a way for him to hide the hurt that was probably eating away at his insides.*

The drummer's count began, and the first few bars of music caressed my ears. Closing my eyes, I tried to calm the thrumming in my chest and ignore the fact that his eyes were trained on me.

I usually never got nervous while in front of a crowd. Music had always been my security blanket—a way for me to control my surroundings. But having Blake there stirred up all new feelings of anxiety throughout my body.

With the music taking over my senses, I allowed the words to flow freely from my lips. Closing my eyes, I caressed the mic with my fingers and let my passion for singing consume me.

The song ended all too soon, and I was practically begging my mind not to look out into the crowd—at him. Turning my back on the audience, I clapped to the beat of the next song and sashayed around the stage a bit, killing time until it was my turn to step up to the mic once more.

Todd followed my movements, moving closer to me so he could speak into my ear while his fingers fumbled with the guitar strings.

"*What is that coon doing here?*" *he growled, causing me to cringe away from his slithering words. I felt the need to wipe the feel of his breath from my skin as I looked at him with disgust.*

"*Don't call him that!*" *I seethed under my breath. I was careful to show my disdain, while keeping my voice to a minimum. The crowd didn't need to know I hated my guitarist at the moment.*

"*I thought you broke it off with him, Gwen.*" *At this point, I was supposed to be singing, but the band kept up with their instrumental façade, realizing I needed a moment to compose myself.* "*You know damn well he's not right for you,*" *Todd said, a little too loud for comfort.*

"*I don't give a shit what you think, Todd. This is a public place, and he's allowed to be wherever the hell he wants.*" *I was fuming, my body shaking like a leaf in a windstorm. I couldn't believe he was doing this to me, and on stage to boot!*

"*Well, I'll give him a reason to regret coming,*" *he grumbled before slinging his guitar behind his back and grabbing my arm—hard. His grip made me holler out as he brought me against his chest and tried to kiss me.*

The feeling of his lips crushing against mine was vile. I felt like I might actually puke on stage—a definite first for me, and it had nothing to do with performing in front of hundreds of people.

Pushing hard against his chest, nearly beating on him like a punching bag, I still couldn't break away. He had his hold on me so tight that I fought for breath as I squirmed beneath his rough arms. As a last-ditch effort, I brought my knee to his groin and could literally hear the wind whoosh from his lungs upon contact.

"*Don't ever fucking touch me!*" *I screamed, tears threatening to swell in my eyes with pure rage.* "*I'm done, Todd. Find a new singer. And if you ever speak to Maya again, I'll press charges.*"

Without looking back at Todd's writhing form on the floor of the stage, I avoided everyone's surprised stares as I bolted from the platform. I'd never left in the middle of a performance before, but there was no way I could stay.

I could hear Blake calling my name. It took all the control I had not to turn around as I continued running for my car. It wasn't until I heard Maya's voice call for me that I stopped dead in my tracks.

Turning on my heel, I scanned my surroundings until I saw her running next to Blake.

"Maya!" I gasped as she ran into my leg and clung to me.

"Don't leave me. I'm sorry I said that word. Don't be mad anymore, please?" Her begging tore at my heart. She thought she was the reason?

Scooping her up in my arms, I held her tight and tried to soothe her fear. "Shh, you didn't do anything wrong, Maya, I promise."

"Gwen, let's go," Blake said in a low voice as he began ushering me toward the parking lot. Looking around, I noticed several gawkers staring, obviously wondering what had gotten into me. "Now, Gwen. Move your feet."

Shuffling, I nearly tripped with Maya's weight in my arms.

"Here, give her to me," Blake said, reaching out for her.

"No," I refused, clutching her tight against my chest and letting her bury her face in the crook of my neck. "I've got her. I'm not letting go of her right now."

"That's fine. We just need to go. Now," he insisted, while looking back behind us with concern. Following his stare, I noticed the rest of my band members approaching us.

My feet began to move beneath me, terror filling my veins with the look of hatred in their eyes—especially Todd.

"Gwen, get her to the car. I'll handle this," Blake said, his deep voice determined to stay calm for Maya's sake. Dread consumed me as I followed his orders. I knew I needed to get her to safety, but leaving him there to defend himself, when this problem was entirely my fault, still reeked of injustice.

Someone from the crowd must've anticipated the situation would escalate, because the cops arrived shortly after Maya and I ducked into my car. I learned later that the other band members heard the whole thing while on stage and testified to the fact that Todd was out of line.

I'm still trembling with the memory of tonight's confrontation. I can't help but wonder if this is something Blake always has to deal with since Maya is a multiracial child. I also can't imagine why anyone would feel such hatred toward a beautiful, innocent human being like Maya.

Obviously, I can't keep my distance from her. In the short time they've lived next door, I've grown attached to the beautiful girl. I just had no idea she felt the same for me. My heart still hurts with the recollection of her words—words that made it evident she thought my absence was her fault.

Listening to the fireworks bang and sizzle outside, I bid you adieu, my trusty journal. Blake insists on coming over so we can talk. Regardless of what happened tonight, I'm dying to see him—even if it's just to make sure he's okay.

Present

The sound of his footsteps on my porch makes my heart race with anticipation. All the sounds around me are magnified as I sit on my couch and allow him to enter my home without invitation.

Sinking down on the couch beside me, he places his arm around the back and says, "She's finally asleep. My friend, Eric, is there with her. She really wanted you though. Wanted to make sure you weren't still mad at her."

Nodding, I keep my head down and try desperately not to let my emotions take over. Snaking his finger beneath my chin, he forces me to look into his golden-brown eyes.

"Talk to me, Gwennie. For Maya's sake, I need to know what the hell is happening."

"I—" My voice catching in my throat causes me to hesitate. Clearing it so I can continue to speak like a normal human rather than a blubbering idiot, I try to remain calm. "I've made a mess of things, Blake. I should have spoken to you, but I was afraid you wouldn't listen to me."

"I'm here now. Tell me," he coaxes, dropping his hand to grasp mine in my lap.

"My band's guitarist, Todd, has been continually making threats, mostly by way of notes, to me about being involved with you. I tried to ignore him, hoping he would eventually accept my decision or give up the fight. It wasn't until he began spouting his threats to Maya that I started to fear the totality of it all."

"Threaten Maya? When? Where?" His voice increasing an octave causes me to cringe. I can tell he's nervous now as he sits up straight, sweat beginning to bead up on his forehead.

"I don't know when, but I do know it was at school. His son is in the same class with Maya. She told me about it a little over a week ago." As I say the words, my gaze flickers over to the drawing hanging on my fridge.

"Why didn't you tell me about this?" he nearly yells. With a few breaths, he closes his eyes and then continues to speak with a more reserved tone. "This is my daughter, Gwen. I need to know about every detail that happens in her little world. Especially if someone is threatening her."

"I know, Blake. And I'm really sorry. Really. I just thought if I could get rid of the problem on my own, you and Maya wouldn't have to be affected by my life. I was trying to protect you both. I just didn't realize Maya would take it so hard or that it would continue to be an issue after the fact."

Placing a soft kiss against my knuckles, he says, "Do you not realize what you mean to me? To us?"

"None of that matters if my so-called friends are hurting you or putting you two in danger," I whisper, sniffling unattractively. My nose burns with the fight to keep the tears at bay.

"My feelings for you are all that matter, Gwen." Placing his hands on either side of my face and looking deep into my eyes, he inhales a shaky breath. "We're stronger than the ignorance that surrounds us. I'm willing to face the world head on if you are."

"How do you manage to deal with all this… heartache?" The question blurts out of my mouth before I can stifle my thoughts.

"I'm not the only one racial hatred affects, you know that, right?" I just stare at him with wonder and confusion, curious what he means.

"Look how torn up you are over this. This type of thing affects you just as much as it does me. I know it sounds selfish and a bit corny, but in a way, it makes me feel like I'm not alone in this… that as long as we stick together, we can deal with anything."

"I didn't think of it that way."

"Let me tell you a story," he offers, settling back on the couch and lacing his fingers with mine. "I was a junior in high school and Maya's mom, Rachel, invited me to meet her and her friends at the mall. We walked around, shopped a bit, and even stepped into the theater to see a movie. She was animated and excited to have me around, but I could clearly tell her best friend's boyfriend felt otherwise. The tension was thick, and his disdain for me was obvious—at least to me. I was just thankful she didn't notice because I didn't want her to feel embarrassed about having me in her life."

Staring up at Blake, I watch his mouth move and twitch as he talks—first a smile, then a frown. His emotions are so fascinating to me.

"It didn't dawn on Rachel that there was an issue until it came time to leave. The city buses had long since stopped running for the night, and I had no way of getting home. She had ridden to the mall with her best friend in the boyfriend's car, so he was also her ride home. With innocence I still admire about her, even though we're separated now, she asked the guy if he would give me a ride home. His response caused her pretty pink face to turn shades of white I'd never seen in a female before." Pausing, he looks to me, obviously noticing my breathing hitch with the thought of someone hurting him, even with words.

"What did he say?" I whisper, curiosity getting the better of me even though I know I probably don't want to hear it.

"I won't repeat the exact words, but let's just say he was not going to allow me to ride inside his car. His final offer was for me to ride in the trunk, even though his initial offer was for me to be dragged behind it."

Hearing the sudden sob that leaves my chest, he tightens his grip around me and quickly continues with his story.

"Here's the thing about that night, Gwen. I wasn't at all fazed by the words he spoke to me. It was Rachel's feelings that concerned me. You could tell the hurt she suffered was much greater than my discomfort. She was raised to accept and love someone, no matter how different they were from her. She in no way anticipated he would respond with such hate. It was almost as if someone had slapped her in the face. The worst part was, she had to go with the prick. She was staying at her best friend's house, and he was her only chance at a ride. It was all I could do to talk her into leaving me there."

"Did you make it home okay?" I ask.

"Yes," he answers with a smile. "Rachel sent her mother to pick me up since my mother was still working. She could have just made me walk home, but instead, she chose to tell her mother what had happened, even though it got her in trouble for riding in a teenager's car without permission. The honesty between family members was something I had never experienced before, and it made me fall for her even harder."

"I'm sorry that happened to you," I say, while lightly snuggling against his neck.

"The point of the story, my Gwen, is my concern was for the person that I loved, not myself. She was more torn up by the whole situation than I was. There was another incident that made me fear for Rachel's safety, but we managed to get through it together," he said, stopping to gauge my reaction.

"And what was that?"

"She was approached by three girls at school and threatened because a white girl was moving in on their territory. Nothing came of it, and it was no more than juvenile threats. But the episode definitely put the fear in Rachel, to the point where she seriously considered the possibility that we'd be better off apart. If she would have been intimidated enough by their anger and hate to break it off with me, I wouldn't have Maya today." He pauses for a moment, staring at our hands tangling together... peach against chocolate... so beautiful. "I will tell you this and hope it makes you feel better. I've never been physically hurt, nor has my family. There may be people who threaten with words, but they're usually too cowardly to act upon their threats.

Tonight was the closest I've ever come to a physical confrontation, and there are obviously plenty of good people in this world willing to stick up for what's right."

"I was so scared. I'm sorry." My sniffling betrays me, causing him to lift my face and examine my tears—tears I can't hold back any longer.

"Quit apologizing. It's not your fault," he soothes. Settling his chin on top of my head, he huffs. "I thought for sure you hated me. I just didn't know why."

"I felt like pushing you away was the only way… I don't know… it was stupid to think I could stay away from you, Blake."

Looking at me again, he smiles and says, "So you don't hate me?"

With those infuriating words swirling around us, I push at his chest and scamper onto his lap, straddling him so I am now eye level with his handsome face. My lips meet his, igniting that fire I've been keeping buried inside me. Only mere seconds pass before he parts his lips, inviting me to take all of him.

His hands snake around my waist, fingers digging into the flesh at my backside, as he presses me tighter against his hard body and growing excitement. I deepen our kiss, clawing at the back of his neck in desperation to be as close to him as possible.

My mouth muffles his gruff moan, causing the vibration to surge through me like a bolt of electricity. Pulling away, he gasps for air.

"Gwen, I need you," he whispers, panting against my skin. "God, what I mean is—I need you in my life. Please, give us a chance."

I am now very aware that staying away from him would be a mistake. There's no denying we belong together. Pressing my forehead to his, I nod, exhaling a trembling breath.

"Blake?"

"Yes, my Gwen?"

"Make love to me." It isn't stated as a question.

"You sure that's what you want?"

Looking into his eyes, swirling with warm honey, I smile. "I've never been more sure of anything in my life. I need you too."

Without breaking our embrace or saying another word, Blake stands and begins to carry me across the room toward my bedroom.

"Oh, Christ. Put me down, Blake. I'm too heavy to be carried!" I yell, squeezing my eyes shut and clutching to his neck.

"You're definitely not too heavy for me," he responds before laying me down on my plush comforter. Gazing down at me, he smiles. "You're perfect."

It doesn't take long for him to cover my entire body with his hands, starting with the removal of my shirt. His touch is gentle, reverent. He makes sure to pay special attention to the sensitive skin around my neck as his hand cups my breast through the thin fabric of my bra.

Before he can pull the scrap of lace away from my skin, I start clawing at his shirt in an attempt to remove it from his body. He makes quick work of sitting up to remove his shirt before reaching for me again.

Looking up at him hovering over me, the glow of fireworks outside illuminate his beautiful body and striking eyes.

Using his long, strong fingers, he traces the trim of my bra and removes my breast from the cup, exposing my sensitive nipple. I can't help but gasp as his lips close around my breast, sucking at the delicate area with gentle torture. Snaking his hands around to my back, he unclasps my strap and pulls the bra from between our bodies.

As he switches to the other breast, I hold onto his head, pressing him closer to me, while he starts fumbling at the button of my jeans. A quivering moan escapes my chest at the feel of his fingers tugging at my panties.

Pulling away, he looks down at me and spreads that dazzling smile across his face, the pearly whites a stark contrast to his beautiful, dark skin.

With slow precision, he removes my jeans and panties all in one move. My pulse quickens and new butterflies take up residence in my tummy at the intimate nearness of this man. He follows by quickly removing his pants and continues to kneel before me.

Grabbing my foot, he brings it to his mouth and places a soft kiss to my ankle. His lips continue to caress my leg, over my calf, to the juncture behind my knee, and along my inner thigh. I watch with amazement and need as he repeats his torment on the other leg, settling his gaze on my sweet spot.

Blazing lips continue their delicious assault like a trail of fire up my stomach, ribs, and breasts, until he finally reaches my mouth and devours me again.

Between heated kisses, I gasp and make my needs known. "Blake, you're torturing me. Take me, please." I'm aching for him, the need for him inside me increasing with each passing second.

"Shh," he taunts, his hissing breath mere inches from my ear. "I don't want to rush this, Gwen. I want to savor every second with you."

Clutching my fingers to his hard biceps, I press my forehead to his and whisper, "Savor how I feel on the inside before I lose my mind."

His laugh sends a new thrill through me, the sound tickling at my senses. I couldn't care less that he's laughing at me. The fact I bring such a sound out of him is completely worth it.

Placing himself at my entrance, he looks into my eyes and sinks into me, making me inhale with the pleasure exploding like the fireworks that still littered the night sky outside my bedroom window.

A masculine grunt emanates from his chest before he speaks. "Gwen, you feel even better than I imagined you would." His words are spoken as a whisper against my lips, while his eyes stare into mine and his thumbs caress my cheeks.

Pressing our bodies together, we move with the rhythm of our hearts, our souls, synchronizing with each thrust. The feel of him filling me is more than just physical. Connecting with him on this level has my love for him expanding like a wildfire in my chest.

It's not long before I feel an intense power building inside me, just aching to be free. Starting deep in my abdomen, the feeling radiates outward to every nerve ending in my hypersensitive skin.

Positioning his elbows above my shoulders, Blake increases his pace, causing an uncontainable shudder to roll over my body. His animalistic rhythm becomes wild and fierce. Jaw tensing, he looks at me with eyes like infernos, burning me up with his gaze.

His smile of satisfaction is glorious and he throws his head back, slamming his hips into me, hard, relentless. Lifting until he is almost completely withdrawn from me, he slams back inside, sending shockwaves over me.

My insides begin to quiver, and I feel the blazing intensity lighting deep inside me.

"Ahhh, yeah…" I whimper, drawing out my sounds. His thrusts are so powerful that it sounds like I am riding over a railroad track as disjointed moans escape my mouth.

Out of nowhere, I convulse around him, embers sizzling through every inch of my body. Still locking my gaze with his, I come loudly as I burst in every conceivable direction and ride the fierce wave of my release. My moans fill the room, drowning out the sounds of fireworks outside.

My mouth opens again, but his lips pressing to mine muffle my scream. My entire body bows, writhes, and I come completely apart.

Still breathless from my release, I can feel him start to tremble as his climax closes in on him. His groan splinters the air with pure pleasure as my world continues to shatter into a million pieces—spasm upon spasm repeatedly ripples through my body.

He slows, taking a more tender pace as I milk the last of his release.

Blake collapses on top of me and rests his head on my shoulder. His hips twitch, continuing to pump against me in short, jerky motions until he finally stops and his harsh breathing rasps against my ear. His lips graze the base of my neck, and his gasps warm my skin.

Finally lifting his head to look at me, he says, "So, my Gwen, I take that as a no."

Wracking my brain, I try to think of exactly what he's talking about. Deciding I don't have a clue, I say, "Throw me a bone here, Blake. What's a no?"

"I asked if you hated me, and you proceeded to jump my bones," he states with a chuckle.

"Oh, geez." I huff. "I never hated you, and you know that."

"I know. I just needed to hear it. Sometimes guys need that little bit of reassurance too," he admits with refreshing honesty.

Placing a light peck on his lips, while still enjoying the feel of him inside me, I decide to be straightforward with him.

"You have my heart, Blake Meyers."

"And you have mine, Gwen Clark."

"I already knew that." I chuckled.

"Is it that obvious?" he asks.

"No. Your beautiful daughter told me. Actually, she illustrated it for me."

His brows pulling together make his confusion evident.

"She drew me a picture of you handing me *your* heart. She was insistent that she could see your love for me in your eyes." A smile crosses my face at the memory.

"She's a perceptive little bugger, isn't she?" He places a kiss to my forehead, sending a shiver through my skin at the contact. "And she's usually always right."

July 5th

Dear Diary,

Watching Blake's chest rise and fall as he sleeps tangled in my sheets has me grinning from ear to ear. The early morning light rising over the lake is casting the most interesting shadows along his slender body. His reassuring words last night has me hopeful for our future and gives me strength that together, we can handle anything.

So, as I scribble my thoughts onto your ivory fibers, I am left with the overwhelming emotion of just how much I love this man and his little girl.

Rene Folsom

Author Dedication

To all those who have loved and lost—know that there is hope and never let others make the decisions when your heart is what hangs in the balance.

About Rene

Rene Folsom, author of paranormal romance and erotica, lives in Florida with her husband and three kids. She has officially diagnosed herself with creative ADD and often has a million and one writing projects going at once. In addition to writing, she is also a graphic artist who enjoys creating custom book covers for indie authors. She is definitely an artist at heart and would love nothing more than to be elbow deep in clay during her waking hours.

Rene believes that all fiction is based on some form of reality—otherwise we would never have the inspiration or knowledge to dream up the realistic situations we portray with our words. She is proud to say that her personal experiences have been inspirational, though perhaps not always identical to that of her fictional characters. Where reality and fantasy diverge, however, must remain her little secret...

Follow Rene

Website: http://www.renefolsom.com/

Facebook page: http://www.facebook.com/renefolsom

Read More from Rene

Shuttered Affections: http://amzn.to/1dHOReI

Home Again

Vicki Green

Chapter One

It's been four years since I found Sterling, Wyoming. Four years. As I sit and watch our son and daughter, Zach and Bailey, playing out in the yard from the deck chair and gaze at the snow peaked mountains, I'm remembering my crazy life when I found my home here. Running from my abusive husband, scared, alone, and the feeling I had when I stepped off the train into a town full of strangers. I'd known the town was going to be my home as soon as I entered the café in the station and felt the friendliness of the owner, Betty. After her suggestion of staying at the boarding house and being befriended by Bailey, the owner, and the gorgeous tenant, Hutchinson Parker, I knew I would be safe here. Unfortunately, my luck would not hold out for long.

Falling in love again didn't come easy for me. I was so unsure of everything after escaping Darrin, including myself. Hutch was too good to be true and my feelings soared as soon as I met him but how could I possibly feel that way when I'd just left the worst marriage, losing my self-esteem and myself along the way? Bailey turned out to be such a good friend and quickly became my adopted grandmother. She told me that I was meant to find Sterling and to be with Hutch. After our long talks, she set me straight on how love finds you when it's right and no matter what happened in your past life that it's okay to have those feelings and not fight them. Oh, she was so right and I'm so glad I listened to her.

I can still remember Hutch and I jogging on the trail, the water fights we had, falling on the ground laughing and out of breath. *"Baby, you sure give me a run for my money."* He'd roll over, put his arm around me and we'd just lie there looking into each other's eyes. *"I can't wait until we're married and have kids. I hope they look just like their mother. So beautiful."* My heart would beat so hard I could hear *it. I remember his gorgeous dimpled smile, his dark blond hair longer on top and shorter on the sides and in back. So sexy.*

I'd brush his hair away from his forehead, his eyes closing with my touch and he would have the sexiest look on his face. "Do you think Bailey's right? Do you think she can look into the future? If she is, if she can, that means we're having a boy and later will have a little girl. Wouldn't that be magical?" He'd lean over, kiss me full on the lips, and smile.

"I'll bet my life she's right. And, they will be perfect, just like you. Our son will be a pro football player like I used to be. Our daughter? She'll be anything she wants to be because her mother can do anything and will be a great teacher," he'd tell me.

"Hey, baby! What are you thinking about so deeply?" Hutch walks up from behind me, leans over and gives me a quick peck on my lips, shaking me out of my wonderful memories. He sits down in the other deck chair, leaning his elbows on his knees and looks out at the kids playing in the yard.

Looking at him reminds me of the day I walked down the aisle and how handsome he looked standing there waiting for me, his hands folded in front of him, his black tuxedo, crisp white shirt, and that dimpled smile on his face. His dimples. I melt every time I see them, especially when his smile widens, making them even deeper. So. Sexy. I remember him taking my hand and the words he lovingly said.

"Um, baby? What's wrong? You're doing it again." He reaches over and takes my hand, kissing the top. "You've been through so much and even though it's been four years, it's still really hard on you, isn't it? I'm so sorry. I wish there was something I could do." I give him my best smile and move closer to him, leaning in a bit and pressing my mouth against his. Our kiss begins to deepen when I hear little feet pounding up the deck stairs. Turning my head I see Bailey holding onto the rail and taking one step at a time with her little feet while Zach comes stomping up with his famous mad face on.

"Mommy! Baiwy pushed me down! She was being a meanie!" He stomps over, stops in front of me and crosses his little arms. I have to hold my breath in order not to laugh. He's so cute when he's all grumpy.

I place my hands in my lap and give him my best concerned look. "Zachary, what happened, sweetie?" Bailey finally reaches the top of the stairs and runs into her daddy's arms, giggling. Hmmm, she doesn't seem real mean to me.

"Well. Baiwy and I were playin' see? And, she ran over to me, fell, and smacked me wiff her hand. Real hard, mommy!" My head turns to Hutch, Bailey in his lap, his hand covering his mouth and his body shaking with laughter. Big help he is.

I reach down and lift Zach, setting him in my lap, putting my arm around him and my face softens as I look at his baby blue eyes. "Do you think maybe it was an accident, sweetie? I mean, if she fell then you probably helped her not to hurt herself when she accidentally smacked you. Don't you think?" His brows crease as he considers my explanation. "I think you're such a great big brother to help her not get hurt. My big boy." Now his brows raise and the cutest smile adorns his face. "That's my boy. Why don't you and Bailey go inside and get washed up for dinner, hmmm?"

Once Zach takes Bailey's hand and leads her inside, Hutch gets up from his chair and I slide over as he sits in mine with me, his arm resting on the back and his fingers playing with my hair. "That was a good one. Good job, mommy." Chills shiver through me as his mouth comes close to my ear. "I think mommy deserves some pampering tonight after the kids go to bed, don't you?" Yelling starts coming from the kitchen, disrupting our little interlude and we both stand up laughing and head inside, our arms around each other's waists.

* * * * *

"Night, my sweet boy. Mommy loves you so much," I whisper as I kiss Zach's little face. Quietly creeping out of his room, I close the door, leaving it open a crack, and blow the hair out of my face as I walk to our room. I stop dead in my tracks when I walk through our doorway and see the lights down low, candles lit on the nightstands, and soft music playing. Hearing soft humming coming from the bathroom I head that way and lean against the doorframe, seeing my love lying in the tub. There are bubbles all around him, the lights are off, and several lit candles flicker on the counter top. *Sexiest thing I've ever seen.* I smile when he looks up at me. He winks and calls me over with his dimpled grin and index finger. It doesn't take me long to remove my clothes and get settled in front of him, my back against his broad, strong chest. "Ah, what did I do to deserve this special occasion?"

He kisses my ear while rubbing soap against my arm. "Baby, you deserve pampering and more. You're incredible." He kisses my cheek, "You take care of the kids and me, keep the house clean, work at the Coffee Shop, and help out at Bailey's Boarding House when you can. And..." His hand turns my head by my chin and kisses me fully on my lips. "You're so sexy," he whispers against my mouth. His tongue quickly invades my mouth, his hand slides down my slippery arm until he places it where I need it the most. My hips buck of their own accord as a finger penetrates me and I barely register the water sloshing around us as he moves around until he's suddenly on top of me. My heart beats wildly when his thumb begins circling my soft spot as he adds another finger inside me. My moan echoes off the bathroom walls as his fingers leave me, and he thrusts inside of me. "I love you so much, Zoey. I'll never get enough of you. You're so beautiful when you are in ecstasy. Come. Come with me, baby." He starts moving in and out of me faster and as I look at his gorgeous face filled with love and desire I reach my peak, crying out his name. I watch through hooded eyes as he reaches his climax, shouts my name and he collapses half on top of me. We lay there in each other's arms, his body still shuddering from his ecstasy. The water has grown cold so he helps me out of the tub and we quickly dry off. I throw on his T-shirt, my favorite sleeping wear, and he gets into his pajama pants. We snuggle in bed until I hear his light breathing and I look at his gorgeous face once more before I close my eyes, drifting off as I think about how lucky I am.

Chapter Two

"Yeah, that sounds great. Thanks so much." I hang up as Zoey walks into the kitchen and I watch her walk over to the high chair. Bailey is in her high chair eating oatmeal with her fingers, ewww, and Zach is sitting in his big boy chair at the table eating his favorite pancakes. "Oh, morning, baby." I give her a quick kiss as she walks by on her way to get a cup of coffee.

"Who was that so early in the morning?" she asks as she takes some of the pancakes and puts them on a plate, spreading some butter on them and then pouring syrup on top. My eyes are glued to her as she walks over to the table, sits down, and takes a huge bite.

"Um, Betty. Was thinking of taking my girl on a date tonight. Maybe dinner, then a movie? Um, baby?" She looks up, fork raised with another large bite, syrup dripping from it, and raises an eyebrow. "You're kind of eating like a pig. I know you had a really big dinner last night and come to think of it... You had a huge breakfast and lunch yesterday. I know you lost all the weight from having the kids but, um, you're gonna get really fat," I tell her laughing.

She pushes the fork into her mouth, closes her eyes and moans. *Sexiest thing ever!* When she opens her eyes, the kids and I are staring at her. "What?" I laugh and sit down in the chair beside her, take her fork out of her hand and hold it tightly.

"Baby. Something you want to tell me, hmmm?" I ask while trying to hold in my laughter. *Something is going on with her. So not like her.*

"Um, no? I'm just starving! What?" She snatches her fork out of my hand and digs into more of her pancakes, devouring them.

Later that afternoon I tell her I'll keep an eye on the kids while they take their naps when she informs me she wants to go workout at the gym. *Really, after eating like that, hmmm.* She's only been gone about an hour when my phone rings. "Sis, how are you?" I hear sniffing on the other side. "Hey, what's wrong?"

"Oh, Hutch. It's Jamie McCoy, you remember her? I used to babysit her when she was younger." I nod like she can hear me but my silence doesn't stop her. "I just found out she has cancer. I'm just so upset. You know she just turned twenty-one a few weeks ago. It's in remission, but we all know that cancer just doesn't always stay away."

"Oh, Lauren, no! I can't believe it. I'm so sorry. I haven't seen or talked to her in years. You know, with everything that's happened." Damn, cancer. Just like my ex-wife. Memories flood my mind and heart; Jodi lying in the hospital bed in pain and there wasn't a damn thing I could do. I felt so helpless watching the love of my life being eaten up with that horrible and deadly disease.

"Hutch?"

"Oh, sorry! I guess my mind wandered. How is she holding up—stupid question I know." We ended up talking for about half an hour and she explained Jamie is in Sterling for a little vacation. She asked if she could call me to teach her some work out techniques at the gym. I told her to give her my number and I'd definitely help her out and she proceeds to tell me she already did—Jamie should be calling me any minute and she's anxious to get started. Right after we hang up, sure enough, Jamie calls me. We make arrangements to meet at the gym in twenty minutes, and then I call Betty. Once she arrived to watch the kids for me, I head to the gym.

Jamie is already stretching over on the weight side when I get there. I walk up behind her and take her arms as she starts to lift some ten-pound weights.

"Hey, Hutch! Thanks for meeting me. So, I saw Zoey on the way in and wow, she's gorgeous. So, that's exactly the body I want to have when I'm done training with you." I try to hide the depression I'm feeling as my heart breaks for the girl.

"Well, you can't have her body 'cause her body is totally mine." We look in the mirror at each other and start laughing. Over the next fifty minutes, I show her as much as I can around the weight room. She's actually in pretty good shape, considering, and did very well. We head our separate ways into the locker rooms and I take a long shower. My mind is full of Jodi and the pain she went through, how helpless I felt knowing I couldn't help her, how I couldn't save her. Once I finally get dressed and start to walk out of the locker room I literally crash straight into Jamie. "Oh, sorry, Jamie," I say, steadying her by grabbing her arms.

"Oh, my fault. Guess I wasn't paying attention." I smile and cross my arms over my chest.

"Hey, wanna get a beer with me? I'd really like to catch up, it's been so long. I wanna hear all about your new life here, Zoey and the kids."

"I dunno, Jamie. It's getting late and I really should get home." She looks so disappointed. Damn, I hate to hurt her feelings especially after everything she's been through but I'm not sure I can handle talking with her. What if she starts talking about the cancer? I look at her again, such a sad look on her face.

"Oh, what will one beer hurt? You know where the bar is? Up Main Street and a right at the last light on Tenth Street." She nods and gives me her sweet smile.

"Great! See you there in about twenty minutes?" She gives me a hug and walks away. Just then my manager of the gym walks over and gives me a concerned look. I'm really glad I bought this place but sometimes it can be a handful. So glad I have Aaron to run the place for me.

"Boss, I need you to look at one of the treadmills. You know, the one you're always fixin'? It's not running right again." I roll my eyes and follow him back, spending the next fifteen minutes fixing the treadmill that I really need to just replace. By the time I get done I race over to the bar and hope Jamie isn't upset I'm late.

Jamie and I had a really nice time catching but once we both had a few beers in us she started telling me about her battle with cancer. "I'm sorry, Hutch. I didn't mean to load all that on you. I know how horrible it was for you to go through that with Jodi."

I pat her shoulder and hiccup. "Nah, I don't mind at all. I'm just glad it's in remission and hope it never comes back. I'm proud of you. You're so strong and courageous. I just can't even imagine." We have two more drinks and by the time I leave and I decide I'd better walk home, or stagger was more like it.

It's late by the time I get to our front door. The walk didn't sober me up a bit and on the way I realized I hadn't even called or texted Zoey. What a shit husband I am. I stumble into the door after taking forever getting my key in the lock—it seemed to keep moving on me. I'm louder than I plan when I crash the door into the wall behind it. Looking over, I see Zoey walking into the entryway, all beautiful and maybe a little pissed.

"Oh, baby! Sorry, didn't mean to wake you, um, what are you still doing up?" I ask, my words slurring really bad.

"Oh, nothing. Just haven't heard from you… all day. Thought I'd find you here when I came back from my workout but, no, found Betty instead," she tells me, her arms crossed and her foot tapping. Stepping forward I try to put my arms around her but she steps back and I give her a confused look.

"Baby, don't be like that. I need some lovin'. Don't be mad. I love you." My speech is so slurred and my body is swaying. "Hey, I'm sorry, baby. I'm really sorry." She finally lets me fold my arms around her and I kiss her cheek, burying my nose in her neck. "I guess I had one too many with a friend down at the bar. I'm sorry I didn't call you." She nods slowly as I release her, keeping an arm around her waist as we head up to our bedroom. She leaves me to go into the bathroom so I lay down on the bed, my eyes so heavy and I'm out like a light.

Chapter Three

The next morning I wake up queasy and find that Hutch is not in our bed. Covering my mouth, I jump out of bed making it into the bathroom just in time to pray to the porcelain God and release everything I've ever eaten in my entire life. After brushing my teeth I walk downstairs to the kitchen in search of my husband and kids, only to find the kids eating breakfast and Betty cooking. *What now?*

"Oh, morning, Zoey. How did you sleep?" She walks over and lays her hand on my forehead. "Dear, you look a little pale this morning. Are you okay?

I give her a little smile as I walk over to the fridge, get the orange juice and grab a glass from the cabinet. "Um, my stomach is a little upset this morning. Where's, um, Hutch? I'm surprised he's not here with the kids," I ask as I pour juice into my glass before returning the bottle back to the fridge. Betty returns to the stove and starts cooking again, looking over at me with a concerned look on her face.

"Oh, sorry to hear that. You need to get some rest and take care of yourself." She flips a pancake and I think I might have to run to the bathroom again. "Hutch called me early this morning and asked if I could come over so you could sleep in, said he had a couple of errands to run," she continues, looking down at the pancake and flips it again.

I set the glass down on the counter, cover my mouth, and run to the bathroom in the hallway. Once I dry heave for several minutes over the toilet, I check myself in the mirror and frown. I do look pale and my stomach is still queasy. Walking back to the kitchen I stand in the doorway and watch Betty as she eats at the table with the kids, talking to them while picking bits of pancake from Bailey's hair.

"Um, Betty? Do you think you could stay a little longer with the kids? I think, maybe, I need to go see Doc. Marrow. I'm not feeling very well." She looks at me and smiles and tells me not to worry, that she can stay as long as I need her to.

An hour later I'm sitting in a room with a lovely paper-thin gown on, swinging my legs back and forth as I sit on the cold, hard patient table. I look up when the door opens and Doc. Marrow enters, smiles at me, and sits on his doctor stool with a chart in his hand. He pushes his thick, black-framed glasses up on his nose and looks up at me.

"Zoey, my dear. So glad to see you, but I wish it was for a better reason. Stomach giving you problems, eh?" I nod, giving him a small smile, and he nods back, pushing his glasses up again. "Zoey, when was your last menstrual cycle?" *Menstrual cycle? Oh! Dang, I can't remember.*

My brows crease together as I concentrate. "Um, I think... Oh, it was about three months ago, I think." I had totally lost track of time with the kids, work, and everything else going on in our lives. Wow, had no idea it had been that long.

"I see. Well, Zoey, the test results I ran show you're pregnant. Given that it's been about three months since your last cycle, I'd say you're about two months. I hope this is happy news for you and Hutchinson." He stands and walks over to me, putting his hand on my arm. *Pregnant. Of course I'm happy, but now, with all this going on with Hutch? This couldn't have happened at a worse time.* "You don't look happy, my dear. Want to talk about it?"

I look at him and quickly put a smile on my face. "Oh, no, David. This is very happy news. Really. I'm just a little shocked is all." I lay my hand over his on my arm and give it a squeeze. "How can bringing another life into ours *not* be happy news? Really." He gives me his fatherly smile and squeezes my arm before turning away.

"Good. Good. I'm so very happy for you, Hutchinson, and your kids. I'm sure they will be excited to have another sibling. I'll just leave a prescription for prenatal vitamins at the front desk. Make an appointment for about a month from now and we'll see if we can pinpoint a due date." Turning around as he holds the door open, he smiles again. "Congratulations, my dear. I wish I could see the look on Hutch's face when you tell him." With that, he leaves me alone. *Yeah, me too. Hmmm, maybe this is good news; maybe this will help turn our uprooted lives back around. I can only hope.*

Candles lit... check. Lights down low... check. Bottle of sparkling grape juice chilling in the bucket... check. Now, if only Hutch was here. I look at the clock on the mantle for the hundredth time. Midnight. Hutch texted me about three hours ago and said he'd be home shortly. What is going on with him? What did I do? I'm so confused and feelings of jealously and fear are filling up my heart and soul. I'm so scared.

I jump and turn in my seat when the door opens loudly. Hutch comes staggering in with a cute and sexy little thing under his arm. His eyes are half closed and glassed over with the alcohol that's in his system. I stand and walk to the entryway, listening to the young girl's giggling and watch her trying to keep Hutch from falling over. "I'll just take it from here, um..." She looks up at me with a surprised look and smiles.

"Of course. Sorry, I'm Jamie. Nice to meet you." She tries reaching her hand out for me to shake but quickly pulls it back when Hutch starts to lean to the side and places her arm around his waist. Quickly, I walk over, put my arm around his waist, and she releases her hold on him. "Well, I'll just... Nice to meet you. Tell Hutch... Yeah, well, goodnight." She walks out the door, shuts it, and I'm left with my drunken husband who has a hell of a lot of explaining to do in the morning.

"Oh, baby. You're here. I wove you so much," he says, slurring while trying to kiss me. His breath is of stale liquor and his body almost knocks me over as he leans into me. "I wove you... I wove you... I wove our kids... I..." He stumbles as I pull him toward the stairs and we both almost fall down them backwards but I finally manage to get him in bed. Once he's tucked in, I head downstairs to blow out the candles before I sit on the couch in the dark and cry my heart out.

* * * * *

"Mommy, Baiwy is playing with her, um, sherios!" Zach yells as I take the last of the waffles from the iron and place them on a plate. Setting them on the table, I lean over and proceed to pluck Cheerios from my sweet baby's hair.

"Thank You, Zach. Now finish eating…" My head turns as I watch a hung-over Hutch enter the kitchen, heading straight for the coffee pot. "Finish eating your waffles and then go get dressed, okay?" Smiling at him, I flick his nose and listen to his adorable giggle as he nods. After cleaning up Bailey, I pick her up out of her high chair and place her on the floor. She runs over to her daddy, who bends over and kisses her on her puckered mouth and then she runs out of the room, Zach quickly following her. I begin picking up their plates, walk over to the sink, and start washing them.

"Uh, sorry about last night, baby. It won't happen again." My head snaps to Hutch who's leaning against the cabinet beside me. I can't help the frown on my face and the sickness in my heart as well as my stomach.

Placing the plates in the dishwasher, I close the door roughly, step back, and lean against the breakfast bar opposite him, crossing my arms. "Hutch. I can't do this. I can't…" He looks down as my words trail off. "I thought I found my home here. My heart is filled with you, the kids, but… I can't live my past marriage over again and it feels like that's where this is going. What's happened to you? Did I do something? Am I not doing enough?" Quickly I'm in his arms, my tears flowing, and he can't seem to get close enough to me.

"Baby. Oh, baby. I'm so sorry. I'm… I'm going through some stuff right now and the last thing I want is to hurt you or remind you of your past." He pulls back, keeping his arms around me and looks deeply into my eyes. "You know I'd never physically hurt you, right?" I nod slightly and he pulls me close again. "I'd never, ever hurt you. But… I just can't talk about what's in my head, yet. I will, but… I just can't yet. I'm so sorry. I love you so much. You're my world. Please be patient with me, please!" I nod my head and lay it against his chest.

"I love you too, babe, but I wish you'd talk to me. You know I am always here for you. It kills me that you're going through something but won't let me in." His arms squeeze me tighter and he sighs.

"I know, baby. Soon. I promise. Very soon. I hate keeping things from you too, but it's something I need to come to terms with before I can tell you. I hope you understand," he tells me. *This makes me even more confused and my poor stomach is tied up in knots as well as wanting to dispose of my breakfast even more now.*

We end up have a great day together. We took the kids out shopping and watched as they played at the indoor play area at the mall. We laughed, kept our arms around each other whenever we could, and it seemed as though things were back to normal. Until that night…

Chapter Four

I've thought about Jamie all day again. She called and said she had to rush back home because she wasn't feeling well and then called later to tell me the cancer is back. I feel so bad about how I've been treating Zoey, but I just can't cope with this. I ended up back at the gym, lifted weights, and did all the machines in there, as well as ran around the track several times. I've managed to get through the entire day and find myself at the bar again, drinking Jack and coke this time.

I haven't talked to Zoey all day and I'm not sure I can. How do I tell her about all these feelings Jamie's cancer is drudging up inside of me? I don't want to bother her with my past that won't seem to let us have a happy future. Oh, who am I kidding? This is destroying me and will eventually destroy us if I don't get a grip on things.

I remember Jodi, our wedding and how beautiful she was. I remember how she filled my heart and my soul, how special she was. Then I remember her body looking so small in the hospital bed, her face as she winced in pain. I went to the cemetery after everyone left and knelt at her gravesite but I knew she wasn't really there. I cried and cried for hours before I went home, gathered up as much as two suitcases would fill, and said goodbye to her forever.

When I found Sterling it was totally by accident. I found it strange that it wasn't on any map but the snow peaked mountains surrounding the town made it somewhat magical looking. When Bailey took me in at the boarding house and started talking to me about everything that is good in life, I wanted to heal. I wanted love again and then Zoey walked into the boarding house and straight into my heart. She was running from an abusive marriage and I wanted to kill her ex-husband for hurting her. I can't imagine anyone being able to physically hurt another person, but a defenseless girl? When she finally opened up to me I knew we would be together. Then he came here and tried to kill her, almost succeeded too. I almost lost her forever. I'm going to lose her now if I don't get my act together.

I'm wobbling in my chair by the time the bartender, Taylor, walks over to stand in front of me. "Hey, Hutch. I think you've had enough, don't you? I hope you don't get pissed, but I called Zoey and she said Chris is on his way to pick you up and get you home." I look up at him, my eyes blinking rapidly and nod.

"Chris is a good guy. He's really a good guy," I say slurring my words badly. I'm almost asleep sitting up at the bar when I feel a hand on my shoulder. Cracking my eyes open, I see Chris standing there with a frown on his face.

"Come on, buddy. Let's get you home." He lifts me to a standing position with his hand under my arm and I almost fall over but he keeps me in check with his firm grip. He helps me to his car and buckles me in.

"You're a nice guy, Chris, and I'm such a stupid idiot." He looks over at me, laughs and then looks back out the front to watch the road. "I mean, really. Look what I'm doing to Zoey. I mean… Who would do that to such a wonderful, loving, and caring person? But I just can't…"

"Hey. Why don't you just get a good night's sleep and sober up. Then man up and talk to her." He looks over at me, the frown apparent on his face. "But, you really need to talk to her."

I'm jarred awake when Chris gets me out of the car and stumbles with me to the front door. I dig for my keys and drop them once I manage to get them out of my pocket. Chris somehow manages to pick them up, while keeping me upright, and opens the door and leads me inside. He walks me all the way upstairs to my bedroom and then to my bed without turning on the lights. He sets me on the bed and backs up a couple of steps.

"You know, Hutch. You're right about one thing: you *are* being stupid and an idiot. There's no one better than Zoey, and your kids for that matter. You have everything. Why would you want to chance losing them by doing what you're doing? I don't get it, man." I look up at him and sigh. "I don't know what's eating you and, not trying to be mean, I don't really care. Whatever it is, wouldn't it be better to talk it through with the person who loves you the most? The one person who cares about you? Not everyone has that in their lives. Not everyone has a Zoey."

With that he leaves, shutting the bedroom door behind him. I lay back, my arm going behind my head and just stare up into the darkness. Tomorrow morning. I'll talk to Zoey tomorrow morning. I have to do this, for her. My eyes grow heavier and then close.

Chapter Five

Simon helped me escape from the abusive marriage I was in. We go back to our college days and I thank the heavens he and his partner of several years helped me. That's how I found Sterling and Hutch. Of course, once my life began to get on the right track, Hutch and I had fallen head over heels for each other, my ex-husband found us and tried to kill me, killing Bailey in my stead. Since then my life turned around with a loving husband, two wonderful kids, and so many friends here that I never imagined anything bad would ever penetrate our happy existence. I was so wrong.

Thank goodness it's spring here in Sterling so all the snow has finally melted. I packed a couple of bags, one for me and one for the kids, gathered up a bunch of their toys, and took them over to the Boarding house across the street. Once I get the kids back into bed, in a spare room on the third floor, I head downstairs to the kitchen where Simon is fixing us some tea.

I rub my face with my hands and when I remove them I'm looking into the concerned eyes of my best friend as he sets my tea down in front of me. "Ok, girl. Spill." Sighing I take a drink, fold my hands around the warm cup, and try to hold back the tears that are threatening to flow. His hand reaches across the table and takes one of mine.

"Well, just in the last week Hutch started acting strange, not himself. He started drinking and I heard he was with another girl, a very young girl, I might add, the other day at the gym and then she brought him home the other night, drunk again, and now tonight." He hands me a Kleenex as the tears start trickling down my face and I start sniffing. After wiping my eyes and blowing my nose I look at him again, the frown on his face matching how I feel. "Something's just not right but he won't talk to me. I knew this was all too good to be true. Nothing in my life goes right, nothing works out for me. What's wrong with me, Simon?" The tears start up again and Simon squeezes my hand gently.

"Hey, now. Nothing is wrong with you and I'm as sure as I'm sitting here, that you've not done anything wrong." He brushes back some of my long hair and smiles. "You're the best person I know. You're kind, loving, sweet, and beautiful. Now stop..." He's cut off when we hear the front door close and Chris walks into the kitchen and directly to me, kissing me on the top of my head while patting my back.

"He's safe and in bed. Didn't even notice you and the kids are gone, but, you know he'll be over here looking for you tomorrow. You know you all can stay here as long as you need and we've got your back, but I really hope it doesn't come to that. Something's just not right, something's weighing on him that he can't let go of. He's not himself." I nod shakily as I watch him pour himself some tea.

We sit and talk for a few hours until I can't keep my eyes open anymore. I kiss them both on their cheeks and head up to the spare bedroom next door to the kids. As I lie in bed and stare up into the darkness, all my thoughts are on Hutch and now I'm wide awake.

* * * * *

BANG! BANG! BANG! DING DONG! DING DONG! My eyes spring open when I hear all the racket coming from downstairs. I hurriedly jump out of bed, put on my robe, all while looking at the clock to find it's only four in the morning, and run down the stairs.

"ZOEY! I KNOW YOU'RE IN THERE! ZOEY!" I stop on the bottom step, my eyes wide and I shake my head no as I look at Chris and Simon standing by the front door.

"Go home and sleep it off, Hutch. Zoey doesn't want to talk to you right now. Sleep it off and maybe later we'll see," Chris yells while looking at me, his hand holding onto the shaking doorknob.

I jump when I hear the bang of his hand on the door and the sound of it sliding down the wood. "Zoey, baby. Please talk to me. I can explain and I will. Please, baby. Don't leave me. Don't take our kids from me. I can't live without you." My heart breaks as I hear his crying and I almost give in when Chris speaks up again.

"Best thing you can do is go home and sober up, my friend. Call Zoey later on and maybe she'll talk, but right now? You need to go get some sleep." My hand covers my beating heart when he lightly hits the door again and I hear his footsteps growing fainter as he walks away. I slide down, my back against the wall, until my legs give out, and I am sitting on the step. Gagging a little, I cover my mouth with one hand, wrapping the other around my waist.

"Zoey, honey. Are you okay? You look really pale," Simon asks, squatting down in front of me, one of his hands on my knee as the other brushes some of my long hair away from my face.

Nodding my head shakily, my stomach finally calms down and I uncover my mouth. "I'm… I'm just pregnant," I tell him as I shrug my shoulders. He immediately puts his arm under my legs, the other around my back and lifts me, carrying me into the living room and places me on the couch. As soon as I look up a glass of water is in front of my face and I take it graciously from Chris. I chug half of it and set the glass on the coffee table. "I just found out a couple days ago. Had no idea except for my queasy stomach."

Chris stands there, his hands on his hips and smiles. "Well, no wonder. Hutch told me the other day he's never seen you eat so much since you two have been together. That explains a lot." I can't help but laugh. It feels so good to laugh right now.

I stand and walk to Chris, first giving him a hug and then Simon. "I'm going to bed. I'm exhausted and I think that Hutch and I will have a lot to talk about tomorrow. I just hope I'm up for it. 'Night, and thank you so much for being such wonderful friends. I love you." They say their goodnights and as I climb into bed I can't help but wonder if my life can ever be happy again. Well, I have the kids and a baby on the way, thank God for that. Now, I'm scared.

Chapter Six

I don't hear from Hutch all day and now I'm even more sad and depressed. Doesn't he care about me or the kids anymore? Doesn't he want to fight for us at all? I don't understand what's happened, what's caused all this, and why he won't talk to me. The kids were kept busy all day by Simon and Chris while I worked at the Coffee House. They love their uncles so they didn't even notice daddy wasn't around.

It's dark by the time I finish cleaning the shop, still not hearing from Hutch. It's been pouring down rain all day and now that it's dark I can barely see outside as I close the blinds on the shop's windows. Great, just what I need... and I didn't bring an umbrella. My phone rings on the counter and I walk over to pick it up quickly.

"Hutch?"

"Um, no, sorry sweetie. It's Chris." I sigh and gather my positive strength from within.

"Oh! Hi, Chris. Sorry. How're the kids doing? Drive you insane yet?" He laughs and tells me he checked on my house a little bit ago and the sump pump is broken and backing up into the basement, there's water everywhere. *Seriously? I just can't catch a break.* He tells me he called a repairman and to meet him over there because Hutch can't be reached. *Oh, really?* I thank him, hang up, and head out of the store.

I'm dripping wet, my stomach is upset, and I can barely see where I'm going. This isn't just a rainstorm, it's a freaking monsoon. Even though our house is only about two and a half blocks from the shop, I feel like it's taking forever to walk even ten feet and is taking all of my strength. I barely hear my phone ringing; digging it out of my pocket I see that it's Hutch. Finally!

"Hutch?" Static. "Hutch, I can't hear you!"

"Baby, wh... ar... ou?" The static is horrible and I can't make out what he's saying. I don't know if he can hear me either but I have to try.

"Hutch! I'm on my way home but I can barely see. I'm by the alley, next to the drug store-" and the line goes dead. *Great!* I keep pushing on but I'm freezing from the cooler temperatures and the wind feels like it's cutting right through me. Looking down the alley as I pass by, I see a small overhang from the drug store roof and decide to try to get some shelter, hoping the rain will let up enough for me to get home soon. Once I'm under the overhang I'm finding it's helping somewhat, but not enough with the wind blowing the rain at me anyway. It's so dark and I'm freezing. Who knew the weather was going to be this bad? Well, evidently not me. I forgot to check the weather forecast this morning. The wind seems to have picked up more and I swear it's going to blow me away when something hits me against my head, hard, and I fall to the ground.

"Uhhhhh," I moan when I fall face first onto the pavement. Lying there in a big puddle of water, I reach up and touch the side of my forehead, watching the blood wash off my hand when I look at it. I try to stand but get the worst pain jolts in my stomach and my head pounds at the same time. My head feels woozy as the pain becomes overbearing. Laying my head back down, I close my eyes.

* * * * *

My wife's out there, damnit, and it's all my fault. I had this whole thing set up to make it up to her and talk to her about everything and now she's out there in this horrible weather, alone, and probably scared. I dial Chris immediately and he picks up quick but the reception is still really bad.

"Hey, what's up? The kids are doing great. Did you get all the candles lit, the wine, roses, and everything set up to spill your guts to Zoey? Ya know, she totally bought the sump pump story and should be on her way..."

"Chris… Zoey's out in this mess and I can't reach her now. When I talked with her I think she said she's by an alley but there are a few alleys in town, and now her phone isn't working. I'm going out there to look for her. I'll let you know as soon as I can," I tell him in a rush.

"Oh, no, Hutch. Do you need help? Simon can stay with the kids and I'll meet you out front. I'll have him call the police to get others out there looking for her, too. Hutch. We'll find her." I agree that it would be better with more than one of us looking for her. We hang up and I throw on my overcoat and stuff a duffle bag with a blanket, tarp, and our first aid kit and head out the front door. I'll never forgive myself if anything happens to her. She's my heart and soul and I can't live without her.

Chris and I meet in front of my house and are pushing against the elements to find my love. We finally get to the first alleyway, flashlights not seeming to help much in this blowing, heavy rain but we manage to go up and down the length of the area and no Zoey. I'm becoming frantic at this point. She's been out here for a half an hour now. She has to be freezing and what if she's hurt? I'm desperate as we head down the street to the next one.

We get to the entrance of the next alley and start heading in. We are both chilled to the bone so I know Zoey has to be in dire need of help even more. Chris is taking the right side and me the left, our flashlights shining back and forth.

"Mmmmm." My head whips up the alley and my pace quickens when I hear a moan. My light lands on a bundle against the wall and I run over, bending down on one knee to find Zoey lying face down. I start to move her when Chris stops me.

"Don't move her, Hutch. She could be hurt and doing that could hurt her more. I'm going to run next door and call an ambulance. Hang on!" He heads off in a sprint and I look at my love, her wet hair covering the side of her face.

I gently move the hair away from her face, the rain pelting on her. Opening my duffle bag, I grab the tarp and throw it over her, raising the end up over her face to help keep the rain away. "Zoey? Baby?" She moans lightly, her eyes not moving at all. "I'm here. Oh, baby. I'm so sorry for everything. Please… Please don't leave me. I can't live without you." My head turns to the entrance of the alley when I hear sirens in the distance and loud footsteps running this way. Moving more fallen wet hair from her beautiful face, I bend down close to her. "Baby. Help is on the way. Hang in there for me."

Chris runs up next to me, breathing heavy from running, and the sirens getting louder as the ambulance approaches. "She doing okay?" I shake my head sadly. "Oh, God. She's got to be okay. She's just got to."

We both turn and see the ambulance stop at the curb next to the sidewalk and a paramedic jumps out of the driver's side. He runs into the alley and straight to us. "Sir. What happened?" He squats next to her motionless body and takes the tarp out of my hands and off Zoey.

"We're not sure. She was on her way home and I got a call from her but it was full of static so I couldn't really tell what she was saying. I got worried and we came out looking for her. She hasn't moved or woken up since we've been here which has been about twenty minutes now," I tell him as he feels her neck for a pulse.

"Ok, sir. I need you to move back so we can check her injuries, please." By that time another paramedic has joined us and I feel Chris' hand on my shoulder, so I stand and move back a couple steps with him. I'm moving back and forth, trying to look around them as they both hover over my love.

"Ma'am? Ma'am? Can you hear me?" The first paramedic asks as he removes his fingers from her neck. My heart races when I hear her moan and I take a step forward only to be halted by Chris' hand on my chest. "Okay, ma'am. I don't want you to move, let us do all the work. We're just going to slowly turn you over so we can assess your injuries, alright?" My heart feels like it's pounding through my chest when I hear her let out another guttural moan as they turn her over. I can see the left side of her face is covered in blood as the paramedic gently pulls back her wet hair.

The other paramedic looks up at us, "Any allergies or anything medically we need to know about her?"

"No sir. Zoey is very healthy and..." I'm quickly cut off by Chris, his hand on my arm squeezing it, my head quickly turning to him.

"Um, actually, she's pregnant." *What?*

"Thank you, sir." The paramedic goes back to helping the other check out Zoey and I turn to Chris, the confusion apparent on my face.

"Chris? Wha…?" His hand still on my arm, he pulls me back more, the sadness in his eyes reaffirming what an idiot I have been.

"When she brought the kids over the other night, when you… Well, she told us she'd just found out she's pregnant." My fingers squeeze the bridge of my nose as I cringe with how selfish I've been, only thinking of myself. How hard it must've been for her to go through everything I've put her through. How could I have done this to her? To the kids? What kind of husband would only think of himself instead of being strong for his family? What is it gonna take to teach me that I'm stronger than I think, that I can handle bad things coming my way as long as I have the love of my life with me?

One of the paramedics stands and runs to the ambulance, returning a few minutes later pushing a gurney. I watch as they pick up my unconscious Zoey and place her on it, cover her with a blanket, place an oxygen mask over her mouth, and start taking her away. Immediately I run after them and thankfully they let me ride in the back with her. Chris yells that he'll head home and get Betty to watch the kids and he and Simon will drive to the hospital. I watch as they set up an I.V. and I pray the entire way for God to keep my love alive.

Chapter Seven

My eyes slowly open and then close quickly. The bed is soft, unlike the hard ground I remember lying on before. I slowly open my eyes again and see Hutch's head lying on the bed, his eyes closed and my heart swells with love. My left hand lifts and I see a needle band-aided on the top, and an I.V. tube running out and up the bed. My hand moves to Hutch's head and my fingers caress his soft hair, pushing it away from his forehead. His eyes suddenly open and he gives me his warm, soft, and sexy dimpled smile. As he sits up he takes my hand in both of his and leans over and kisses my wedding rings.

"I thought I lost you, baby." Tears instantly form in his eyes and I see his chin quiver. "God, I thought I lost you." He loses it completely, his forehead resting against my hand he's holding and he sobs.

I reach across with my other hand and stroke his hair. "I'm here, my darling. I'm here. Everything's okay now. Everything's..." Flashes of rain, falling, the hard ground, and a stabbing pain in my stomach. "The baby," I whisper.

His head snaps up, his eyes watery but full of love. "The baby's just fine, my love. There was a big piece of glass that had penetrated your stomach but didn't go deep enough to hurt the baby, but you do have a few stitches there," he says as he rubs his thumb over my hand. "Another baby." His feelings can't be denied with the huge smile on his face.

"I'd only just found out when... When you... When everything changed," I choke out, my eyes drifting down to the bed. My chin is lifted by his hand and he leans into me, his mouth pressing against mine. I feel all the love pouring out of him with his kiss and just as I'm needing more, he pulls back. He places both hands on the sides of my face, kisses me chastely once more and then smiles.

"I know I've been a horrible husband and father..." I start to protest but he gently presses a finger against my lips. "Lately. I'm so sorry, love. The girl who brought me home that one night? Jamie? She's a friend of the family and Lauren called to tell me that Jamie has cancer." I gasp at his news and he kisses me quickly again then presses his forehead against mine. "I just couldn't handle it. It was like Jodi all over again but I didn't drink like that when we found out about Jodi. I was strong for her, stood by her side the entire time, but I just couldn't..."

My chin rises and I kiss him this time. "Shhhh, my darling. I understand and it's okay." I feel the tears from his eyes on my face and he quickly wipes them from me and himself.

"No, it's not okay." His face moves back from mine a bit and he looks deeply into my eyes. "Don't you see? I was selfish. I only thought of myself this time. I wasn't thinking of you. The kids. I couldn't face it again so I hid. I'm a coward." He starts to rise and I grab his hand, stopping him.

"You were scared. You were reliving some of the most horrific moments in your life and were trying to come to terms with it the best you knew how. It may not have been the best way; I would have hoped you'd feel you could talk to me and know that I love you enough to try and help you get through it, but, it was the only thing you could do, at the time. It's okay, my love." I'm suddenly in his arms as they wrap around me and I wince in pain as he pulls me up.

"Oh, no!" He helps lay me back down and sits on the side of the bed. "Baby! I'm so sorry! I just wanted to hold you…"

Smiling a little I place my hand flat against the side of his face, his eyes closing with my touch. "It's okay. I wanted you to hold me… I want you to hold me so very much."

He takes both of my hands in his and gives me a teary smile. "I will never *ever* hold anything back from you again as long as I live. It took almost losing you to realize that if I had only talked through it with you, my love, then I wouldn't have put you through all of that and you wouldn't be here right now." My smile is huge as I squeeze his hands. He leans down and I latch on to his full lips and we kiss like long lost lovers.

Epilogue

Zoey ended up having to stay in the hospital for a few days but it was some of the best days of our relationship. We rekindled our love and talked about everything! Why didn't I just talk to her when I was depressed in the first place? Because, I was stupid. Never. Again. I finally get her home and, of course, the doctor said she still needed to be careful and get plenty of rest. Simon and Chris had the kids waiting for us when we walked in the door and I had to gently hold them back—they were so excited to see and hug mommy. I cooked. I cleaned. I even put a pillow under her feet on the coffee table as I served her milk and she lazed on the couch. I made sure to treat her as I used to—like a queen.

A week later, while she was putting the kids to bed, I rushed around, turned off all the lights downstairs, lit the candles I had placed all over the living room and waited. I heard her walk down the stairs and through the entryway and then her gasp. I had lit a fire in the fireplace, laid our big pillows on the floor in front of it, the candles glowing all around the room, and I had a bucket of chilled sparkling grape juice on the floor next to me with two wine glasses.

"Hutch! What's all this?" she asked, smiling, as she walked towards me and then knelt in front of me. I sit up, take out the bubbly, pour a wine glass full and hand it to her before filling the other for me. Once I've placed the bottle back into the bucket, I raise my glass to her, her eyes wide but watery.

"Here's to my loving wife. I promise to have and to hold, I promise to love, cherish, honor, and respect her. I promise to pamper and spoil her, every minute of the day. I promise to make love as often as humanly possible..." She giggles and closes her mouth quickly. "I promise to always tell her everything, never, ever, keeping anything from her ever again." I clink my glass against hers but she sets hers down on the hearth, removes mine from my hand, and pushes me down onto a pillow. Her mouth presses against mine and I swear it's the best kiss I have ever had in my entire life.

* * * * *

A few weeks have passed and I'm sitting out on the deck watching Zach and Bailey play out in the yard. Zack is swinging on the swing set and Bailey is playing in the small sand box with her toys. I look up at the mountains in the distance and remember everything that we went through when I couldn't release all the bad feelings from inside me and Zoey walks out the sliding door, kisses my cheek, and sits in the chair beside me. I take her hand and she smiles at me as she squeezes it.

"What's got you thinking so deeply, my darling?" I'm mesmerized by her beautiful face, her deep blue eyes with a twinkle in them, her long, black lashes, her luscious full lips and the smile that melts my heart. She giggles. "You're doing it again."

Leaning over, I kiss her as if I've been missing her for years. "I'm just thinking about how lucky I am. Having the best wife that fills my heart and soul, the best kids..." I place my hand on her stomach, my thumb rubbing over her t-shirt. "The best baby on the way. How can life get any better than this?" Her hand lies on top of mine and the glow in her smile brightens up her face, making her look heavenly.

"Well, how about twins?" My eyes spread wide and then soften as I smile. Twins. Life just got a whole lot better and I'm home again.

Vicki Green

Author Dedication

This to my husband and two teenage sons, for without them I wouldn't be able to do what I love: write. To the readers who have purchased this anthology, thank you, for without you this would not have been written. Love is a powerful thing, none should be without.

About Vicki

Vicki Green grew up in Overland Park, Kansas and currently resides in Olathe, Kansas. Along with her husband and two teenage boys, she shares her home with her cocker spaniels, Shadow and Mocha. She worked full time at the same company for 35 years but now is enjoying some time as a full-time writer.

She had a dream that played out for over a year, came home one day after work, and decided to put it on a word document to see how it read and that became *My Savior Forever*, the beginning of her Forever Series.

Follow Vicki

Website: http://www.vickigreenauthor.com/

Facebook page: http://www.facebook.com/VickiGreenAuthor

Read More from Vicki

Finding My Way Home: http://amzn.to/1gBub8t

Masked Encounters: Extended Edition Intoxicating Passion #1

Felicia Tatum

Chapter One: Korah Daniels

He slurped his drink entirely too loudly, making me want to rip the glass from his hands and throw the ice cold Coke in his face. I didn't, of course, but I imagined. A few times, actually. The liquid spraying as it impacted his small, weasel-like expression. His eyes bulging as he realized what happened. Yeah... I'd thought about it. Tonight was the worst date of my life. I glanced at the clock, once again, hopeful enough time had passed for it to be acceptable to leave.

This was why I hated being set up on blind dates, especially from the neighboring frat house. I got creepy men who obviously never spoke to a girl before, or slimy losers who saw me as another lay. It got old. My friend, Leela, insisted on setting me up, and who could resist her adorable pout? Not me, obviously. So here I sat, poking the food around on my plate, head sunk in hand not caring it squished my cheek in an unflattering manner, while this weirdo droned on and on about who knows what. I quit listening at least fifteen minutes ago.

The sudden silence from Mr. Talker caught my attention, only to be skewered by his eager eyes. "I'm sorry, what?" I asked, hoping I sounded as bored as I was. In all honesty, I didn't even remember his name. John? Josh? Or maybe it was Jacob. It was a J name. I think.

He leaned closer, giving my slight cleavage a hungry gaze. "I said, *The way you look in that dress makes me want to do things to you only Prince would sing about,*" he repeated, in what I supposed was his seductive voice. It sounded more like a snake hissing, or a balloon deflating... as I hoped his ego would be doing soon.

The urge to vomit was fairly strong at this point. I pushed my plate away, took a pointed look at the clock, and pulled my purse from the chair back. "Thank you, for that, I think. It's time for me to go. I have a bedtime, you know. I assume you'll be paying?" I asked rhetorically, not really interested in his answer. I stood, straightened my dress, and sauntered out. The weight of his beady eyes followed me, no doubt imagining my body beneath his, but I didn't care. Perverse fantasy would be as far as he ever got with me.

* * * * *

Slipping quietly into the apartment I shared with Leela and Windi, I slid my shoes off hoping they wouldn't hear me enter. I turned the knob, closing the door silently, before tiptoeing across the living area to my bedroom. I was almost there, seconds from being free of interrogation, when I heard my name.

"Korah!" Leela exclaimed sharply. She reminded me of a stern schoolteacher in 1950.

I turned, seeing her with hands on hips, staring me down. Her long blond locks fell in curls around her shoulders, while deep blue eyes quietly assessed me. She was in her last year, while I was only in my second, so she embraced the big sister role with fervor. Holding my hair while I threw up, helping me treat hangovers, giving me boy advice, etc. I loved her immensely, but the jerk she set me up with tonight was not her best choice. Judging from her stance and, blazing eyes, she'd already heard how I left. Unfortunately, this wasn't the first bad blind date I'd gone on, and they always seemed to call her before I got home. It was pathetically annoying how immature some boys were.

"Well?" she challenged.

I shrugged, smiling at her. "Well?" I mocked back.

"You just left him there! He was so embarrassed. Poor, Zane," she sympathized, trying to guilt me.

Zane... that was it. I was all kinds of wrong about his name. "Yeah... he said something that made me uncomfortable. So, I left." Shifting my weight to the right, I bent my left leg up to lightly scratch the back of my calf. Finally starting to unwind from my difficult evening, I folded my arm across my chest, standing with my purse dangling from my hand.

"Korah... I just want you to be happy. Ever since Christopher..." she started, her expression torn and sad. Leela captured her bottom lip in her teeth, clenching her hands together before she hooked them behind her back. She knew she'd gone too far.

I didn't want her pity, nor did I need it. "I don't want to talk about him," my exasperation coming through more clearly than I intended. Catching myself and knowing her concern was well meant, I sighed crossing my arms. "I don't need a man to be happy. You don't have to keep setting me up. I'll be fine. Now, please, can we be done? I'm going to study." For the second time in less than an hour, I didn't wait for an answer. Turning, I hurried to my bedroom, ignoring her calling my name. My misery didn't like company

Dating had never been kind to me, but recently, my disastrous love life was on a completely different level of crazy. Abusive relationships, level five stalkers, and desperate types who proposed after two dates. I refused to deal with it anymore, not even wanting to bother with romance because of all the torment, which inevitably resulted. At nineteen years old, I knew it was not normal to have this much drama.

I had friends who were married, some with children already. I wasn't ready for either of those responsibilities, but... why couldn't I find a decent guy? What was so wrong with me that I attracted all the whacky ones?

I flopped on my oversized bed, sinking deep into cotton covers and feathery pillows. Darkness settled in around me, the only light a half-moon peeking through the curtains. Looking guiltily at my desk, strewn with papers for my speech assignment, I groaned inwardly. Turning to my side, I found Elle under the abundance of covers. Worn oversized ears, trunk now bent at an awkward angle, she had been a source of comfort since I was a little girl. Snuggling her to my chest, I drew my knees to my stomach. My eyelids fluttered against the pillow before I fell into a restless sleep.

* * * * *

"Korah… Korah…" a sing-song voice called.

The world shook as I bounced around. Complete dark surrounded me, the only sound a voice calling me by name. I slowly came to consciousness. Peeling one eye open, I saw Leela's ginormous face smiling down on me. "Good grief," I groaned, burying my head under the pillow, tucking Elle deep enough to avoid detection.

"Wake up, Korah! I need to tell you some exciting news," she exclaimed. The bed continued to move under her weight as she thrashed about, jostling me to and fro.

"Go away," I mumbled. The nightmares continued to haunt me, causing sleepless nights and the unattractive dark circles under my brown eyes. Thank goodness for make-up.

"Korah, we need to go shopping," she lured, teasing me with one of my favorite past-times.

I lifted the pillow cautiously exposing the side of my face. Peering at her with one squinted eye, I raised a brow and clarified, "Shopping?"

She nodded eagerly, finally standing and relieving me of her weight." Yep. We have lots to get."

I eyed her suspiciously. "Such as…?" Leela despised shopping with me. I *took too long,* or I *tried on everything,* or some other nonsense. She seemed miserable every time we went together. Which meant she was up to something, probably something I wouldn't like.

"A Halloween costume," she shrugged in feigned nonchalance before escaping out my door.

And there it was. I propped on my elbows, staring at the spot where she had been standing. There was only one reason Leela would want me to have a Halloween costume and that would be for a party. I'm no math major, but: Me + Parties = Disaster. I propelled my body upward, still drowsy from sleep. Rubbing the crust from my eyes, I turned, putting reluctant feet on the floor. Finally, I staggered upright and shuffled into the common room. "Lee?"

"Yes, sleepyhead?" she sounded way too chipper, her eyes twinkling in delight as she glanced up from her books strewn over the coffee table.

"You have a party for us, don't you?" I accused, yawning.

"Did you not sleep enough?" She always avoided questions I desperately wanted answers for.

"Don't do that, Lee. Don't tell me it's more frat guys?" I scoffed, rolling my eyes.

"Maybe," she shrugged, picking up the pink highlighter and fake studying.

I flopped down on the couch she leaned against from her seat on the floor, rubbing my face vigorously with my hand. "Come on, I told you I'm not interested in dating." I was practically begging at this point. After six months of her nagging, enough was enough.

"I'm not setting you up, Korah," she stated, dropping the marker and angling her body to face me. Her shiny blue eyes implored in a loving but determined way. "You don't get out enough. I feel like you're stuck in this hole... I worry about you. You're basically my little sister, and it hurts me to see you like this. You mope around, refusing to give any guys a chance..."

I interrupted, "If they weren't losers or assholes, I'd give them more of a chance."

"Korah," she pleaded, taking my hand in hers. "You haven't been the same since Christopher. And I get it, totally, but you can't withhold trust forever. Some time, at some point, you have to give someone a chance."

"No, I don't," I huffed. Her words were correct, but I wasn't ready. I couldn't forget what he did to me, all the trauma I endured. Trusting men was too risky.

"Then will you go for me? Be my date?" she smiled. Her lower lip twitched, and I knew she would give me the pout if I didn't agree.

"Fine! But I'm not going for guys. I'm not dating anyone. I'm not even dancing with anyone," I warned.

She squealed, a high-pitched sound that stung my eardrums. "You are going to have *so* much fun! Go, go, go. Get ready! We are leaving after I get us some breakfast," she instructed, snatching her keys off the table. "I'll be back in a few!"

I sat there, glaring at the door, for longer than I should have. She meant well, I knew, but that didn't stop the sinking feeling in my gut.

Halloween was just days away... and this was so much more than a party. Something was going down. I didn't know if she planned it or not, but I knew more than dancing and haunted houses would be happening on Halloween.

Chapter Two: Dane Davidson

She lay beneath me, panting and writhing from pleasure. I couldn't remember her name... only that her breasts were double Ds, her hips large enough to grab, and her body willing and able to take mine. I buried my face in her shoulder, not wanting to see hers. Seeing their faces made it real. I didn't want to think of the feelings or the person, just the body and relief I desperately sought.

I grew closer to release, finally lifting my face and pressing my lips to hers. They always liked it when I kissed them right before we finished. It was the least I could do. I thrust until I exploded, her enthusiastic cries loud in my ears as I brought her to the brink again. I jerked my head away, not wanting her to see my lack of emotion.

"Dane," she sighed breathlessly, pulling me to her by the base of my hair and assaulting my mouth with her tongue.

I let her, not wanting to be a complete jackass about it all. Did I care about her? No. Did she know this? Yes... but that didn't mean I couldn't pretend, at least for the duration of our romp. She pulled away, tracing my lips with her tongue, giving me her sexiest look. She was attractive, I'd give her that, but blondes were never my preference. This chick, whatever her name, was short, round, and more than willing. She'd been eyeing me at our local bar for the past two weeks, and I finally, selfishly, gave in to her advances. I knew she'd want to go again, but I didn't. I made it clear when we left the bar, sex and nothing else. I hoped she wasn't one who would beg for more.

I slid out, seeing disappointment cross her face as I climbed out of her bed. I slipped into the bathroom, closing the door and dousing myself in the face with water. The women, the sex, the drinking was all a part of daily life for me. As a junior in college, a brother of Alpha Kappa Pi, and a Bio major, I epitomized the college playboy, classes by day, drinking and ladies by night. I enjoyed the no strings sex, knowing I wouldn't have to see the girl again. There were times, naturally, I'd run into a woman later. Embarrassment generally held their tongue; rarely did they say anything, but if they did, they cried or screamed at me. One slapped me, and while it stung, it didn't affect me.

Nothing really did.

I stepped out, in my naked glory, to see the chick propped on her bed, legs open and waiting for me. "Dane, I'm ready," she invited, while sliding a hand up and down her body.

"I've got class," I offered with less-than-sincere-regret, grabbing my clothing and pulling them on as quickly as possible. I guessed where her hand was headed and I needed to escape. *Fast.*

She didn't stop, however, or take the hint. Double D Blonde continued, adding what I knew she thought were sexy sounds to her display. She threw her head back, shaking her hair around her, the image not unlike a dog after a bath.

I cringed, looking away, as she explored her body, desperately trying to entice me back to her. Unable to stand it any longer, I moved forward grasping her hand, pulling it away from her, and made eye contact. "I have to go. I had a good time," the lie a practiced, parting gift. In reality, she was neither good nor bad, it was what it was.

She captured my mouth with hers, darting her tongue in and out while pressing her breasts into me. I broke free, desperately wanting to wipe the saliva she left on my face, but I couldn't be rude to her.

Her gaze fell, the realization striking her hard. Dropping her hands from my shoulders, she accused, "I won't see you again, will I?"

Straightening, I stuck my hands in my pockets as I backed away. "I don't know. I told you I wasn't looking for anything," my tone, intentionally, a chiding reminder.

"Do you even know my name?" she demanded, jumping from the bed. Her breasts bounced attractively, momentarily distracting me from her tantrum.

Quickly tiring of her games, I looked her square in the eye. "No. And I don't care to."

Tears formed, anger replaced with an abrupt wash of hurt. Not my intention, but Double D Blonde left me no other way. I really needed to screen the women better, because I was getting more of the crazy ones lately. She scrambled to cover her body, large green eyes looking childlike with glossy sad tears.

"Bye," I called. I left without looking back.

* * * * *

Class let out early, so I sprinted across campus, past the student center and registration hall, through the commuter parking lot, and met my brothers just as they started a new game of basketball. Slightly out of breath, but pumped nonetheless, I slung my backpack to the side of the court and ripped my shirt off.

It was October, and most of the days were spent with fifty and sixty-degree weather. I didn't complain, but I missed the hotter Georgia months. The short skirts, shorter shorts, and long, long legs. The girls on campus didn't bother to cover themselves often, and I appreciated it very much. Today wasn't a particularly warm day, but my mad dash across campus left me sleek with sweat. I knew the basketball game wouldn't allow any cooling down.

"Hey, got room for one more?" I called, stretching my arms above my head before slugging a quick drink of stale water from the bottle in my pack.

"Don't you have some chick's pants to be getting into?" Jack mocked, giving me a few suggestive hand movements for good measure. He was the biggest asshat I knew.

"He left with someone last night," Cale reasoned, throwing the ball at my chest.

I caught it, carelessly dropping the bottle on my pack then dribbling a few times, before passing it to Jack. "So, can I, or not?" Jack and I didn't get along. He was a ladies man wannabe, and I, well, I wasn't a wannabe. Several times a girl Jack was interested in, ended up leaving with me. He held it against me or something.

Jack threw it back my way with more force than necessary, nodding grimly. We spread out, dividing into teams, and began the game. Jack wasn't overly aggressive, but it was obvious he was intentionally trying to press his luck with the fouls. We didn't play basketball by the regular rules, we played Alpha Kappa Pi style. We were men, strong men, and a few fouls here and there weren't a problem. Jack took advantage.

I was happy to oblige.

By the time the score was 15-14, my body felt bruised and beaten. Jack had gotten in a few good elbows, landing hits to my back and head, though I managed to dodge a cheap shot at my groin. My anger rose with each unnecessary assault until my blood was near boiling. I was done, but I wasn't leaving before giving Jack a nice taste of his own medicine.

I dribbled the ball lazily, appearing tired. Jack watched me closely. I waited, continuing to casually dribble even though others were calling for me to pass and finish the game. I ignored the confusion and frustration they threw at me, patient. Finally, Jack looked away. I threw all my strength into the ball, passing it harshly and quickly.

The ball made a satisfying crunch as it impacted with his face. I was unable to hide my smirk as blood began to pour from his nose. I didn't think it was broken, but I was sure it wouldn't look pretty tomorrow for the Halloween bash our frat house was throwing.

"Dammit, Dane!" he screamed, using his palms in a desperate attempt to catch the pooling blood.

"I thought we were playing. Why did you turn away?" I questioned innocently. His pride wouldn't allow him to call me out in front of all the guys. He'd look like a wimp.

Jack's eyes narrowed. "We're done," he growled. He turned and grabbed his shirt, using it to cover his nose, before stomping off.

I shrugged, allowing the snicker I'd been holding to escape. He deserved that and more. I was glad I had been the one to put him in his place. Bending to get my shirt, I used it to wipe the sweat from my face then threw it over my shoulder. Resting my backpack on top of the sweaty garment, I turned and ran right into Cale. "You scared me, Buddy."

"We need you to help decorate tomorrow morning," he grinned, knowingly. Cale was sure the throw was intentional; I could see it in his eyes.

"Ok. I need to get a costume. What are you going to be?" I asked, starting my walk back to the house.

"I dunno yet. You going now? I'll go with."

"Sounds good," I stated. I walked at a steady pace, returning back to the house in record time. Jack was nowhere to be seen, which wasn't surprising, but I guessed he'd already been through and told everyone. I got a few stares, a few high fives, and a few glares. Most of the dudes wouldn't mess with me; I was older, I'd been here longer, and I could make their life hell if I needed to. Turning to Cale, I said, "I'm gonna shower, be back down in ten."

* * * * *

Going shopping was a pain in the ass. Especially this close to the holiday, but I'd forgotten about our party. I needed a costume with a mask. We searched several stores, but I couldn't find one I wanted. I'd gotten two phone numbers, however. The last one, a feisty brunette with amazingly tight pants, would probably be getting a call from me tonight. Last night's release was only temporary. I wanted to sink myself deep into every nook and cranny she possessed.

I leaned against the counter, contentedly waiting for Cale. Two girls walked by, one blonde and petite, the other a gorgeous brunette with the most amazing body I'd ever seen. She wasn't too skinny, not too big. Curvaceous and stunning. Her hair fell to mid-back, her eyes as rich as the near black strands. She was the sexiest woman I'd ever laid eyes on. I couldn't stop myself from staring.

She glanced at me, furrowing her brows, before moving to the other side of her friend. *Odd,* I thought. Women don't react that way to *me.* I stepped forward, eager to speak to her, but Cale's timing stunk. I turned, responding to his calling my name; he was standing impatiently, holding two large bags. I held up a finger, signaling him to wait, but when I looked back around, she was gone.

Chapter Three: Korah

The stores were clustered with people and some of them smelled. The stores, not the people. Leela was in super-happy-hyper-mode, while I was ready to go back to the apartment and take a nap. She tried on outfit after outfit at store after store. We were at our sixth stop of the day and it was barely noon.

"You haven't tried on anything," she scolded, giving me her signature "I'm-disappointed-in-you" eyebrow raise, before disappearing in the dressing room with armload of clothing.

"I haven't noticed anything I like," I called sweetly. It wasn't a lie, nothing looked good to me. I didn't want to be a cliché witch or princess for Halloween, and most adult costumes were slutty. It seemed impossible to find what I envisioned: a classy costume, with a mask.

Leela stepped out of the dressing room, her long legs showing all the way up to her butt cheeks. The outfit, a little red riding hood get up, was just that... little. Her boobs poured out the top while the bottom left little to the imagination. Exactly what I meant by slutty. She looked gorgeous, don't get me wrong, but slutty, nonetheless.

"What do you think?" she asked excitedly, spinning in front of the mirrors to check herself out.

"Honest?" I questioned, giving my bottom lip a gentle bite. She was my best friend; I didn't want to make her feel bad.

She gazed at me, nodding emphatically.

"You look like a little red riding whore," I admitted, letting my eyes travel her body. "Those guys won't have to wonder about *anything.*"

She laughed loudly, jumping up and down. "Exactly what I was going for!"

Rolling my eyes, I left Leela preening in the mirror while I perused the racks. Everything showed too much skin, or in the case of the nun costume, not enough. I wasn't a prude by any means, but I didn't feel comfortable running around with a bunch of masked people nearly naked. It just wasn't me.

I wandered the store aimlessly. In my minutes of solitude, I decided I wouldn't go. She would be mad, and probably cry, but I couldn't find a costume. That was a good excuse, right? I argued internally for a bit, finally taking a deep breath for courage, I turned on my heel heading back to the cash registers. That's when a piece of heaven caught my eye.

A long, silk white dress with large feathered wings was hanging on the mannequin. It looked like it would be snug, but it would cover most of my body. The neckline was low, but not embarrassingly so, and there were small beads lining it. A mask, also white with a feather jutting off each side hung from the mannequin's hand.

How could I say no to this costume? A sales associate obviously saw me gaping, because he walked up, smiling. "Want me to get it down so you can try it on? I think you would look lovely as an angel," he purred, eyeing me closely for a reaction.

Too in awe for words, I nodded. He got the ladder, brought the costume down, and directed me to the dressing area. Leela was MIA, but I didn't care. I needed this dress to fit. Something about it was... special.

I undressed in a hurry, then indulged my fingers in traveling along the material, feeling the fabric whisper in a seductive smoothness. It was amazing. I slipped it over my head, keeping my back to the mirror. Setting the mask in place, I closed my eyes for a brief moment, before spinning to see my reflection.

The dress fit me perfectly, showing off every curve I possessed. My breasts looked larger, rounder. The mask hid most of my face, revealing only my lips and eyes. My dark eyes appeared nearly black contrasted against all the white. My hair, long and loose around the dress, became a rich brown hue, more chocolate than faded milk chocolate. Even the wings were perfect, peeking just beyond my shoulders.

A knock at the door shook me from my assessing. "Korah? You in there?" Leela called.

Still unable to speak, I opened the door, eyes wide, and waited for her reaction.

Her mouth fell, her pupils grew large. "You look amazing, Korah," she whispered reverently.

I ran a hand down my side and across my hip, "Is it ok? Too much?"

"Too much?" she quizzed, placing her hands on my arms. "You look amazing. Beautiful. And not slutty like I'm going to look. I say get it," she smiled with all the sincere warmth I loved her for.

I nodded, going back in to take it off. Closing the door, I stared at myself for several more minutes. My insecurities regularly brought me down, but something about the way I looked right now... it mesmerized me. I *must* have this dress. I felt crazy, but I thought this costume was meant to be mine. After changing back to my clothes, I stepped out to find Lee eagerly waiting for me.

"You're getting it, right?" she questioned. Leela knew me too well.

I normally would back out, but not this time. "Yeah, I'm getting it." A smile bloomed on my face all by itself.

She squealed loudly, causing everyone to turn and look at us. I made my purchase, ignoring the flirtatious comments from the guy who helped me earlier, and led Lee out the door. "Lunch?" I asked, nodding toward the small café we liked to eat at during our trips.

She nodded, linking us at the elbows, and bouncing down the street. Leela chatted about nothing in particular, in an animated way that allowed my mind to drift and overanalyze our day. The bad date last night caused the Christopher nightmares to resurface. Leela startled me awake, demanding I go with her to a party, knowing how much I despise them. Why was I going? Good intentions aside, she always set me up with men who were totally wrong for me.

But... were all of them wrong? I was broken, damaged goods, unable to love or be loved. Every guy had some sort of issue; a reason I was not interested. He wore too much cologne, or his toenails were too long. Sometimes they did have serious issues, such as being unable to commit. No matter who it was, I found a problem. A deal breaker that completely turned off any and all emotions I may have been considering.

I'd been this way since breaking up with Christopher eight months ago. I couldn't stop it; well, more accurately, I didn't know how to.

"Korah?" Leela prompted. We stood outside the café, her giant blue eyes filled with concern, clearly waiting for an answer to the question I hadn't heard.

"I'm sorry, what?" I refocused my attention, feeling bad for ignoring her.

"I asked you what exactly happened with Zane last night. I know you don't want to talk about it, but he gave me some crazy story and I want the truth."

I told her everything, including the creepy crawly feeling I got when he leered at me. Her face showed disgust, while her eyes lit with fury. Leela was overprotective, a mother hen, and even though she set us up, she wasn't going to let some punk treat me badly. She kept quiet, as we walked into the restaurant and requested our usual table.

"Are you mad I left?" I was not sure how to approach her after confessing.

"No. I'm mad at him. He promised he wouldn't be a douche and he treated you that way. These guys need to stop thinking with their pants," she ranted, picking up her menu, then slamming it back to the table. "I don't understand why guys are so awful around here. Are there none that have any decency? Manners? How hard is it to take a girl out a few times before trying to get her back to your apartment?!" she exclaimed. Throwing her arms up in frustration, she once again gained attention from onlookers.

"I just have bad luck," I shrugged, and resumed perusing the menu.

"Maybe I should quit setting you up," she thought aloud, tapping her finger to her chin.

I giggled at her seriousness, while nodding my head in solemn agreement. She *should* stop setting me up. It never went well. "So, this party... you don't have some connection planned?" I asked wearily.

She shook her head, "I told you, you're *my* date."

"But you try to set me up so often, I wasn't sure," I mused, affectionately.

"This is true," she agreed with a laugh. "I'll stop... *if* you promise to be open-minded and not shut someone out if you have feelings for him."

The server came, bringing our water and taking our orders. After she walked away, I thought about what Leela said. I shouldn't be so opposed to love and romance. Not all guys were Christophers. "Lee,

I'll try, but no promises. I can't stop the insecurity that comes with dating. And I know all people have it, but I still have nightmares about him and everything he did. If someone decent comes along, I promise I will *try*," I paused. She knew this but saying it out loud was difficult. "I'm broken."

Leela's eyes brimmed with tears as she reached across the table, taking my hand gently in hers. "You aren't broken," she reassured softly. "Maybe a little torn and tattered, but definitely not broken. You're one of the most amazing women I know, Korah. I wish you could see that," she gave me a watery half smile.

I smiled back, my heart swelling with love. Leela meant well, and always had my back. She was the sister I never had and always wanted. I squeezed her hand, happy to be having this talk with her. "Thank you," I said. "Sooo... the costume, is it really ok?"

Her expression brightened. "Girl, you are going to turn every head in the place! You won't know what to do with all the attention," she giggled in happy anticipation.

I had to agree with her last prediction. I wouldn't know what to do. I'd be nervous, for sure, but I hoped I could keep my cool. Having a mask would help. Before I could contemplate and worry myself more, our plates arrived. We talked about the party between bites. My excitement grew with each word, and every quick peek at the beautiful promise in the bag next to me. It was time to step out of my shell, to be a new Korah. The shy, timid Korah wasn't much fun. She was too scared of life and feelings. If nothing more, for one night, I would be someone else. Someone confident. Someone fearless. Maybe even someone sexy.

Chapter Four: Dane

"You sure that's your costume?" Cale asked, *again*, as I pulled out my debit card to pay the cashier.

I offered it to the older lady, giving her a charming smile that made her blush as she took it from my hand. "Yes," I said through gritted teeth. "I'm sure. Why do you keep asking?"

He shrugged, "I dunno. It doesn't seem... you."

I let his words roll off my back, signing for my purchase and stuffing everything into my wallet. I decided to ignore his badgering. "You ready?" I questioned, taking the bag and nodding my thanks to the still smiling clerk. "I'm starved." I started out the door, my thoughts drifting back to the girl in the third store we had been. It was unusual, the effect she seemed to be having on me. She wasn't interested, that had been clear, yet I couldn't stop thinking about her. Her onyx eyes had touched my soul, stirring something I hadn't felt in a long time.

I wasn't sure I liked it.

"Let's go back and order pizza," Cale suggested.

Completely distracted, I answered with a short nod, before walking aimlessly to the car. I fought to not think of her, but I couldn't stop. Would I ever see her again? Would it matter if I did? She'd obviously disliked me. The questions rolled around in my mind the entire drive home.

* * * * *

"It'll be $25.83," the delivery girl flirted, batting her long lashes at me. She was short and petite, a redhead with brown eyes. She wasn't ugly, but she wasn't spectacular either. She eyed me, her gaze apparently favoring my biceps and chest.

It was obvious she wanted me.

I pulled out the cash, giving her $30 and telling her to keep the change. Balancing the pizzas on one hand, I attempted to close the door with the other. A small foot lodged between the frame and the door, stopping me. I had to look down to even see what caused the blockage. "Yes?" I asked, slightly annoyed.

"Is this where the party is tomorrow night? The Masked Nights theme?" she smiled, reaching through the still cracked door to grasp my forearm.

I nodded, knowing where this was heading and not liking it.

"Is everyone invited? Will you be there?" she asked, not trying to hide the hopeful lilt in her voice. I could see the desire in her eyes, growing as I indulged her in conversation. Her panties were probably soaked at the thought of having a chance with me.

She didn't, though. No one did, for anything more than a single session.

"Yeah, it's for everyone. You need to have a masked costume to get in the door. There will be bouncers," I explained. I hoped I didn't sound interested.

"What are you going to be, big boy?" she cackled, falling short on sounding sexy.

"It's a secret. Whole point of the party is to make connections with people without knowing who it is," I clarified, pulling my arm from her grip. This chick wasn't getting the hint.

She pulled a pen from her pocket, scribbling a number on top of the pizza box. "Why don't you text me what time the party starts so I don't miss it." She sounded expectant, and slightly desperate. An unattractive combination.

I gave her a tight smile, not agreeing to anything, and told her bye as I firmly closed the door. Trudging to the kitchen, I wondered how in the hell I got to this point in my life. I used to be able to love… to care… to feel, but not now. No, I couldn't do it anymore. My heart had been ripped from my chest, stomped on and shredded to pieces. A bear could have torn me apart and it would have hurt less than the pain I'd felt when my heart shattered. Loving a woman was dangerous, a risk I couldn't take anymore. Feeling for someone was a gamble, and I was broke.

Bet on everything and lost.

Dropping the boxes on the table, I grabbed two slices before leaving the dining room. I couldn't deal with any of my brothers right now. I shuffled up the stairs, closing and locking my door so I could get some much needed studying accomplished. Stuffing half of one slice in my mouth, I searched for my books.

Technically, I was in my third year of college, but careless drinking my freshman year put me a few classes behind, so I still registered as a sophomore. Apparently slamming back shots of whatever I could get my hands on wasn't a good studying technique. Now I knew.

I pulled my backpack to the bed, shaking the contents out and arranging them by classes... kind of. Half my classes were still general requirements while the other half were upper level. I had to take my second biology term and a calculus course next semester and that would be finish the all the requirements. I couldn't wait to really dive deep into my major and learn things I wanted to, rather than repeating shit I'd already learned over and over again in my younger years.

I finished my pizza in four bites before sprawling out for an afternoon of studying. Tonight and tomorrow we would decorate, but at the moment, I had to do everything I could to divert myself from the dark haired goddess I'd seen this morning. Reaching into my pocket, I pulled out my phone and a slip paper fell to the bed. *Tight pants girl*, I shot her a text, requesting her address so I could come by later. A much better way than studying to forget the girl causing my distraction.

* * * * *

The rays of sun fell on my face, warming me to consciousness. I threw my arm over my face, blocking the light as I turned to see who was in bed with me. The tight pants girl, Stacey, lay completely relaxed, her leg thrown over me as she pressed her warmth against my thigh. Memories from last night flooded back, causing me to get turned on again. Her long brown hair draped over me as she rode, her tight warmth enclosing me, hot breath on my face as her mouth devoured mine. It had been a better than average night full of lust.

It wasn't her I thought of, though.

Her tight body was making my need grow, so I lifted the slender leg off me, pulled protection over my shaft, and positioned my body behind her. She stirred, but didn't wake until I sunk myself deep inside. She moaned against me, arching her body so her taunt ass pressed against me firmly. She didn't question what I was doing, didn't even really seem surprised, she was as ready to go as I was. I pumped into her, releasing quickly, but bringing her over the edge even quicker. She was spent, lying there holding onto her pillow and panting. Grabbing my clothing, I headed to her restroom.

Hurriedly peeing and dressing, I was relieved to slip out of the door as she dozed. I jumped in the car, resting my head against the steering wheel briefly. The black-eyed beauty had been the one on my mind for every touch, every kiss, every entry. I'd seen her for two seconds and she was consuming my thoughts. The feelings she caused were the exact reason I didn't date, why I didn't fall in love.

Women were dangerous creatures.

I turned the engine over, backing away before Stacey noticed my departure. I needed to shower and start decorating for the party tonight.

* * * * *

Halloween decorating was actually enjoyable. For one night a year, we could be scary and gory without chicks freaking out, but we *were* men, so we had to call on our sorority sisters to help out. Tablecloths, table placement, and all that crap was way over my head. I was more of a "tell me where it goes, and I'll move it" kind of guy.

So that's what I did. I let the girls boss me around until our whole bottom floor was transformed into a haunted house. Even the bar we set up in the kitchen was spooky, with heads and various body parts appearing to come out of the wood. Fake blood dripped from the walls, from the ceiling, basically from anywhere we could get away with. It was gross, it was fun, and it was going to be an epic night. Being a Saturday, I didn't have to worry about classes or work, so all my attention was on the party. Sexy women were due to start arriving in a few short hours, in what I hoped would be even sexier costumes.

My testosterone filled hormones were pumped and ready for tonight's entertainment. I could hardly contain my excitement. Jack tried to piss me off, but after yelling at him a few times, he retreated to pout in his room. The day was shaping up nicely.

"Ya about ready, Buddy? I think we're done," Cale sighed, sweating from running every which way while we put the sister's ideas into action.

"Gonna need a nap," I chuckled, "I had a late night."

Giving me a proud grin and slapping me on the back, he thrust his hips in a mocking way. Laughing, he said, "I knew it! I figured you were meeting a girl when you left here at midnight."

"They can't resist me," I shrugged.

He scoffed, turning to go upstairs. "Good job, Dane. I'll see ya later," he called.

I waved two fingers, standing there with my arms crossed as I surveyed our haunted house. The large "Alpha Kappa Pi presents Masked Nights" sign hung in the entryway, its edges slashed to make it look like a wild animal took to it.

Some lucky girl would get this wild animal tonight.

Chapter Five: Korah

The party was a couple hours from starting. I was nervous, and nauseous, no longer wanting to go. Leela anticipated me doing this, because she'd been in my room a few hours back, threatening my life, and all of my precious journals if I tried to back out.

She knew me all too well.

So I sat on the living area floor, legs tucked under my butt as she curled and sprayed my hair with at least ten pounds of spray. *To keep it in place,* she'd said. *It'll be hot and it may come undone,* she worried. Her words meant nothing, because at this very moment I felt like one of those poor children in "Toddlers and Tiaras." I'd throw a tantrum, but I knew it wouldn't help.

I was stuck.

Though I sulked as she made my hair pretty, I was grateful she found a hairspray that didn't leave it feeling hard as a brick. My dark brown mane, probably my best feature, still shone in the light and looked silky. I allowed her to do my make-up, though I sternly warned eyes only. I didn't like foundation; it made me break out, and my skin didn't need it.

When she finished, I felt like a princess... a princess going to a dreaded ball where some prince-wannabe-charming would try to get in my pants, or in this case, up my dress. We switched spots, me now making her pretty, as she chattered on and on about how excited she was.

"What's wrong with you, Korah?" she questioned after I burned my finger for a fourth time.

"Sorry, just not thinking clearly."

"You don't want to go, I know, but you *promised* to try. It's normal to be a little nervous. It'll be fine. *You* will be fine," she assured me.

I sighed, straightening the last of her bouncy curls. "I worry, Lee. You know this. I don't want to ruin the event for you because I'm scared or something."

"You won't," she stressed. "I want to have a fun night with my best friend. That's all. I won't even dance with anyone, so you don't have to be all huddled in a corner waiting for me to return," she promised.

I would have laughed at her, but it was true. I would go find a spot and hide myself until she found me, begged me to come back, or promised we would leave. It really was ridiculous. "You don't have to, Leela. I'll be ok by myself. I'm a big girl. So if some sexy amazing guy comes by and has to take you away, I want you to go. Don't think twice. I'll be alright," I promised. I wouldn't allow my insecurities to ruin her night.

I finished applying her make-up, allowing her to do her own eyeliner. My hands were unsteady and I didn't want to blind my roommate today. We hugged awkwardly, not wanting to mess up each other's masterpieces, and headed to our rooms to dress.

My angel costume was the only part of tonight I was excited about. Drunk guys would go for the girls showing boobs and butts, so I would be in the clear. I hoped to go in, find a drink, a corner, and people watch. As a journalism major, people watching was a favorite pastime of mine. People were strange creatures and observing them was an amazing way to get inspired for stories. Someday, I hoped to work for a newspaper or magazine while writing novels, so I could use all the inspiration I could gather.

Carefully stepping into the neckline and pulling the satin softness up my body, a feeling of awe washed over me, calming my nerves. This dress was truly spectacular, I felt more right than I had in a very long time. I chose to go shoeless, wearing foot jewelry instead. The glass diamonds lining my feet matched the glass beads trimming the dress. My wings and my mask matched. The organizer in me jumped with joy.

I finally stepped out of my room, eager to see my friend's reaction at how I looked... nothing like the Korah Daniels I'd known all my life. I felt beautiful, a word I never used to describe myself. And now that I had the mask on, I felt brave. I could do anything, including going to this party and actually socializing with people I didn't know.

I heard her gasp and my gaze met her masked face. Leela looked hot, her costume showing all her curves. The men would drool when she walked in the door. She gave me a thumbs up while shaking her head slowly, causing mutual giggling to ensue.

"You look sexy," I said, giving her a huge smile.

"So do you!" she exclaimed.

Shocked, I stared at her. My body was covered. Leela's costume was typical while mine was modest. I would stand out like sore thumb. She was trying to tell me I looked sexy? "I do not," I countered. Grabbing the small clutch I was taking, I put in some money, my ID, and phone. Leela did the same, shaking her head at my disagreement. Her purse arranged, she walked over, trying to slip condoms in my bag, but I jerked it away from her. "I won't be needed those and you know it."

"Come on," she groaned, sticking the little wrapper in my face. "When was the last time you got laid, Korah?" she questioned.

I was uncomfortable, not wanting to answer. She already knew, but saying it would cause her to go off on an annoying tirade of how I need to feel a man's warmth beside me, or some more vulgar generalization. "It doesn't matter."

"Take one," she pleaded, trying to hand it to me once again.

I shook my head, turning and opening our door. "Are we going or what?" I called over my shoulder. She threw the condom at me, hitting me on the forehead. We left in a burst of laughter.

* * * * *

The Alpha Kappa Pi house was nestled on the street behind our campus, smack dab middle in the large row of fraternities. It was different, larger and more menacing than the others. I didn't know if it was years of donations, or if it was because they truly were a superior fraternity, but it was daunting to approach. We parked what felt like a mile away, causing me to instantly regret not wearing actual shoes. Small scrapes lined my soles and every rock I stepped on caused me to yelp.

"I told you not to wear those things," Leela griped, hands on hips as she waited for me to catch up.

"No you didn't," I threw back, biting my tongue as a piece of wood pierced the skin beneath my toes. "You said they were cute."

"I told you yesterday, when you insisted on getting *foot jewelry*, that they were a bad idea."

I stopped, the faint recollection of her saying something like that playing in my memory. "Oh, yeah."

"*Oh, yeah*," she mocked. "It's the next house. Surely they have carpet," she speculated, offering her hand.

Holding my dress in one hand and hers in the other, we slowly but surely made our way to the Alpha Kappa Pi house. The music was blaring, an eerie, haunting sound that resonated everywhere while seeming to come from nowhere in particular. The whole outside was decorated, phony blood dripping from every window, a few fake hands and arms sticking out like people were trying to escape. The front door opened as soon as we made our way up the steps, but no one stood there.

It was phenomenal.

We stepped inside, my feet sighing with relief at the cool tile floor. I stood a moment, letting the cold soothe my aching arches. I'd need to go wash them and maybe snoop around for some Band-aids, which I doubted I would find in this place, but it wouldn't hurt to try.

We made our way inside. I finally let my dress fall to my feet and released Lee's hand. The place was packed with bodies in every corner, on every piece of furniture, and lining the walls. Every single face was covered with a mask, a surprising thrill coursed through me. All of these people, and none of them knew who I was. I glanced around, taking in my surroundings, when a deep voice spoke in my ear.

"You seem to be bleeding on my carpet," he whispered, sending a tingle up my spine.

I spun, finding myself face to face with Zorro. Dark hair peeked from under his large hat, big brown eyes gazed back curiously from behind the black mask. I couldn't see his entire face, but I knew he was gorgeous. As my eyes met his again, I saw the surprise in his as they widened. He reached out, grasping my hand, and said, "Come with me."

I couldn't speak. The warmth from his hand flowed through my body, a warm pulse that caused parts of me to awaken from a deep slumber. I nodded obediently, wincing softly as my feet touched rough carpet on the stairs.

In a swift motion, his arms went around my back and under my knees; he lifted and carried me the rest of the way up. My heart pounded in my ears, all the blood rushing to my head. Well, maybe not entirely to my head. I didn't know what was happening, who this was, or where we were going... but I knew my body was reacting to him and I kind of liked it.

Chapter Six: Dane

The second Angel Eyes walked through the door, I knew I had to talk to her. Her pouty lips showing obvious pain, but her hauntingly familiar eyes were the strongest draw. As soon as she turned, her endless gaze met my soul, and I knew who she was.

The girl from the store was here, looking even more beautiful, and bleeding on my carpet.

My heart hammered in my chest; my palms grew wet with sweat. I rushed to snatch her away for myself, and now here we were, in my room. Angel Eyes sat on my bed, her dainty feet propped on a chair I placed in front of her while I searched for a first aid kit. "What happened?" I asked, oddly unsure of what to say. She made me nervous. I hated it.

"I didn't wear shoes," she explained, her voice angelic, matching her costume perfectly.

I stared at her, wanting nothing more than to press my lips to hers and take her right now. "Oh," I replied lamely, my response making even less sense than her explanation.

Quick dash to my bathroom, so I could wet a washcloth to wipe her feet clean of the blood and gravel. I went to work, amazed I was sitting in my room at the biggest party of the year washing a chick's feet. Not that I cared, I would do anything to touch her. The whole minute she was in my arms was heaven. I had tunnel vision for this gorgeous angel who wasn't ignoring me like she did before.

She didn't know who I was this time, though.

Angel Eyes watched me intently, insisting she could do it herself every so often. I shook my head each time. After placing some ointment and bandages on the worst cuts, I sat beside her.

"You're beautiful, Angel Eyes... but you should have worn shoes," I gently teased.

She smiled, lighting my whole life with that small curve of her mouth. "I know, pretty stupid, huh?"

Reaching out, I brushed a stray curl from her cheek. "You don't strike me as stupid," I admitted softly.

She blinked several times, her long lashes brushing the mask below her eyes. The white showed off her darkened irises, and I couldn't deny myself what happened next. I leaned toward her, hungrily taking in her lavender scent as I watched her large eyes grow even larger in surprise.

I pressed my lips to hers, feeling the soft skin against mine. I moved gently, prodding her mouth open and slipping my tongue in ever so slightly. She was hesitant, timid, but she met my kiss. Her tongue was shy, as she cautiously darted it in my mouth.

That one tiny move set me over the edge.

I leaned over her, pressing her to lie on the bed as I stood and kissed her with every ounce of passion now barreling through my body. She moaned in my mouth, causing me to want her even more, although I didn't know how that was possible. The more our mouths moved, the more I wanted to touch her, feel her, please her.

Shifting, I settled myself beside her on the bed. Moving my lips to her neck, I sucked and kissed as she wiggled beside me. My hand found her face, caressing her cheek as I stared into those intoxicating eyes. She made me drunk on her, causing all common sense to fly right out the window.

Dragging my fingers down her neck, I slid my hand inside the top of her dress. Her eyes closed as she gasped, so I continued. Kneading and stroking her breasts, flicking her nipples with my thumb before moving my head to assist my hand.

Angel Eyes roughly tossed my hat across the room, before tugging at my hair. Nipple still in mouth, I traced my hand the length of her, pausing briefly at her ankles. I moved back up, this time under her lovely dress, and watched her eyes grow even blacker with desire.

"Please," she begged, arching her body to me.

She was going to be the death of me. I couldn't have sex with her. This woman was different than the others. She made me *feel*, and I couldn't ruin that… but having her here, begging for me on my bed, was more than I could take. I couldn't say yes, but neither could I say no.

Slipping two fingers in her panties, I found her sweet spot and stroked her wetness ever so slowly. She watched me intently, eyes heavy and hooded. Relaxing, she moaned a few times, grinding herself against my hand, causing me to groan into her chest with my own desire. I continued, stoking her while suckling her breasts until she cried out. Eventually, her body grew limp and she sighed contentedly.

I pulled my hand away, tenderly moving her clothing back to cover her body. Moving upright, I kissed her gently. She met me with a renewed passion, her tongue more aggressive while it darted around my mouth, tangling with my own. Then Angel Eyes nibbled at my bottom lip, pushing me to my back with her hands.

Stunned, I watched as she slid her hands up and down my body, slipping them inside my shirt to feel my chest, down to my pants and finally delving inside. She leaned down, placing those sweet, soft lips on my neck as she gently wrapped her small fingers around my rock hard shaft.

She was going to be my undoing.

Her movements were tentative at first, sliding her hand slowly, softly in each direction. My mind grew cloudy with desire and lust. She kept on, driving me mad. "I'm going to…" I warned, watching her as she delighted in making me explode. She didn't take her eyes off me the entire time, a small smile playing on her lips as she pumped me rougher, faster.

Finished, and still panting, I leaned back on my pillows and closed my eyes. I breathed deeply trying to calm myself. She stayed beside me, tracing my jaw line with her finger. "You didn't have to do that," I said quietly. I looked at her, appreciating her beauty all over again.

"I know, but I wanted to," she cooed, placing a gentle kiss on my cheek.

She started to stand, but I grabbed her wrist. "I have to know your name, Angel Eyes."

She looked panicked, her eyes grew wild and she began fidgeting. "Wh..wh… why?" she stuttered. Angel Eyes tried to get away, but I wouldn't let her. I didn't hold her hard enough to hurt her, but I wasn't letting go easily.

We stood together, her wrist still clasped in my hand even though she was on the other side of the bed. "I'll go first," I offered, letting go and hoping she didn't leave. "I'll turn, take my mask off, then you can do the same."

She sighed, motioning for me to go ahead. As soon as I turned, I heard the rustle of her gown and the door open. I flung my mask off and turned, but she was gone. Rushing out, I flew down the stairs, past the couples making out, past the drunken guy hanging of the banister, singing loudly and obnoxiously. I pushed through the throngs of people, their sweaty bodies congested throughout the house, making it difficult to move. Each room housed a swarm of people, women grasping at me, pressing their bodies to mine. I kept on, searching for the angel in white. I caught a glimpse of dark, flowing locks and a white mask, so I desperately maneuvered through, using my elbows to make a path. People yelled, cursed, and pushed back, but I didn't care. I kept on. I saw her from a distance, urging a girl in a short costume to come with her. I screamed at her, begging for attention, but it was useless. The house was booming with music and people, she would never hear me. I watched them slip out, barely missing them by just a few feet.

I followed them outside, almost tripping over a couple draped all over each other at the bottom of the stairs. A few feet forward, a freshman puked in the bushes. She'd disappeared. I walked aimlessly up and down the street, hoping to find her again. I wasn't even sure why I wanted her so badly. No girl had this effect on me. Something about her reached into the hidden depths of my soul, touched my heart. It was disturbing, but I also knew what it meant.

I had to find her.

Felicia Tatum

About Felicia

Felicia Tatum has been writing since the age of twelve. A lover of chocolate and all things book, she's been writing since May 2012. She's the author of a YA paranormal romance series and two new adult romance series. Masked Encounters is the first in a five part novelette series titled Intoxicating Passion. Sign up for her newsletter to get new releases directly in your email!

Follow Felicia

Website: http://www.feliciatatum.com/

Facebook: http://www.facebook.com/feliciatatumwriter

Read More from Felicia

Mangled Hearts: http://amzn.to/Kub4l7

No Details

Marie Wathen

I chuckle at the two princesses dressed in designer jeans, pastel silk blouses, and overpriced heels softly arguing over who would be the first to enter the outdoor restroom. Shaking my head at them, I glance down at my attire and sigh happily, feeling relaxed in my favorite comfy clothes, although I know that all too soon they will demand I play dress up with them. I find nothing wrong with my charcoal gray hoodie, dark wash jeans, and black Chucks, but unfortunately my comfort zone attire won't suffice for all the high society events they've penciled into our agenda over the next month.

Upon retrieving the tiny key attached to a gigantic piece of driftwood from the attendant working in the dilapidated, fifty-something year old gas station, my best friends, Willa and Penelope, shuffle toward the ladies room while I top off the gas tank. With grimaces frozen in place on their faces, they suspiciously eye the half-busted door, virtually covered in cobwebs.

After replacing the gas nozzle into the pump, I stroll over and snatch the key out of Willa's hand. Stepping a good five feet away from the door, as if she's afraid something is going to jump out at us, Penelope teases, "Always the brave one, Cheney."

It's not that I'm brave, really. I just don't have anything that scares me. I'm not a girlie-girl. I don't get freaked out by bugs or creepy places. I don't buy into superstations, at all. I'm willing to try anything once, but, if it isn't for me, I'll never do it again. The only real fear I have is getting my heart broken.

No worries!

That sucker is guarded by a defense system the likes of Mr. T and Stone Cold Steve Austin. It will be a cold day in hell before I'm vulnerable again.

My parents divorced when I was a teenager after a nasty incident. What I thought was a relationship epitomizing true love, blasted me out of my fantasy world when my father cheated on my mother with some skank bitch, bar-troll he'd met at some seedy club during his business travels. When he came home and told my mother that he couldn't continue the charade of loving her, he didn't even have a smidge of remorse about the damage he inflicted. Abandoning us, he proved to me he didn't care that it wasn't just my mother's heart he crushed that day. His actions and reckless attitude about the whole event created the untrusting and callous woman that I am today. Don't misunderstand, I'm not a prude. I have shared more than one man's bed, but I do have *some* morals and a bit of dignity.

A bar-troll will *never* have me. *Ever*!

"I'm just sick of watching this endless debate, Penelope. If we're going to make it to Memphis by nightfall then we need to get on the highway," I reply to her snippy attitude. Twisting the key into the padlock dangling precariously from the doorframe, I force open the wedged door with my shoulder. "All clear," I offered, gesturing with my hand inside the room before grabbing Willa by the arm and shoving her in. She obeys, creeping inside with her hands raised high like she's scared to touch anything. Penelope shivers and I chuckle while shaking my head. "Hurry your asses up, Brookies," I shout over my shoulder, walking back toward the rental car.

We planned this road trip to Las Vegas six months ago after I heard a commercial on my drive into work one evening. The *iHeart Radio Music Festival* is something we decided to include on our bucket list of things we'd do together. With JT performing, it was an absolute for me. Willa and Penelope share a love for rock concerts with me, but neither was too keen on the idea of traveling across the country via automobile. It took months to convince them that traveling the countryside together, doing a slow crawl through local festivals in several towns that we've always wanted to visit, could create memories we will regret not having if we didn't take a chance. They made demands, of course, but finally relented and we left Birmingham just before dawn. Memphis: the first leg of our adventure awaits us.

Now if we can just get on the road.

"Ready," Willa singsongs, slipping behind the wheel of the tricked out Lexus SUV she insisted on as one of her road trip requirements.

"Set," Penelope clicks her seatbelt in the front passenger seat before twisting around and scowling at me for lying on my side across the backseat.

I smirk before shouting, "Vegas!"

And we're off.

Penelope, Willa and I met our freshman year at the University of Alabama in Birmingham. They are lifelong friends from the richest part of the city, Mountain Brook. Where I'm from we call everyone from the filthy-rich suburb, Brookies, hence the nickname. I'm from a section of town just a little east called Inverness. It isn't a poor area, but it doesn't compare to the Brookie lifestyle at all. Although my two best friends insist on the best of the best, they somehow managed to overlook my low class imperfections and adopted me as their sister.

Insert big eye roll here at my self-deprecating snarkiness.

With the exception of my two girls, the only thing I care for in the Orange-County-wannabe-town is the best damn pizza parlor in the nation, Davenport's. We've dubbed the infamous restaurant, 'The Scene of the Crime,' because it's the place where we met. After being shoved together into a corner table in the backroom, and over several pitchers of beer, we discovered that other than them being born into privilege and me, not so much, we could've been born triplets. All three of us have long blonde hair, me being the only one with a slightly darker natural tone, because I can't imagine spending money for the bottle-blonde upkeep and them because they believe in the old saying that blondes have more fun. We have varying shades of blue eyes, mine are the darkest. Our most important similarities? We are identically loud, opinionated, and independent women.

Six hours and several stop offs later, all at Penelope's demand to quench her Starbucks fix, we arrive at the Madison Hotel in West Memphis. It's the nicest accommodations in the area, another of the Brookies requirements. After checking in and admiring our three gorgeous art-deco rooms, we slip into cocktail dresses and make our way downstairs for dinner at the swanky *Eighty3 Grill*. The food is excellent, the drinks are flowing, and we celebrate our last bit of freedom with our all-girl's trip before facing the world of grownup jobs, adult responsibilities, and mature relationships.

After scanning the room, noting several single men and then inspecting me and Penelope, Willa's eyes sparkle as she chirps, "Hot damn ladies, we are *so* getting some tonight."

I roll my eyes and she snaps, "Cheney Reid, do not roll your eyes at me. We're on this trip because of you. Now, unlock that damn chastity belt safeguarding your lacy thong and live for once."

"My thong is none of your concern, Willa Barlow. I live, but you know my rule."

"One of these days you're gonna jinx yourself, Chey," Penelope adds her two cents worth to the ridiculous conversation.

"Whatever!" I counter.

"Oh yes!" Willa giggles loudly. "He'll be perfect in every way and you'll toss him because of that stupid-ass rule." Willa shakes her head, smiling wickedly before adding, "I bet if you met JT in a bar you would annihilate that senseless self-imposed decree."

"For the millionth time, JT is unavailable and I'm not a home wrecker," I clip, hoping that I've shut her down. This discussion is as old as our friendship. It's only a matter of time before she brings it up again.

"One day you'll get over yourself and I pray to the sweet heavens above that I'm there to see it for myself." She smirks.

Willa is *that* friend. You know the one who loves being right and will do anything to make it happen so she can rub it in your face later. I still love her, but what a bitch. "I'm excited about our first stop at the local festival tomorrow, but I need some entertainment tonight." Willa peeks over her wine glass at me suspiciously. "Are there any landmarks you want to check out?"

"Mm hmm," I smile happily, knowing that my one other request is easily accepted. "Alchemy for bourbon." Just because I'll never date a man I meet in a bar doesn't mean I can't go to them.

"Let's do it," Penelope cheers enthusiastically.

"Alright, I'll get the taxi," I offer, leading the way out the front door.

After exiting the cab and tipping the driver, we push our way through the heavy Friday night crowd and successfully locate two empty seats at the bar. Passing on sitting for the time being, I stand wedged between them while we begin our tastings. Sample testing has become our *thing* recently, all part of our transition into being 'grownups.' What I've discovered about bourbon is that it can become an addiction, especially when you find a great one. We sip for half an hour before the live music begins, begging us to move. Without a dance floor we are left wiggling in place and getting sillier as the liquor warms us from the inside out.

"We *need* to find a club," Willa begs, scanning her eyes around the room. "Preferably one with lots of hot men." Disagreeing completely with the idea of hooking up, I groan, not wanting or *needing* that.

"Yes, or we can snag a couple here and drag them with us," Penelope agrees seductively and I shake my head more adamantly now that they're both considering diverting from our original plans of 'no boys allowed.'

"This seat is open," a husky voice murmurs over my shoulder.

I twist around, finding a pair of warm brown eyes sparkling down at me. My gaze drops slightly south to a pair of the sexiest red lips I've ever seen. They're quirked up on the corners, rising higher the longer I stare.

Oh damn, do I stare? Hell yes. The man is a god in human form. Oh, the humanity.

I'm so mesmerized that Penelope must elbow me before I can break from my stupor. Awkwardly, I also must pry my teeth off my bottom lip because I've been biting the hell out of it while entranced by this guy's mouth. I blink and glare over my shoulder at Penelope, who gives me an obvious eye waggle before I turn back to *those* lips.

And damn, I'm completely speechless.

* * * * *

"Hi there," Mr. Perfect-lips says, dropping his face to the side a bit so that he's closer to my eye level. Still stuck between Willa and

Penelope's barstools, I take a step back, pressing against the bar to take him all in. He is spectacular, towering every bit of six-feet-five inches over my five-feet-seven. From what I can tell through his black dress shirt and slacks, his body is equivalent to those lips, if not more perfect. Broad shoulders, dark blonde hair, thick arms, deliciously large hands, and a sprinkling of tiny freckles on his cheeks, a small amount of imperfection on his flawless face that make him even more handsome.

"Hi." Of course, once I do find my voice after inspecting Mr. Perfect-everything for an indecently inappropriate amount of time, my epic reply comes out raspy and lustful. From the glint in his eyes he can clearly tell the effect he is having on me. Not immune himself, his warm, honey colored eyes darken into molasses and his eyelids barely hood his own desire. Clearing my throat, I recover finally and calmly add, "Thank you, but I'm fine."

"Oh." He blinks twice as if he's trying to compute my innocent rejection. "Sure. I just..." He glances at Willa and Penelope before stepping closer to me. His heady scent slams against me, forcibly overtaking my sense of smell. "I thought you'd be more comfortable sitting next to your girls."

"Your offer is *really* sweet, but I'm not uncomfortable standing," I assure him, happy that I pulled my head out of my ass before I did something completely foolish. Well, more foolish than drooling over his hotness. Oh, and selflessness! Turning away quickly, I run my thumb over the corner of my mouth, confirming that I'm in the clear.

Get a grip dork!

His warm breath glides over my bare shoulder, and an exhilarating shiver runs up my spine like a silk scarf over a nude backside "It wasn't as chivalrous of an offer as you may be thinking. I wasn't giving up my seat for you." I glance back at him and he smiles.

Ah damn, dimples too?

He points with a long thin forefinger. "I'm in the next one over."

"Oh?" I glance at the two empty seats on the other side of Willa. "Okay, but this *isn't* a date," I joke, grabbing my purse and sidling into the wooden high-back chair.

"Good," he counters playfully, dimples on full display while taking his seat, "Because our first date won't include your friends."

Shocked by his audacity, my lips part slightly and I lick them before countering, "You're confident. What if I told you I'm not from Memphis?"

"Well, then I either need to see you again before you leave, or get your address so I can pick you up when you return home." Dripping sex, he stares at me with a teasing smirk that could mean he's playing with me, but his eyes confirm that he is dead serious.

Shaking my head and crooking my finger for him to come closer, I lean in and break it to him gently. "Except for tonight, my plans don't allow for a night out and I'm not from Tennessee. Also, I have one rule that I stick by, no matter how much I might want to break it." Slightly dejected by my first two bits of information, he appears intrigued by the last one with a playful grin tugging up those perfect lips. With my face mere inches from his and our eyes focused on each other, I whisper, "I never date men I meet in bars." His smile drops instantly and I crinkle my nose, feeling like an ass at the cruel bleakness.

"Damn girl," he whispers, staring at me while reaching one hand for a half glass of amber liquid. After taking a long drink, he pulls a smile before continuing, "You could be my one shot at true love, but you're not even going to give me a chance to test out that theory because you met me in a place that I've never been to in my life?"

Matching his disappointment in my tight and strict standard, I shrug and confirm, "That's the rule."

"Harsh one, too." His eyes penetrate mine seriously for several moments while I sip my bourbon again, feeling deflated after my confession. "No getting around it?" Hopeful, he lifts an eyebrow.

"Unfortunately, no," I offer firmly. However, something about this man makes me want to pour caution down the sink like a tumbler of bad whiskey, breaking my ridiculous rule.

"Hmm." He nods his head slowly as if he's working out some masterful plan. "What if I told you that I'm a rebel, who always breaks the rules and that I'm willing to travel to wherever you're from?"

Feeling like he's reading my mind, I twist around, facing him directly, finding true determination blazing out of his silky, sunset colored eyes. He smiles a sexy lopsided grin that does something odd to my chest. Besides clenching tightly, it feels like a weight has dropped on me, applying a ton of pressure. It's strange really, because it isn't uncomfortable. It actually feels… nice. After an extended moment, realization sets in and I discover that it's his smile causing this never before experienced sensation.

Going against everything I've ever done with any man that I've ever met in a bar before, I reciprocate his expression with a hint of a smile before responding. "I would say you are my first official stalker."

"Really?" Amused, he narrows his eyes on me observantly. "A woman as intriguing and beautiful as you are doesn't have at least a dozen men chasing you?"

"Oh, I didn't say that," I tease. "I just don't feel freaked out by any of them."

"I freak you out?" He licks his lips slowly and I can't help but mimic the action.

Oh, shiny perfect lips. *Mm, I want to taste them.*

What the hell?

"Uh, no." I stutter, pulling my gaze back up to his eyes, currently locked on my glossy lips. Due to the intensity of his stare, my breath catches before I can answer. "You… don't freak me out," I pant.

This man is making me sound so dumb.

"What do I…?" Pausing with a hint of blush tinting his cheeks, he looks directly into my eyes and tilts toward me, making our proximity much more intimate than I'm comfortable with. Usually. "Forgive me for not introducing myself. I'm Ace." Oh man, he smells so nice and that name is just so sexy. It's perfect for him. Completely unnerved by everything about him, I blink several times, inhale deeply, and respond like my sweet grandmother taught me.

"Nice to meet you, Ace. I'm Cheney," I offer before tipping my drink for a sip.

"As in Dick?" He snorts, catching his question and I smirk while offering him a nod. Trying to recover from his outburst, Ace apologizes, "Sorry, Cheney, I didn't process beforehand how that was going to sound coming out of my mouth." He glances over his shoulder to hide his laughter. He totally made that playfully sexual and for some reason it didn't creep me out so I join him in laughing. *Damn this guy is adorable.*

"You're cute, Ace," I admit through the remainder of my giggles.

Running a hand through his rich blond locks, he turns back to me slowly all laughter gone. "I don't know anything about you, Cheney, but I'd be willing to bet that this is you," he waves a hand in front of me gesturing from my hair down to my feet, "only when you're with them." He thrusts his chin in the direction of my friends. "I'll bet under all this," he touches the back of his knuckles against the cap sleeves of my light blue cocktail dress before sliding them down slowly over my arm. A shudder runs along my blazing flesh caused by the warmth and tenderness of his caress. He notices and those damn dimples appear, tauntingly. "...is a woman who is more beautiful than designer clothes and flawless makeup."

Focusing on his words instead of the way his touch ignites my desires, I ask, "Are you insulting my friends?"

"I would never do that. Just one humble guy's honest opinion." His eyes smolder while he leans forward as if being pulled by some invisible force demanding our connection. "I just really want to get to know *that* Cheney," he claims, looking deeply into my eyes like he's searching for the real me behind them.

Suddenly unable to catch my breath, I pause to regroup after feeling an unfamiliar desire flare deep within my chest.

What the hell is happening to me?

I want Ace to know me. *But, that can't happen.* I'm only in Memphis until tomorrow. Although Ace definitely could satisfy my physical need for tonight it can't happen because I met him in a damn bar. Of all the places for a meet-cute with a guy who can hold my interest for more than two minutes, why did it have to happen here?

"Come on, Chaney, bend the rules just a tiny bit," he whispers into my ear, grazing his smooth face against my head, his breath brushing against my hair. Mustering all the control I have in my reserve bank, I close my eyes, swallow audibly, and breathe through the moment.

"I can give you tonight, but," I offer, lifting my eyes to meet his. "We can share general information about our lives. No details. And when the night is over, we leave it." Ace stares for a short moment before nodding, but I can see the disappointment blazing fiercely in his features.

"Tell me everything you can about Cheney," he demands, sweetly taking my hand into his, linking our fingers together and drawing his body closer. Feeling a striking sensation coursing through my body caused by this gorgeous man agreeing to play this my way, I uncharacteristically relax. Starting with random facts, we learn very little *real* stuff about each other over the next hour.

* * * * *

"Yes, I'll be fine," I tell my two friends who are abandoning me for a couple of guys trolling the bar. "Ace doesn't have the scary-thirst-for-blood look in his eyes." I wink and wave my hands in an attempt to shoo them off to enjoy their romp in the hay.

With true concern looking over at Ace, Penelope asks, "See you at the festival?"

Nodding to reassure her that I'm perfectly capable of taking care of myself, I smirk at Willa, wiggling her eyebrows appreciatively at me because of Mr. Perfect Lips. Oh, that girl thinks she knows something, but she will never wrench the admission out of me. "See ya tomorrow, Brookies."

Turning back to the bar after watching them walk out the door, I catch the bartender's attention. "Another Buffalo Trace."

"Have you tried the MaCallan?" Ace indicates toward his tumbler before taking a long pull from the dark liquor.

"No," I reply and he slides his glass over. My eyes latch onto the edge where his perfect lips were just moments ago and even though I want to cover my mouth over the spot, I don't. "Hmm," I moan smelling the heady scent, feeling the slight burn, tasting the fruitiness mixed with something exotic that I just can't put my finger on. I smack my lips absorbing the deliciousness while swirling my tongue inside my mouth trying to guess the extra little something that makes it so good.

Ace notices and offers, "It's chocolate."

"It's perfect," I correct, giving him a sideways smile before reaching out for the BT the bartender places in front of me.

"So, tell me more," he leads.

"I was just thinking that this isn't an easy game. I'm not sure what else there is to tell that won't give away too much."

After sharing a plethora of incidental information, we've discovered that in addition to our adoration of great bourbons, we have a lot in common. Just to name a few, music, OCD arranged closets, and being outdoors hints at what Penelope would consider kindred spirits. My friend believes in all that soul mate BS.

While thinking about how much I can share, I recline back into my seat, seeing his eyes sparkle with delight. He really wants to know me, but I continue hesitantly. "I adore moonlight, scary movies, college football, and without question my granny makes the best cornbread dressing in the free world. I am an only child and the first in my family to graduate college." He applauds and I bow playfully. "I may or may not have a weird obsession with Justin Timberlake. The beach is my serenity, but I adore the thrill of the city, especially when it's alive at night and..." I glance down at his hand resting on the edge of the bar just inches from my arm before looking back into his direct gaze. His closeness brings to life tiny goose bumps and I move my hand across my forearm to calm them. "This may sound weird, but I get turned on by large hands." Ace breaks away from his riveted staring, shifting his eyes down to his hand. From my peripheral, I can see him move it toward me, but he hesitates before glancing back at me with a sexy smolder in his russet-hued eyes.

"You seriously can't tell me those things and expect me to not want to date you, Cheney." Finally, his thumb moves, grazing against my arm and making my prickled skin feel scorched from this small movement. "Especially the part about JT." He smirks covering his other hand over his heart teasingly. I bite my lip, holding back my laughter at his roguish banter. "The guy is a god, making every woman weak in the knees leaving us mere mortals looking like pathetic second choices."

"I know, right?" He grunts. "Okay, Ace, your turn," I suggest reaching across his arm to steal another taste of his Scotch. His muscles bunch up from our contact and I think I hear him hiss softly. Pressing the rim against my bottom lip, I suck the delicious liquor through my closed teeth. My eyes drift shut and I moan enjoying the enchanting flavor.

"Stop," Ace growls softly, wrapping his wide hand around my wrist and taking his glass away from my mouth. I pout playfully and he mumbles under his breath, "I don't know how I'm going to get through this damn night." Ace sets his cup down and stares hard at me. I smile deeply and watch the corners of his lips curl upward.

There's that perfect smile.

"Ah, girl you're going to drive me straight into madness." He sighs. "More about Ace, huh?" I nod hungrily, really wanting to know more about him. *God, this damn game is turning into some freaky, forbidden shit.* Shifting his eyes toward the doorway, he hesitates briefly. "My parents are obsessed Kiss fans, which explains my name. I'm the youngest of four so I'm sure you can guess my brother's names." With a hint of a smile, he pierces me with a steely glare. "Understand this; I take *all* sports seriously, especially my guy's night beer pong game." I nod dramatically at his wit and he winks. "My serenity comes during the quiet minutes before dawn and I don't really have any weird obsessions, unless you count my recent need to know *everything* about the beauty I met tonight." I shake my head and he reiterates, "No details. I know."

"Right," I confirm.

In deep thought momentarily, Ace finally reveals what's on his mind. "Can I take you somewhere?"

I quirk an eyebrow up curiously. "Where?"

"I heard you convict your friends with jumping-ship from your dancing plans. Would you let me take you to a club?" Man, I would love to take him out on the dance floor. Risqué dancing is a guarantee with a slamming hottie like Ace. *But the rules*, my conscience reminds me. I sigh seeing the hope swirling in those sexy brown eyes and battle against my internal line-judge. *I'm bending the rules, not breaking them!*

"Why not?" I clutch my bag, point a finger against his chest and restate, "But this isn't a date." My demand is more for my pesky conscience than Ace.

"Of course not," he replies, smiling like he just hit the Powerball lottery.

Ace takes me to Rum Boogie Café and from the moment we enter I feel transported. There are over one hundred guitars decorating the walls from almost every legendary guitarist you can imagine. My mouth hangs open as we pass the priceless, autographed instruments just hanging there, suspended for all to fondle. I'm flabbergasted. They should be locked behind cases in a museum somewhere.

With his fingers laced through mine, Ace guides me toward the dance floor. The hard beats lead my body into a grooving, spinning, dance-machine. It's positively euphoric, but my true elation comes from the deep rich eyes roaming all over my gyrating body. Ace smiles through a few songs, but he's a terrible dancer so I give him a break and drag him off for a drink.

"Jameson," I order from the busty blonde working the counter.

"I'll have the same," Ace adds, passing her his credit card.

Sitting and watching the mass of bouncing bodies, we chat while sipping on several more drinks until the band plays one of my favorite songs. I close my eyes and sway to the seductive beats of Candlebox's *Far Behind*. Spotting my smile, Ace leans forward, his mouth a breath away from the tender spot just below my earlobe when he whispers, "Dance with me." I nod and accept his hand.

He spins me around, pushing us toward the couples swaying to the low, entrancing tempo. Stopping along the edge of the dance floor and with his chest pressing against my back, Ace drapes his arms over mine and presses his hands over the top of my thighs. His hips grinding deliciously into my backside and I press back against him impulsively. He feels so amazing, but I remind myself that no matter how he makes me feel, I refuse to go home with a man I met in a bar.

I've enjoyed every moment of this night since falling victim to Ace's hypnotic gaze, but whatever is happening between us can't be more than this night, a few ridiculous clues about our lives and some... *oh!* Ace's hands trail up my ribs, edging against the swell of my breast and... *Mmm,* now we're naughty dancing.

"God, you feel so good." He growls and I moan in agreement with breathless anticipation.

Lifting my arms up to wrap my hands around his neck, I allow my head to fall back against his chest. Ace's fingers dig into my waist painfully and I hear him groan while feeling the vibrations push through my veins like a sweet liqueur. He bumps harder against me before moving us into a deliberate rhythm that makes me hot all over. Ace drops his face on my exposed shoulder, his perfect lips grazing up to the crook of my neck.

"Cheney, you're captivating."

His cheek rests against my hair, his warm breath fluttering my eyelashes and warming my cheek. With this man worshipping me with his body and seducing me with his mildly controlled whispered desires a wanton pulse shoots straight to my core. Fortunately, the live music blares over my lustful moan saving me from total mortification.

"What are you doing to me, beautiful?"

My heart whirls end-over-end hearing the full-on passion in his desperate question. We're both so turned on right now and for a moment I'm completely caught up in the heat radiating between us. I face him and slide my hands down his chest, feeling his drawn muscles and erratically beating heart. His look is severe and needful, matching mine exactly. A vision of us kissing in this sea of swaying couples flitters through my mind, verifying that I want him like I've never wanted any man before.

Kiss me, my heart cries.

Standing on my tiptoes so Ace can hear me, I shout, "Can we go?" Without hesitation, he pays the bill and we leave. Stepping outside the cool air settles some of the excitement stirring around in my stomach. Once I glance up at Ace, staring hopefully down at me, I lose all possibility of being in control.

Run.

"Are you alright?" He moves close, sliding the back of his hand over my sweat-covered neck, pushing away damp hairs. A sweet caress typically meant to be an innocent gesture is anything but while he looks at me like I'm the only woman in the world.

"I'm just tired and ready to go to my hotel." Disappointment flourishing in his face and shockingly his reaction is relatively upsetting to me: he doesn't argue. Instead, he stretches out an arm, flagging down the cab approaching. He holds the door open, allowing me inside, and he just stands there leaning his head in, looking miserable.

"Thank you for tonight, Ace. It was great getting to know you."

Before shutting the door, he drops down onto one knee, looks me in the eye and tilts his head slightly as if in deep thought before responding. "If I had met you on the sidewalk in front of the bar, would you have gone on a date with me?"

Reaching up I stroke the side of his face feeling my heart beating wildly in my chest. There is no doubt I would have dated Ace. From the frenzied butterfly effect my stomach is experiencing while looking at this incredible man, I know for certain I would have done so much more with him. I probably could have fallen hard for Ace, but it wasn't meant to be.

"Yes," I whisper.

* * * * *

With a resigned pout, Ace lowers his gaze to the ground. "Could I at least get your number so I can text you sometime?"

"There's nothing in the rulebook against it." Surprised by my answer, he looks up with a sexy as hell smile before reaching for his phone. He hands it over to me and I store my number quickly, but hold it away and remind him, "Just remember, no details." Chuckling he nods his head and I pass his cell back. His fingers sweep over mine and a buzzing energy trickles up my arm from the contact. Afraid I'll encourage him inadvertently, I hold my breath, suppressing a moan from the mind-blowing sensation.

After dropping his phone into his back pocket he leans forward and grasps the sides of my face with both hands. He strokes his thumbs tenderly across my cheeks while moving his eyes slowly, looking back and forth from each of my eyes as if he's waiting for my permission to do the one thing I don't think I can deny him. He notices when my lips part slightly a second before he crushes his mouth against mine. Ace moves slowly, but roughly in this enthralling kiss, controlling the mesmerizing tempo and I literally feel my heart skid nearly to a halt. The force of this demanding kiss sears into my memory like a black ink tattoo of *mine* scrawled onto my soul.

This feels so right.

He pulls away from my mouth, pressing his forehead against mine and sighs. Ace is teetering dangerously close to an edge that could cause me harm if he pushes the boundaries I've given him.

With his eyes pinching shut Ace breathlessly whispers, "Cheney, I don't want to let you go." Understanding exactly how he feels I nod agreeable, but wrap my hands over his and pull them away from my face, letting him know that we must stop. I can't explain it and I damn sure don't want it, but this man somehow now holds a piece of my essence. Without a doubt, I have to get away from him now before I do something stupid. I've already gone too far past my limits with him than I have any man before him. Allowing this game to continue would be unfair to both of us.

"I'm sorry, I can't. Good night, Ace." I manage to hold my resolve.

Unwillingly, he stands up, steps away, and closes my door. He watches as I speak with the driver before he turns, walking away. A beautiful woman steps out of the bar stumbling into him. With her hands strategically placed on his chest she smiles up at him and drags her hands down his stomach. He helps right her from the tilted position and then shakes his head, moving away, leaving her standing and drooling after him.

My cab driver complains about the heavy traffic, but finally merges onto the busy lane. Our pace drags, but my eyes stay transfixed on the beautiful man walking ahead down the sidewalk. Suddenly it hits me that he's walking the same direction my cab is going. I tap on the driver's window and after hearing him grumble a few moments I convince him to pull up alongside Ace.

"Ace," I shout and smile watching his foot stop midair before he plants it and turns toward me.

"Cheney?"

"It looks like you're going my way." Pointing ahead, I smile. "Want to share?"

"Are you sure?" He steps up to my window, ignoring the blaring honks from the impatient drivers behind us. "What about your rules?"

"It's not like I can figure out much about you just by knowing which hotel you're staying in," I offer sweetly before pushing open the door and sliding across the seat. "Just remember, this isn't a date."

Smiling proudly, Ace slides in without hesitation. The cab driver glares at us through the rearview mirror and I quickly avert my gaze to the gorgeous man sitting next to me. His perfect locks are a disastrous, yet beautiful, mess and his eyes sparkle with a renewed joy that wasn't there when I said goodbye to him. He leans forward and speaks to the driver, but I'm completely enraptured with his seductive scent; a combination of a woodsy bourbon and sweaty man that I don't think I've ever been fond of before this moment. My stomach knots. I'm feeling more for him than I should.

Playing with fire!

Leaning back against the seat, Ace faces me and those dimples are more pronounced than ever before. "I have to say I'm completely and pleasantly surprised." He shakes his head before asking, "Did I look that pitiful?"

"What? No, of course not. I just noticed you walking the same direction. It would be rude not to ask you to share with me."

"Oh," he sighs. "I was hoping that you just didn't want our time together to end." Embarrassed, he shrugs and I notice him blushing before he glances away. It's his most adorable gesture yet. Ace is right. I don't want our time to end either.

Fire!

Taking advantage of our last few moments together, he grips my hand and laces our fingers, pulling them up to his warm lips. He kisses the back of my hand tenderly, melting my insides into molten lava. I swallow audibly and his eyes travel from our connection, up my arm, straight to my face. He holds my gaze and a million things pass between us. It feels like a thread in time has knotted for us specifically, like something magical and unexplainable is happening between us. *This totally sucks.* Why couldn't I have met Ace anywhere except that damn bar? He pulls his lips away from my hand, releasing the hold he has on it, and wraps his arm over my shoulder. Tugging me gently, he snuggles me into a side hug and nestles his face into my hair.

"I need to hold you for as long as I can, beautiful." He inhales deeply and I shiver. At a loss for words, I offer a weak nod.

My body heats instantly from our contact and my heart seriously can't find a steady rhythm. I don't think I've had one since I first looked into his enthralling eyes. Before long, the cab veers right and then stops in front of his hotel. He pulls away enough to tip my chin upward so that he can look deeply into my eyes before placing a sweet kiss against my cheek.

"I don't believe in fate, but I have a feeling we'll meet again." He pulls away, reaching for the door handle before adding, "And when we do, you're tossing out that damn rulebook." He leaps from the cab, turns, and offers me a wink before shutting the door. I smile and nod, but he doesn't see it.

"Miss?" The cab driver shifts around in his seat facing me. "What are you doing?"

"Huh?" I stare at him confused by his question. "What do you mean?"

"You have to follow him." His tone is forceful and there's a challenging glint in his eyes.

Shaking my head slowly, I lower my eyes in defeat and whisper, "I can't." I don't offer an explanation; he wouldn't understand. Even the Brookies don't get it. But if they had been hurt by a two-timing-piece-of-trash-bar-troll like my father, they would all back off me and my one simple rule.

"You must," he demands in a harsher tone than before. I snap my attention back to him and see him pointing. "This is your stop too."

Jerking my head to the side, I look out the window and realize that he's right. We are parked in front of the Madison Hotel and Ace just crossed the threshold of the front door. I scoot out of the cab after tipping the driver and hustle to catch him.

"Ace," I call in breathless anticipation after pushing through a couple exiting the hotel. Standing in front of the wall of elevators, he presents me with another brilliant smile and damn if those yummy dimples don't do something to my insides. It feels like someone struck a hornet's nest in my belly and the queen bee has issued a full alert flyby commanding them to remain on standby until she orders the attack. "It looks like you're going my way, again." I smile, not nearly as bright as him, but only because I'm biting the corner of my lip trying to keep from looking like a complete idiot. "Want to share?"

"You're in this hotel?" He turns his entire body toward me. "I don't believe it."

"Yeah." I nod as the doors open. Walking into the elevator, I push the floor number for my room and press my back against the far wall. His strides are long and quick when he strolls in and he doesn't bother glancing at the number panel. A moment before the doors close, Ace's hands fist tightly in my hair and his lips press sweetly against mine.

"Beautiful." Ace's voice is raspy and that one word is barely a hum against my mouth. Pinching deliciously against my bottom lip, he sucks it in between his and I open to him willingly. He tenderly glides his tongue in and with a happy sigh I give into his desires. *Our desires.* Dropping his hands from my hair, he wraps both around me, pressing his fingers against my sides like a vice holding me against him. His kiss entrances me the entire trip up to my floor. When the chime indicating we've reached my destination sounds, Ace pulls away only to lace my fingers through his. Quickly he checks the floor number before drawing me out of the elevator.

"What's your room number?" He keeps his gaze fixed tightly on me.

Even though he's left me breathless from that hot-ass kiss, I don't even hesitate. "404."

"That way," he points right and we walk toward the far end of the hallway.

Stopping in front of my door, he kisses me tenderly, both hands framing my face. He drops his forehead to mine and sighs. In his eyes I can see that he wants to say more, but he doesn't. Instead, he steps back a few feet and watches me slide my key into the lock.

"Cheney," he calls out before I slip into my room.

Glancing over my shoulder, I spot him holding up his key and watch as he inserts it into the door across the hallway from mine. Without much effort the door opens and he steps inside with a grin on his face so wide you'd think he found the pot of gold at the end of a rainbow. "Coincidentally, I'm just across the hall if you decide that you want to..." He points inside his room. I smile, but realize taking him up on his offer would lead to things that I would only regret. "I wasn't kidding when I said I don't want this night to end." Before slipping into my room, I offer a soft goodnight, close the door, and shut Ace out of my life for good.

* * * * *

At two a.m. I wake up from a restless sleep. The air conditioning is blasting from the vents, but I'm doused in sweat and feel like I've been swimming. My mind is cloudy from the crazy dreams that I've had of Ace. Of all the things I could dream about.

My father is walking me down the center isle of the MGM Grand Garden Arena toward a man with the most breathtaking smile plastered on his dimpled face. Ace spots me inching toward him hesitantly and winks. He knows my insecurities. He knows everything about me and yet for some unexplainable reason he still loves me.

Just a few feet away from reaching the man of my dreams, my father leans over and whispers, "I'm so proud of you Cheney-doll. A bar troll is the best a daughter of a bar troll can do."

Hearing his words, my feet falter before stumbling backward one step at a time. My eyes drift from my father's satisfied snarl to the panic-stricken look on my lover's face.

"No," Ace pleads from atop the stage when he recognizes my anxiety forging my escape plan. Unable to breathe, I continue withdrawing until the max-capacity crowd eclipses his view of me.

"No," Ace yells.

I turn and run.

Climbing out of the bed, I flip on the light and stagger into the large en suite bathroom. I gulp down an entire glass of water and force down a couple of ibuprofen.

"It's just a stupid dream, brought on by too much alcohol and punishment for breaking my freaking rule," I explain to the woman in the mirror staring accusingly. If I didn't know better, I would swear that she just rolled her eyes at me. Turning away, I flip off the light and stand in the middle of the room, looking intently at the door that leads to my fantasy man across the hallway.

"Ace can't have what I don't give him, right?"

I pace over to the door, squinting through the peephole seeing that the floor's empty. I press my head against the door and release a heavy breath. Uncertain as to why I do it, I jerk open the door and step out. There, just eight feet away from me stands my dream's leading man.

No emotions display on his perfect lips, but his eyes search mine for any sign of life and I blink rapidly and suck in a heavy breath before responding.

"Hi." Oh good lord, another epic response. I'm sure he's dazzled by my mastery of brilliant repartee.

"Can't sleep?"

"No, I slept," I admit, nervously clutching the door for support.

"Bad dream?"

How could he possibly know that?

"Umm…" I run a hand through my ponytail and glance down at my tank top and shorts, hoping that I don't look that disheveled.

"Uh no, I didn't mean it like that. You don't look too bad." His attempt at recovering from implying that I look like shit tumbles out of his mouth like a three year old doing flips across the floor. "I mean, you don't look like you've been thrashing around in the bed." His eyes darken acknowledging visions of me in bed and his cheeks redden. Shaking his head with a smile twisting on his perfect lips, Ace mumbles, "You look beautiful."

"Okay," is all I can say.

"Would you like to come over?" He gestures toward his room and suddenly all I can think about is us thrashing around in his bed. When I don't respond he adds, "Just to talk. It's still night and you promised that I could have this one."

Glancing over his shoulder, I spot the perfectly made bed and wonder why he hasn't slept. "Yeah, I would like that. Let me grab my key." I rush into the bathroom, brushing my teeth at rapid speed before snagging my room key and returning to the hallway. Ace is standing in the same spot I left him moments ago with his hip leaning into his open door. I cross the hall walking into his hotel room and stop right in front. "Just remember…"

Cutting me off, he finishes my sentence. "This isn't a date." His gorgeous lips are marked with a proud smile, displaying radiant, white teeth. Unconsciously, I return the goofy look and then nod.

Entering the large space, I notice the differences in our rooms are only the slightly darker accents. I spot a chair positioned in the corner that is furthest from the bed and climb into it, tucking my feet under my behind. The click of the door closing and slide of the lock engaging draws my eyes back to Ace. Strolling over to the other chair next to the small table separating him from me, he sits with his legs stretched out and his hands draping over the armrests. He's wearing low hanging black sweat pants and a baby blue American Eagle tee shirt. The contrasting shades bring out his blond hair and dark tan perfectly.

"Want to talk about your dream?" Twisting his head against the top of the chair, he faces me, looking casual and sexy as hell.

"Nothing to tell really," I lie. My eyes move toward the bed. "Why are you still awake?"

"Usually I'm a night owl, but after the drinks and dancing I'll admit that I was tired when we returned to the hotel, but…"

I straighten out my legs and stand. "I'm so sorry. I'll go so you can get some sleep."

"Oh, no you don't." He blocks me from leaving, holding his hands up in front of me without touching. "You're not keeping me awake. I had some work emails that couldn't wait. Besides, I was hoping a special visitor would drop by and I didn't want to miss her. I got tired of waiting so I was coming for you. And that's when you found me at the door." He smiles while gesturing toward my vacated seat. "Please stay."

"As long as you promise that I'm not keeping you from your beauty sleep," I joke.

"Do I look like I need that much rest?"

"Yeah, you're ugly as sin," I lie again and he roars a hearty laugh.

"I should have used that line on you at the doorway earlier instead of stumbling through that ridiculous shit I spouted." This time it's me who laughs. Actually, I snort which causes him to laugh and before I know it we're both nearly doubled over gasping for air.

"I appreciate honesty in all things, but if you ever tell me I look like shit I might hire an assassin to take you out."

"Wow, with the threats." Seeing that he really is okay with me staying, I drop back down, keeping my feet on the floor this time. He sits too.

"Thank you for a really nice night. I know it wasn't exactly something out of a romance novel. And I'm sure that women usually just throw themselves at your feet, understandably so." Smiling he shrugs like he's heard this line before. "But you've totally respected my need to keep things relaxed and ambiguous. As irregular as I am, I know it may seem ridiculous to play along, but I totally appreciate it." I pause before adding, "I'm sorry."

"Why are you apologizing?"

"Well, I…" I'm just as confused by my apology and I'm not really sure how to explain.

"Cheney," Ace spots my confusion. "I'll admit that when I approached you tonight I was attracted to you. I would be lying if I said that I wasn't envisioning you in this very room doing more than talking." *Bar troll*, my conscience screams within my head. "But you shot me down. Sure there are women who come on as strong as you suggested, but none of that interests me. You are unique, strong-willed, intelligent and cautious…"

"You mean to say that you get turned on by the oddly stubborn and smart ass women with hang-ups?"

"That right there is exactly what I'm talking about." He chuckles. "You don't see things the way other people do and I like that about you."

"Ace..."

He cuts me off again. "Let me finish." I shut my mouth and nod. "Tonight could have gone the way I hoped it would and then tomorrow we would go our separate ways forgetting each other's names, but definitely remembering the night." He waggles his eyebrows and I roll my eyes. "However, now that I've spent a little time getting to know you I think the way you've dictated this relationship is much more preferable and better given our situation. I want to be your friend, Cheney. I said it before and I'll repeat myself." He leans forward, pressing his elbows into the top of his thighs and clasping his hands in front of him. "I want to know everything you want to tell me about yourself and, one day, when you're ready to give more than just the surface info, I want that too." He says the words coolly, but his meaning hints to much more.

There's no denying that I like Ace. If he's willing to leave the pace of this relationship in my hands then I know we won't exceed what I'm capable of giving.

No more kissing is paramount.

"Okay, friends it is." I smile. "Thank you."

"Now, let's go to bed." Standing up quickly, he takes my hand, guiding me toward his bed.

"What do you think you're doing?" I tug away from his hold.

"Taking you to bed," he repeats and I deadpan a look at him implying that he's lost his ever-loving mind. "Friends sleep together, Cheney. I know you've had sleepovers with your girls."

Placing both hands on my hips, I counter, "Yeah, but that's different."

"No, not really, not in *my* rulebook. Seeing that you're never going to throw yourself at my feet and I'm serious about being your friend, you'll sleep safely on your side because I'll stay on mine."

"You think this little game is clever don't you? Nice plan. You get me into your room, tell me that you want to be friends, and then you casually suggest that we sleep together. Clearly, you think I'm dumb enough to believe that this will remain platonic." I cross my arms defensively.

"Not sure *what* you mean by that, but the only thing I'm planning in bed with you is talking. Oh, and sleeping... like closing our eyes and heavy snoring kind of sleeping." One of my eyebrows arches upward. "I'm totally serious. So don't look at me like that."

"Mm, hmm," I scoff suspiciously, but he genuinely seems insulted that I don't believe him. Pointing at him, I issue a warning. "No hanky-panky. You blow it and there won't be one good thing to remember about tonight. And I promise, you *won't* forget my name."

"Get your sweet ass in my bed, woman!" He swats my tush playfully when I crawl onto my knees.

"Ouch, you're starting off on the wrong foot already." I rub the tender spot mimicking pain, but really... I liked it. A lot. Ace's eyes zero onto my hand covering my backside and it's as if shutters drop, darkening them once again. He's turned on by the action too. Getting into his bed may not be a good idea after all. Digging my feet under the covers, I scoot to the far edge giving him more than half of the bed. After watching me settle in, he lies down onto his side facing me and props his head on his hand.

"I'm a Cancer, born in July. Got caught spray painting the train overpass on Main Street when I was sixteen. First girl I ever kissed was Lorelei Jenson—we were eight. It was compensation for sharing my oatmeal crème pie with her. My first car was a faded yellow Datsun with hunter green interior. The thing was older than me by fifteen years. I sent it off to its final resting place at the scrap yard two summers ago." He sighs. "May it rest in peace."

"Wait," I interrupt turning onto my side, sliding my hands under my pillow. "What did you draw on the bridge?"

"Oh no, that one you can't have." Smirking at my disappointment, he shakes his head, places his hand against his mouth and whispers, "It could provide some insider information that will lead to you figuring out who I am and you're just not ready for that yet."

"Ass." Huffing, I roll onto my back.

"As I was saying…" He pauses. "I'm not from Tennessee, Cheney."

Covering my arms over my eyes, I sigh and then whine, "Ace, no details."

"Huh, you think with me admitting that tidbit you'll be able to guess which one of the other forty-nine states I'm from." He chuckles. "You're smart, but it's highly unlikely unless I give you forty-nine guesses."

"Oh god, you're hilarious."

"Oh, that's another thing. I did open-mic night at a comedy club in college and won."

"No kidding? I hope you kept your day job."

"Har har, you're a funny girl." Turning to glance at him, I see his wicked smile and get goose bumps. "Sooooo, what's your sign?" I laugh, I can't help it. His whole charade really is cute.

"Aquarius." Knowing that he wants more random details, I give in. "I played every sport in high school and was in every club possible. My parents divorced when I was a teenager and I still feel split down the middle because of it. No," I pause. "That's not true, I'd say I'm more eighty-five slash fifteen."

"Yikes." Ace grimaces.

My breathing becomes ragged while my heart thunders viciously teetering on a topic that threatens to weaken my stronghold. "Fifteen is too generous really."

"Mom or dad?"

I refuse to show Ace any part of this madness. "Some other time." I fake a yawn, not wanting to let our simple conversation veer anywhere near my real issues. Honestly, I can't believe I gave him this much. My sentinel is apparently taking a siesta like I should be doing.

"Sure, Cheney," he whispers, rising up so that he's hovering over me.

Ace smiles sweetly and I feel my heart do a back flip inside my ribcage for a reason beyond my private terror. As if he senses my inner turmoil, his hand lifts hesitantly awaiting my approval. Accepting that I really do want this, I offer one miniscule nod. He touches his fingertips to my jaw line, whispering tender strokes across my sensitive skin. My eyes drift shut and for a brief instant I sink into the bliss of being with Ace. Drifting skillfully along, he inches over all of my face before dipping down to the center of my throat. His sweet caress makes my eyes flutter and I struggle with keeping them open. Reaching the dip at the base of neck, Ace's hand trembles and he places a warm palm flat against my chest. Through my broken stare, I've watched Ace's eyes travel the path of his fingers. Now he stares at his stilled hand for several long moments. Pulling himself out of a torturous self-induced spell, he blinks, breaking the fog an instant before shifting his eyes upward. Lingering briefly on my lips, he settles his gaze back on my eyes. The distinct flash of passion blazes deeply in his chocolate shaded irises, revealing so much more than words ever could while liquefying all of my unwillingness to deny him anything. His eyelids pinch together tightly a moment before he presses his lips to my forehead.

"Sleep, sweetheart." Ace rolls away from me and I instantly miss his touch. His hand sneaks back toward me, I offer mine and we link fingers.

I am so comfortable being in Ace's bed, letting him know more about me and enjoying his caressing enough that I drift into a pleasant slumber. The most shocking aspect out of all of this is the fact that I've never slept overnight in a man's bed. Usually, I turn into the dude, dashing away after a night of physical exertion. After the way this enchanting night has been, I wonder if this is the last time I'll sleep with Ace.

* * * * *

A shrilling racket slices through the darkness twice before someone grumbles an unpleasant greeting. A moment later I feel a shift on the bed. Scattered memories of the night before floods my mind the exact moment I hear a sharp expletive.

"Damn," a gruff tenor repeats after a pause. "Sure, I can be there immediately, Izzy… Agreed, I want it done fast, like last week… If it's postponed again, I won't be held responsible for the ass-whooping... *chuckle*... You know me too well, babe... Get the old man to agree to a date and I'll fly home for the ceremony." His voice softens. "Yeah, me too. I'll see you soon."

Izzy?

Ceremony?

Me too? Like the incognito phone call *I love you too*, me too?

Son of a bitch!

Did I actually almost fall for Ace's game without asking if he's single? Once again the darkness veils my pathetic heart. *BAR TROLL!*

Hearing him slip into the bathroom and start the shower, I kick off the comforter and leap out of his bed. I snag the key to my room and bolt across the hallway. Lethargically forcing my steps into the bathroom after calming my heart, I stare at my reflection and notice the harsh scowl marks between my eyebrows. Running both hands over my face, I drop my ass onto the edge of the tub and prop my elbows on my knees.

I shake my head through my self-reprimanding. "You are so stupid. One simple freaking rule? You chose to risk it all on a guy who is no different from every other bar troll." Dropping my hands, I stand and glare back at the reflective twit. "You are so stupid!" I repeat pointing an accusing finger. "Thank God he doesn't know any real thing about me."

Time to get my shit together and disappear!

At breakfast, Willa calls my cell telling me that she and Penelope are out shopping. No surprise there. They shop for sport and thankfully know that I am not a team player in that game. Tucking my room key, along with my cash and identification, into my laptop case, I slip out of my room in stealth mode. I chance a quick glance at Ace's door before rushing down the corridor. Luckily, I don't find him standing there, all sexy and shit, like he was the last time I exited my room. I don't realize that I'm holding my breath until the front doorman wishes me a good morning.

Following my phones GPS, I locate a tiny hole in the wall coffee shop a couple of miles away, on the route toward the Cooper Young festival. Pushing open the door, I bask in the warm essence of dark roast and sweet pastries, easing away my sullen mood. After picking up my cappuccino, I settle into a short leather chair near the front window. The small business is a hub of activity, effectively distracting me from thoughts and more regrets over last night's fiasco. I plug in my ear buds, open my email and read through several job offers.

Currently, Duke University Medical sits at the top of my wish list of facilities that I'm considering. It tips the scale, making it the best of the best in neurology. Graduating at the top of my nursing class gifts me the option to choose according to my desires. The only downfall is the distance away from home. But turning down this offer would literally make me look like a fool. I just need to face the facts that I may be calling North Carolina home sweet home very soon. Now, if I can convince my mom to relocate, we can put Alabama behind us. There's nothing wrong with moving, per se, but I feel like something is pushing me out or pulling me away. I just feel like something has to give.

A beep interrupts one of my many road trip playlists indicating I have a new text message. Glancing at the clock I sigh noticing I've spent three hours reviewing the proposals. Stowing my laptop, I pluck my cell phone off the table and my fingers still when I read the text.

ACE: *U left w/out a goodbye.*

Dammit, I completely forgot that I gave the bastard my phone number. If I don't respond maybe he'll believe that I gave him a fake number and eventually get the hint. *Not likely!*

Hopefully he'll remember that I'll only be here another nineteen hours and will stop feeling like he needs to call for the sake of manners. Oh, who the hell am I kidding? A tiny part of me misses him.

I am such an idiot.

Trekking down Nelson Ave, I mesh with the crowd, zigzagging my way toward the main stage. I spot Willa and Penelope lounging with several guys on blankets stretched out in the grass near the band.

"What's up chica?" Willa scoots over to make room for me to sit.

"How long have you been here?" I ask waving at her companions.

"About fifteen minutes." She points to two guys. "Jasper and Rob."

"Hi, I'm Cheney."

They leer at me and the one named Jasper offers a, "Sup?" that I ignore along with Rob's lustful stare.

"Triplets?" Rob growls deep and low.

Penelope replies with a huff, "No."

"We found the cutest store today." Willa begins her instant replay of their day. She likes to hear herself talk so much that it's not even important if I'm paying attention so I zone out immediately.

"Dig in, Chey," Penelope orders pointing toward her cooler filled with Pabst Blue Ribbon.

The sunset brings cooler temps. Even with the heavy amount of liquor coursing through me, I begin to shiver. Willa invites a few more guys to join our little picnic, increasing the numbers up to eight in our party. A guy name Spencer begins chatting me up and with the beer's assistance we hit it off easily. Remembering how comfortable I was last night with Ace, I begin comparing Spencer to him. The tick marks are stacking up against poor old Spencer. It's unfair to this sweet guy... and me.

Damn, why did he have to turn out to be a two-timer?

Disappointed or not with Ace's lying, I can't help scanning the festival for any signs of him. I finally spot him near the back of the stage speaking with a guy in the band performing next.

God, he looks good. Better than last night, if that's possible.

The moment his conversation ends, he whirls around and begins walking toward me. My heart zips up and fist in my throat with excitement. He's speaking rapidly on his phone and is distracted by whoever's on the other end. Fortunately for me, his in-depth conversation prevents him from noticing as he passes me. Some tiny part of me feels let down that he didn't even look my way.

What the hell, Cheney? I mentally slap the shit out of myself before turning back to Spencer.

"So yeah, Willa said you're staying at the Madison. Cool place." I nod and shiver. "Hey, it's cold as hell out here. Want to catch a taxi and hit up Hard Rock?"

Spencer is a handsome man, maybe a year older than me, with medium brown hair, cropped closer than I prefer. His body is trim under his fitted long sleeve tee and ass-molded denim jeans, giving him a classic frat boy look. He could be a great diversion that will get my mind off another guy I met in the city just twenty-four hours ago.

"Hard Rock is perfect," I confirm.

We clear our trash and tuck the blanket into Penelope's bag. I relay our plans to the girls, who decide to hang out here and we push our way through the drunken crowd. Spencer laces his fingers through mine. I blame my intoxicated state for numbing the energized sensations that I should be feeling from our contact. I may be drunk, but I know exactly why I don't feel anything for Spencer.

My heart is screaming at me, *he's not Ace.*

Clearly my heart can't handle her liquor.

After another mental slapping, I resolve to enjoy every moment with Spencer blocking out all thoughts of the unavailable jerk. Once inside the packed club he locates some friends and we join them at their table. A local band plays several upbeat cover songs before a slow song begins billowing through the small space like a restless wind through the sails of a monsoon-targeted ship. The beats surge and roll through the tight area and a desire unlike anything I've felt before urges me toward the dance floor. I grab Spencer, but he shakes his head. Undiscouraged by his lack of enthusiasm, I seek out an empty spot among the swaying couples without a second thought. Tilting my head back, I feel the music. With my hips shifting side to side, my arms drape loosely behind me and I become one with the seductive rhythms of Daughtry's *Waiting For Superman.*

Warm hands brush over the swell of my hips and an intense heat presses against my back. A distinct and familiar scent washes over me, compelling me to remain like this for as long as possible. Through the end of the song he holds me possessively. The fingers on one hand splays wide across my lower belly, the other digs deliciously into my hip while his face nuzzles against the hair behind my ear. I don't fight it. For a fleeting moment, I pretend he's mine and melt into Ace. The final notes of the song hangs in the air as if time stops just for us. Slowly, he turns me around to face him, and every bit of the conviction I had to hate him combusts due to the concentrated desire in his eyes.

"Missed you, beautiful." Ace presses his forehead against mine.

Missed you.

Feeling my inner-rebel consuming my struggle, I swallow down the bitter cough syrup that will surely sicken rather than restore me because at this moment I want this bar troll more than I need my own fucking sanity.

"Take me out of here," I plead staring into his needful chocolate eyes. Ace doesn't wait for further prompting before whisking me off to the Madison.

Back inside Ace's hotel room, he guides me toward the same bed I fled from twelve hours earlier. His eyes scan over every inch of my face, searching for any sign of resistance. Slow moving fingertips touch the center of my forehead, gliding over my temple and then edging down my jaw line before stopping on my bottom lip. Ace's eyes pierce mine and our silent exchange confirms mutual desire. But he waits. Pushing my lips out, I kiss the rough pads softly acknowledging his soundless request. One finger tugs lightly, parting my mouth before he pulls a kiss with his perfect lips making me whimper. A satisfied moan rumbles deep down within his throat.

"Stay with me tonight, Cheney?" Ace holds me in an intoxicating embrace, studying me again.

Can I?

Is he with someone?

No details!

My self-governing battle halts in utter defeat like the way the south fell to the north in the American civil war. For the first time in my adult life, the defensive lines keeping me from becoming the type of woman I despise fades away and I surrender. Common sense tells me this status is irreversible.

"Yes, Ace," I whisper pulling his lips to mine.

His mouth, hands, and body dominates all of me and I descend into his temporary bliss. "Ah god, Cheney," Ace moans, kissing the curve of my neck. "I wish you were mine."

One night.
No details.
I'm already *his*.

No Details

Marie Wathen

Author Dedication

This story is dedicated to all the amazing bloggers who have supported my writing during this amazing journey. The Indie writer world is chaotic at best, but with your friendship, I find peace, happiness and inspiration. You all rock my damn world everyday! Thank you to all My Sweets!!!!

About Marie

Marie Wathen, author of the Amazon Best Selling novel *Be All*, book one in the *All* series, is a writer, wife, mother of two and Lola to her grandchildren by day. By night, she is a law enforcement dispatcher. Storytelling all of her life, Marie has made her family and friends laugh with crazy, vivid details and clever sense of humor. In 2012, Marie decided to share some of her stories with the world. Including the *All* series, Marie is currently collaborating with a friend on a Paranormal Romance and has several other unnamed projects in the works.

Follow Marie

Facebook: http://www.facebook.com/MarieWathenAuthor

Twitter: http://www.twitter.com/MarieWathen

Read More from Marie

All This Time: http://amzn.to/1evYMke

Surrender

Sarah M. Cradit

Author Note: This story is an expanded version of a flashback excerpt from the novel, *The Storm and the Darkness*, Book 1 in the Southern Fiction Paranormal series, *The House of Crimson and Clover*.

Chapter One: Anasofiya

Anasofiya Deschanel sat in the parterre garden of *Ophélie*, pretending to read. Back in the garçonierre, Oz and Nicolas were still sleeping, and likely would be until noon.

Although she enjoyed their company more than almost anyone else, sometimes Ana needed the comfort of solitude, more than the comfort of others.

The Scarlet Letter had been assigned by their Honors English teacher, Mr. Nelson. He requested an essay on the town's treatment of Hester Prynn. Ana could have completed this assignment in her sleep; she'd read the book a half dozen times long before it was ever assigned. But her mind was restless, as usual, and she couldn't stop it from winding a direction of its own choosing.

Her thoughts were currently floating around what happened with Clancy Sullivan. He was a senior, and a cousin of Oz's. Clancy, with seemingly endless patience, had tirelessly vied for her attention the last year. Where most boys eventually gave up, realizing Ana was not girlfriend material (or at least not like the other girls her age were), Clancy held strong in his pursuit.

It would have been simpler had he been like some of the other, crude boys who normally chased after her. But Clancy's kindness always threatened to penetrate her well-armored heart. When he smiled at her, his whole face lit up, from his perpetually flushed cheeks, to his inquisitive blue eyes. His requests came from a place of sincerity, and left her feeling confused rather than exasperated.

She knew she could do much worse, but that wasn't the point.

Why had she let him walk her home yesterday? Maybe it was the way he always smiled at her, whether his friends were around or not. Or perhaps she was simply tired of always saying no. Secretly, she sometimes wished she *could* return his affections.

"See, this is nice," Clancy had observed as they meandered through the Lower Garden District, down Prytania. *Eight blocks. That's all.*

Ana had merely smiled, lacking any engaging contribution to the small talk, something she'd never particularly enjoyed or excelled at. But then he'd laced his slightly damp hand tentatively through hers, and suddenly eight blocks seemed like eighty. Her toes curled in her shoes as they continued their walking, an involuntary mannerism; one of many Ana had developed to control anxiety.

"Have you started Nelson's assignment yet?" he queried, swinging their hands gently as they walked. The warmth of his large, soft hands distracted her in a way she didn't understand.

"Not really," Ana replied, not adding the assignment wasn't even a challenge for her. Immodesty was not only unbecoming, but it left you vulnerable to scrutiny.

"We could study, together," Clancy shyly suggested, his hopeful smile pleading from the periphery of her gaze. He really was handsome; truly was kind.

"I'm working with Oz on it already," she lied, quickly.

"Oh." His face fell. "My cousin is a lucky guy. He gets to see you all the time."

Yes, Ana thought. *Though hanging out and doing nothing is hardly anything to be jealous of.*

When Clancy finally deposited her on the porch of her father's Greek Revival on Second, she muttered an awkward, but still gracious, goodbye, hoping to disappear behind the oaken door before things could get any more uncomfortable. But then she'd dropped that book bag of hers in a completely ungraceful trip up the top stair. Before she'd gained her composure, Clancy was kneeling across from her, sliding books back in the bag, before tucking her hair behind her ears. When she looked up to thank him, he pressed his lips to hers in a hasty, impulsive kiss. His mouth was warm, soft, and unpredictably inviting. Ana surprised herself by not only letting him do it, but by lacing one hand over his shoulder, indicating she didn't mind if the contact lasted.

Ana was forced to admit, it wasn't altogether unpleasant. She would always remember the moment she broke away, his periwinkle eyes sparkling at her, his smile, as always, genuine. Ana's father once told her you could only really trust a man if he displayed the same emotions when no one was looking.

He really does like me.

She watched Clancy walk away, down the crumbling sidewalk. Once he disappeared from sight, she let out a shy, nervous giggle, pressing her hand to lips that, only moments ago, had been joined to his. Then she sighed, a long exhale which caused her shoulders to sag, as the weight of it hit her.

Anasofiya, at sixteen, had experienced her first kiss. But it was with the wrong boy. The wrong Sullivan.

Inside *Ophélie*, the *right* Sullivan slept the deep sleep of a teenage boy. She would never risk sharing with him the feelings recently growing within her.

Friendships were safe. They were predictable, and reliable. You could count on them. They were persistent, and reassuring.

Relationships were not.

Ana had known Oz Sullivan since she was a very young girl. The connection existed initially through her cousin Nicolas, Oz's best friend, but the Sullivans were always a welcome addition to any Deschanel table.

Ana was not one to take inventory on the relationships in her life, so she had never made an official assessment of Oz growing up. She knew he was one of the 'good guys' in a time when it seemed like goodness was in short supply. Even her cousin Nicolas, whom she loved beyond measure, was not one of the good guys, although she knew he was not really a bad guy either.

Dating Oz had never occurred to Ana as they grew up, despite how very much alike they were. Neither fit into the greater world especially well. Both preferred the comfort of a book to people, because books provided an innocuous protective blanket, buffering them from the reality of knowing the world might never understand them. Ana felt safe with Oz, in a way she only would have realized if the constancy of his presence were removed entirely. Oz understood her, and more broadly, he accepted the unusual abilities, which were scattered about the Deschanel bloodlines. Some called it a gift, others a curse; to Ana it was a practical excuse for her personal inclination to remain distant.

Dating was something that required an openness and sharing of oneself that Ana found uncomfortable. As she grew older, she would understand she enjoyed physical connections, but at sixteen she had not experienced her sexual awakening yet. Relationships meant exposing herself, and worse, being put in a position where she would be required to at least try to explain who she was, and why she was the way she was. She envisioned her mind laid bare, all her thoughts exposed and analyzed. Ana did not understand that friendships and romantic relationships didn't have to be so different, and that she had already, without realizing it, shared herself with both Nicolas and Oz.

But Oz was her friend, as Nicolas was. They were three against the universe, and that was enough. Whatever other feelings had recently sprung up simply didn't matter in the larger equation.

Boys mostly left Ana alone when she was younger. She had not been a child who needed a great number of friends, and never sought the approval of anyone. Many of Ana's family, including her own father, had an extraordinary ability to influence others. Gifted in other ways, winning everyone over was of no great importance to her. She focused on schoolwork, looking forward to the moments after school where she could be herself, with Nicolas and Oz.

Some of her classmates dismissed her as being weird, while others seemed not to notice her at all. But as she grew out of girlhood, genetics and hormones guided Ana on a metamorphosis from the awkwardness of youth to the loveliness of a piece of art coming into completion. She had her mother's bright, thoughtful blue eyes, while her grandmother gifted her with dark strawberry hair, freckles, and dimples. From her father, Ana inherited a fresh, youthful complexion.

Nicolas often joked she had the body of an Irish ballet dancer. "You have the grace of a swan... but we're going to need to do something about those boobs and hips." She hid behind sweaters and jeans, but it was no use. Her juxtaposed beauty and aloofness piqued everyone's curiosity. She was no longer weird, but mysterious.

"All the girls want to be you, and you want to be no one," Nicolas said to her once. "There has to be a ridiculous cliché in there somewhere. My heart bleeds for you."

Unlike many of the family, Nicolas was benign; he had no special abilities. Well, that was if you didn't count his prowess with women and apparently high tolerance for alcohol. Ana wished she could be "normal," too. However, even though Nicolas teased her, Ana took comfort in knowing he understood her torment was very real.

Oz, though, had a slightly different insight. "Even if you showed them all who you were, they'd never understand," he said one day, as they studied beneath a tree in his parents' backyard. Ana still remembered the way the sun shone crudely through the fall storm, and how the leaves from the banana tree provided complete shelter from the incessant rain.

"But you do," she'd replied, nose down in a book.

Oz responded by smiling from behind his own book, resting his hand on her leg before resuming his reading.

Oz reflected his understanding in a much different way, instead choosing to date girls who were exactly his opposite, rather than one who might offer him a comforting reflection. Ana watched with fascination as he went from one vapid debutante to the next, never seeming to realize how each made him completely miserable.

Ana, in contrast, refused any of the boys who asked her out. Eventually, there came a time when boys asked less and less. Only Clancy persisted. But his kiss had terrified her, simultaneously awakening something within, while also bringing her to the realization she might never be normal enough for a sweet boy like Clancy Sullivan.

* * * * *

Several months later, Clancy asked her to prom, and she turned him down. *I don't understand,* he'd said, both of them thinking about that early fall kiss on her father's porch. *Did I do something wrong?*

Even Ana understood the "it's not you, it's me," line would be a cruel response. True or not.

It was her stepmother, Barbara, who persuaded her to accept Calvin Whittaker's invitation to her junior prom. *You will regret it if you don't go,* she'd said. *You don't have to marry him, Ana.*

Calvin was an okay guy. Ana knew him from the school paper, where she was the editor. He wrote mainly sports features, one of the few popular kids who wrote for the paper. While he exhibited many of the typical, annoying tendencies around his friends, he wasn't so bad when working with the editorial staff. The only real problem she ever had with him was his tendency to turn things in too close to deadline. He didn't have her focus; but then, few did.

Ana knew he was interested. He hadn't been especially shy about it, always asking for her advice about how he worded things in his pieces. Ana had little interest in sports, and Calvin knew that, but it didn't stop him from seeking her advice. When he finally asked her out, it hadn't been much of a surprise.

He wasn't sweet like Clancy, but, somehow, that felt safer. There was no chance of Ana falling for a boy like Calvin Whittaker.

It was her father who convinced her to wear her mother's wedding dress to the dance. Well, it wasn't *exactly* a wedding dress. It was a strapless white satin gown with a sequin-beaded top and a wide taffeta skirt that resembled the White Swan costume from Swan Lake. Ana had always adored the gown, but only because it had been her mother's, and there was an air of magic and mystery around anything belonging to the woman she had never met.

There were few images that brought Ana joy more than the pictures of her happy, smiling mother wearing the dress, clutching her new husband's arm.

Ana's father never got excited about anything outside of his company, and even then it was a subdued kind of excitement. When Ana agreed to try it on, at his suggestion, she was rewarded with a smile unlike any she'd ever seen from him. Her heart swelled with joy at the sight of it.

"It fits you perfectly, Anasofiya," he had said. There were tears in his eyes. "You look so much like her…"

Ana felt it was an unfair tactic from her father. He knew invoking the memory of her mother would sway her. She commiserated with Nicolas about it, but he had little sympathy this time.

"The bells are ringing with pity," he'd said, with an exaggerated roll of his eyes. Then, a moment later he added, "It's not wrong to enjoy looking pretty from time to time, Ana. You're going to be stunning no matter what, so why not also make your dad a little less cranky for once?"

It was so rare for Nicolas to be the voice of reason in their relationship. However, when she put the dress on and looked at herself in the mirror, it was her mother looking back at her.

This realization gave Ana an unexpected burst of courage, and she began to look forward to the evening.

Chapter Two: Oz

Oz Sullivan watched his best friend toss back three glasses of Hennessy without taking a single breath. It never ceased to amaze him the amount of alcohol Nicolas Deschanel could consume. The responsible side of Oz wondered at what this might mean for his friend's future. But tonight wasn't a night for serious considerations.

"Is my shit straight?" Nicolas asked as he squinted toward Oz, tugging at his vest. They were in their limo, on the way to pick up their dates. "Fuck, this is hideous."

"It's fine," Oz insisted, though his mind was far from whether or not Nicolas' vest was straight.

"Good thing I won't be wearing it for too long," Nicolas replied with a wink.

"I'm not even sure why you bother going," Oz teased drolly. He would be surprised if Nicolas even lasted a full hour before breaking away to head to his own party, upstairs.

"Because if I don't go to prom, I can't throw a prom party. Duh!"

"Of course," Oz agreed, with a distracted glance out the window. They were racing down the Expressway toward New Orleans, and the closer they got to town, the worse he felt. "Your reasoning is, as always, without question."

"Do you remember what I told you?" Nicolas asked, arms spread out across the entire seat.

"About?"

"Don't play dumb."

"Maybe I'm tired of talking about it," Oz replied, with a pointed glance.

"I would think you'd be more tired of never getting laid," Nicolas chastised. He went to pour himself another drink, discovered the bottle was empty, and tossed it on the carpeted floor. "Ozzy. She's a sure thing. I should know, I hit it a month ago."

"Yeah, well, you've been having sex since you were twelve, so the list of girls you *haven't* hit might be smaller than the ones you have," Oz snapped. "I'm not like you."

Nicolas leaned forward, on to his knees. "Hey. What crawled up your ass?"

"Nothing crawled up my ass. I'm tired of talking about whether or not I'm going to bang Melodie Cantwell, who, for the record, I can't even stand!"

Sympathy washed over Nicolas' expression. "Ozzy, why didn't you *ask* Ana?"

"You know why."

"I know the bullshit reasons you keep giving me, but not the real one."

Why hadn't Oz asked Ana? There were a hundred reasons. She was beautiful. She was terrifyingly insightful. She was his best friend. She had never, not once, had a boyfriend, and had refused so many boys Oz lost count. And she'd never given Oz any indication she might have a different answer for him.

Mostly, he knew she was afraid of opening herself up. He empathized and cared about her enough not to ask it of her.

"I guess I don't want things to change," Oz said finally. It was as close to the truth as he could find himself comfortable to share.

"Fucking *life* is about change!" Nicolas exclaimed, rummaging through the liquor cabinet for a suitable replacement for his Hennessy. "It's gonna change whether you want it to or not, Ozzy. You gotta decide whether you're gonna grab it by the balls and choose your path, or whether it's going to turn around and take your balls for its bitch, instead. Here's a secret: it won't be gentle."

"Gross," Oz dutifully replied. But he understood, in the way he always understood Nicolas' messy but sage logic. Understanding didn't make it any easier, though.

"Well, it doesn't matter, right? You're going with miss Melodie, with the tits her daddy gave her for her sixteenth, which, by the way, will feel awesome pressed against your-"

"Stop!"

"Fine," Nicolas said, retreating with his new drink. "You can tell me I'm right later."

Well, there was zero chance of that. Oz had no pious reasons for preserving his virginity, but he respected himself enough not to give it away to a girl like Melodie.

But what kind of message am I sending her? Oz thought, as he watched Nicolas go back to fiddling with his vest. *Maybe she's expecting exactly what Nicolas thinks.*

And then Oz's heart sank to the floor, as he realized Ana might be walking into a similar situation with Calvin.

She's a strong girl. She wouldn't give herself so easily, Oz reminded himself, but his heart was playing devil's advocate, unraveling all the heartbreaking ways Ana might end up in Calvin's arms by night's end.

"Pour me one of those, Nic, would 'ya?"

Chapter Three: Anasofiya

It did not take long for Ana's night to sour.

Calvin was drunk before they even arrived at the dance. He stumbled into the ballroom, with Ana tripping to catch up. Then, as they stood near the punch bowl, he whispered crude things in her ear that were decidedly sexual in nature.

Finally, while dancing, he tried to slip a hand under her dress. "I know you wanna know what it's like," he muttered, his muggy breath hot against her ear. "Let me show you."

"I appreciate your thoughtfulness, but I'll pass," she'd replied, pushing her hands against his chest to add some much-needed distance.

He disappeared to talk to his friends and never returned. Like an idiot, she sat and waited, pretending he'd lost track of time, when she knew very well he wasn't coming back. And truthfully, she didn't want him to. She cursed herself for listening to Barbara, knowing she should have gone with her instincts and stayed home. She'd guessed all along Calvin was only hoping to get lucky, and this was precisely her motivation for *not* wanting to go. Worse, it was why she chose him over Clancy. She knew it would be easier to walk away.

She never wanted to lead him, or anyone else, on. Ana wasn't protecting her virginity for any moral or romantic reason. She didn't harbor those kinds of hang-ups on anything, for the most part. The real, raw reason was that intimacy terrified her, and she had never met anyone who could make it less frightening.

Nicolas also disappeared early with his date. He had rented out a suite of rooms at the Monteleone, for an event that people would talk about for years after. Ana hadn't expected him to stay at the dance long, but still felt a knot form in her stomach at being left to fend for herself.

She sat in the corner alone, watching the events of her prom unfold around her, like an outsider. This feeling never bothered her when she was surrounded by the safety of Oz and Nicolas, but tonight they had their own plans. She was alone.

People moved from group to group, talking, laughing. Ana envied those who were good at small talk. It wasn't that she couldn't think of anything to say, because there were always a million things on her mind. With Nicolas and Oz, she could talk for hours. With the rest of the world, she wished only that they would leave her alone.

Her classmates continued to leave the ballroom in droves. It was still early, so she knew they must be heading to one of the many parties going on; most likely Nicolas', which was expected to be the most extravagant of all. The chaperones had to know what was going on but either they didn't care, or they understood the kids behind the shenanigans were the children of the men and women who kept the city's economy afloat.

Ana knew she should be joining them; as a Deschanel, she should be at the center of the events. But that was not who she was. She would never be that girl. She was just Ana, and she was alone.

Chapter Four: Oz

Melodie spent the first hour of their night thinking of new and creative ways to pass judgment on the various females she called "friends." She would start with a compliment to their face, and then, as they went to mingle with others, the venom would emerge. *Hell hath no fury like an insecure teenage girl.*

Like many of the girls Oz dated, he could find no common ground with which to relate to her. Instead of trying, it was easier to pretend, and to let her think they were in accord. Agreeing was always easier.

"What the *hell* is Cassidy Weatherly *wearing*?!" Melodie exclaimed rhetorically, with a crude wrinkle of her tiny nose. "She looks like a whore."

Oz wouldn't tell her he quite liked Cassidy's dress, and the way her long legs peeked from beneath the tassels like stems from an expensive glass. Or that every other male in the building was probably thinking the same thing. Instead, he took a long swallow of his punch, and let her continue to rant.

"And *Tanya* needs to tuck herself back in her dress," Melodie continued. "It would help if, 'ya know, she hadn't tried to shove her boudin, sausage ass into a dress two sizes too small!"

Oz didn't point out that Melodie's dress didn't fit exactly right, either.

Melodie Cantwell was the daughter of Judge Cantwell. Of course, everyone here was the daughter or son of someone important, including Oz. His own father was the Senior Partner of Sullivan & Associates, a New Orleans law firm which had been in the Sullivan family since the early 19th century, and that Oz would one day join. His father was pleased to hear Oz was taking Melodie, as the connection certainly couldn't hurt business.

"Ugh, and have you *seen* Ana Deschanel? Is she *actually* serious with that dress? She is such a total and complete *weirdo*!" Melodie cackled, dangling her glass as if it were a martini and not simply sparkling punch.

Yes, Oz had seen Ana. She was the first person he'd noticed when he entered the elaborately decorated ballroom. She was *always* the first person he noticed when he entered a room.

She sat in the corner, alone. Abandoned by the jerk she came with, most likely. Her slender arms were crossed self-consciously over the dress Melodie now insulted. But Oz saw only the beautiful, embarrassed flush to her cheeks, and the way curled tendrils of her artfully styled red hair tickled the brilliant white of the dress she sought to hide.

While Oz had endured Melodie's cracks about others throughout the night, the slight upon Ana offended him so greatly he had to resist the urge not to dump his drink on her.

In fact, it was at that very moment he decided he'd reached the limit of his patience with Melodie Cantwell.

* * * * *

Oz could not remember a time when he was not enchanted with Anasofiya. The cousin of his best friend Nicolas, Ana was a constant in his life since he could piece together his earliest memories. She was present, always, in every important event of his childhood, and knew all his darkest secrets, keeping them close to her heart. Similarly, he guarded her secrets protectively, treasured insight as to what made Ana special beyond her beautiful packaging.

Early on, his view of her was as neutral as any child regarding a friend of the opposite sex. She could climb trees as high, or higher, than he and Nicolas. She raced them across the grounds of *Ophélie*, the plantation home Nicolas' family owned and lived in, and told some of the scariest ghost stories when they hosted sleepovers. She spat, cursed, and laughed with both of them, from childhood, to adolescence and beyond.

It was hard to pinpoint the moment he began to love Ana, for it was a little like watching a flower bloom. Somewhere between his voice deepening, and her hips widening, his heart was no longer his to give.

"Fuck's sake, Ozzy, ask her out, already!" Nicolas exclaimed one day. They'd stopped by the Sacred Heart to pick up his sisters, and found Ana sitting at the end of the hallway, reading a book by her locker. Oz's heart skipped at the way her hair fell down over her face, glancing the edges of the pages. His expression was obviously a transparent window to his thoughts.

"It's not like that," Oz evaded, watching her.

"What the hell do you mean, it's not like that? It's *always* like that!" Nicolas insisted.

But it wasn't. Not with Ana. She was afraid of being hurt. Nicolas and Oz were the only two people she trusted, and he feared he would somehow let her down. His choice in dates was intentional. Girls like Cassidy, and Melodie, and Jessica, demanded nothing more from him than compliments and time. He wasn't going to disappoint them.

Oz had so much more to give and he didn't fear giving it, only that it would not be enough. Ana deserved the best of him. One day, he would be ready to give it to her.

* * * * *

"Oh, how sad, even Calvin abandoned her!" Melodie cawed, as her long, extended finger pointed once again in Ana's direction.

Patience previously expended, Oz frowned, as he watched Ana retreat even further into her corner. Melodie erroneously interpreted his silence as support and went on, "There's only one reason someone like Calvin would have gone with her to begin with. But even *I* could have told him she wouldn't put out! I mean, she's probably not even a *girl!*"

"She's the most beautiful girl I've ever seen," Oz corrected, and walked away, leaving Melodie's slack-jawed expression to gape after him.

Chapter Five: Anasofiya

Ana's gaze fell on a familiar face: Oz. He had taken a girl named Melodie as his date, and Ana wasn't even sure of her last name, but she was blonde and popular and otherwise unmemorable. Ana was often surprised at the girls Oz dated, but other times, like tonight, she gave him silent credit for his intelligence. Oz was different too, but he had found a way to fit in, while she was still hiding in corners. He had someone tonight, and she did not.

He spotted her and walked over to her corner. There was comfort and relief in a familiar face, although she knew it would not last long as his date was already glancing over in their direction. All of a sudden she was struck with a pang of awkwardness; somehow, wearing her mother's dress in front of someone she knew so well felt more uncomfortable than around others whom she knew very little. It was as if his knowing her brought more attention to it.

"Don't say a word," she warned him, looking straight ahead.

"About?"

"The dress," she said, shifting. The taffeta rustled and she felt horrified, as if everyone could hear that small noise over the loud music. "It was my father's idea. I feel ridiculous."

"Oh, the dress. I figured nothing needed to be said about that," he teased. Ana readied a look that suggested he was a jerk, but upon seeing his playful smile, she laughed instead.

"I see you've made quite the impression on your date," Oz said, scanning the room and noticing Calvin was nowhere to be found. "Did the dress run him off?"

She sighed in feigned irritation, when in truth Oz's presence was already putting her at ease. "I really shouldn't have come."

"Not with him," he agreed, then raised an eyebrow at her dress again. "Though, it's possible he just wasn't ready for marriage. Surely, you understand."

"I have little choice in the matter."

"He's the one missing out," Oz returned. His gaze lingered on her a moment longer and they both seemed to notice at the same time, each looking down at their own hands in unison.

Then he asked her to dance.

"I might injure myself... or more likely, you," she said, looking at his extended hand. A hand she'd held many, many times over the past sixteen years; a lifeline to safety.

"Well, my father has good insurance," he replied. "And if things get too bad, he is also a lawyer."

"Well, here's to being the first person to get sued for terrible dancing," she predicted, but took his hand and let him lead her to the floor.

Ana had never been in the arms of a boy before; not like this. The warmth she felt when Oz put his arms around her waist made her realize how real he was, and the weight of that realization overwhelmed her. His breath was hot near her ear; she detected his heartbeat through their joined hands. She would never forget that feeling: the subtle pulsing through his warm hands transferring through to her like soft vibrations. She wondered if everyone noticed things like this, or if Oz had always felt like this, and she'd simply missed it.

She found this feeling not only bearable but somehow welcoming. Realizing once this moment was over, they would go back to the way things were, brought upon her an unexpected sadness. Oz would go back to being simply her friend.

The sudden rush of despair sucked the air right out of her. It took great self-control not to break away and leave Oz standing there on the dance floor. Ana's heart raced so fast that, to her horror, Oz actually asked if she was okay. When the song ended, she squeezed his hand and walked away from him, threading through the crowds, into the quiet hallway.

Alone, she leaned against an empty desk and tried to regain control of herself. It was at times like this Anasofiya wished she knew how to escape from her own head, and become someone else entirely. Someone who could embrace the complexities of the world around her, and thrive within it.

She looked up to see Oz standing there. He said nothing, and his face was not full of pity, which she would have resented greatly, but understanding. If anyone could understand, it would be him, although no one would ever really know the intricacies of Ana's mind. Not even her.

Someone else might have stood there helplessly and asked polite questions, but Oz merely nodded at her. She understood all the things left unsaid and appreciated them, especially as she needed to say nothing in return. Ana was too young and inexperienced at the time to recognize it, but this would be one of the most intimate moments of her life.

"So, I know you get about as excited to party as I do, but I think I could get drunk. You?" he asked.

Ana offered him a half-laugh and smiled, her face, as usual, not matching what was in her head. "I've never been drunk," she admitted.

"Never? I've never known a Deschanel holiday that did not include its share of liquor," Oz challenged.

"Oh, that. Deschanels like to get drunk properly, in private," she said and they both laughed. "What about your date?"

He bit his lip and looked down guiltily. "Would you believe me if I said I wasn't her biggest fan?"

"Would you believe me if I said that's not entirely shocking?"

"Sooo," he continued, moving closer to her, "maybe we can rescue each other from the horror of going back to our shitty dates?"

She laughed. "Okay, let's do it."

He led her to one of the suites upstairs that Nicolas had rented out. By the time Ana and Oz had arrived, it was already packed.

Everything about the party had an air of gratuitous wealth; from the champagne fountains to the high-end dancers flown in from New York, to the live entertainment. The music was unbearably loud and it was evident half the suite would be in shambles by night's end. But Nicolas was a Deschanel; this would all be swept under the rug, like everything else he did.

Ana could read Oz's amazement. He grew up on the outskirts of their world, only a visitor. Even after all his time with the Deschanels, things like this could still shock him.

"You said you wanted to get drunk, right?" Ana prompted, taking his hand as they entered the party together.

Ana felt a sense of ease knowing she was in Nicolas' realm now; as if she belonged here second only to him. She drank down her first glass of champagne, quickly emptied a second, and then grabbed two more as she walked ahead of Oz, in search of her cousin.

"Easy," Oz laughed, catching up to her.

She smiled and led him to where Nicolas was sitting with his date and another girl. Both women were beautiful, and far too old to be hanging out with Nicolas, but there was nothing unusual about that. His face brightened to see her, and he fist-bumped Oz. "Didn't expect to see you here!" he yelled over the music.

She nodded at Oz. "Your friend is a bad influence."

"Or a good one," Nicolas said with a knowing wink. "Try not to be so uptight. You have all of this at your disposal and a place to crash afterwards. Live a little tonight, Anasofiya!"

Ana decided to embrace his advice, wishing to block out all the things that made the night start off wrong. She accepted drink after drink, dance after dance, and at some point during the night her hair had literally come down and was flowing wildly down her back. The world was spinning and she saw everything in colors brighter than she had ever seen. She danced with everyone and did not shy away from the hands on her, on her hips, waist, back, neck. For one night, she was free of herself and the confines of her own self-imposed limitations.

At one point, she locked eyes with Clancy. Before he could move toward her, she marched his direction, throwing her arms around his neck as she kissed him with twice the passion of their first time.

"What was that for?" he asked, a look of dazed happiness plastered across his face.

"For being one of the good ones," she replied, then melted back into the crowd of her peers, her thoughts moving on to the next thrill.

All night, Oz was there. He didn't leave her side for more than a minute or two; when he did, always he would reappear, arms around her waist, leading her, guiding her, watching over her. Her childhood friend, looking after her, as he always had.

As the night crept into morning, he declined drinks on her behalf, and stopped her from taking a pill she was ready to take without question.

"Ozzzzzzz," she'd whined.

"Ana Banana, sweetie," he replied, as she distractedly played with his hair, twirling it through her fingers as if she'd never seen hair before, "you will thank me later."

As people started to leave, or retire to private rooms, Oz finally said to her, "Ana, I am going to take you back to your room."

She stumbled on his arm, too intoxicated to argue or even care. As he walked her down the hall, she threw her arms in the air, in submission of inhibitions. In happiness. For the joy of freedom. Surrender. His arms never left her, even when he put the key in her lock and let her in.

Oz laid her gently on the bed, and as he stood, she wrapped her arms around his neck and pressed her lips to his, feeling emboldened by her actions with Clancy earlier. *This time, the right Sullivan.* The taffeta rustled brusquely as she held onto him, but it didn't bother her as it had earlier.

He returned the kiss, but then he pushed her back gently. "Not like this," he said, and disappeared, returning when he had a nightgown for her.

He helped her change and, that accomplished, she stood up to kiss him again. But then the room began to spin and she could not make it stop, no matter how tight she clenched her eyes shut. "Ahhh!" she cried, reaching to grip the bed, finding only air instead. Once again, his arms were there to catch her.

"You okay?" he asked, and she shook her head no.

"I am going to be sick."

He led her to the bathroom, holding back her hair, and patted her back for several hours as she threw up everything she regretfully consumed throughout the long evening. She sobbed, wondering if she was dying, and he comforted her, assuring her she wasn't. Finally, when she was done, he took her to bed.

Oz lay down next to her, holding her as she fell asleep.

When she woke up several times during the night, he was still there, still holding her, watching over her.

Chapter Six: Oz

Oz hardly slept. He kept watch over Ana, fearful the amount of alcohol she'd consumed might somehow be toxic. He'd let her do it, too. Foolishly, he thought she might relax and enjoy the freedom from herself, even if only for the night.

Then she'd kissed him. *Anasofiya had kissed him.* And he'd pushed her away, understanding innately it was the alcohol in charge, and not her. He'd refused her partly for her own protection, and partly in protection of his own bruised ego, which insisted she could never love him under better circumstances.

As he fought to stay awake, his mind drifted toward a recent memory. All three of them, Ana, Nicolas, and Oz, were sleeping in Nicolas' garçonierre, his private living quarters, detached from the rest of *Ophélie.* Sleepovers with the three of them were common, and had been for many years. Growing up didn't change that.

The three often slept in the same bed, passed out at odd or uncomfortable angles as they grew from children to young adults. The comfort level in their triad was such that they never, not once, felt there was anything awkward about the arrangement. Their closeness never waned; it evolved.

One evening, Nicolas snuck out after Oz and Ana had fallen asleep, likely off to his usual shenanigans. Oz awoke as the door closed downstairs, and his eyes caught the glint of moonlight dancing off Ana's fiery hair on the pillow beside him.

Then, he saw the tears in her eyes.

"Ana Banana, what's wrong?" Oz whispered, positioning his face across from hers on the same pillow.

"I had a bad dream," she said, but did not drop her eyes. She didn't need to; he'd seen every side of her.

"Do you wanna talk about it?" He reached over and gently pushed her hair back from her face, where it was matted in sweat. He'd always done it. It felt so natural.

She shook her head, clenching her eyes shut. Then, opening them, she said, "I saw you out on the levee. And then a wave came up from the Mississippi, behind you. I saw… saw it, and tried to call to you to move, to get out of the way. But you just smiled at me, not understanding. And I ran, I ran so fast, so hard, faster than I've ever run, but the wave grew higher and higher. And then it swallowed you whole." She choked back a guttural sob. "It was so real, Oz. You know how real my dreams can be."

He did know; he'd seen how cruel her sleepwalking and night terrors often were. "It was just a dream," he reassured her, but wanted, more than anything, to hold her and silence the trembling. "I'm okay, see?"

Ana pressed her lips together and nodded, but the tears continued to form under her tired lids. "I'm afraid to go back to sleep."

Oz watched one of his oldest friends, now the keeper of his heart, dissolve before him. She was not the quiet, strong girl at that moment, but vulnerable and needing a comfort he realized only he was capable of giving.

He felt like an adult for the first time in his life, as he gathered her into his arms and held her. "I won't let go, then. If you feel me, you'll know the dream isn't real," he whispered, his heart soaring as she clung to his shirt with one tiny fist, the other looped round his waist. "This is how you'll know I'm real."

"Promise?"

"Cross my heart."

His senses were overwhelmed with how *real* she was to him at that moment. She slept in her t-shirt and underwear, as she always had, but now her soft legs were twined through his, and he felt the cotton of her panties pressed against his thigh; her heat. The smell of her sweat and shampoo produced an intoxicating, drowsy effect, reminding him she was no longer the little girl he used to climb trees with. Her breasts against his chest removed all final doubt of it.

* * * * *

As memory Ana faded, the Ana before him snored softly at his side. Mascara stained her pale face, and her breath stank of her transgressions.

But Oz loved her no less than he had that night at *Ophélie*. In fact, he loved her more.

Chapter Seven: Anasofiya

Ana woke before he did the next morning, and her first thought was: *I am a damn fool.* She remembered every last moment of idiocy from the night before, with painful clarity. Her body, gifted with the unique, Deschanel ability to heal itself, was clear of all effects, but her mind viciously held onto every nuance.

Wanting to cry at her complete loss of self-control, she would not allow herself that relief. She would not lose further control with tears. *Live a little*, Nicolas had said. Ana could not understand how living like this was enjoyable for anyone. She was ashamed of her behavior, and horrified that both Nicolas and Oz had seen her like that.

Oz. Ana had thrown herself at her friend. *The right Sullivan.* Of all the behaviors of the night before, this one was the most dismaying to her. Then he had rejected her, and even her bruised ego understood that he had shown restraint for her sake, though that didn't make it an easier pill to swallow. It didn't make it hurt any less.

Face buried in her hands, Ana sat at the edge of the bed, her mind whirling. She did not hear Oz wake, but felt his strong legs slide on either side of hers as his arms moved around her waist. He kissed the back of her neck, resting his face against her shoulder blades.

Ana put her hands over his, and he squeezed her fingers. An electrifying jolt passed through her, and she stopped breathing for a moment.

Tipping her head back so he could see her face, Oz rewarded her bravery by gently kissing her chin, and cheeks and neck. She led his hands over the curves of her hips, her stomach; her chest. *All things he's seen, and touched, before. But never like this.*

Turning fully to face him, they reclined together on the bed. He pushed her back softly, peeling her nightgown up, kissing her stomach, hips, and softly between her legs. She ran her hands through his hair… that soft, raven black hair of his that she had always found lovely and mysterious. His body brushed lightly against hers, sending chills throughout her; his hardness, his soft skin, and his lips met hers. "Colin," she said, using his given name as she realized the intimacy she had been missing was upon her, it was happening, and it was real. "I've never done this before."

"Woken up next to a hot man in a strange hotel room?"

She laughed. "You know what I mean."

"Me either, Ana," he said, serious now. "But I want to. With you."

"You do?" Ana asked, with an innocence she never realized was within her.

"I've always wanted to," Oz admitted, pressing his forehead to hers.

And then he was inside her, her Oz, once again protecting her by showing her the full extent of his care for her, and how safe she was in returning it. *This is how you'll know I'm real.* Nothing had ever been more so than the sensation of her best friend bringing her over the precipice of girlhood.

Later experiences for Ana would be more wild, more creative, more carnal, but none would ever be as intense for her as this first time. Ana opened herself up to Oz and laid herself completely bare, without a hint of self-consciousness. She surrendered to him, without fear. Understanding then, for the first time, intimacy could be so much more than a burden or something to fear; that her desire to be with Oz could be beautiful, not terrible.

Later, they lay in the bed, talking for hours and hours. He played with her hair; she traced pictures on his belly. These things they did naturally, as they always had, but there was something else now mixed into the gestures. Something deeper and more serious than either of them had ever experienced.

"I can't believe that happened," Ana said, with a nervous laugh.

"Can I make a confession?" Oz asked, not waiting for her answer. "I've wanted to for a long time."

Ana scoffed, making light of the serious words. Despite how safe she felt, years of training herself to be guarded couldn't be erased in one night. "Not my fault you couldn't control your attraction to me after that exciting night of vomiting."

Oz smiled, as he traced a hand lazily across her bare back. "Do you remember the bad dream you had a few weeks ago? At *Ophélie*?"

Ana nodded, wondering why he did.

"You felt safe with me, right?" Oz asked. Ana nodded again. "I hope you know you always will be."

Ana kissed him again, by way of answer. One kiss turned to many, and many turned to further, welcome exploration.

As the morning passed into day, and day passed into evening, their playful escapes returned to conversation. Then, as the evening passed into morning yet again, the eagerness of their conversations turned to silence.

Oz looked at her thoughtfully. "I can probably guess what you're thinking."

"Yes," she said after a pause and a sigh. "You probably can."

"Because it is probably what I am thinking too," he ventured.

"Yes," she agreed. "Probably so."

"You're thinking relationships suck, and maybe this has potential but maybe it doesn't."

Ana nodded slowly.

"But you're thinking the odds are in our favor, and you just don't want to be the one to say it."

Ana was surprised he came out with it so directly, but then everything about the last twenty-four hours surprised her, and not necessarily in a bad way. She cared about him. Maybe more than cared, because for Ana, strong feelings did not come easily but they did come intensely. Her trust and comfort level in Oz only confused her further.

Yet, there was still fear this surrender would leave her exposed and inevitably bruised. It would be safer to go on as before and pretend it had never happened.

Oz leaned over her. "Look at me." After a moment, she did. "I get it. I do. But since we are both feeling the same way about this, isn't that a good sign?"

"I want it to be," she said. *More than anything.*

"And I want you," he concurred, rewarding her with more kisses. "So it's settled."

Ana smiled, closing her eyes to accept the many gifts he'd given her over the past two nights. "It is."

As she drifted off to sleep, in the arms of a boy she'd slept next to her whole life, Anasofiya Deschanel knew she had embarked on the first important journey of her life. She had no foresight as to the final destination, but knowing Oz was by her side, in a role somehow so much more than it had ever been, filled her heart with the first real gladness she had ever known.

Sarah M. Cradit

Author Dedication

For Anasofiya. Sometimes it's easier to understand who we are, when we know where we've been.

About Sarah

Sarah is the author of the Paranormal Southern Fiction series, The House of Crimson and Clover. She is always working on the next book in the mysterious world of the Sullivans and Deschanels.

Sarah lives in the Pacific Northwest, but has traveled the world from Asia to Europe to Africa. When she isn't working (either at her day career, or hard at work at writing), she is reading and discovering new authors. The great loves of her life (in order) are: her husband James, writing, and traveling the world.

Follow Sarah

Facebook: http://www.facebook.com/houseofcrimsonandclover

Twitter: http://www.twitter.com/thewritersarah

Read More from Sarah

The Storm and the Darkness: http://amzn.to/1bIimht

The One

The One

S.L. Dearing

"C'mon. Katie. Let's go already."

Kate Flannery applied her lipstick and ran a middle finger along her bottom lip, making sure it hadn't bled off the edge. She assessed her work in the mirror. Her long, wavy brown hair was piled loosely on her head, as tendrils fell gently around her face. The red cocktail dress she wore accentuated her curves, but was subtly sensual, yet not overtly sexual. She smoothed out the rough edges and sighed.

"I guess that's as good as it's gonna get."

"Well, if that's it, let's go," said Lana.

Kate turned around and raised an eyebrow at her best friend.

"Really?"

"Yeah, you look great. You always look great. Let's go!"

Lana motioned for them to walk as Kate sighed again and grabbed her clutch, following Lana to the door and out to the car. Lana started the engine as Kate snapped her seatbelt.

"Maybe I should have brought a coat?" asked Kate.

"Maybe you should just relax and enjoy the evening."

"Who is this artist?"

"Artists. Fram Cooley…"

"I'm sorry, Fram Cooley? That's not a real name." Kate laughed.

"Probably not. He's some little douchey guy from Columbus," Lana responded. "Anyway, Fram Cooley, Peter Cross, Kami Ashley, Ron Kretz and Matthew Eisner."

"Okay, I don't know any of them."

Lana laughed as they drove out of the circular driveway.

"Thanks again for being my date. These artists are all on the rise and I really need a big client; and I couldn't go stag and if I'm networking I can't take Bill. He's too needy."

Lana rolled her eyes and Kate laughed.

"You're the best date I've had in months, Lana."

"I swear, Kate, you really need to pick better guys. You're so out of their league. Why can't you see how wonderful you are?"

Kate shrugged and looked out the passenger window.

"They're the only ones who ask me out. I keep hoping one of them is the one, but I'm getting tired of hoping."

Lana frowned.

"I don't understand how a woman as wonderful and beautiful as you are doesn't have men lying down at her feet."

"I'm just not the one, Lana."

"What the hell are you talking about?"

"You know, all those girls who get a guy and are convinced they are the one. I've never thought I was the one, maybe I'm just not the *one*."

"That's the dumbest fucking thing I've ever heard. You just haven't met your *one*. You've been busy. You're a successful writer, which takes time and effort. You finally have the time to find the guy to light your fire."

"Not sure he exists."

"Of course he does, you just haven't met him yet."

"Okay, I'm over this. Change of subject, so, none of these artists have agents?"

Lana shook her head, but didn't press.

"Okay, fine. No, not yet, and since Eliza left me and went with Dan, I don't have a really big name. I need to get a super big client."

"But these guys aren't big yet, are they?"

"Well," Lana replied, "they're big, just not huge, but they are super close to breaking through and becoming huge. I need huge."

Kate turned her head and looked out the window, smirking. Lana Fowler had left New York and the EXA to create an L.A. agency for fine artists two years earlier, but it had been difficult to convince the L.A. artists who were already established to go with an agent who had no agency. She had worked hard and finally landed Eliza Shan, but three months ago Eliza had left Lana to go to her major competitor, Dan Portner. Lana was still trying to recover her confidence and Kate knew she was Lana's moral support, even though she was much more of a museum girl rather than a gallery girl.

"I'm sure you'll dazzle them."

"What if Dan is there?"

"I don't know, what if Dan *is* there?" asked Kate, looking at her best friend, eyebrow raised.

Lana glanced at Kate and smiled.

"Nothing."

"Exactly."

Lana pulled up in front of the Boga Gallery and parked her Black Audi A5, leaving the motor running. The valet opened Kate's door and helped her out. She smoothed out her dress as Lana walked around the back of the car.

"Ready?" asked Kate.

Lana nodded and smiled.

"Good. Go get 'em, killer."

Lana laughed as they walked into the gallery.

The clear modern lines of the gallery's design were typical of the L.A. exhibit scene. The white walls, upon which hung various kinds of artwork from paintings made with oils, to acrylic to charcoal renderings. The stone pillars, which showcased several different kinds of sculptures, stood sporadically throughout the gallery. Kate had been to enough openings with Lana to know what was in store— pseudo-intellectual sycophants, pretentious critics, and rambling artists. She took in her surroundings, sighed heavily, and deftly grabbed a large glass of wine from a bypassing waiter.

She took a sip as she watched Lana take action, shaking hands and schmoozing. Then she turned and quietly wandered the maze of slate floors and white walls, seeing if there was anything she found interesting about these up-and-coming artists.

* * * * *

Matt Eisner was trying to look interested in the words coming out of Fram Cooley's mouth, which was no small feat. Although Matt loved being an artist, he hated all the social bullshit that accompanied the success train. He tried to focus on appearing fascinated by Fram's ramblings when he saw her, a stunning brunette in a red dress. Matt felt his gaze being pulled to her. She moved with a subtle confidence as she walked slowly, absorbing the art around her. Matt's eyes narrowed as he assessed her. The fine line of her jaw, her full red mouth, her bottom lip resting against the edge of the wine glass, just hovering for an eternity before she tilted the glass and drank the fruity nectar contained within, then the subtle wetness as her bottom lip disappeared beneath the top for only a moment.

"Eisner? Eisner!"

Matt heard Fram's voice needling him out of his trance. He inhaled and turned back to the little man. Matt smiled as he looked at his diminutive frame, arms crossed in annoyance, that petulant frown on his face as his shaggy Fab-Four haircut hung down in his dark beady eyes.

"Sorry, Fram, I just noticed someone I know. I'll be right back."

"Well, I haven't told you about Milan, Eisner…"

"Later, Fram."

Matt pointed and winked at Fram as he started to walk away. Fram Cooley just stared after his fellow artist, appearing shocked that he had been left without an audience. He looked around and saw Kami Ashley, smiled and sauntered over.

Matt then tried to zero in on the brunette in the red dress. Wandering around where she had just been, he looked behind several walls and finally found her standing in front of one of his pieces. He was awestruck and just observed her.

Kate stood staring at the massive oil painting in front of her. The canvas was ten by ten feet square. The scene was a city with tall white buildings looking down a hill or mountain and into an ocean. She wasn't familiar with the city, but the area looked almost rural and foreign. She could see the soccer field in the distance and the point of view was that of a window in a room.

She moved her eyes over the soft brush strokes the artist made, noting the use of acrylic underneath to change the texture and perception of the oil on top. The piece made her yearn to be in that room, to see the ocean and who might be playing on that pitch. She lifted her glass and downed the last of her wine, placing the empty glass on the tray of a waiter passing by, never letting her eyes leave the painting.

Matt saw an opportunity, grabbing two more glasses of wine from another waiter. He walked up behind her, and handed her a glass.

"Here you go," he said.

Kate turned and looked at the glass being handed to her. She raised an eyebrow and took the glass, casting her gaze to the man who passed it to her. Her breath caught slightly as she took in the vision before her. He was smiling down at her, his shoulder length wavy, dark brown hair gently cascaded around his face, fray hairs catching against the artfully trimmed beard that surrounded his generous mouth. She noticed the glint of silver hoops in both ears, then let her eyes travel to the exposed skin above his unbuttoned collar and the black ink looping up his neck and disappearing under his hair. His eyes danced behind small wire frame glasses and she noticed that they seemed to change from deep green to blue, mostly resting somewhere in between.

She felt her teeth find her bottom lip as she tried to keep her composure, her heart thrumming a little faster in her chest.

"Thank you," she said, sipping from the glass.

"Sure," he said, grinning. "You see something you like?"

Kate turned back to the painting and sighed. It truly took her breath away. She nodded, holding the chilled glass to her cheek as she wistfully studied the piece.

"I do... very much."

"You don't think it's a little... juvenile?" he asked.

Kate raised her eyebrow in annoyance. Maybe she had misjudged the vision to her left; her attraction meter seemed to always be broken. The guys she wanted always turned out to be douche bags. Why couldn't just one of them not be a pretentious ass? She opted to engage; at least she would have some fun.

"Juvenile? What's juvenile about it? It's lovely. Soft lines, rich texture... a beautifully inviting scene. Please, tell me, what is juvenile about this painting," she chided, obviously annoyed.

He was thrilled. Not only was she beautiful, she was feisty. A trait he admired in a woman. No wilting flowers for him. Matt beamed inside, but shrugged, feigning hurt at her tone.

"Well, I was only eighteen when I painted it. I just wanted to make sure that it didn't look juvenile... some critics think so."

Kate felt her stomach turn.

Oh, shit... an artist... she thought, cringing.

The last thing she wanted to do was mess up any opportunity for Lana. She perused the painting and found the signature. *MEisner.* She took mental inventory of the names, delicately ticking them off, mouthing each one until...

"Matt Eisner," he said.

"Yeah," she sighed, her lips had mouthed his name as he said it. "Look, I'm sorry, I thought you were a critic, or..."

"Some pretentious jackass? Yeah, I didn't think I put off that vibe."

Kate winced, and shook her head, waving her hand for him to stop. She gazed up at his face and was again stilted by the crooked smile beaming down at her. She forgot what she was going to say.

"Do I make you nervous?" he asked.

She shook her head. "Um, no... it's just that..."

"You find me incredibly attractive."

"Excuse me?"

An incredulous smile spread across Kate's face. He laughed.

"I didn't expect you to be so easily flustered," he said.

He raised the glass to his mouth and sipped, never taking his eyes from hers. She had to remind herself to breathe. Of course she found him incredibly attractive. In addition to the lean muscular frame and ruggedly-handsome-ever-smiling face, he exuded a confidence and charm that was all-powerful, like a tractor beam, and she felt herself being drawn to him.

"So, you're Matt Eisner."

Kate breathed a sigh of relief as Lana walked up, hand extended to meet a new artist.

"Yeah," he responded, his smile never faltering as his gaze turned to the petite blonde.

"When I saw you talking to Katie, I knew I had to come over and introduce myself. I'm Lana Fowler."

"Nice to meet you," he said, taking her hand. "So, you're friends with Katie?"

Kate raised her eyebrows and continued to keep her mouth busy by consuming more of the liquid grape, letting Lana take control of the conversation, while she directed her attention back to the painting.

"Best friends. She didn't tell you?"

"Didn't have a chance," Kate mumbled.

"Oh, well, we are… BFFs," Lana continued, turning to Kate with her brows raised.

Kate nodded and smiled as Matt chuckled softly.

"I see," he said. "I heard you might be here tonight, Ms. Fowler. Sorry about Eliza."

Lana dismissed the notion.

"Well, she did what she thought was best for her. I can't fault her for doing that, and please, call me Lana. Have you considered any representation, Mr. Eisner?"

"Matt, please. I have actually, I met with Dan Portner yesterday."

Kate looked at Lana's face and saw a tiny fissure, as she tried to hide her disappointment. Kate inhaled.

"Did you sign with him?" asked Kate.

Matt looked at the fiery brunette, the corner of his mouth curled up again.

"No, no I haven't."

"Well, good, then you can meet with Lana, see what she has to say."

Matt chuckled, nodding.

"Ok, tell you what, I'll meet with Lana tomorrow for lunch, if you spend the evening with me."

Kate furrowed her brow.

"Excuse me?"

"Not in an *Indecent Proposal* kind of way," he answered, laughing. "Just hang out with me, tonight. No agenda, I just want to spend time with you, get to know you."

"Why?"

"You're beautiful, intelligent, you love my art, and you make me laugh."

Kate watched him ruefully, and then glanced at Lana. The mask was still intact, but Kate could see the desperation in her friend's eyes. She sighed.

"Ok, Eisner, you've got a deal."

"Great!" Matt turned to Lana. "So, I'll meet you tomorrow at…"

"La Scala?"

"Ok, La Scala it is. Say noon?"

"Noon is perfect," Lana beamed, as she handed Matt her card. "In case something changes, you can call my cell. Otherwise, I'll see you tomorrow."

He took the card, gazed at it, and then placed it in his pants pocket.

"I won't be canceling. Now, if you'll excuse me one moment, I have to let Pietra know that I'm leaving. I'll be right back."

He turned and walked towards Pietra Goonst, the owner of the Boga Gallery. Kate watched his long legs carry him to the tiny pinched-faced woman. She downed her wine as Lana grabbed her arm.

"Thank you, thank you, thank you!"

"I didn't do anything, Lana."

"Yes, you did. I know you really aren't into dating, especially since breaking up with Anthony, dick that he was," Lana mumbled. "But that was almost a year ago, you might have fun."

"It's fine, really. It's not like he isn't dishy, I mean I can't imagine what he wants with me, I mean, I must be like ten years older than him."

"Um, you're hot, older or not."

"You just love me."

"Well, I do love you, but that has nothing to do with what you look like, or even who you are as a person. You always sell yourself short, Kate. I wish you would stop."

Kate shrugged, smiling as she chewed her bottom lip.

"Just have fun, Katie. You *do* remember how to have fun, right?"

"I'll try," Kate said, giving her best friend a toothy grin.

"I hear he's a great guy."

"He smiles a lot. That's a nice change."

Lana laughed, then nodded as Matt strode back to the women.

"Sorry about that. She's a pain in the ass. You ready?" he asked Kate, who nodded. He turned to Lana and extended his hand. "You, I'll see tomorrow at La Scala at noon. You wanna make an impression, pimp me out while I'm gone."

"La Scala at noon, and I will definitely pimp you out," Lana said, shaking his hand. "Take care of my girl, Eisner."

Matt winked at her and turned, offering Kate his arm. She slid her hand through the crook and smiled as they made their way outside. At the curb Matt raised his hand and a few moments later a valet returned with a silver Dodge Viper. Matt opened the passenger door for Kate and held her hand as she slid into the soft leather interior, shutting the door softly when she was securely inside. She inhaled the scent of leather and sandalwood. All Matt Eisner, delicious and male. She still had no idea why he had singled her out. She looked out the windshield of the sports car and watched as Matt handed the valet a tip. In one fluid motion, he had opened the door, glided in, and revved the car to life.

"Where to, beautiful?"

Kate blushed, raising her eyebrows.

"This is your road show, what do you want to do?"

"I'm hungry, how about you?"

"Yeah, I could eat," she answered.

"Oh, by the way, my name is Matt Eisner," he said leaning over, extending his hand.

Kate laughed and shook her head, took his hand, then leaned in as well.

"Kathleen Flannery, but you can call me Kate."

He let his digits close around her hand, softly pulling her fingers to his mouth, where he lightly pressed his full lips against her skin. She felt her breath hitch. The blood pumped furiously through her body, pounding in her ears, as the electric touch of his mouth radiated through her, leaving butterflies in her stomach.

Matt let his lips rest on her soft delicate fingers, inhaling the jasmine on her skin. He raised his head, and gazing back at him were those warm amber eyes. He breathed deeply.

"Nice to meet you, Kate."

Kate blushed again, but didn't try to take back her hand. She couldn't believe the effect this man had on her.

"Nice to meet you, Matt."

Smiling, Matt reluctantly released Kate's hand and put the car in gear. They pulled out on to the main street and Matt rested his arm on the ledge of the open window, the wind gently blowing his hair around his face.

"How about Canter's?" Matt asked.

"Love Canter's," she replied.

Matt grinned.

"So, tell me, Kate, why hasn't some guy snatched you up?"

Kate raised her eyebrows and shrugged.

"I have horrible luck with men. They all end up being asshole douche bags."

Matt laughed loudly and glanced over at her, shifting down as the light turned red. The car rolled to a stop and he turned to her.

"Are you telling me that not one of these guys knew what they had?"

She gazed at him, those green-blue eyes staring into her soul.

"I don't think I was what they wanted," she stuttered, turning away. She was so unaccustomed to his bluntness. It unnerved her, and yet she was drawn to his honesty and forthright personality.

"I find that hard to believe, Kate."

"You don't even know me, Matt."

"You're right, but that's why were here, right? Find out more about each other? Well, that's why *I'm* here. I want to know everything about you. I kind of extorted this date, I know. I wasn't sure if you would go out with me if I just asked you."

Kate couldn't help but grin as he spoke.

"I'm glad you extorted the date," she mumbled.

"Ah, there we go! You do think I'm incredibly attractive!"

Kate's grin turned to laughter.

"God, do you always say everything that comes into your head?"

"No, that would be inappropriate," he answered through a toothy grin.

The Viper pulled into the parking lot on Fairfax and slid into a spot. The attendant walked over and handed Matt a ticket through the window. He twisted to Kate, still beaming.

"Stay there."

She watched his long, muscular body easily exit the sleek car and moments later her door opened and a hand was offered in front of her. She sighed as she took the hand and swung her legs out of the vehicle.

He easily pulled her up, but her shoe slipped and she stumbled. Strong arms caught her as she fell against Matt's chest. She raised her face to his.

"Easy, beautiful."

She felt her face flush, the corner of her mouth curling upwards. Her face was inches from his chest and his scent drifted around her. It was delicious, and it sent her blood whooshing again, that thunderous beating filling her ears.

"Sorry. I'm kind of a klutz."

She started to move back, but Matt didn't let go. Instead he held her in his gaze, his strong hands gently holding her against him.

"No worries," he replied, his deep voice willing her to keep staring into those deep pools of distraction.

She stayed for what felt like an eternity when he finally loosened his hold and she immediately wanted to pull him back. She shook her head as Matt closed the door and they walked past the furniture store to the deli.

From the back of the restaurant, music blared into the dining areas. The manager walked up.

"Two?" she asked.

"Yes, please, but could we sit here in the front, maybe over on the side? Away from the Kibbutz Room."

"Sure, this way."

Matt put his hand on Kate's back, the charge of his touch easily permeating the fabric of her dress. She tried desperately to get her desire under control, but he was already the oxygen feeding a blaze in her body. She slid into the booth, he on the opposite side. Neither one picked up a menu.

"You already know what you want?" he asked.

She smirked.

"Of course."

A white-haired waitress of seventy-years-old walked up.

"You ready?"

"Yeah, I'll have the pastrami on rye, fries, and a chocolate egg cream," Matt answered.

"I'll have the corned beef Reuben, but instead of rye, I'd like sourdough. Fries, a side of ranch and Thousand Island dressing, and a chocolate malt, please. Oh, and pickles please."

The waitress sighed and nodded as she waddled off. Matt raised his eyebrows and nodded.

"You really gonna eat all that?"

"Have you seen my ass? Of course, I am," answered Kate.

Matt snickered, shaking his head.

"I *have* seen your ass and it's amazing. I'm impressed. I love a chick who can put away that kind of food and still look as outstanding as you do."

"Chick?"

"Yeah, chick... you're a chick, a girl, a woman, a honey, a Betty... do I need to continue?" Matt asked, jokingly.

Kate bit her bottom lip, shaking her head, and looking down. What was she doing here? Why was he interested in her? She suddenly felt all those insecurities surge up and submerge her entire being. She didn't feel sexy, she felt foolish. Why was she here with this gorgeous younger man? She felt like a joke.

Matt frowned, then knocked on the table.

"Hey, where did you go?"

Kate looked up, and shrugged.

"I'm here," she answered.

"No, you just flipped on me. Where's that feisty woman who challenged my taste back in the gallery? Where is that confidence you just had?"

Kate sighed and leaned forward, apprehensively looking into Matt's eyes.

"I don't know what you want from me. I'm not who you think I am. I'm not the one... I'm never the one."

"I'll decide that for myself, thank you. I don't think you're anyone other than Kathleen Flannery. I want you to be you. I want to know who you are. If you think I'm an ass, say it. If you think I'm obnoxious, say it. If you think I'm wrong, say it. If you think I'm sexy, say it. Don't try to be anything other than who and what you are, Kate."

Kate inhaled a trembling breath, unsure of who she was or who she should be. The unkind words of previous men, the constant barrage of demeaning comments, the rejections, all flooded her psyche. Her eyes welled with tears as she chewed the inside of her cheek.

Matt reached across the table, taking her hands in his own. He wrapped his fingers firmly around hers and pulled them to the middle of the table, his gaze never leaving her face. Finally, her lovely amber eyes lifted, and Matt could see the fear trying to take up residence.

"Nobody's perfect, Kate. I happen to think you are the most beautiful woman I've ever seen, and any guy who has told you the opposite needs to have his ass kicked. Do me a favor? Drop all that baggage, you don't need it."

Kate felt her mouth begin to curl upward and, for the first time in a long time, she believed the words that fell crashing on her soul. He thought she was beautiful. She wasn't sure why she believed him, but she did. She nodded.

"Sorry, I'm a girl. I get a little crazy sometimes."

Matt's wry smile returned.

"There she is."

He leaned over and lightly kissed her fingers again. The gesture caused Kate's heart to race, and when he tried to release her hands, she held fast.

"Not yet."

Matt cocked his head. The smile on his face now wrought with want as he moved his hands, and laced his fingers with hers.

"Ok."

She beamed as the warmth of his touch filled her heart with hope and yearning. She was amazed that his contact grew more and more electric. Every time her skin met his, it was as if she needed it. She was exhilarated and terrified, but those eyes seemed to give her strength.

They finally released one another when the food arrived. Matt looked at their plates.

"Well, we're quite the stereotypes aren't we?"

"What do mean?" Kate asked.

"The Jew with the pastrami and the Mick with corned beef."

Kate laughed loud and clear, and Matt grinned broadly in response.

They ate and talked, sharing stories about their families, friends. Kate told him about Lana, her sisters and her writing. He told her about his parents and growing up in L.A. and Israel. They finished and left the delicatessen.

As they stepped out onto the sidewalk, Matt reached down and grabbed Kate's hand, holding it gently, but fixed. She curled her fingers over the area between his thumb and index finger, lacing her pinky into his digits.

They walked slowly back to the car, meeting the attendant. Matt paid, never letting Kate's hand leave his own. As the attendant walked away, Matt opened Kate's door and helped her into the silver Viper. Moments later, the driver side door opened and Matt saddled into the driver's seat.

"Still up for more, beautiful?"

Kate nodded.

"Yeah, what's next?"

"How about I show you a secret?"

"Ok."

The Viper roared to life. Matt backed the car out of the spot, pulled out of the parking lot and onto the street. They traveled down the side streets of Los Angeles until they came to a gray building near Third and La Cienega. Matt pulled the car alongside the curb and turned off the motor.

"So, I used to live not far from here when I was, like, fourteen. Anyway, I was kind of a delinquent. C'mon, I'll show you."

Kate went to get out of the car, and again, Matt was there to help her out. She thought she could get used to being treated like this. Chivalry wasn't dead, at least not in Matt Eisner's world. He took her hand again and led her to an alley. There on the back of the building were several garage doors and each one had a full mural— the beach, the city, cars, and palm trees. The essence of L.A. was painted on the doors. Vibrant greens and blues enhanced by the sunshine and sand, as the mountains and desert all blended together on the doors.

"I was a graffiti artist."

"It's outstanding, Matt."

Matt squeezed her hand as they continued to stare at the aging street art.

"Yeah?" he asked.

"Truly."

"I'd like to show you more of my work."

"Is it on a street near here?" Kate asked.

Matt chuckled and shook his head.

"Alas, this is all that's left of my criminal art. But I do have a bunch of pieces at my studio, if you're not too tired."

"Not tired at all," she responded.

"Cool, c'mon."

Kate watched the scenery zip past her as they drove out of the city and into Malibu, then up the hills above Pacific Coast Highway. Through the tree-lined, winding roads of the Santa Monica Mountains, the silver Viper hugged the asphalt until it reached a rod-iron gate. The gate opened and Matt pulled into the circular driveway that lay before a large white Mediterranean home.

The motor rolled into silence, while Kate leaned forward taking in the massive domicile. She twisted her head to Matt, who was smiling and watching her.

"I thought we were gong to your studio."

"It's here."

"Is this your house?" she asked.

He nodded.

"You do well for an artist."

Matt laughed, and Kate's heart leapt.

"I'm also a graphic artist. A very sought after graphic artist."

"Ahhh, I see."

"If you're not comfortable, I can take you home. I never want you to be uncomfortable around me, Kate."

She leaned back and breathed deeply.

"I've already had my insecurity breakdown for tonight. I'm not uncomfortable at all. I'm not sure what it is about you, Matt, but the more time I spend with you, the more time I want to spend with you."

"It's because I'm sexy as hell."

"So cocky."

"Oh, you have no idea," he grinned like the Cheshire cat, as Kate laughed.

"Get out of the car, Matthew."

Kate spun around and opened the door, as Matt tried to jump out of the car, but she had already pulled herself out as he rounded the vehicle.

"You're supposed to wait for me, Kathleen."

"You gotta move faster, Matty."

"Glad you're back, feisty."

"Show me your studio, cocky."

Matt offered Kate his arm and after slipping her hand along his forearm, they sauntered into the house. Kate marveled at the hard wood floors and floor to ceiling windows. She imagined that the light was outstanding in the daytime. A curved double staircase filled the end of the foyer.

They ascended the staircase and walked down a wide hallway. Matt opened a door and they entered the studio. The windows from below had extended up the entirety of the home and one wall was entirely glass. The hard wood floors were covered in paint and dust from charcoal. Scattered around the room were easels, covered in muslin, while blank canvases of many sizes were leaned against the stark white walls. Every so often a piece was hanging on the walls. They were all landscapes. Kate found herself drawn to each and everyone of them. The realism and passion bled through, pulling her into each and every location. She wandered the room, running her fingers over the edges of the work, trying to somehow touch these places.

"Do you prefer landscapes to people?"

Matt stood by the door and looked around, folding his arms in front of him.

"I can't seem to get the faces right. There's always something missing."

"Missing?"

"Yeah, my 'face' muse is missing."

Kate laughed as she turned to face him. He was watching her, but instead of feeling self-conscience she felt confident, sexy, and desired. In those green-blue eyes, she saw herself as he saw her. She was beautiful. She smiled, and began to walk towards him.

* * * * *

Matt saw Kate move in his direction, her gaze on him never wavering. He took several steps to her and they met in the middle of the room. Matt unfolded his arms, gently caressing Kate's cheek with the back of his hand. Her eyes closed as the electricity of skin on skin unfurled its magic, racing through her veins, calling to her heart.

"I am incredibly attracted to you," she said. "You're sexy as hell. Invite me to stay the night, Matt."

Matt felt his breath catch, and then exhaled a soft shuddering breath. His hands cupped her face, lacing his fingers into the mass of brown silky curls, as his thumbs lightly caressed her skin.

"Stay with me, Kate. Let me show you how amazing you are."

Matt pulled her face to his and let his full mouth envelope her lips. Soft and sweet, the electricity of their touches paling in comparison to the coupling of their kiss. They each felt the tendrils of ecstasy following each synapse, popping and snapping, creating a massive desire that neither could control.

Kate's mouth responded to Matt's in wet passion as she fell against him, allowing her body to mold to his. Her head swam with longing, as she realized for the first time she fit. Her body was made to be with this man. They fit together perfectly.

Matt let his lips lift and opened his eyes, gazing down at the woman in his arms. He lightly brushed his lips against hers. Her eyes were filled with craving— glassy and bright.

"Are you sure?" he asked.

"Show me, Matty. Show me."

Matt devoured her mouth again, hot and moist, passion pumping though his body. He felt himself growing firm as he caressed her soft skin. He let go of her face and ran his hands down her body, tracing her curves as he reached her thighs. He lifted her up, and she wrapped her legs instinctively around his waist, feeling the length of him pressed against her sex through fabric, hard and unyielding. Her heart thrummed in her chest as she felt him carry her to another room. Within moments, she felt the soft billow of a comforter and mattress.

Kate felt him pull away and every part of her yearned to have his hot mouth on her lips, but instead he found her throat. The wet trail of kisses sent shocks of rapture straight to her mound, and a moan escaped her throat. His fingers found the zipper of her dress, sliding the apparatus to open, then nimbly pulled the red fabric from her luscious curves, exposing soft, porcelain skin. His fingers continued to nimbly remove her bra, exposing perfect pink nipples and round, satin breasts. He sat up and took her all in. She watched his eyes roam over her body and for a moment the ugly fears and insecurities tried to rush in. She watched him. Then he let his hands roam over her skin, soft, but firm, as he lowered his head.

"So fucking beautiful," he mumbled, as his mouth captured her sensitive peak, gently tugging and nibbling causing it to pebble. His thumb and index finger twisted the other until it throbbed, aching for his mouth. She arched her back, moaning under his touch. He finally let go of his first assault and attacked the other crest, nipping and rolling it along his tongue.

Kate let her fingers tangle in his mass of curly locks, pressing his mouth onto her delectable flesh. Her bud throbbed in anticipation of being assaulted. She tugged on his hair, pulling him back to her, crushing his mouth to hers. Her hands pulling and tugging at his clothes, he pulled back.

"Please, Matt. I need you inside of me."

"Say it again," he commanded, his voice husky and mad with longing.

"Fill me. I need you inside of me."

He disrobed in mere moments and stood before her a mass of lean muscles. She could finally see the tribal tattoo that surrounded his left upper body, a mass of black-inked swirls and Hebrew characters intertwined with a Star of David. His hands pulled at her silk panties. She felt his fingers lightly trace her skin up her long smooth legs, gently pressing them apart and exposing her dampened curls to his touch. She squirmed as he stroked her wet folds, crouching above her. She felt him long and hard as he pressed against her.

Matt looked down into her stunning amber eyes and laced his fingers in her sable locks, lightly brushing his lips against hers. He consumed her mouth as he entered her slowly; her moan was dripped with bliss. He filled every inch of her, lighting the fuse of rapture. She rose to meet him with every thrust.

Kate felt her body start to lose control, tears filling her eyes. Her control shattered as she shuddered under Matt, muscles convulsing in pleasure accompanied by audible cries of gratification. Matt didn't stop. When Kate had finished, he assaulted her neck again, sucking and nibbling her soft skin. Bringing her back to the edge with every thrust, as each touch of his mouth and hands caused the fire in her belly to engulf her. Soon her whimpers led to cries and together they crashed in elation, exploding again and again. Kate lost track of how many times Matt brought her to crest, causing her to lose herself in his touch.

* * * * *

The sun poked through the slit in the curtains, hitting her in the face. She opened her eyes and stretched as she rolled over, a hand searching for Matt. The bed was empty. She sat up and looked around. On the edge of the bed was a pair of sweats and a t-shirt. She scratched her head and breathed deeply.

Bacon.

Her stomach rumbled, and she smiled.

Matt stood in the kitchen wearing only a pair of sweats. He ran a hand through his long curls, and then cracked an egg into the skillet. The sizzle of butter and bacon filled the air, only interrupted by the soft padding of feet. He smiled.

"Morning, beautiful. Hungry?"

"Mmm, very."

"Good."

"Do I smell bacon, Matthew?"

"Yes," he replied, laughing.

"You're Jewish."

Matt turned and leaned on the counter, staring into the lovely face of Kate Flannery.

"Some Jews eat bacon. I'm one of those Jews."

A wry smile crossed Kate's mouth.

"Awesome."

Matt turned back around and flipped the eggs.

"Matt?"

"Hmm?"

"What's the name of that painting I was looking at last night? The window view of the city?"

Matt smiled.

"View of Holon."

"Where is Holon?"

"Israel."

"I want to go there."

"I'll take you."

"Seriously?"

Matt twisted around, eyebrows raised.

"Seriously."

Kate smiled, blushing, as Matt shook his head and turned back to the eggs. He turned off the stove and slid them deftly onto two plates, already filled with bacon, potatoes, tomatoes, and toast. He picked them up, slid them across the counter, and joined Kate on the other side, jumping up onto a stool.

Kate picked up her fork and dove in with gusto. Matt smiled as he watched her eat.

"I made you something."

"Yeah, breakfast. It's delicious," she said, her mouth full.

Matt laughed and reached to his left, picking up a pad of paper.

"No, I made you this."

Kate looked over, still chewing, as Matt handed her the pad. She swallowed and reviewed the masterpiece in front of her. It was a charcoal rendering of her, asleep. It was perfect. The line of her jaw, her nose, her mouth— all perfect.

"I thought you couldn't draw people."

"I found my muse."

Kate lifted her gaze to his. In that moment, she knew she was home. From the depths of her soul, he was the one, but was she?

"Me?" she asked, timidly.

"You. You're the one, Kate… the only one. I knew it the moment I saw you. I knew it here."

Matt placed his hand over his chest.

"You are the only thing I've been missing."

Kate closed her eyes letting his words fall over her like a waterfall, drenching her in warmth. She opened her eyes to see those deep liquid pools anxiously waiting for a response.

Kate leapt out of her chair, snaking her arms around his neck and pressing her mouth to his. The electricity was still there and still as intense. She pulled back and smiled.

Matt traced his fingers gently over her jaw line and pulled on her bottom lip. He nodded to her food.

"Eat your breakfast, beautiful. I'm not going anywhere. Oh, and don't forget, we have lunch with Lana at noon."

"We?"

"I don't feel like going anywhere without you just yet, if that's ok?"

Kate nodded, sat down and smiled, shoveling a big forkful of potatoes into her mouth. Matt laughed and began to eat. Kate watched him as she happily chewed and processed it all.

He lit a fire in her no other man had ever done. He thought she was beautiful.

He desired her, he wanted her, he loved her.

She was... the one.

S.L. Dearing

Author Dedication

This story is for all of us who believe in soul mates and love at first sight.

They could be anywhere at anytime, so never give up hope and never settle.

And remember... beauty is in the eye of the beholder.

About S.L. Dearing

Although she grew up in Arizona, S. L. Dearing was born and raised in California and considers the Golden State her home. Shannon attended Cal Poly San Luis Obispo, studying biology, then moved to Los Angeles where she spent several years studying at Los Angeles City College's renowned Television/ Film program. She learned the art of storytelling from her father when she was very young and has been writing since the tender age of five. As an author of many genres, she is always hoping to learn more by exploring the world of story. Shannon currently resides in Los Angeles.

Follow S.L. Dearing

Website: http://www.sldearing.com/

Facebook: http://www.facebook.com/SLDearing.Author

Read More from S.L. Dearing

The Gathering: http://amzn.to/M8lN5Q

The End

Follow Novel Grounds

To stay up to date with information about all these and many other great authors, sign up to follow Novel Grounds.

Website: http://www.novelgrounds.com/
Facebook: http://www.facebook.com/novelgrounds
Twitter: http://www.twitter.com/novelgrounds

Made in the USA
San Bernardino, CA
11 March 2014